ears

dress.

*"I felt
your gaze
on me."*

"Perhaps it was someone else's."

"No, I'm rather sure it was yours. You have an intensity about you. Do you often stand up here, gazing out, spying on those below?"

He skimmed a bare finger along her nape. Beneath his touch, she shivered.

"You should be aware I employ any means to get what I want."

"You sound ruthless, Your Grace."

"I want you, Rosalind. I have wanted you from the moment you walked through the door."

"I am not quite so easy to obtain."

"Are you not?"

She turned to face him. "No."

"I am prepared to convince you otherwise."

He claimed her mouth as though he already owned it.

By Lorraine Heath

THE DUKE AND THE LADY IN RED
ONCE MORE, MY DARLING ROGUE
WHEN THE DUKE WAS WICKED
LORD OF WICKED INTENTIONS
LORD OF TEMPTATION
SHE TEMPTS THE DUKE
WAKING UP WITH THE DUKE
PLEASURES OF A NOTORIOUS GENTLEMAN
PASSIONS OF A WICKED EARL
MIDNIGHT PLEASURES WITH A SCOUNDREL
SURRENDER TO THE DEVIL
BETWEEN THE DEVIL AND DESIRE
IN BED WITH THE DEVIL
JUST WICKED ENOUGH
A DUKE OF HER OWN
PROMISE ME FOREVER
A MATTER OF TEMPTATION
AS AN EARL DESIRES
AN INVITATION TO SEDUCTION
LOVE WITH A SCANDALOUS LORD
TO MARRY AN HEIRESS
THE OUTLAW AND THE LADY
NEVER MARRY A COWBOY
NEVER LOVE A COWBOY
A ROGUE IN TEXAS

LORRAINE HEATH

THE DUKE

AND THE

LADY IN RED

AVONBOOKS

An Imprint of HarperCollinsPublishers

AVON BOOKS
An Imprint of HarperCollins*Publishers*
195 Broadway
New York, New York 10007

Copyright © 2015 by Jan Nowasky
ISBN 978-0-06-227626-1
www.avonromance.com

First Avon Books mass market printing: May 2015

Avon Trademark Reg. U.S. Pat. Off. and in Other Countries, Marca Registrada, Hecho en U.S.A.
HarperCollins® is a registered trademark of HarperCollins Publishers.

Printed in the U.S.A.

10 9 8 7 6 5 4 3 2 1

For Cayce
Every author should be so fortunate to have a fan as
wonderful as you.

Chapter 1

London
1874

*S*he could make a killing here.

Rose did nothing to reveal her delight at the discovery although she doubted anyone would derive the true meaning behind a beaming smile or eyes glinting with satisfaction. All the ladies in attendance were agog at the magnificent display of opulence and the evidence of sin, avarice, and gentlemanly indulgences. The fairer sex had finally been allowed entry into one of the men's most notorious and gossiped about inner sanctums, and they were relishing the discoveries of all that had been held in secret and denied them.

The express purpose of tonight's event—a grand ball, entrance by invitation only—was to entertain current members and introduce potential future ones to all the benefits that the former gentlemen's club offered. Since her arrival in London a fortnight before, Rose had discovered the Twin Dragons was the talk of the town.

Not surprising as she'd caught sight of its owner half an hour earlier when he'd emerged through a doorway that apparently led to back rooms. With a purpose to his stride, he had caught her attention because she recognized in him a kindred spirit. Not ten minutes later, he'd taken a woman into his arms and kissed her quite thoroughly and entirely inappropriately—right in the center of one of the dance areas. Based on his fervor and the lady's enthusiasm, Rose eliminated him as someone with the potential to assist in her endeavors. He was obviously spoken for, and unattached men were much less complicated with which to deal.

Ignoring the men scrutinizing her, she familiarized herself with the surroundings that would serve as a second home during the coming weeks. A portion of the room contained tables that dealt with various games of chance. She suspected on the morrow that the remainder of the room would as well, but tonight the area absent of games served as a place for people to visit or dance. Huge crystal gaslit chandeliers provided the lighting. The paper along the walls was neutral in tone, not particularly masculine or feminine.

Rose would have liked to have had the opportunity to view the club before the renovations that sought to strike a balance between what would remain of interest to males and what would not offend females. No doubt it had proven a bit more decadent and far more interesting. But she wasn't here for the trimmings. Rather it was the building's heart and soul—those upon whom its very existence depended—calling to her.

Wandering through the crowd, smiling here and there, she knew those to whom she'd given a nod of acknowledgment would be confounded, striving to remember from whence they knew her, some would even swear on the morrow that they had recognized her, were old acquaintances. None would admit they'd never seen her before in their lives. She had mastered the art of appearing as though she belonged, had mastered a great many things.

Walking into the ladies' salon, which after tonight would be off-limits to gentlemen, Rose knew she wouldn't make a habit of frequenting this room, but it might provide the occasional opportunity to cement the *right* relationships.

"Hello."

Turning, Rose faced a small woman with mahogany hair and eyes as dark as Satan's soul—and full of suspicion. Another kindred spirit perhaps.

"Good evening," Rose said with authority, as though the room were hers to command. Control, imperative to winning the game, had to be kept at all times, at any cost. "I don't believe we've been properly introduced. I'm Mrs. Rosalind Sharpe."

"Miss Minerva Dodger."

Shoving down her surprise, Rose merely arched a brow. "You are rare, my dear. An unmarried woman of means."

"Why would you draw such conclusions?"

"It was my understanding that only the nobility and those of wealth were invited to this exclusive affair. As you do not appear to be nobility, that leaves wealth."

The woman smiled slightly. "Yes, invitations were rather limited, but it is my father who has the means. Not to mention that he was the previous owner of the establishment, when it was Dodger's Drawing Room."

Ah, yes, Rose should have recognized the name. She'd castigate herself later for failing to do so. A careless slip could cost her dearly, put a crimp in her plans. "I suspect he's a rather interesting chap. I look forward to meeting him."

Miss Dodger glanced around casually although there was an alertness to her that Rose didn't much favor. "Is your husband about?" the younger woman asked.

"I'm a widow."

Miss Dodger swung her gaze back around, sorrow evident within the depths of her dark eyes as she settled them once more on Rose. "I'm terribly sorry."

"A tiger attack while we were touring through the jungles of India. But he went as he lived—adventurously. I draw comfort from that. He would have hated dying of old age, infirmed, in bed."

"I suppose there is something to be said for going as one wishes rather than as one is forced. Are you new to London, then? I don't mean to pry, but I'm not familiar with your family."

"No need to apologize, my dear. I've been here only a fortnight. It's my first foray into town."

"That's unusual."

"Before India, I lived in the north, a small town hardly worth mentioning as few have heard of it." Nowhere that she'd lived was really worth mentioning, especially as it was risky to provide breadcrumbs for anyone who might take an interest in retracing her journey. "I believe my solicitor was instrumental in garnering me an invitation to tonight's affair." She was sure of it, in fact. Daniel Beckwith had been bending over backward to accommodate her since she had walked into his office. Widows who were to inherit all their husband's holdings were rare and greatly appreciated. Based upon what she had told him of the estate, he was well aware that he stood to make a tidy sum by assisting her. He wanted to keep her more than content. "I'm eternally in his debt."

"Would you like me to show you about?"

"I couldn't possibly impose to such an extent. Besides, I have a bit of the adventurous in me and prefer exploring on my own."

"Well then, I'll let you get to it. I do hope you enjoy your evening."

"Oh, I shall most certainly strive to do exactly that."

Miss Dodger took her leave then, and Rose made a mental note to ask Beckwith about the girl's father. It was quite possible that she might want to form a friendship with Miss Dodger, even if she wasn't nobility. Unlike most people, Rose was more interested in coin than rank. As the new owner had opened the establishment to those who were not peers, it seemed he, too, valued coin over birth. A wise principle as one could not choose family.

She knew that well enough.

Rose walked into a dining room. Such a tremendous amount of food adorned the sideboards that they were in danger of buckling. People sat at round linen-covered tables, enjoying the fare. The lights were dimmer. Candles flickered in the center of the tables. The room would serve as a romantic rendezvous. She would dine here when the time came, would do a good many things here.

They had allowed her in. Her skill and cunning would ensure she took advantage of their lack of good judgment.

*T*he woman in red drew his attention as soon as she walked through the entrance doors as though she were the queen of England herself. His notice of her surprised him, as nothing about her was particularly eye-catching.

Looking out from his perch in the shadowed corner of the balcony at Dodger's—

Avendale growled. The Twin Dragons. Why the bloody deuce had Drake changed the name of the decades-old gaming hell? Not only the name but almost everything else about it? Avendale didn't like it. He didn't like it one bit. He especially didn't like that women were now allowed inside, would be members, would be strolling about, just as the lady in red was doing now.

Her hair, piled up and held in place with pearl combs, was blond silk. Not vibrant or fiery or different. It should have ensured she blended in. But she didn't.

It was her mien. The elegant slope of her neck, the way she carried those slender shoulders as though they'd never known a burden. The way her gown hugged her curves, made men wish they were hugging them as well. She had a rather nice full bosom, displayed to perfection, drawing gazes from her face to the gentle swells. He suspected a good many of the gents here tonight would recall the lady in red over breakfast, yet he doubted a single one would be able to accurately describe the features that formed her face, but they would be able to expertly mold her shape in the air before them.

He knew the majority of the women in the aristocracy. He did not know her, which meant that in all likelihood she was one of the wealthy commoners that Drake was enticing into his club. Or an American. From what he'd been able to gather, they were all as rich as Croesus. She certainly gave the appearance of someone who was no stranger to the finer aspects of life.

In the main salon, she'd spoken to only one person—a footman. Shortly afterward, she'd disappeared into the ladies' private chambers for a bit. He'd almost gone after her, but he didn't like this curiosity about her plaguing him. No doubt it was simply a result of his growing so blasted bored of late. His partner in wickedness, the Duke of Lovingdon, had recently taken Lady Grace Mabry to wife, leaving Avendale to carouse on his own. Not that he required a male companion when he had female ones aplenty.

But sometimes it was nice to have someone with whom he could carry on a halfway intelligent conversation. Someone with an intellect. Someone who appreciated his ribald jokes. The women usually in his company tended to mewl, sigh, and whisper naughty things in his ear. Not that he didn't enjoy them. He did. But they were so alike. They seldom varied. Oh, their hair, their eyes, their shapes were different, but at their core they were all the same. Exciting while in his bed, but dreadfully dull out of it.

Yet the lady in red didn't appear at all dull.

He knew a very private card game—without women—was being played down the hall. He should be there. It was where he'd been headed when he decided to peer out over the crowd. And spotted her.

She'd held him enthralled ever since. Even when she wasn't visible, she toyed with him. Generally with women, for him, it was out of sight, out of mind.

Not very gentlemanly of him, really, but he tended to spend his time with loose women who didn't expect—and probably preferred not—to be remembered. He avoided those crowding the main floor, except for occasions like weddings or this event tonight, which involved friends of the family. He usually made an appearance for appearances' sake, when the mood not to be an arse struck. It pleased his mother. Gave them a couple of moments to catch up.

He'd spied her earlier meandering about with her second husband, William Graves. Avendale's father had been her first. A sorry affair that had been.

He shook off the memories, shoved them back down. They were not the sort he liked to examine. But the lady in red . . .

He would very much like to examine every inch of her.

*S*he knew she was being watched. She could feel the gaze homed in on her, was aware of little shivers cascading along her skin. The fine hairs on the back of her neck had risen. But she gave no outward appearance that she was bothered by the scrutiny while inside her heart pounded with the fierceness of a regimental drum beating out the call to battle.

She'd overheard someone talking about an inspector from Scotland Yard who was wandering about. But he was supposedly a guest and not searching for her. She hadn't been in London long enough for alarm bells to be ringing, for anyone to suspect—

"Champagne?" a deep voice asked behind her.

She would dearly love some, but needed to remain sharp and focused. Spinning around to decline the footman's offer, she came up short.

The man extending a flute toward her was most certainly not a servant. Nobility, entitlement, privilege screamed from every pore, every finely stitched seam, every thread of exquisite cloth that cloaked his magnificent frame. His dark eyes blatantly assessed her, and the hairs on her nape quivered once more. So it had been him watching her. He possessed an intensity that was slightly unsettling, made her fear that he could see straight through her.

But if he could, he would be calling for that inspector who was around here, not offering her champagne. His gaze wouldn't roam over her as though he were taking measure of every curve, dip, and swell while imagining how each would fill his hands.

If she had to guess this man's rank, she would put him as duke. He wore power and influence like a second skin. She could make do with a duke.

She gave him her most alluring, sensual smile. "I am quite parched, and so appreciate a man who can fulfill my desires. Thank you."

Wrapping her gloved fingers around the stem of the flute, she made sure that her fingers touched his, lingered for a moment. His eyes widened slightly, and a corner of his luscious mouth curled up almost imperceptibly. Anyone else might not have even noticed, but she had trained herself to discern the smallest of details. People communicated far more truth with their bodies and facial expressions than they ever did with their words.

She tapped the edge of her glass to his. "To an interesting night."

Peering over the rim of her flute as she slowly sipped, she watched him as he did the same, inspecting her. She'd never been so intrigued by a gentleman. Most fawned over her once they made their move and got her attention. This one was more cautious, more assessing. He would be a challenge, but if she was right about his position, she was more than willing to welcome it. She licked her lips, satisfaction coursing through her as his brown eyes darkened. He was not as skilled as she at appearing unaffected.

"Isn't it rather scandalous for a gentleman to approach a woman he doesn't know without someone at his side to make introductions?" she asked.

"I am nothing if I am not scandalous."

"Should I be wary? Is my reputation at risk?"

"Depends on your reputation. Considering that you arrived without chaperone or escort, I assume your reputation is of little consequence to you."

So he'd seen her arrive, had been observing her for a good long while. Nearly three quarters of an hour now. It was a good omen that she had managed to hold his interest for so long. "I'm a widow. I don't require a chaperone."

"My condolences on your loss, although it appears you're out of mourning."

She didn't fail to notice the way his gaze dipped to the plumped up mounds of her bosom. They drew men much more than her face, which was lacking in beauty. But it served to her advantage, as a dipping gaze seldom noticed the shrewdness in her eyes. "It's been two years now. We were exploring the jungles in India when he was attacked by a tiger. Terribly gruesome." She visibly shuddered, ensuring he was distracted by the quivering flesh of her breasts. Men were so easy to manipulate. She should be ashamed, but she had learned long ago that one shouldn't be regretful about what one was forced to do in order to survive. "I don't wish to dwell on it."

She took another sip of the excellent champagne, allowing her hand to tremble slightly. "I fear I need a distraction. It has been lovely visiting with you, but I should like to tour the gentlemen's salon. As I understand it, after tonight, ladies will no longer be welcomed within its walls. I want to see what we are being denied."

"I'll accompany you."

"Surely you have a wife somewhere who would not appreciate your attentions to me."

"No wife. No betrothed, no paramour. I've no interest in attachments of a permanent nature."

"I can't blame you there. Having had one, I now find myself feeling quite the same way."

He offered his arm. "Then shall we?"

She placed her hand in the crook of his elbow and was greeted with firm muscle. A man who didn't just lie about with no purpose. Her head barely reached his shoulder. He was a towering man, large and broad. But it was more than his physical traits that made him appear powerful. She suspected if his height did not extend past her knee, he would still dominate his surroundings. He seemed to dwarf everything around him. She didn't know if she had ever met a man who commanded such supremacy.

As they strode—as this man could do nothing except stride with confidence—through the room, he acknowledged a few but was greeted with deference.

"Your Grace."

"Avendale."

"Duke."

She'd been correct about his title. She wondered how many lesser ones he might possess, how much property. What was he worth? Based upon the excellent tailoring of his black swallowtail coat, trousers, and waistcoat, along with the jeweled pin nestled in his cravat, he was worth a princely sum.

They arrived in a room that was much darker than any of the others she'd viewed. The walls were papered in rich burgundy and forest green. The furniture matched. A massive fireplace dominated one of several sitting areas. Glass cabinets held an as-

sortment of spirits. Liveried footmen served amber
liquid.

She finished off her champagne and set the flute on
the tray of a passing footman. The man beside her—
Avendale—did the same. She didn't like noticing that
he seemed to belong here more than in any other
place. That he was made of—and for—debauchery.
He was comfortable with his surroundings, would
flourish here as well as in the bedchamber. She was
rather certain of it. Even in shadows, he would stand
out, prowling toward her, conquering every aspect of
the night, conquering her. She wouldn't so much as
whimper in protest.

"Would you care for something darker?" he asked.

He grinned wolfishly, and for a moment she feared
he read all her thoughts. A shiver went through her
before she grasped his meaning. He'd distracted her.
Normally she kept her head around men, even handsome ones. Or perhaps she was giving him too much
credit, had simply sipped the champagne far too
quickly so that her mind had dulled for a moment.

"Is it allowed?" she asked innocently.

"It is. That's Darling's purpose here—to open up
every manner of vice and decadence to the ladies. But
wouldn't it be far more enjoyable if it weren't allowed?"

He held her gaze and she was no longer certain
they were discussing liquor. Things not allowed generally were more enjoyable. How did he know that
was what she preferred? What she thrived on? The
forbidden was always more alluring. She suspected
many of the ladies would soon wonder what all
the fuss had been about now that they could walk
through the doors whenever they chose.

"Did I hear my name taken in vain?" a deep voice
asked.

Turning to the side, she came face to face with the man she'd earlier seen kissing the woman in the dance area. That woman was now beaming with happiness and inappropriately nestled against his side. But then Rose supposed in a place like this nothing was completely inappropriate. That was the entire point to it.

"I've been taking your name in vain ever since you came up with this ghastly idea to allow women into our sanctum," Avendale said, clearly disgruntled.

"Yet here you are walking about with one of those ladies," Drake Darling said. "Are you going to introduce us?"

"I fear we have not yet been introduced." Avendale's gaze ran over her. "Names are unimportant to me."

So he had only a temporary interest in her. Perhaps for just tonight. A tryst, something wicked. She was insulted enough to take offense, but not so much that she wasn't also flattered. Yet both emotions were schooled not to show. Much more satisfying to make him pay later for his arrogance. Oh, and how he would pay. She could hardly wait, but taking her time would make it all so much sweeter.

"My apologies, Mr. Darling," she said softly. "I am Mrs. Rosalind Sharpe."

A dark eyebrow arched over dark eyes. "You know who I am?"

"You had an invitation delivered to me. I made inquiries after I arrived here and someone pointed you out. I had planned to make your acquaintance straightaway but you seemed rather busy." Smiling, doing all she could to blush, she looked at the woman.

"Yes, I was rather," he admitted.

"You do realize you're going to have to marry Lady Ophelia now," Avendale said, "after that spectacle you made earlier."

Rose fought not to show her surprise that a commoner had snagged nobility.

"I shall do so with great pleasure. And I'm being rude. Lady Ophelia Lyttleton, allow me to introduce Mrs. Rosalind Sharp."

"A pleasure," Lady Ophelia said.

"The pleasure is all mine, my lady. I do hope we may have an opportunity to know each other better," Rose said. "I am quite fascinated with the place. I can see myself spending considerable time here."

"I'm sure I'll pop by from time to time, but for the immediate future I'm going to be extremely busy arranging our wedding." She looked up at Drake Darling with adoration, and Rose fought back the little bite of envy. Love was not for her and well she knew it.

"If you'll excuse us," Mr. Darling said, "we need to finish making the rounds."

Their arms linked, they wandered off.

"And so another one falls," Avendale said somberly.

Rose looked up at him. "You seem to be friends, which surprises me. He is a commoner, and based upon the manner in which people greeted you, you are a duke."

He shrugged laconically. "Our families share a past and a deep friendship."

"That makes it even more odd."

"We are quite a mixture of commoner and nobility, far too complicated to explain with few words. I'm not in the mood for words, but rather drink." He snatched two glasses containing amber liquid from a passing footman and offered her one. "Something darker than champagne."

"Thank you." She took a small sip. "Excellent brandy."

"A woman who enjoys the finer things."

"Oh, I am most certainly that." She glanced around. "So within this room, men drink, smoke, read, and converse. Where do they play cards when they don't wish to remain civilized?"

He nodded toward the back of the room. "A door over there takes them to another room where they gamble to their heart's content without ladies seeing how dashed awful they are at gambling, and how much they lose without blinking an eye."

"You don't strike me as someone who loses."

"You don't have to flatter me, Mrs. Sharpe. You have my attention."

"But for how long without flattery?"

He chuckled low. "Until I grow bored. And flattery bores me."

"Well, then, without further ado, I would like to finish my tour of the place. You are welcome to accompany me or not. Makes no never mind to me." She could be as cool and aloof as he required. She did like that he didn't crave adulation, but it did leave her a bit discombobulated, as she'd never before dealt with a man who didn't react to being fawned over.

He showed her the gaming room that was for men only. It was much like the salon: dark and ominous. Masculine. It spoke of power and wealth. How she would like to be a fly on the wall in here.

With few words uttered, he escorted her back to the main salon. But he was a man who communicated nonetheless. With a touch to her elbow, the small of her back, her shoulder. Light and quick caresses, but still there was an air of possessiveness to them. He was not completely immune to her charms. He was simply striving not to be sucked in too far.

"Dance with me," he said.

His words startled her. Inwardly she cursed herself

for losing her composure for a moment, for letting him take her off-guard. "I'm not certain why but I didn't think you were one to dance."

"Normally, I'm not, but my mother spent a fortune on lessons. I should put them to use now and again. Would you prefer to dance here or in the ballroom?"

"There is a separate room for dancing? I somehow missed that."

"Something tells me you don't miss much."

And neither did he. She considered making her excuses, leaving now before things went too far, before she was the one sucked in, the one not thinking clearly, but it had been a good long while since anyone intrigued her. He was mysterious. Based upon how few people stopped to speak with him, she suspected he was not known for being interested in their affairs and was known for not sharing his. She could take advantage of his tendency toward privacy.

"I should like to see the ballroom," she said.

"If I must walk that far for a dance, I shall have to have two."

"That would be rather scandalous, wouldn't it?"

"You're past the first blush of innocence. I suspect scandal suits you."

"In all honesty I try to avoid it, but I have not danced in ages, not since my husband's passing," she felt obligated to say. Wrapping her hand around his arm, she gave him a smile intended to charm, to make him feel as though he were the only man in the room worthy of her attention. "Lead on."

As he escorted her through the rooms and hallways, she caught the speculative glances, the raised eyebrows. It was to her advantage to garner attention, but not too much. A woman was always best served by keeping an air of mystery about her.

The ballroom was magnificent. Glittering chandeliers. Mirrored walls. A balcony with an orchestra of
at least a dozen. Lilies emitted their sweet fragrance
into the air. Ah, yes, Drake Darling was providing a
place for the untitled wealthy to socialize with the
nobility. Clever man. He had brought all she sought
into one convenient place. She would have to send
him a note of appreciation when the time came.

"You seem impressed," Avendale said.

"I appreciate elegance." And it was important that
she remember every detail. She would no doubt be
grilled on them when she returned home. "I shall
have to do something similar with my ballroom. It's
in need of a touch more stylishness."

"You have a ballroom?" he asked, and she heard
the surprise in his voice.

"My husband, bless him, left me quite well off. I'd
have thought you intelligent enough to discern that
I'm a woman of independent means. How else might
I have garnered an invitation?"

"Quite right. I wasn't thinking. I forgot that Darling has certain requirements regarding his members.
At least it should keep out the hoi polloi." He nodded
toward the center of the room. "Shall we?"

"By all means. I would be most delighted."

With a smoothness that set her heart to tripping
over itself, he swept her into the fray of dancers. She
realized a tad too late that waltzing with him was a
mistake. He held her close and firmly, possessively.
Yes, she could see the peril now. He was a man accustomed to owning what he desired.

His dark eyes never left hers. She was acutely
aware of his blatantly assessing her. Every strand of
hair, every eyelash, every blush. Which was only fair
as she was assessing him. Not a strand of his dark

brown hair was out of place. Sometimes when the light hit it just so, she thought she detected shades of red in it, but mostly the dark had its way. She suspected it dominated all aspects of his life.

Nothing about him seemed light or carefree. Everything was intense. While others conversed and smiled at their partners, he merely studied every line and curve. She could tell that he preferred the curves. She was accustomed to that when it came to men. Her bosom was her finest asset, and she took great pains to show it off. She'd long ago shed the mantle of timidity.

His face was composed of hard lines and harsh angles. He would never be considered beautiful, and yet there was beauty in the ruggedness of his features. Handsome, manly. Appealing. He appealed to her in ways no other man ever had.

That made him very dangerous indeed. She kept a wall between herself and men. They were to be used, then discarded. She didn't think this man would be easily tossed aside. She needed to escape his company as quickly as possible, while she could. She was far too attracted to him. That would not suit her purposes at all. He would not suit.

The final strains of the waltz drifted into silence.

"That was lovely," she said. "Thank you. I shall leave you to enjoy the remainder of your evening now."

His eyes narrowed. "I thought we had agreed to two dances."

"I don't wish to dominate your time."

"There is no one else I would rather dominate it. Is someone expecting your company?"

She should say yes. But then he would no doubt keep an eye on her to discern who was of interest to

her. She didn't want him observing her. Best to give
him a bit more time tonight and then move on. "No."

"Then it seems another dance is in order."

The music began. Another waltz. Did the orchestra know naught but waltzes? Did her skin have to
welcome the press of his hands? Did she have to feel
his touch cascading through her entire being? It was
at once disconcerting and exciting to have these reactions to his nearness. What was it about him that
affected her so? It was more than his handsome features, something deep within him that was calling to
something in her, something that had been dormant,
that was awakening. She needed a distraction from
these unsettling thoughts.

"Where is your estate?" she asked.

"Cornwall."

Yes, she could see that. His being part of the
rugged coast. Perhaps he was even descended from
pirates. She could well imagine thievery and plunder-
ing in his heritage.

"You're not one for conversing, are you?" she asked.

"Not with words, no. I prefer other means of communication, especially when a lady is involved."

She was losing her edge with him. She didn't know
how to get it back. "That sort of communication
deals only with the surface. There is no depth to a
relationship of that nature."

"I care for only one sort of *depth*." His eyes smoldered with his innuendo and she nearly stumbled.

She was out of her league with him. He would
not be easily manipulated. But something inside her
yearned to accept the challenge. Things had become
too easy of late. She was bored. She hadn't realized it
until that moment. There was no life, no excitement

in her anymore. She simply existed. But he brought a spark to her. He interested her. She thought he might have secrets as dark as her own. Drawing them from him would be a challenge, might prove to be to her advantage.

"You offend me with your insinuation," she said.

"If that were true, you would have slapped me by now. You're a widow, not an innocent miss. The other ladies here interest me not in the least, because they are naive. I prefer a woman who is seasoned."

"And you judge me to be seasoned?"

"You intrigue me, Rosalind."

"You're taking liberties with your informality."

"I believe your protests are false. You want me to take liberties. It's the reason you haven't left in a huff." He narrowed his eyes. "No, you are not one to huff about. I think you would make me pay in other ways."

Oh yes, he had the right of it. She most certainly would make him pay in other ways. Might still do so. But for now they were merely taking measure of each other.

"I find you equally intriguing, Your Grace, but I fear I have been too long away from the social scene. My skills at being coy are sadly lacking."

"You don't have to play false with me. I prefer honesty."

"Then know that I find myself attracted to you, although I'm not sure it's wise on either of our parts."

"But it could be enjoyable."

She had no doubt of that. He was a man not lacking in confidence. He could show her a jolly good time, but she knew far too little about him. Her purpose here tonight was not to settle on one, but to amass many admirers. He was distracting her from her plans.

The waltz came to an end, but he didn't release her immediately. He simply held her scandalously close, allowing the minutes to tick by as though there were no one to see, no one who possessed a tongue to wag. If she were a young girl of nineteen, with a father or brother to speak for her, she would find herself betrothed by midnight.

"What else is there to see here?" she asked.

"I believe you've seen it all. Perhaps we have run out of reasons to stay."

How she was tempted to accept his invitation, to go with him wherever he wished to go. But she had planned too long to be reckless now.

"I spied a draped balcony in a far corner of the main salon." She suspected it was from there that he'd observed her earlier. "I should very much like to see it. How does one get to it?"

"One must possess a key."

She angled her chin. "Do not take this as flattery, Your Grace, but rather the truth being spoken. You strike me as a man who would possess a key."

*H*e did indeed possess a key. It was no doubt unwise to take her up there, as he wanted to do things with her that were best done within shadows, and there were shadows aplenty within the balcony, and his passions were on a weak tether. She was not an innocent miss, only recently presented to the queen. She was a widow. She had to know men, had to know that he was with her at that moment because of his desire to know her in the biblical sense. Without guilt, he could give in to his desires.

But she was not quite what she seemed. Of that he was fairly certain. He had spent a lifetime avoiding entanglements and relationships. He never looked below the surface of a woman, but something about her urged him to explore a little deeper.

She wasn't an American as he'd first wondered. Her speech was refined, definitely English, deliberate, but now and again he caught the lilt of something else, as though she were putting on a performance and forgot for a moment her role in the play.

That little aspect to her intrigued him all the more but was no cause for alarm. He didn't want anything permanent with her. He merely wanted to explore all that lay beneath the red gown. His hands would span her waist. Her breasts would overflow his cupped palms.

He guided her through the crowd that was becoming more populated by the hour. How many blasted invitations had been dispatched? He doubted he would seek sport here after tonight. The club would no longer be as exclusive as it had once been. But then he'd long ago found darker places in which to vent his shame and anger.

They came to the door that opened into the hallways where offices and secluded rooms provided very private entertainment. Removing the key from his waistcoat pocket, he extended it toward her.

She gave him a delighted, wicked smile, filled with mischief and daring. She enjoyed doing things she ought not. He liked that about her. Before the night was done, he anticipated that they would do a great many things they ought not.

Inserting the key, she turned it, twisted the knob, and opened the door. She hesitated not even a heartbeat before walking through and passing the key back to him. After closing the door, he once again offered his arm.

"Everything here seems older," she said.

"Darling didn't bother refurbishing this part, for which I'm glad. There is something comforting about the familiar. It has been this way for decades."

"You don't look old enough to have been visiting it for decades," she said.

"I got started quite young." Although she was right. He'd visited for only a little over a decade. "I know its history. It's legendary among those of my acquaintance. The stairs that lead to the balcony are here."

With his hand on the small of her back, he guided her up them and down the short hallway that ended at the balcony.

"As long as you stay behind the draperies, you can't be seen," he said quietly. "The shadows serve as cover."

She eased forward slightly and gazed out over the assembled guests. "Is this where you were when you spotted me?" she asked in almost a whisper.

He came up behind her, only a hairbreadth separating his body from hers. "Yes."

"It's odd, but I felt your gaze on me."

"Perhaps it was someone else's."

"No, I'm rather sure it was yours. You have an intensity about you. Do you often stand up here, gazing out, spying on those below?"

"Darling did. He liked to watch the money coming in. Dodger, the previous owner, did as well." He removed his gloves, stuffed them into the pockets of his coat, and skimmed a bare finger along her nape. Beneath his touch, she shivered. "I was simply striving to determine if it was worth my time to go downstairs tonight."

"What would you have done if you hadn't gone downstairs?"

"There is a private game in one of the rooms up

here. The stakes are high, but those who play cheat."
He pressed his lips to the juncture where her neck
and shoulder met. "You should be aware I employ
any means to get what I want."

"You sound ruthless, Your Grace."

"That is putting it kindly. I want you, Rosalind.
I have wanted you from the moment you walked
through the door. There are rooms here. We can
make use of them. Or I can take you to my residence."

"I am not quite so easy to obtain."

"Are you not?"

She turned to face him. "No."

"I am prepared to convince you otherwise."

He claimed her mouth as though he already owned it.

*S*he shouldn't have been surprised that he took ad-
vantages of the shadows. She knew she'd been toying
with a man who was far more daring than his civilized veneer let on.

She was, however, surprised by her reaction to his
generous mouth blanketing hers. She welcomed it.

Acutely aware of his arms banding around her and
pressing her flat against the hard planes of his body,
she should have protested. Instead she indulged her
curiosity and her own flagrant desires that she had
held at bay for so very long. She couldn't remember
the last time that she'd taken something she wanted,
that she had done something for herself.

She was certainly indulging now.

Scraping her fingers up into his thick hair, she regretted that she wore gloves. Tasting the richness of
brandy on his tongue, she regretted they'd not had
more to drink. As the pleasure coursed through her,
she regretted that she was not free.

With that thought, guilt speared her. She did not

resent that she was not untethered. Freedom came at a terrible price she was not yet ready to pay.

She forced all those thoughts back and concentrated instead on the moment. It was always best to focus on the moment. The sweep of his determined tongue. His large hand caressing her back, her backside, coming up along her hip, dipping in at her waist, and resting just below her breast. She felt the stroke of his thumb along the underside. She should have been appalled. She should have struck him.

But a woman did not reach her years without yearning for things that eluded her. She was certainly no stranger to kissing, but this man was doing far more than pressing his lips to hers. He was claiming her, branding her. She would forever remember his taste, his strength, his fragrance.

Sandalwood and bergamot. Dark and rich.

She would remember rising up on her toes to welcome his mouth. His deep groan rumbling within the small confines of the balcony. The dizziness. The sensations swirling around her.

He dragged his mouth from hers, along her neck to the sensitive spot just below her ear. "We'll never make it to my residence," he rasped. "There is a room only a few steps down the hallway."

"No." She said it too softly. He must not have heard because he began worrying her lobe between his teeth. She nearly sank to the floor with the absolute pleasure of it. He could have her here. "No," she stated more firmly.

Breathing harshly, he drew back, his dark eyes pinning her. "Just as you require no chaperone, you have no innocence to protect."

"I am not a woman with no morals. I don't fall into bed with a man simply because he wishes me to do so."

"*You* wish to do so. Your moans and sighs are proof of that."

"Unfortunately, life is such that we are not always granted our wishes. I have been absent from the gaiety too long. I must return to it lest rumors begin."

He curled his hand around her neck, stroked the underside of her jaw. "You do not strike me as a woman who cares about rumors."

"I care about the opportunities that tonight affords me." She could not have spoken truer words. "I am here to meet people, to become part of Society. To be accepted and welcomed. It would be reckless of me to risk all that I might gain for one night of pleasure."

"I promise it would be worth your while."

Of that, she had absolutely no doubt, but the price was too high—to her plans, quite possibly to her esteem. To have him walk away afterward . . . she was always the one who walked away, who decided when it was time to move on. Swallowing hard, she pushed back the temptation plaguing her. "Good night, Your Grace."

She had taken a mere two steps when he wrapped his large hand around her arm, turned her back to him, and again took her mouth. His was lush and hot and so very skilled at making her forget her responsibilities, her duties. What would it hurt if just once in her life she did something for herself? If she took something she craved?

Tearing her mouth from his, she shoved on his massive shoulders, frustrated when she couldn't even make him stagger back a step. "No."

His eyes were as heated as his mouth. "You've been teasing me all night, Mrs. Sharpe. You can't possibly think I'm going to let you walk away without doing my damnedest to convince you to stay."

Another kiss would probably do the trick, damn him. "It's been a long time since I've been with a man. I'm not ready for what you're proposing." Reaching up, she combed her fingers through his hair, straightening the strands she had mussed. "Please let me go."

Slowly, agonizingly slowly, he released his hold. "At least allow me the honor of escorting you home."

"We both know that would be most dangerous. Alone, in a small space, in the dark. I do not believe I would arrive home unscathed. Besides, I have a carriage. So again, good night."

"I won't give up."

She'd barely turned when his words froze her on the spot.

"I will have you," he said, his voice a whispered promise that caused a shiver of foreboding, a quiver of pleasure to ripple through her. "Because you want it as much as I do."

She nearly denied the words, but she feared if she delayed, she'd find herself back in his arms, this time without the wherewithal to deny him, to deny them both what she thought might be a glorious night. She wanted to flee, to run, but she kept her pace slow and measured as she left the balcony, surprised her trembling legs managed to carry her down the stairs. Twisting the knob, she opened the door and strode into the main salon. She had planned to continue with the rounds, to be seen, perhaps to make a few other acquaintances, but he had unsettled her. She was not accustomed to being unsettled.

As calmly as possible, she walked to the entrance, acutely aware of his gaze following her the entire way. She'd made a mistake tonight, misjudged. She would have to be more careful in the future. The Duke of Avendale had the power to destroy her.

Chapter 2

 By the time Rose strode in through the front door of her residence, she was back in control, her heart no longer pounding ferociously and threatening to crack a rib. A part of her was grateful she'd managed to escape. Another part, one she seldom allowed to come to the fore, wished she were still in the shadows of the balcony captivated by a kiss.

Merrick shuffled out of the parlor, his brow deeply furrowed. "Wasn't expecting you home so soon."

Removing her wrap, she handed it down to him. "See what you can uncover regarding the Duke of Avendale." She'd given the man too much power. To avoid that happening again, she needed to learn everything she could about him.

"Duke? That's a bit bold, even for you. He could be influential enough to see you hanged once he realizes what you're about."

"The trick there, then, is to ensure he doesn't realize what I'm about. Any problems this evening?"

"No." Merrick scrunched a face weathered by a harsh life. "He seems happy enough here. He's sleeping now. Maybe we could stay this time."

"You know that's not possible." She headed for the stairs, aware that Merrick traipsed along behind her.

"Maybe we could find another way."

She spun around. She'd misjudged his nearness and he rammed into her. Grabbing his shoulders, she prevented him from tumbling over. When he was once again steady, he peered up at her and repeated, "Maybe we could."

"What would you suggest? What could I possibly do that would provide us with the means to live in the luxury that we do?"

"Mayhap we don't need as much luxury."

"But Harry should have it. I owe him that."

"Ain't your fault the way your father treated him."

Merrick had not witnessed all that she had. He could not possibly fathom all the ramifications of her father's cruel actions. "Remember, Merrick, you are here by my good graces, not to question me. Now, let Sally know I've returned so she can assist me in preparing for bed." She carried on up the stairs, refusing to feel guilty over the life she led or consider the consequences it might heap upon her. Life was filled with choices. She'd made hers. It was too late for regrets, and they served no purpose except to distract.

In her bedchamber, she peeled off her gloves and tossed them onto the dressing table before walking to the window and gazing out on the fog-shrouded gardens. She'd not accomplished all she'd meant to tonight. She had hoped to make associations with women who would invite her to their balls and dinners. The more she was seen within high Society, the more she would be trusted, the more people would wish to assist her. But the duke had distracted her from her purpose.

After the blistering kisses he'd leveled on her, she

could hardly stay at the affair. It had not been until she was halfway home that she'd been able to think properly again. How could she scheme when her mind had turned to rubbish? Oh, she'd been given kisses before, but none that spoke of possession, none that consumed. She was quite surprised they'd not erupted into a conflagration on that balcony.

As she heard the door opening, she swung around and smiled. "Sally."

"Did you enjoy your evening?" Merrick's wife asked.

"Tonight's purpose was work, not enjoyment." She walked to the center of the room where a short stool rested and turned around. Sally stepped up and began loosening buttons and ribbons.

"Seems like you could mix the two."

"I might end up concentrating too much on one and losing sight of the other."

"Wouldn't be so bad if it was the work you lost sight of. When was the last time you had a bit of fun?"

With the gown loosened, Rose worked her way out of it. "I read an entire book just last night before I went to bed."

Scowling, coming around to take the gown, Sally said, "I'm talking about fun with others."

Rose smiled. "I have a jolly good time with you."

"You're being difficult now."

"Yes, I am, because I don't wish to discuss it."

After removing the remainder of her underclothes and slipping into her nightdress, she sat on the bench in front of her dressing table. If she could, she would have a home absent of mirrors, but she needed to know how she appeared before she went out. Appearance was crucial to the game.

But here, within her bedchamber, not so much.

When she looked at her reflection, she saw a woman nearing thirty, one who would never have a husband who loved her or children to adore. One who was so remarkably lonely that it was all she could do not to weep. She despised these moments of weakness when her lost dreams nudged her to be refound.

She had no right to complain, not when others suffered far more than she.

"You look sad," Sally said, as she moved near and began brushing Rose's hair.

"Simply tired. It was a long night."

"Merrick mentioned that you're inquiring about some duke."

"We danced." The reflection caught her smile. It appeared almost dreamy, as though she were a young girl filled with hope after her first waltz. "He was quite charming."

Deliciously so. And tempting.

"Was he handsome?" Sally asked.

"Do you know of a duke who isn't?" Rose asked.

"Don't know any dukes."

Rose laughed lightly. "Yes, he was handsome. Dark hair and darker eyes. Haunted eyes. He is not a joyful man."

"You was always so skilled at reading people."

She needed to be in order to do what she did. She'd learned the talent at her father's knee, not that learning anything from him was worthy of boast.

"Did you like him?" Sally asked.

Did she? "I don't know him well enough to know whether or not I like him."

"Was he a pleasant fellow?"

"He was intense. Most intense. He didn't visit much with people, although it was obvious a good many knew him. I think he was there for one purpose: to indulge in whatever sort of misbehavior became most convenient."

"And he thought to indulge with you." Sally moved around, draping Rose's plaited hair over her shoulder. "But you held him at bay."

The words were not a question but a declaration, and Rose knew Sally would be disappointed if anything untoward had happened—such as a kiss in the shadows. "It would not suit my purpose to give in to temptation."

"Were you tempted?"

Rose twisted on the bench, which put her on eye level with Sally. "No."

The lie should not have come so easily. It was slightly disconcerting that it did. If she could lie so easily to her dear friend, could she lie as easily to herself?

"Thank you, Sally. I'll see you in the morning." Rising, she walked to a corner table and poured herself a splash of brandy, as was her nightly ritual.

"You're troubled," Sally said.

"Tired, as I stated earlier." Glancing over her shoulder, she smiled. "I'm well. Good night."

She waited until Sally left, then walked over to the sitting area and curled up on the corner of the sofa. She inhaled the intoxicating aroma first. Taking a slow sip, she savored the flavor more than she ever had before. It reminded her of him. She imagined again his lips on hers.

And she tried not to regret that she had not left with him.

Avendale strode into his residence and staggered to a stop as a couple weaving toward the stairs nearly stumbled into him.

"Your Grace," the young swell slurred with an awkward salute before tumbling into a heap on the floor, dragging the woman at his side with him.

Avendale thought there was little worse than a man who could not hold his liquor.

With a delighted laugh, Aphrodite untangled herself from the drunkard and pushed herself to her feet. She swayed toward him. "Avendale, I seem to have lost my partner. I'd prefer to have you anyway."

Her gossamer gown revealed all her curvaceous attributes. Her blue eyes glinting with desire, she slowly ran a hand up his chest, over his shoulder. "I'm yours," she said with a sultry voice.

Yes, because he paid her—not in coin, but in excess. Clothes, jewelry, baubles, perfumes.

"Not tonight, Aphrodite." What he desired tonight, he'd been unable to obtain, which only served to make him want Rosalind Sharpe all the more. He couldn't recall the last time he'd been denied anything, the last time his thoughts had been so occupied with one woman.

Without guilt or remorse, he edged politely past Aphrodite—she'd find a new partner easily enough—and strode down the hallway to his library. A footman—not only standing at attention, but also standing guard as no one except servants was allowed in this room—opened the door. Avendale stepped inside. As the door was pulled closed behind him, he walked to a glass case that housed his spirits. A marble table rested beside it with glasses and decanters. After filling a tumbler with scotch, he took a chair near the fireplace and downed half the glass's contents, before sighing and dropping his head back.

How had his life come to this debauched existence? Beauties of questionable character were always on hand. Young swells were continually dropping by for a taste of women, drink, or cards. He didn't know the names of half of them, but they all knew orgies were carried on within the confines of his residence.

It had all begun when he was much younger, when he spent more time lost in women and wine. But of late, he'd begun to grow bored with it. He seldom accepted the ladies' offers anymore. He could no longer differentiate one from the other. Perhaps he never could. They'd been a means to deliver surcease for his aching loins. They'd provided a few moments' respite from dark thoughts—just as the drink did. It seemed of late he was relying more heavily on the drink.

He took another sip, forcing himself to savor it. He savored so little. He plowed into pleasures as though they were the answer.

When he didn't even know the bloody question.

Another sip. A dark chuckle. Had he really thought to bring Rosalind Sharpe here? To witness his madness, to see how far he'd fallen into depravity?

He could have explained his guests by saying tonight was merely a party—

Why did he feel he needed to justify the way he lived? He didn't. Not to her, not to anyone. He did what he wanted, when he wanted, as he wanted.

He got up, strode to his desk, and yanked the bellpull on the wall behind it. He walked to the window. Gaslights illuminated the gardens and the people cavorting about, some dancing naked in his fountain. There was a time when he would have joined them. Tonight he merely found them wearisome.

The door opened.

"I want them gone," he announced before his butler had taken half a dozen steps into the room.

Silence. Finally, *"Them?"*

"All these people. The women, the gents. Have the women call upon my man of business if they need assistance settling elsewhere."

"Yes, Your Grace. Will there be anything else?"

Avendale continued to stare at the gardens. "Have all the mattresses replaced. Pillows, cushions. Replace what can be replaced, get rid of what can't. Any furniture that reeks of sordid activities I want gone. This residence is to appear as though no one has ever been here save myself and that I have lived as chastely as a monk."

"I shall see to it posthaste."

"And ensure there is a servant on hand who knows how to attend to a lady."

"Yes, sir."

Avendale could hear the question in Thatcher's tone: Was the duke on the verge of taking a wife?

"That'll be all."

"As you wish, sir."

After Thatcher left, Avendale leaned against the window casement. He planned to entertain Mrs. Rosalind Sharpe in his residence in the very near future. He wanted her to feel comfortable, for everything to be to her liking, so the preparations needed to begin in earnest now.

She would not be an easy conquest, but conquer her he would.

*L*ying in bed, Rose stared at the ceiling. She'd had a dreadfully fitful slumber, sleeping a mere two winks, if that.

It was blasted Avendale's fault she had grown so warm that at one point she'd considered divesting herself of her nightdress. Even knowing it was nigh impossible, she could have sworn that she still felt his lips moving so determinedly over hers. He'd displayed no hesitation as he guided his hands along her side. He was a man who knew precisely what he wanted. And he wanted her.

Over the years, other men had as well. She'd grown skilled at enticing them near, yet holding them at bay. She wasn't certain Avendale would be quite as easy to manipulate. He was dangerous, not likely to settle for the crumbs with which she was willing to part.

She would do well to seek out another benefactor, but Avendale fascinated her. "I will have you," he'd said. As she wasn't likely to shake him off easily, she might as well embrace the challenge of besting him. Could be fun and include a few additional pleasantries. Kissing him was certainly no hardship. As long as she remained in control and held him to that, she thought she could gain everything she wanted.

A quick glance at the clock on the mantel revealed that it was midmorning. Tempted to pull the covers over her head to see if she could fall more easily into slumber, she resisted, knowing that Harry would be enjoying breakfast now. She should have checked in on him last night, but she'd had the insane notion that if he awoke he would be able to look at her and know the sort of mischief she'd been up to with Avendale, had even wondered if he might have caught the scent of the duke on her skin.

Guilt could certainly make her irrational.

She rolled out of bed and began to prepare for the day: washing up, brushing her hair and pulling it back, holding it in place with a ribbon, donning a simple blue dress that required no assistance. As soon as she was satisfied with her appearance she wandered down to the breakfast dining room.

"Hello, dearest," she said to Harry as she walked in. He was four years her junior, not that many would guess that, as life had not been particularly kind to him and the hardships had taken a toll. Leaning down, she pressed a kiss to the top of his head. "How are you this morning?"

"Well," he replied, his eyes sparkling with joy as he gave her the smile that never failed to warm her heart.

He sat at the head of the small square table. Sitting opposite him so it would be easier to carry on a conversation, she lifted the teapot and poured some of the brew into her cup. A few covered dishes rested on the table. As it was only the two of them each morning, they kept the meals small and simple. No sideboards laden with assorted items. They could not afford the waste.

"Did you have fun last night?" he asked.

She dropped four cubes of sugar into her tea, stirred. "I did indeed. Although I missed you terribly, not to mention our reading. I'm most anxious to discover where Gulliver's travels take him next." Her reading to him was their nightly ritual. "I shall stay in tonight."

"Tell me about the place you visited," he urged.

"The building was incredible, the people adorned magnificently. We shall begin as I walked through the doors." Then recalling every detail memorized, she set about to paint a vivid portrait of the night, which she hoped would give him a memory he would never be able to acquire on his own.

"I wish I could see it," he murmured when she was finally finished.

"I wish you could, too, my love. I'll draw pictures for you later if you like."

He gave a barely perceptible nod, before returning his attention to his food. She knew sketches were a poor substitute, but she could not risk his ruining her plans. Their future depended on them.

Chapter 3

"You are beginning to make my employees uncomfortable with your lurking about in the balcony."

Avendale had been up here, scouring the crowd, making note of who entered, who left, for the better part of three nights now. He glared at Drake. "Shouldn't you be off tending to your wedding?"

"Phee and her aunt are managing that. I merely need to acquire the license, so I have time to see to my business. Right now the club is a novelty, its acceptance still questionable. However, I did not invite women to join so men could engage in voyeurism. You're going to damage the reputation of my establishment, of what I'm trying to achieve, if you continue in this vein. I shall be forced to relieve you of your key."

Ignoring the rebuke and the threat, Avendale asked, "What do you know of Mrs. Rosalind Sharpe?"

"Who?"

"You don't know who she is, yet you invited her to your ball?"

"The name is somewhat familiar."

"The lady in red," Avendale said impatiently. "I

introduced her—or rather *she* introduced herself—to you in the gentlemen's salon."

"Ah, yes, I remember now. I'm afraid I was rather preoccupied with other thoughts that night."

"So how did she come to your attention?"

Drake brushed his fingers through his long, dark hair. "Her solicitor sent me a missive, thought she might qualify based on my standards."

"Which were?"

"A well-turned ankle and money."

Avendale did not like that the solicitor might have seen her ankle. "How would he know what her ankle looks like?"

Drake sighed. "He was referring to the fact that she is female. Why do you care?"

"Has she been here since the ball? I've not seen her."

Crossing his arms over his chest, Drake leaned against the wall. "Have you an interest in her?"

Avendale saw no point in mincing words. "I want to bed her."

Drake narrowed his eyes. "The ladies welcomed to my club are not here for that purpose."

"I'm not going to force her, but I certainly intend to seduce her. Nothing I do will reflect badly upon your establishment."

"I should hope not. I would hate to revoke your membership."

"Has she been here?" Avendale repeated succinctly.

"Not that I've noticed."

"Did she purchase a membership?"

"I would have to check my records."

"Then check them."

"That information is private."

"We have long been friends—"

"We've never been friends. Acquaintances—due to our family connections and our friendship with Lovingdon. But other than that, I would be hard-pressed to refer to us as friends."

Avendale scowled. For a man who catered to vice, Drake was far too upstanding. And irritating as the devil, even if he was being generous with the definition of their relationship. "Is there anything you can tell me about her?"

"Not really, no." Drake held up a hand before Avendale could lambast him for his unwillingness to cooperate. "I don't truly know her. As I said, I invited her because of a recommendation."

"But you must have researched her a tad. And you would have obtained her address in order to send her an invitation."

"Again, private."

"Devil take you." Avendale turned his attention back to the main floor. What if she never returned? What if she hadn't been intrigued by what the Twin Dragons had to offer? What if she'd not been intrigued by him?

The kisses they'd shared indicated otherwise. But perhaps the attraction had frightened her. Just because she was a widow didn't mean that she'd known passion. Her husband could have been one of those sanctimonious sorts who believed only men derived pleasure from copulation. What had transpired between her and Avendale had been heated—

Blond silken strands caught up into a perfect coiffure with a few curls dangling along a slender neck snagged his attention as a woman walked through the door. The air backed up painfully in his lungs. She wore a deep violet gown that left her shoulders bare so that he could nibble on them more easily. White gloves rose past her elbows. He would enjoy leisurely peeling them off.

"What's garnered your attention?" Drake asked.

"She's here." At last, at long last. He released his breath. It was unconscionable that she affected him so. To maintain the upper hand, he would remain up here for at least half an hour. Then he would slowly make his way—

To hell with it. He couldn't risk her leaving before he ensured their paths crossed.

"Have a room prepared for a private card game." He strode briskly from the balcony.

"Is the elusive Duke of Avendale smitten?" Drake called out.

Ignoring the mocking tone, Avendale carried on. Smitten was too tame a word for what he felt. Regretfully he had no words to describe this madness that was in possession of him because he'd never experienced anything like it. He simply knew he had to have her. One way or another. At any cost.

*S*he'd waited three nights before returning to the club. Best not to appear too eager. But they might have been the longest nights of her life, even though she'd spent them with Harry, reading, playing whist, walking through the gardens. He preferred the gardens at night. Although the flowers had closed their blossoms, their fragrance still lingered.

Here, the fragrances were very different. Tobacco, spirits on the breath, dark masculine colognes fought with lighter feminine perfumes for dominance. She was surprised not many women were about, but then simply because a place was accessible to ladies didn't mean they would frequent it, particularly if they had domineering fathers, brothers, or husbands in their lives. She was fortunate to rule her own life. She had since she'd reached the age of ten and seven and run off from her cruel father.

She handed her wrap to a young woman at the counter by the door, received a slip of paper with a number on it, and tucked it into her reticule.

She wondered if she should first visit the women's salon and private gaming area, if she should strive to strengthen connections there. With her last visit, she'd met very few ladies, and while her ultimate plan involved a gentleman, she knew that women had quite the influence over males, even if those males were domineering.

On the other hand, she was sure to be noticed with so few women about in here. Being noticed was paramount.

As she approached a roulette table, she caught a gentleman's eye. Winking at her, he eased over slightly, allowing room for her to get nearer to the excitement. She watched the little ball spinning, heading toward a numbered slot. Five, she thought. It landed on twenty-one. A single groan, composed of nearly a dozen voices, rose up. No sooner had the wooden tokens been gathered up than others were being set down.

A hand came to rest on the side of her waist, and she was remarkably aware of a broad chest at her back. She might have been startled if his presence wasn't so powerful, if she hadn't sensed his approach before he arrived.

"Have you ever played?" Avendale whispered low against her ear, and she fought not to alert him to the tiny shiver that coursed through her at his nearness.

"No, but it seems rather easy."

"Which means the odds of losing is greater." He

set some coins on the table. The man who had spun the wheel gave him a stack of green disks and placed a small metal token on it. Avendale held the disks out to her. "Place them wherever you like."

"I don't want to lose your money."

"It's only money."

She ground her back teeth together to withhold a scathing retort. Only money to him. Life to her.

Peering at him through lowered eyelashes, giving him a gamine smile, she took the wooden circles and placed them all on twenty-five, Harry's age.

"You can spread them out if you like," Avendale said.

"I believe in all or nothing."

She felt a subtle tightening of his hand on her waist.

"As do I," he rasped so low she suspected no one else heard.

The croupier waved his hand over the table, spun the wheel, dropped the ball—

Rose was acutely aware of Avendale's inappropriate nearness. She should elbow him, get him to move, and yet she relished the heat of him, his fragrance, his breath feathering along strands of her hair. She didn't want the ball to ever roll into a slot. She wanted to stay as she was forever, which was remarkably stupid and shortsighted. She had responsibilities. A plan.

"Thirty-three black," the croupier called out.

Rose slammed her eyes closed, released with a great huff the breath she'd been holding. Opening her eyes, she peered up at Avendale. "I'm so sorry."

"Have dinner with me, and I'll forgive you."

She released a light laugh. "Forgive me? When I had no control over the outcome?"

"You chose the number. Besides, you apologized so you must be feeling a measure of guilt. I merely wish to relieve you of it. Have you eaten this evening?"

"Nothing substantial."

"I've yet to sample the dining room here, but I do know the cook is excellent."

"I suppose I'm feeling a bit peckish."

"Splendid." He offered his arm, but the intensity of his gaze gave her pause. He could destroy her plans so easily. Or perhaps he would turn out to be her savior.

She placed her hand in the crook of his elbow. Merrick had discovered that Avendale was quite well off. A lot of activity was going on at his residence, as though he were moving out a previous mistress in hopes of moving in a different one. If he was thinking of her for that role, he was going to be disappointed, as Rose had no plans to be his mistress, to visit his bed. But his interest indicated that she could taunt him, make him want her until he was willing to give her whatever she asked. Only to discover too late that he would not acquire all he desired.

She had some standards, arbitrary and low though they might be.

As they made their way along hallways, she caught the occasional inquisitive, speculative glance from gents and ladies, but was relieved to see—once they entered the dining room—that at nearly every occupied table was a man and a woman. Two gents were seated at one table. At two others were solitary gentlemen. But this seemed to be a place that catered more to couples.

Avendale spoke low with a man in red livery. Then they were escorted to a distant corner that housed more shadows than light.

She had the irritating notion that he was ashamed to be seen with her. "Would it be better to not isolate ourselves?" she asked, not bothering to hide her pique at being hidden away.

"I want to get to know you better," he said. "Being away from the others suits my purpose."

"They may think we're up to no good."

"They all know me well enough to know that I'm always up to no good."

"You say that with such pride."

"One must excel at something and I excel at being fodder for gossip."

Had he no shame? How wonderful it must be to be in a position not to care what others thought. He nodded toward the footman or whatever the man was, and the servant quickly pulled out her chair.

Hesitating, she considered the other couples. Surely they were not all married, surely sitting with Avendale in a darkened corner would not cause damage to her reputation, to her goal. On the other hand, sitting in the shadows with him might make everything else moot, might allow her to gain what she wanted that much more quickly.

She sank onto the seat and proceeded to peel off a glove. Before she could blink, Avendale was kneeling beside her, taking her hand. "Allow me."

She fought not to appear stunned. "Get up. People are likely to think you're proposing marriage."

"As I said, they know me well enough here, and so they know I'm not engaged in any such nonsense. Although before the night is done I intend to propose something quite wicked."

His eyes smoldered as they met hers. With that devilish smile of his, how could she take offense? She couldn't blame him for his forthrightness when she'd accepted his kisses the other night. In fact, she preferred it. The game he was playing was more honest than hers. "I believe, Your Grace, that you have mistaken me for a woman of questionable moral character. I assure you I am no light-skirt."

"I'm counting on it."

What the devil did he mean by that? Then all thoughts fled her mind as he slowly stroked a blunt-tipped finger along the inside of her upper arm, above the glove. Down. Up once more. Pleasure skidded along her skin, warmed her to the core.

When he reached the glove again, he began slowly rolling it down, the edge of his fingers caressing her skin, a hint of a touch, more a promise, until the supple kidskin was gathered at her wrist. She wondered if he could feel the throbbing of her pulse there.

Gently he tugged on each finger, until he finally peeled away the glove. He held her fingers, strength and assurance in his hold. He wasn't cocky. She didn't even think he could be classified as arrogant, but he was a man who understood his place in the world was at its peak, and he could not be toppled from it. She imagined his ancestors on a battlefield. They would have led the charge; even if they had been the last ones standing, they'd have not gone down in defeat. She had an insane realization that she should have stayed at the roulette wheel. The odds might have been with the house, but she thought she stood a better chance at beating them than beating him. Then again, she did so love a challenge, and outfoxing him would bring such satisfaction.

He took her other hand, gave the exact same ministrations to the skin above her elbow, caressing with soft deliberation before removing her glove. Only this time when he took her fingers, he turned her palm up and pressed a kiss to its heart. Her lungs froze. Everything within her told her to run, but she had run only twice in her life. The first time had resulted in failure and a beating. But she had learned the hard lesson. The second time, no one had been able to catch her.

In the years since, wisdom had taught her the value in standing her ground. He could only win if she let him. "You're taking liberties you shouldn't."

He lifted his gaze to hers. She saw the amusement there, and a hint of victory. It appeared he was one to stand his ground as well. "This is a place of vice and sin. Ladies should comprehend the significance of that if they want entry."

"You're using me to set an example. That could be most dangerous, Your Grace." Leaning over, she bussed a kiss against his cheek, before sliding her mouth to his ear and whispering in a low, sultry voice, "Know that two can play this game."

*H*er kiss nearly unmanned him. Her words did the deed.

It took Avendale a moment to regain his bearings so he could stand to take his chair. He knew women who were coy. He knew women who didn't pretend to be anything other than what they were. But none of them were as straightforward as she. She would challenge him at every turn, but he welcomed it, was excited by the prospects. It had been a good long while since anything had excited him.

The footman came over and handed them each a card upon which the night's delicacies were printed. "Will you want wine this evening?" he asked.

With an arched brow, Avendale met Rosalind's gaze.

"Wine," she said. "Red. I prefer heavier ones that linger on the tongue."

Avendale thought of her tongue lingering on him,

lapping at his throat, his chest, lower. Inwardly, he cursed the hoarseness in his voice when he ordered the most expensive bottle on hand.

When the wine was poured, he lifted his goblet to hers. "To making the most of the night."

Her lips curled up slightly. "Well worth drinking to." She tapped her glass against his, took a sip of wine, closed her eyes. "That's marvelous."

She opened her eyes, and he regretted that they were in shadows, that he couldn't see the sapphire depths as clearly. When he made love to her, he would do so with lights blazing. He wanted to see the fire in her eyes, the passion, and ultimately the apex of pleasure.

He ordered the finest fare on the menu. For her, he wanted only the best. She was not some cheap bawd. She was like no woman he'd ever experienced.

"Tell me about this odd family of yours," she demanded. "With its commoners and nobility."

He swirled his glass, watched the wine create a vortex that could suck him under if he wasn't careful. "People met, fell in love with no consideration for rank or propriety, married, had children. Boring. I'd rather talk about you."

"Presently, I'm dreadfully boring. I've been in respectable mourning for two years. Now I am ready to experience life again. I want to make the most of it."

Reaching across the table, he took her hand and stroked his thumb over her knuckles. "I can help you achieve that goal."

She once more released the light laughter that teased the edges of his soul. "You're not at all arrogant, are you?"

"I know what I want and I'm accustomed to acquiring it."

She slipped her hand from his. "If you discover the price is exceedingly high?"

"I think you would be worth any price."

"I'm not a whore, Your Grace."

"Neither are you an innocent. You know we're engaged in a game of seduction."

She angled her head, peered at him through lowered lashes. "Yes, and I also know I hold all the cards."

$\mathcal{R}$ose was grateful when the turtle soup arrived. Not that her stomach was relaxed enough to truly enjoy the delicacy.

She'd never had a man be so bold in insinuating what he wanted. He both frightened and excited her. The way he watched her, the way his gaze slowly roamed over her as though he could quite clearly envision her without her clothing. The odd thing was that she found herself wondering what he might look like beneath the gentleman's attire.

She had never found herself drawn to a man in this manner, had never itched to loosen buttons or remove a neck cloth. Had never wanted to order him to stand perfectly still while she unwrapped him as though he were a gift. She had little doubt that Avendale was a gift—probably from Lucifer himself. He was certainly no angel.

At certain moments, she forgot that they weren't alone here, that her thoughts were entirely inappropriate, that his innuendoes were deserving of a slap.

Yet at the same time, the lonely woman inside her was flattered by his attentions, even though she understood that she was merely a novelty. Once he acquired what he wanted, he would be done with her. He was a man of passions that she suspected changed with the wind.

Presently the wind was blowing in her direction and she needed to make the most of it. Who knew when it would begin gusting elsewhere?

"What is your name?" she asked, noticing that he'd barely touched the soup and was again indulging in the wine.

"Avendale."

"Your mother gave you a name when you were born. What was it?"

"Actually, I suspect it was my father who provided the name. As I understand it he was very specific regarding how things were to be done."

"How old were you when he died?"

"Four when they told me he was killed in a fire."

Odd phrasing, she thought, but she suspected any specific inquiry regarding it would be rebuffed, so she moved on. "Do you remember him?"

"Benjamin Paul Buckland, Earl of Whitson, Duke of Avendale," he said abruptly, obviously not intending to answer her question about his father. "From the moment I was born, I carried the courtesy title of the Earl of Whitson. To this day, my mother calls me Whit more often than she calls me Avendale. No one, absolutely no one, calls me Benjamin or Paul. That, sweetheart, is the extent to which I will share anything about my family or my past. They have no place in my life."

"The past is always there," she told him. "You might ignore it, but you would be a fool not to recognize its influence, and you don't strike me as a fool."

"I'm interested in you, aren't I? That should prove me not to be a fool."

The opposite, she thought. It proved the opposite.

The next dish was brought out. Duck glazed in some sort of orange concoction that she wished she could take home to Harry. Sally cooked but her skills leaned more toward hearty food that put meat on bones, not that one could tell by looking at Rose. She was quite conscientious regarding her figure since she considered it her most alluring asset when it came to capturing the attention of the males of her species.

"Have you a box at the theater?" she asked.

He took a long swallow of his wine, and she wished she could remove his neck cloth, watch the movements of his throat as he indulged in the red bouquet. She didn't know why she had this blasted obsession with removing his clothes. No other man had ever caused these thoughts to spiral recklessly through her mind, but then no other man she'd encountered up close was as fine a specimen as the one before her now.

"I believe it is mandatory for dukes to have a box at the theater," he finally said.

"I've never been to the London theater. It is on my list of things I should like to do in my life."

"Did Mr. Sharpe not take you?"

She was surprised he'd brought up her husband. She would have thought it bad form to mention another man to a woman one was attempting to seduce. "We never visited London. Instead, we moved to India two seconds after we were married."

"Why India?"

She gave him a small smile. "You expect me to reveal my past while you refuse to reveal yours?"

"I'm sure yours is more interesting. Where else have you traveled?"

"Only to India. My husband had business there."

"Where were you raised?"

"To the north."

His luscious mouth that no doubt tasted of dark

wine now spread into a slow grin. "Seems you are as forthcoming as I."

"Stubborn more like," she said, sipping her own wine. "I won't reveal my past if you won't reveal yours."

"Then we must concentrate on the present."

She paid little attention to the number of courses brought out, but she knew their dinner was coming to an end when a piece of cake coated in chocolate was set before her. As she enjoyed her first bite, she released a little moan. "That is scrumptious."

Reaching across, he stroked his thumb at the corner of her mouth. She saw a bit of chocolate on it just before he slipped it between his lips. "Indeed you are."

Molten heat spiraled through her. Why did she have these reactions when he barely touched her, merely gazed at her, smiled? Dare she risk another kiss tonight?

After he signed his name in a small book the footman brought him, Avendale got to his feet and helped her out of her chair. As they walked through the dining room, his large hand lighted on the small of her back, nonchalantly and yet possessively. She could not help but feel he was laying claim to her in front of anyone who was here.

"Perhaps you would join me for a private card game," he said quietly as they stepped into the main area. "I've had a secluded room arranged."

Stopping, she shifted slightly to face him and fought to appear as innocent as possible. "How many will be playing?"

His eyes darkened with promise. "Only you and I."

She considered, but knew it was too soon. It was always to her advantage to leave them wanting. "I am tempted, Your Grace. *You* tempt me, but I think we both know that it could prove very dangerous and lead to destinations to which I am not yet ready to travel."

"I would be on my best behavior."

"Your *best* could prove to be very bad indeed. I truly appreciate dinner, but I must be off now. Perhaps another night." Rising up on her toes, placing a hand on his shoulder for balance, she lightly brushed her lips along his cheek before whispering in his ear, "I shall be riding in Hyde Park tomorrow at four."

Then without a backward glance, she left him standing there. Once again, she was aware of his gaze homed in on her, was aware of everything about him. She was spinning a web and knew that with him, she had to be careful that she wasn't the one who became ensnared in it.

Chapter 4

"*T*he duchess is here to see you, Your Grace," Thatcher announced.

At the desk in his library the following afternoon, Avendale looked up from the note he'd been penning to his mother. Thatcher continued to refer to her as the duchess, although she'd not been a duchess for a good many years, not since she'd married a commoner. But for Thatcher, who had been in her employ long before he was in Avendale's, she would always remain the duchess.

"Inform her that I'm not at home."

Thatcher merely looked at him.

Avendale sighed. "You are in my employ now, Thatcher, not hers."

"She is your mother."

"I am well aware." But their relationship was strained, had been for years. It was difficult for him to be with her and not reveal what he suspected, what he knew, what he'd seen. He'd lost count of the number of times he'd almost confronted her, but what could come of it—except to put more distance between them?

Thatcher did not move, did not avert his gaze.

"I should have you sacked," Avendale said.

Thatcher lifted a brow that had once been black as Satan's soul and was now almost as white as angel wings. "Does that mean you are home?"

"Yes." But only because, upon reconsideration, he needed her to know he would be making use of the theater box this week. Easier to tell her in person than to pen the missive. He allowed her to use it, as he seldom went to the theater. Truth be told, he couldn't recall the last time he'd gone. When he was much younger and had taken a fancy to an older actress. She had taught him the value of seasoned women.

His mother swept into the room, radiating poise and self-assurance.

Avendale got up, rounded the desk, and pressed a kiss to his mother's cheek. "You don't have to be announced."

She gave him a wry smile. "I worry about interrupting you and one of your paramours."

"Yes, I suppose that might prove uncomfortable." He walked over to the sideboard. "A bit of sherry?"

"It's only just past noon," she admonished.

"Then it seems I'm getting started late." He poured himself some scotch, indicated two chairs near a window that looked out on the gardens. As she daintily took a seat in the plush brown velvet chair, he sprawled in the one opposite her.

"The residence seems different somehow," she said.

"I dispensed with the company I was keeping and had the servants give it a thorough cleaning."

She brightened. "Does this mean a nice lady has caught your fancy?"

"A lady yes. Remains to be seen how nice she is. I'm hoping not very."

"Oh, Whit," she chastised. "There is more to life than naughty women."

"Not for me."

"It's high time you settled down. Lovingdon has married, and now I hear that Drake Darling is betrothed to Lady Ophelia Lyttleton. Seems something is in the air this Season."

"Then I shall immediately take to holding my breath as often and as long as possible so that I don't become infected with whatever is in the air to cause such bad judgment," he assured her.

"Why are you so against love?"

"Surely you didn't come here to discuss the state of my heart."

"No, but sometimes I wonder where my sweet little boy went."

Her sweet little boy had seen something that had irrevocably changed him. He recognized she would never forgive herself if she knew.

"He grew up," he told her. "By the by, I shall need my box at the theater this week."

"Oh dear God, not another actress."

He grinned. "On the contrary, she may be the most unpretentious woman I've ever met."

"Who is she?"

"You won't know her. She doesn't run around in your circles."

"You would be surprised by how wide my circles are these days."

That much was true. She met a good many commoners through her husband. "Mrs. Rosalind Sharpe."

"A married woman?"

He heard the disappointment in her voice, and it pricked that she would suspect the worst. He didn't know why, because he had entertained married women on occasion, so his mother's assumption was valid. "Widowed."

"Old?"

"Young."

"Dark?"

"Fair. She's new to London."

"Marvelous. I'm hosting a dinner party Thursday next. I stopped by to issue an invitation. You should bring her."

"My relationship with her—or what I intend for my relationship with her to be—is not something to which you want to expose your other children."

His mother looked at him for long assessing moments that made him want to squirm in his chair. "I know you're searching for something, Whit. I wish I knew what the devil it was."

So did he, but he hadn't a bloody clue.

Chapter 5

"A horse? What you be needing a horse for?" Merrick asked.

Rose watched as her coachman, Joseph, examined the beautiful white mare. Mr. Slattery, who had just delivered it, was standing off to the side out of earshot, thank goodness, as Merrick had no command of dulcet tones.

"For rides in the park," she answered softly.

"You've got two legs. They seem to work well enough."

She sighed with exasperation and bent down until she was on eye level with him. "Honestly, Merrick, you do try my patience. I intend for this to be our last haul for a while and I need to make it count. In order for that happen, I'm required to project a certain image. If you must discuss this, we'll do it later."

She straightened as Joseph turned away from the horse and winked at her. "She's good."

Smiling, she trod across the ground behind her residence where a small stable and livery was kept. She held out her hand. "Thank you, Mr. Slattery. I shall notify Mr. Beckwith to send you the funds with interest as soon as he has finished settling my husband's estate."

"Thank you, m'um," he said, tipping his hat to her before he left.

She saw no reason to alert him that her solicitor had stopped by that morning to inform her that he was having a dreadful time locating the people with whom he needed to speak in India in order to settle the estate and ensure she received all her husband had left to her. Over tea, she had flattered him for his determined efforts and encouraged him not to give up. He was her last hope in acquiring what was rightfully hers. She knew it was a nuisance having to work with foreigners, but there you had it.

He had reiterated that she was to send any merchants his way so that he could assure them her credit was good and payment would be forthcoming. She had also convinced him to lend her two thousand pounds in cash for anything for which she could not be billed. After all, a woman alone in the world could not be expected to get by with no coin whatsoever.

"Joseph, saddle her up for me, will you?" she asked. "I'm going to change into my riding habit and then I'll be off."

"I don't like this," Merrick muttered as they walked to the house.

"You don't have to."

"It just seems that this time you're taking a lot more risks."

"For greater rewards." Stopping, she faced him. "He's not like the others, Merrick. He can't be won over with flattery or words designed to puff up his pride. It's a very different sort of web I'm weaving. It requires more finesse, a more elaborate deception."

"Then leave off. Find someone else to fleece."

She hadn't half considered it. "No. I'm enjoying the challenge of it, of him. Besides, he is too intrigued with me to simply walk away if I appeared to have lost interest. He wants me too badly."

"Sounds as though it's *your* pride that's being puffed up here."

Did Merrick have the right of it? She couldn't deny that Avendale's pursuit was a balm to her wounded soul, but it wasn't affecting her decisions. They were as they'd always been: calculating and made without emotion. "My pride has nothing to do with it. As I said, he won't give me up, but when the time comes we need to be able to move with urgency and to a location quite far away. I'm thinking Scotland, especially if I'm able to gain enough so we can live comfortably for a while without worrying about creditors or obtaining more funds. If you don't like the way I keep food in your belly, clothes on your back, and a roof over your head, you're welcome to leave."

He scowled. "You know I won't find anything better than this. Least you give me respect."

"I ask only that you do the same of me."

An hour later she was sitting astride Lily—the name she'd decided on for the horse—as the mare trotted along Rotten Row. It was a gorgeous afternoon. A slight breeze in the air, the sun warming her face. So many people were about. She recognized a few from her sojourns to the Twin Dragons. Three gentlemen tipped their hats to her. A couple of ladies smiled.

But she needed more.

Patience, she cautioned herself. The key was patience.

Then she saw him. He was here, trotting toward her on a large black horse. Magnificent. Avendale, not the horse. Although the beast was a beauty.

The thrill of his presence, the excitement of his near-ing nearly toppled her from her saddle. Here was the more she wanted, the more she could never possess.

She wished circumstances were different, wished she were different. But if she were, she wouldn't be here now, would have never met him. He was a duke and she was completely undeserving of his time and attention. But it didn't stop her from craving it.

Slowing Lily to a walk, she gave no pretense that she was doing anything other than what she was: waiting for him to catch up to her. As he came closer, she pulled back on the reins, stopped.

Bringing his horse to a halt, he swept his hat from his head. "Rose."

She loved the shortened version of her name on his lips. One syllable, but he said it in a way that was both provocative and sensual. Whatever was wrong with her, to be so affected, when others had called her that for most of her life? But no one else made her want to sway toward him. No one else made her heart patter against her ribs. No one else made her seriously consider adding fornication without benefit of marriage to her lengthy list of sins.

"Benjamin."

He growled. "I knew I shouldn't have shared that with you."

"If you're going to be familiar with me, it seems I should be equally familiar with you."

"If you can't call me Avendale, call me Whit."

"Your mother calls you that. The last thing I want is for you to think of me as your mother."

"The things I want to do with you . . . trust me, my mother will be the farthest thing from my mind regardless of what you call me."

The blatant sexual yearning in his eyes nearly had

her sliding to the ground in a pool of heated desire. How was it possible that he affected her so with little more than a gaze? Never before had she wanted to run her hands up a man's arms, over his shoulders, along his chest and back. Never had she wanted to see exactly what lay beneath his clothing, how it might be sculpted and shaped, how the lines might fan out and meet.

With a little nudge she urged her horse forward. Avendale—she could not think of him as Whit or even Benjamin as his title suited him much better—brought his horse round so it could plod along beside hers.

"How long will you be in London?" he asked.

She looked at him askance. "I intend to make it my home. I have found much here that . . . appeals to me." With any other man, the last sentence would have been a lie, spoken merely to give him reason to preen. But Avendale was not one for preening, and speaking honestly about her attraction to him served her purpose.

"I prefer you not stroke me with words, but with your hands." He leaned over so far that she was surprised he didn't topple from the saddle. "Or your mouth."

She was quite certain she turned as red as her favorite evening gown. "You do take liberties with your innuendoes." She wondered why she sounded so breathless, as though she were galloping over the green.

"You're not untouched. I see no reason to mince words or to pretend that I want anything other than what I do."

"Just because I'm no longer virginal does not mean that I don't deserve to be wooed. I require affection."

"I assure you that you won't find yourself noticing any lack of affection."

Those heated eyes again, the promise of passion that she feared would leave her scalded for life.

"Let's stroll, shall we?" he asked.

Stroll? Did he truly believe that her legs could support her after the way he looked at her, the words he uttered? She didn't want to be so affected by him. It muddled her thinking. On the other hand, perhaps being nearer to him would muddle his.

"Yes, that would be delightful." At least her breath had recovered, and she sounded more like herself.

As he drew his horse to a halt, she did the same with hers, then watched in fascination as he swung his leg back and dismounted. Why did every movement of his, no matter how common or small, have to intrigue her? He could hold her attention for hours by doing nothing more than taking in breaths. It was utterly ridiculous that he should have a claim over her senses.

He came to stand before her and wrapped his hands around her waist. Such large hands, such capable ones. Hands that could effectively close around her throat and stop all breath from entering her body should he discover her plans, should they fill him with rage. She should have chosen a smaller man, but the truth was that she'd had little choice once he'd approached her, once she'd lured him in.

He wanted her now, and she knew he was not one to turn his back until he'd gained what he wanted.

Which was the reason she momentarily considered facing his wrath, because what he wanted, she would not give. She'd done a good many things in her life, a good many that brought her no pride, but she had managed to do what she needed without spreading her legs to obtain what she *wanted*. She was every bit as determined to gain what she coveted as he was.

Although the advantage was all hers. She knew the true game being played, the rules. While he was engaged in another sort of sport. The trick was to ensure that he didn't realize they weren't on the same playing field until she'd already won.

Dropping her gaze to his luscious lips, she thought of their previous kisses, knew visions of them were enough to flush her skin, cause her eyes to become molten blue. She knew a moment of satisfaction as she saw him swallow, felt his hands tighten on her. She placed her gloved hands on his shoulders, relished the strength there, even as it caused trepidation to slice through her.

Slowly, so slowly, he lifted her up, lifted her off, lowered her feet to the ground, bringing her in close so her breasts skimmed along his chest. Her nipples puckered painfully, her heart pounded, her stomach clenched. She locked her knees, ensuring she remained upright.

Because of his blasted hat, the upper portion of his face was in shadow as he looked down at her. She wanted to knock it off with one quick swipe, see his eyes clearly, know his thoughts, his feelings, his desires. With his thumbs, he stroked her ribs, once, twice, thrice before finally releasing his hold, stepping back, and gathering up the reins for both horses, holding them loosely in one hand before offering her his free arm.

It would be wiser to ignore it, but she couldn't deny her fingers the luxury of the firmness in his muscles. Against her better judgment, she nestled her hand in the crook of his elbow.

While she was not particularly diminutive in height, she was well aware that he shortened his steps to accommodate her as they walked leisurely along, leaving

Rotten Row behind. At first he acknowledged a few people with a nod, a touch to his hat brim, but then he seemed to grow bored with it. No one approached to speak with him. He somehow managed to give off the aura of a man not wanting to be disturbed.

Any hope she might have held for an untarnished reputation fluttered away like the butterflies that frolicked around them. She was well aware that he was claiming her here. In the afternoon sunlight, in the crowded park where those with leisurely lives strolled about, making note of who was spending time with whom. With his demonstration of possessiveness, her options became fewer.

But then if she were honest with herself, they had diminished to one the moment she turned to find him extending a flute of champagne toward her. She might as well enjoy his company for as long as she would have it, as far as they would take it. Although not as far as he insinuated.

She had spoken true last night. She did hold the cards. While she had nothing on which to base her judgment other than her assessment of him, she knew he was not a man who forced a woman into doing something to which she objected. They might kiss, they might touch, but ultimately he would be left wanting. She wondered at the regret that filled her with the thought.

"How many estates do you have?" she asked.

He glanced down at her, and she shrugged. "I'm curious about you and you seem hesitant to discuss anything too personal. I can ask around to find out about your estates. I daresay the solicitor seeing to my husband's estate could tell me. He seems to know the well-heeled and the aristocracy quite well."

"Who's your solicitor?" he asked.

"Beckwith."

"Which one?"

"Daniel."

"The youngest."

"You're familiar with Beckwith and Sons?"

He gave one curt nod. "Their father handled much of my business until he passed it on to his eldest. The other two sons have solid reputations. I don't know that you could have gone to anyone better."

"I fear he's finding it a bit frustrating to settle everything. My husband did not leave his affairs in good order. Beckwith is having a time of it straightening things out. Meanwhile I rely on the kindness of strangers. Although I do worry that those to whom I am in debt will soon lose patience."

"If anyone can hold them at bay, Beckwith can."

"I shall depend on it. So your estates?" she prodded, wanting to get them away from discussing Beckwith. She wasn't too concerned about Avendale approaching the man about her business, as it was obvious that he was more interested in his own.

"Two plus my residence in London. Ghastly large, but it came to me through my father. I suspect I shall always have it."

"You mentioned that he died when you were four. Have you many memories of him?"

"Very few, none of them worth your time."

"Anything about you is worth my time."

He released a dark laugh. "Not that. Why all the questions, Rose?"

"Aren't you accustomed to ladies asking you about yourself?"

"No, not really. The ladies whose company I keep generally want but one thing and it requires little conversation."

"You never explore a lady's mind?"

"I find a lady's mind tedious. I prefer exploring other aspects of her."

"I fear I'm rather insulted. I don't find my thoughts tedious at all."

"Perhaps you shall prove an exception."

They had reached a copse of trees. As he led her into them, she glanced over her shoulder. People were too far away for her to tell if they were paying attention to Avendale's destination. But what did it matter? Being alone with him was damaging enough. Although in the end, nothing would deter her from gaining what she wanted.

The boughs were thick with leaves, the sunlight dappled the ground. Avendale wrapped the reins around a low bush, before taking her into his arms and lowering his mouth to hers. She'd known the kiss was coming. Still the impact of it was a shock, because he did not go gently, but rather he ravished as though he were a man who'd been too long without sustenance.

Immediately her knees went weak even as she wound her arms around his neck. She backed up a step, another until her spine was pressed to bark and Avendale was flattening her breasts with his broad chest. His tongue conquered, possessed, luxuriated.

The velvety silkiness of it lured her, had her knocking off that blasted hat that kept far too much of him in shadows, had her running her fingers up into his hair, tugging on the coarse thick strands, holding him near, encouraging him to stay.

His hands skimmed her sides, her bottom, her hips. Down and around, up and over until at last one cupped her breast. In some far distant place she heard a moan, a whimper—was that she?—followed by a resounding growl of triumph. He flicked his thumb over her turgid nipple, causing it to ache for something more, causing every aspect of her body to ache for something more.

He dragged his mouth over her chin, down her neck until it met her collar and the hollow at her throat. "Why the devil do riding habits have to cover you up as though you're a blasted nun?" he ground out.

Thank God hers did, thank God, thank God. If she felt his heated mouth against more skin she thought her resolve might vanish and she would find herself giving him everything before she had the opportunity to weigh all the consequences.

Damn him for having the ability to kiss her senseless. Damn him for making her welcome him.

He nibbled on her lobe and there was that damned whimper again. Heat pooled between her thighs. Her fingers tightened on his hair.

"Come with me to my residence now," he rasped.

Her voice seemed to have deserted her. She almost nodded in acquiescence. She would give him anything, anything, if he would but make the glorious ache go away, would return sanity to her senses. She knew, without doubt, that he held the power to bank the embers he was flaming to life.

"No," she said, her voice rough and raw. "I told you. I require affection."

"I'll give you more than you've ever known."

Shaking her head, she somehow found the strength to shove on his shoulders. "No."

The fire in his eyes frightened her—not because it heralded anger, but because it was naught but smoldering passion. She saw the desperation with which he wanted her. She knew a moment of triumph, before she was swamped by a sadness she didn't understand. This man had everything: wealth, power, prestige, influence. He owned the world. He had handed her coins to gamble away. *It's only money.*

All he had he took for granted. All he possessed meant so little to him.

And he wanted to possess her. In the possessing, she would cease to matter, would lose her value. She would become like the coins he gave away without compunction, without even bothering to count them.

"No," she repeated, and watched the fire dim to smoldering acceptance.

"Attend the theater with me," he said. "Tonight."

She blinked. She'd expected him to curse her, to state his displeasure over her refusal. She'd not expected him to offer an invitation.

"I'm not available tonight," she told him, uncertain where she found the wherewithal not to immediately jump to his bidding. She'd never been to the theater. The thought of going excited her. The thought of going with him excited her even more.

"Tomorrow," he stated bluntly in a manner that sounded like an order.

She'd let him have that small victory. "Yes, I'd like that."

"Give me the address of your residence. I'll pick you up in my coach at half past seven."

She hesitated, but where was the harm in his knowing? While it might have seemed otherwise to him, she was as private as he was. After she gave him the address, he very slowly peeled away from her. She was surprised the imprint of his body didn't remain in the red wool of her attire.

Reaching down, he retrieved his hat and settled it on his head. Then he gave her a slow smile that made her think she might have misjudged his goal, that he had in fact gained precisely what he wanted.

"Tomorrow night then," he said. "We shall make it one never to be forgotten."

Chapter 6

With affection.

Rose read the note again, then stared at two dozen of her namesakes that had been delivered in an exquisite crystal vase that Avendale must have purchased separately. Surely flowers were not normally delivered in something so fine.

She had told him she required affection, yet she could not help but believe that he was mocking her, although why would he risk upsetting her when he was striving to entice her into his bed? Reaching out, she feathered her fingers over one of the red petals.

"I don't trust a man what sends flowers," Sally said.

"Only because Merrick has never sent you any."

"Why would I?" he asked. "She knows I love her."

"Sometimes a lady just likes to be reminded," Rose said.

He crossed his arms over his chest. "There's better ways to remind her."

"This duke is trying to win you over," Sally said.

"Mayhap, although I suspect it's more habit than anything, something a gent does when he wishes to gain a woman's favor."

"What does the note say?" Merrick asked. He was often into Rose's business far more than Sally ever was.

Rose tucked the folded parchment into the pocket of her skirt. "He merely provided his name so I would know who they were from." He hadn't provided his name at all, yet still she'd known who had sent them. It wasn't because no other gentleman was vying for her attention. It was simply that she *knew*.

"We're going to the theater tonight," she announced.

"Oh crimey, I've always wanted to go to the theater," Sally said. "How did you manage to get us all admission?"

Rose felt a thud in the center of her chest. She hated to disappoint. "Sorry, love. I meant Avendale and I."

Sally's face fell. "Of course. I was silly to think otherwise. What will you be wearing?"

"The red one without the flounces. I want to look sleek and elegant tonight."

"Will you be telling Harry where you're going?" Merrick asked.

"Naturally. I don't keep secrets from him."

He would be crestfallen as well that he wasn't going with her. He would love attending the theater. She would have to memorize every aspect of it.

If only Avendale wouldn't distract her.

As his well-sprung coach traveled through the streets, Avendale found it odd that he was anticipating an evening at the theater. Even when he'd been spending time with the actress he hadn't looked forward to a night in his box with such expectation.

It was Rose. The challenge of her.

Most of the ladies he knew would be accommodating his every whim in hopes of becoming his duchess, while she challenged him at every turn. Because she was a commoner, because she knew he would never ask for her hand in marriage? She flirted with him, gave as good as she got. Because she wasn't a simpering miss. She was a woman with experience. She'd been married, survived the loss of a husband, was on her own now.

Hearing the driver call to the horses to stop, he glanced out at the residence to which they'd just pulled up. It was probably a fourth the size of his, but still large enough to accommodate several rooms. It appeared recently built.

His footman opened the door. Avendale stepped out just as Rose emerged elegantly from the residence. She was dressed in red again. Truly she should wear no other shade. Smiling, she hurried down the steps, along the short path, and through the gate.

"Normally a lady waits until the gentleman fetches her from inside," he admonished lightly.

The bow of her mouth curved up as she squeezed his arm. "I was too excited to wait."

"I would have been less than a minute."

She rubbed where she had squeezed as though she feared she'd hurt him and now needed to offer comfort. "Don't chastise. I've never been to the theater. I don't want to dally a second longer. Shall we be off?"

Looking over her head at the residence, he was disappointed he'd not been allowed inside. He wanted to see the furniture, the paintings, the little touches that he was certain she would have added. He wanted more of a flavoring of her, and he'd thought he might discover additional information when he saw how she lived.

From windows on either side of the door, light

spilled softly out into the night. Other than that, the windows were all shrouded in darkness, and yet he had the distinct impression that he was being observed. A nosy servant perhaps. Who else could it be?

"Avendale?" she chided, taking him from his thoughts.

"You are singular in purpose," he said.

"Yes, quite. I've been looking forward to this evening all day."

And preparing for it, he thought. Her red gown was a simple, sleek style that flattered her curves. The skirts were not so voluminous that he didn't have a good idea regarding the width of her hips. A velvet choker with a small cameo at its center circled her throat. She needed rubies, a host of them, spread across that bared décolletage. He thought about how much he would again enjoy removing the gloves that rode past her elbows. He wanted to free her blond tresses of the pearl combs that held them prisoner. Although he found no fault with the slender slope of her neck being exposed. His lips could find a home there.

After handing her up into the coach, he glanced back at the residence, thought he saw a drapery flutter in an upstairs window. Perhaps he would get a glimpse inside when he brought her home.

Leaping into the conveyance, he took the bench seat opposite hers. He'd had the lantern lit so he could enjoy her without the shadows intruding. It amazed him how much he enjoyed simply looking at her.

With a lurch, the horses took off. She sat there prim and proper, glancing out the window, watching the neighborhood go by as though she'd never seen it before.

"Your home seems hardly large enough to accommodate a ballroom," he said.

With her eyes half lowered, she peered at him. "You shouldn't judge anything by its façade."

"I suppose you have a point. But the neighborhood is nice. You seem to have managed quite well without the estate yet being settled."

"That is all Beckwith's doing. He has vouched for me so businesses will extend me credit."

"Two years seems a rather long time for matters not to be resolved."

"I fear that is on me. I remained in India far too long striving to put my husband's affairs in order. Eventually I had to accept that it was beyond my skills, so I came to London. I spoke with Beckwith yesterday and he is most optimistic that he is very close to having all the little ducks lined up."

"That's good." Thinking of her husband's estate led him to thinking of her husband, which led him to—"Do you have children?"

She smiled sadly. "No. We were not married all that long and sometimes it's just not meant to be."

"How long were you married?"

"Nearly a year."

He fought not to show his surprise. He was not impolite enough to ask her age, especially as the truth was that it mattered not one whit to him, but he reckoned her close in years to him, which meant she was on the shelf when she'd married.

"Married only once?" he asked.

"Only once. Probably only once for all eternity."

"You're young. You don't see yourself marrying again?"

She shook her head. "My husband was a good man, a kind man, but he held all the power. I miss him terribly. I wish he hadn't died, but I have a bit more freedom now." She gave him a dazzling smile.

"To go to the theater, for example. He thought it would be a dreadful bore."

"Most men do."

"Do you?" she asked.

"Depends on the company. Tonight I do not think it shall be boring at all."

He cursed the light for not being strong enough for him to see if she flushed. He suspected she did, that a pink hue would have risen up her chest, over her throat and cheeks like high tide. She glanced back out the window.

"Sometimes you frighten me," she said softly.

He furrowed his brow. "Why? I'm not the sort who harms women."

"But you go after what you want." She turned back to him. "Relentlessly."

"Not usually," he admitted. "Not when it comes to women. I generally have them falling into my lap. Literally. Take it as a compliment that I am still in pursuit."

"And if you knew for certain that you would not gain what you want?"

"There are no certainties in life except for death. So I shall simply have to work all the harder to change your mind."

"You might be quite disappointed, Your Grace."

"I rather doubt it, when it brings me such pleasure to be in your company, to be near enough to inhale your rose fragrance."

"You might discover that I'm rather thorny."

"I don't mind getting pricked when the rewards are watching such beauty unfurl."

Her sweet laughter filled the confines of his coach, circled round, and settled somewhere within the depths of his soul. Other women had laughed in his presence, but he could not remember the sound of any of them. He would never forget hers. On lonely nights he would bring it out and examine it, recall it with such specificity that he would fully appreciate every note of it as though she were present.

He had a fleeting thought that one night with her would not be enough, that every facet of her would need to be explored from different angles. That she was composed of uncharted depths, that a man could never know all of her. He knew a momentary pang of jealousy that Sharpe had known her, had probably known her far better than Avendale ever would.

"Did you love him?" he heard himself ask, and wished he had bitten off his tongue instead, because he had no desire to come across as a jealous lover.

Her eyes widened in surprise, her head jerked back ever so slightly. "My husband?"

"Yes."

"I would not have married him otherwise."

Hardly an adequate answer. He wanted to know the depths of her love. Had she wept uncontrollably at his death, had she thought her life over, had she slept with his nightshirt, run her fingers through the hair in his brush, sniffed his cologne late at night? Had she done all the things that no woman would ever do for him?

He had known many women during his life, but he knew with complete confidence that not a one—other than his mother—had truly loved him. Liked him, yes, enjoyed him certainly. At his passing, they might feel a touch of sadness, but they would not mourn or weep or carry on. He envied Sharpe that this woman had mourned him.

Where the hell had those morose thoughts come from? He shook them off. He didn't need her love or even her affection. He wanted only her willingness, her desire, her passion.

The heart need not be involved at all. Better if it wasn't as their association would be short-lived. Like an explorer who charted an island before reboarding his ship and going in search of something new and different to explore, Avendale bored easily. Always had.

It was her unwillingness to give in to him so easily that kept him tethered. Once she granted him access to the treasures, the quest would end, and with it the thrill of the chase. Without the thrill, nothing would hold him.

He saw the excitement brimming in her eyes as they neared Drury Lane. Her delight was almost contradictory to the woman he'd come to know. For an insane moment he thought how rewarding it would be to travel the world with her, to show her a thousand discoveries. What was he thinking? She'd journeyed through India. Yet never attended the theater. Interesting. What else had she not experienced? He was looking forward to finding out—and to ensuring that she experienced them with him.

The coach came to a halt; the footman quickly opened the door. Avendale stepped out, then reached back to hand her down. For a moment as the streetlights lit her face, he thought he might have misjudged her age. She reminded him of a child unwrapping a gift on Christmas morning and discovering the doll she'd coveted. His gaze dipped to the gentle swells of her breasts. No, nothing about her reminded him of a child, but still he wouldn't mind that look of delighted discovery crossing her face while she was in his bed.

With her hand tucked into the crook of his elbow, they made their way into the theater, and he was acutely aware of her head swiveling about as she took in everything, as though there wasn't an inch of the place that she wanted to escape her notice.

"I find it inconceivable that you've never attended a play," he said.

"I've seen traveling performances, but nothing in a place as grand as all this. It's quite remarkable."

"I can take no credit for it."

"But you brought me, so you get credit for that."

His box was near the stage. As Rose peered over the balcony, Avendale was glad that he was able to offer her such a splendid view. Smiling, she looked back at him, her eyes wide. "This must cost you a fortune."

He shrugged. "I can't recall. I've had it for years. My man of business simply ensures that it is paid for."

Her smile dimmed just a bit and something he couldn't quite place crossed over her features. "It must be wonderful not to have worry about something as mundane as pennies spent."

Was that disapproval in her voice? Envy? Jealousy? He couldn't accurately identify it, but he was rather sure she was not pleased at the ease with which he acquired things. Nor did he understand why he felt this overwhelming need to ensure she understood that he could have anything he wanted.

"You're welcome to make use of my box anytime you like."

She angled her head thoughtfully. "Even after you move on to giving your attentions to someone else?"

He would move on, he knew he would. He always did. And yet he couldn't quite envision it. "We'll discuss it when the time comes. Meanwhile, let's enjoy tonight, shall we?"

"Yes, of course."

They settled into their chairs just as the lights began to dim. He'd forgotten how seductive the box could be as the shadows moved in. He couldn't make love to her here, of course, but who would notice the occasional brazen touch? He could skim a finger along her arm, across her nape, her bared shoulders.

The curtains were drawn back, and she shifted up in the chair, actually shifted up as though entranced by the stage. He found himself equally entranced with her. He'd never seen anyone watch a performance with such intensity, such dedication, as though she feared missing a single word spoken, a single movement of the actors across the stage. She didn't speak, didn't glance over at him, never took her gaze from the stage. So engrossed, she was almost a statue. Halfway through as the drama intensified, she reached across and wrapped her hand tightly around his, squeezing as though she needed to reassure herself that she was not alone.

He might have leaned over to whisper something naughty in her ear, to nibble on that delicate shell, but he couldn't bring himself to distract her. Nor could he understand why he took pleasure in watching her enjoy the performance. She quite simply mesmerized him.

When the curtains were drawing to a close, she abruptly came to her feet and began clapping enthusiastically. "Bravo! Bravo!"

He stood as well. She looked at him then, her face beaming. "Thank you," she said. "Thank you ever so much!"

He couldn't recall ever having so much gratitude showered on him for something so simple. She acted as though he'd been responsible for the actors, the play, the building of the theater. His chest tightened as a gladness swelled. He'd given her this joy and it had taken so little. Would she be so appreciative of everything? Quite suddenly he wanted to bestow everything on her.

Because of the crowd, it was slow going leaving the theater, but he kept his hand on her elbow, creating a path for her. Once outside, he spotted his coach, guided her to it, handed her up. He settled in opposite her, but it was a few minutes before they were able to begin the journey home.

"It was truly wonderful," she said on a sigh. "More than I could have imagined."

"I'm glad you enjoyed it. I don't believe I've ever seen anyone quite so engrossed with a performance."

"You must think me quite unsophisticated to get excited over something that you no doubt take for granted."

"On the contrary, I was thinking how remarkable you are."

She bit her lower lip, then ran her tongue over it. "I find you quite exceptional."

He could not miss the desire that rasped through her voice, the sultry lowering of her lashes. He considered diminishing the flame in the lamp, but he wanted to see her. With briskness, he drew the curtains closed over the windows.

"What are you doing?" she asked as they were shrouded in shadows. He heard no fear, no trepidation, merely curiosity. Or perhaps a feigning of innocence for surely she knew what he wanted. He'd been forthright about it and would continue to be so. He wouldn't force her, but he certainly intended to provide opportunity.

"Giving us some privacy."

"For what purpose?"

"To do what I've wanted to do all night. Kiss you." He removed his gloves before crossing over and drawing her into his arms.

She came willingly, eagerly, her mouth meeting his, her silken tongue stroking over his, stoking the flames of his desire. He'd had women aplenty but they always followed his lead. But not her. She met him without artifice, without hesitation. He'd known experienced women, but even they had held back. She withheld nothing. She explored, demanded he do the same. She might be a commoner, Society might have the audacity to place her below him, but when it came to passion they were on equal footing.

He liked it, he liked it a lot. He liked her. There was an honesty to the way she moved her mouth over his, plowed her fingers through his hair. There was truth in her desire. She wasn't seeking an extra bauble or a few more coins. She wanted what could be between them.

He felt it in her slight shimmering, heard it in her sweet sighs and moans, tasted it in the eagerness of her lips, smelled it in the headiness of her perfume as it was heated by her skin. Her skin, flushed now, he had no doubt.

He dragged his mouth along her throat, not missing how she dropped her head back to give him more access. He nipped at her collarbone, dipped his tongue into the hollow of her throat before trailing his mouth over the upper swells of her plump breasts.

Peeling the silk down, he took a nipple into his mouth and suckled. She whimpered. Her fingers dug into his shoulders. He skimmed his hand along her hip, her thigh, lower still until he reached the hem of her skirt, then he slipped beneath silk and satin, skirts and petticoats, gliding his hand over stocking until he finally reached the heaven of her skin. Silky smooth. Hot, damp. Higher yet, his fingers parting material until he reached curls and her simmering core. Wet, so wet, so hot. Heated honey.

She gasped, but not with indignation. With wonder. Her wide eyes met his, her lips formed a small circle. She panted. Short breaths. She clutched his shoulders as though she might fly through the window without purchase.

He stroked, long and slow, increasing the pressure. Fingers, thumb pinching, pressing, tiny loops, returning to her core, firmly—

With a cry, she shattered in his arms.

Drawing her in, he held her tightly, felt the tremors cascading through her. She buried her face against his neck, and he cursed the neck cloth that prevented him from experiencing the feel of her lips and rapidly falling breaths.

"Oh my God," she whispered, her voice rough and raw. "Oh my God, I had no idea."

He went completely still, not even drawing in a breath. He could not have heard . . . she could not mean . . . "Your husband never—"

"My husband?" she repeated as though it were a word foreign to her tongue.

"Yes, your husband. Did he never give you those sensations?"

She shook her head. "No."

She eased back until she held his gaze, her face wreathed in awe. She shook her head again. "No."

"Then he was a selfish bastard."

Wrapping her hand around the arm that was still buried beneath her skirt, she gave it a little push. "I need a moment. Please."

Very slowly, he removed his hand, straightened her

skirts and then her bodice. He pressed a kiss to her temple, kept his voice low. "Come back to my residence. I can show you so much more."

"No, no I can't." She scooted back into the corner, licked her luscious lips. "I can't."

In spite of the fact that he had no desire to do so, he returned to the bench opposite hers and simply studied her. "Had I known—"

She held up a hand to stifle his apology. "Please don't say you're sorry. I'm not. I just didn't know."

"I find that criminal."

"Perhaps my husband didn't know either. I don't believe he had your experience." She looked at the curtained window as though she could see beyond it. "I feel rather silly to have made such a fuss, to have cried out."

"Trust me, I enjoyed very much your reaction."

"I must trust you to have let you touch me so intimately."

"Are you certain you won't come back to my residence?"

She turned her attention back to him. "You are quite persuasive, but I'm not ready for the more you promise. I need to savor this for a bit. I don't know if I'm quite comfortable with it. And I want to be if there is ever more between us."

He almost reassured her that there would be more. He was not going to give her up without knowing her fully. As it was, his body was aching with need, but he'd never forced a woman. He wanted her willing, as she'd been before she understood the destination of the journey they were on.

He would have her, and it would be sweet, so sweet.

The coach slowed, came to a halt.

"Let me know when you're ready to depart," he said. "My footman will not open the door as long as the curtains are drawn."

"Do you often misbehave in coaches?"

"I misbehave everywhere. I especially want to do so with you, as I seem to have little control when I am with you."

"Yet you stopped when I asked."

"I'm not a barbarian. I want you, I want you completely. But I want you willing."

She released a long, slow sigh. "I should go in now."

He drew back the curtains. The door opened and he stepped out. Then he handed her down, walked her to the door.

"It was a remarkable night," she said. "Thank you."

With one hand, he cupped her chin and tilted up her face. "We are not yet done, Rose. Take whatever time you need, but know that one night very soon you will be mine completely and absolutely."

He brushed his lips over hers, then stepped back.

"Sleep well, Your Grace," she said, before opening the door and slipping inside.

As he strode back to his coach, he doubted he'd sleep at all. Never in his life had he ever wanted to possess a woman as much as he wanted Rosalind Sharpe.

*W*ith tiny tremors cascading through her, Rose pressed her back to the door, surprised her legs had retained enough strength to support her. Never before had she lost such control of a situation, of herself. Never before had she been so frightened by the power that a man could wield over her. He could cost her everything.

She had to look beyond pleasure but it was so

blasted difficult when her nerve endings had been transformed into tiny stars sparkling in the heavens, alive with some sort of electricity shooting through them. She loved kissing Avendale, loved the play of their mouths, loved the warmth he generated. When he slipped his hand beneath her petticoats, she knew he was traveling where he ought not, but she could not bring herself to stop him, to bring a halt to the wondrous sensations that he so easily brought to life.

Had she understood where the journey would end—

She'd not have stopped him. She was still struck by the magnificence of it. Who'd have thought? Could she bring the sensations to him without full copulation? She hadn't considered it while in the coach, but now the possibilities were invading her mind. Unfastening his trousers would be the first step, obviously, and then—

"Are you all right? You look like you've had a bit of a shock."

With a start she jerked away from the door, grateful to find her knees didn't buckle. She bestowed upon Merrick a stern look. "I'm perfectly fine."

And she hoped that nothing in her face gave away what she had experienced in the coach. It was too personal, too intimate, too wondrous.

"Will you be preparing for bed now?" he asked.

She wasn't certain she'd ever sleep again. "No, I'm going to visit with Harry for a bit if he's still up."

He was, in the library sitting in a chair by the fireplace. The only light in the room was provided by the small fire dancing on the hearth. Holding a glass of amber liquid, he scrutinized her as she approached. She did hope the flush had left her skin, did hope she didn't carry the fragrance of pleasure.

Bending down, she brushed a kiss over his cheek. "Hello, dearest." She noticed the book resting in his lap. "What are you reading?"

"*Last of the Mohicans.*"

Straightening, taking the chair opposite his, she asked, "Is it any good?"

"It's interesting. He put his hand on your back on the way to the carriage."

She almost teasingly asked if he was referring to the last one of the Mohicans but she could tell that he was troubled. "You were watching from the window, were you?"

He gave a subtle nod, his eyes, the same piercing blue as hers, containing no guilt or remorse.

With a sigh, she said, "He was being solicitous. It's how gentlemen behave."

"It seemed—" His jaw tightened. "Possessive."

"It wasn't. He doesn't own me, Harry."

"He's big."

She offered him a slight grin. "Not as big as you."

"Would I frighten him, do you think?"

It was difficult but she held his gaze, because she didn't want him to suspect that Avendale might hurt him. "He's a duke. I doubt he's afraid of anything."

Harry looked into the fire. "Will I ever meet him?"

"No, I don't think so. We won't be here much longer." After experiencing a taste of Avendale's talents, she couldn't risk losing control again.

His gaze came back to fall heavily on her. "Do you love him?"

Even though her heart clutched at the question, even though she feared the next word she spoke would be a bit of a lie, she laughed lightly. "No."

Not completely. But she could see the danger of it happening. A man as powerful as he, once he learned the truth, he'd take everything she held dear away from her.

"Because of me?" Harry asked.

"No, sweeting, because of him. His interest is purely—" God, the room was suddenly far too warm as she remembered where his interest had been earlier, where his hands, fingers, mouth had journeyed. "He's a man who only enjoys the chase. It's like that time when you and I went fishing and you insisted we toss the fish back after we caught them. The fun was in catching them, not keeping them."

His brow furrowed. "He could have put his arms around you tonight and caught you."

"It's not quite that easy between men and women." She needed them to tumble off this path before it became more awkward. "Shall I describe the theater to you?"

His eyes glittered with anticipation. "Yes, please."

The towns they'd lived in before hadn't had theaters, not that she would have taken Harry if they had. London offered so much more than any place else they'd visited. She was going to miss it when they left.

"Our seats were in the balcony and I could see everything. I memorized every detail." As she began to elaborate, she couldn't help but remember how difficult it had been to focus on them when she'd been acutely aware of Avendale studying her. She had been so cognizant of his presence filling the box, the nearness of his body. She was fairly certain he'd been bored with the play. Still she'd been unable to refrain from taking his hand during the climactic moment.

As much as she appreciated that Avendale had taken her, it saddened her that he took so much for granted. Had Harry been there, he would have been enthralled. It would have made attending the theater just a little bit sweeter.

It was an hour later before she bid Harry good night and retired to her bedchamber. Sally helped her prepare for bed. When all was done and Rose was again alone, she sat at the window and gazed out. She ran every moment of the night through her mind. Every subtle touch, every hungry look, every determined caress, every whisper. Her panting and gasping, his groans and encouragement. His holding her tenderly afterward as though he'd known how effectively he'd shattered her and how hard she was fighting to pull herself back together.

When she'd been struggling to regain control, to not beg him to take her away from everything, to do with her as he would. Her entire life had been lived for others, and he made her feel as though for once she came first, even as she recognized that it was his own selfish needs spurring him on. He wanted her. He would play any game to have her, just as she would embrace any tactic to best him.

She could not risk his gaining the upper hand again. Yet even as she sat there she knew how desperately she wanted him to have it. She cursed him long and hard for what he'd given her tonight. What woman could resist it? But she must, she would.

They would leave London sooner than she had planned, because she knew with certainty that he had the power to easily capture her, and once he did, all else would be lost.

Chapter 7

Avendale had never been a man obsessed. He
didn't care about anything enough to become obsessed with it. But he was obsessed with Rose.

She flittered into his thoughts, his dreams, his
fantasies. His mind wandered to her at the oddest
moments: while he was reading the newspaper over
breakfast, sipping scotch, shaving, glancing out the
window of his coach at the bustling city. He would
see her in red, always in red. Sometimes in satin
or silk, sometimes in a gossamer veil that swirled
around her and taunted him with glimpses of what
might lie beneath the cloth.

He had not called on her this afternoon, was de-
bating whether to go to the club this evening, because
he didn't want her to know she had this power over
him. But sitting at the desk in his library, when he
closed his eyes, he could still feel her trembling in his
arms. He wanted to be buried deep within her during
that climactic moment, wanted to be flung off the
same peak at the same—

"Avendale?"

His eyes flying open, he found himself staring at

the Duke of Lovingdon, a man who had once shared his penchant for wickedness, but who had recently married and become as docile and uninteresting as a sheep.

Lovingdon arched a dark brow. "Am I disturbing you?"

"No, I was merely resting my eyes." He waved his hand over the papers scattered across his desk. "I've spent the afternoon going over the tedious reports sent by my various estates' managers." He realized the afternoon was waning, dusk was settling in beyond the windows. He shot up out of his chair. "Scotch?"

"I wouldn't mind."

Avendale went to the marbled table, lifted a decanter, and poured its contents into two glasses. "What brings you here? Already bored with your wife?"

"Grace shall never bore me."

Avendale heard the absolute conviction in the words. He couldn't envision having such faith in one person, to know her so well. He had once had the same belief in his mother, but it had been a childish thing. He suspected Lovingdon would one day find his belief in Grace tested. He hoped not, but in his experience people were created to disappoint. Turning, he handed Lovingdon his glass, clinked his against it. "Cheers." He savored a deep swallow before asking, "Then what brings you here?"

"Curiosity. I saw you at the theater last night."

With a groan, grateful for the muted light of evening, Avendale dropped into a chair near the window. Lovingdon joined him. Both men stretched out their legs, lounged in comfort. They had been friends too long to pretend manners mattered between them.

"She was quite lovely. I can't recall ever seeing you with a woman who appeared respectable at first blush," Lovingdon said.

"She is a widow," he felt obligated to explain. "I intend to teach her that respectability is overrated."

"Who was her husband?"

"Some chap named Sharpe. She's a commoner. I doubt we knew him."

"A commoner, a widow, and a woman who is for the moment respectable. Not your usual fare."

"She makes me feel as though I have spent my life sampling pudding. She is something far richer, far more tasty."

"Where does she hail from?"

"I'm not really sure. Her husband died in India. A tiger apparently fancied him for a meal."

"Recently?"

"Two years ago. Not to worry. She's properly out of mourning."

"I'm not sure anyone really comes out of mourning. They simply learn to live without the ones they loved and lost." Lovingdon would know. He'd lost his wife and daughter. But then he'd found Grace and seemed to be embracing life again. He learned forward, planted his elbows on his thighs, and turned his glass between his hands. "It's not my place to say—"

"Then don't say," Avendale suggested.

Lovingdon lifted his gaze. "I know it would not be intentional, but you could do irreparable harm if she is not ready."

He wondered if he'd already done so, last night in the coach. No, he didn't believe he had. She had been taken aback by what had happened, but only because she hadn't experienced it before. She hadn't wept or slapped him or called him a blackguard. "She strikes me as being quite strong. I won't harm her."

"As I said, it wouldn't be intentional."

Avendale swirled his scotch, downed it. "Why do you care?"

"For as long as I have known you, last night was the first time that you looked as though you were precisely where you wanted to be."

"Theater? I abhor theater."

"But not the woman you were with."

Avendale came out of the chair, returned to the marble table, and refilled his glass. "Because I want her, Lovingdon. I want her in my bed as I've never wanted anyone else." Turning he met his friend's gaze. "And I intend to have her."

*T*hanks to Lovingdon's visit, Avendale was in a foul mood when he entered through the doors of the Twin Dragons. He wanted a private card game where the stakes were high and the men at the table ruthless. He didn't care if his finances took a beating, preferred it in fact. He'd almost gone to Whitechapel in search of a brawl. He felt like taking a pounding. He felt like—

Pounding into her.

His Rose was here. Somehow he'd known she would be. She wasn't innocent as Lovingdon insinuated, she wasn't going to get hurt. She was a widow who had obviously not experienced life to the fullest, and so she came here, just as he did, searching for something that would fill the emptiness inside.

He would very much like to fill her. He could avail himself of one of the secluded rooms. Drake wouldn't object. But Avendale wanted her in *his* bed. He wanted her scent lingering there after she left.

He began striding toward her. She was standing

near the roulette wheel. Close enough to observe, but not near enough to have placed a wager. He'd never understood the pleasure to be found in simply watching. If nothing was at risk, where was the excitement, the thrill? Even losing was better than not having participated at all.

As he approached, she glanced over, smiled, but there was an oddness to the upturn of her lips that he couldn't quite place. He might have attributed it to an uncomfortableness with him after last night, but he thought if that were the case, she'd have not come here at all, knowing in all likelihood he'd be present. But then he also thought her pride wouldn't allow her to cower in her residence. No, she would face him, but she would do it with a challenge in her blue eyes and a lifting of her chin.

Something else was amiss. He'd bet his life on it.

He realized that his gloved hand rested on the small of her back, that it had gone there of its own accord as soon as he'd reached her. He resisted the urge to snatch it away, but allowed it to settle into place, to claim her. She didn't so much as raise an eyebrow at his forwardness. He wondered if she'd object if he leaned down and captured those lips as he desperately wished to do.

Probably.

Although he'd welcome the reaction. From the beginning her vibrancy had appealed to him. She seemed to have misplaced it tonight. And that bothered him. Not so much that it was absent, but the reason behind its disappearance. He didn't like knowing that something—or someone—had caused her to wilt. Not that he was considering taking up the role of being her champion. That had never been his way. Truth be told, he was usually the one who caused the wilting.

Not that he was particularly proud of that realization at the moment. But he did know that her present state was not because of his actions the night before—unless she'd spent the day battling the demons of propriety and piety. "What's wrong?" he asked.

She shook her head slightly. "Nothing."

A lie. He prided himself on his ability to read women, not that he'd ever found her particularly easy to read—which meant that she wanted him to read her. It was not in his nature to prod and dig until he uncovered the reason behind a woman's strange mood. They came, usually with no reasonable explanation. A woman's moodiness never appealed to him. He generally walked away and found someone more fun, more obliging, less complicated.

But he couldn't walk away from her.

Not yet at least, not until he'd had her in his bed. It was that unfulfilled need that kept him anchored to her side. "Why aren't you gambling?"

She lifted a bare shoulder. "I don't believe I shall tonight. I simply needed to be surrounded by those having a jolly good time."

"What's wrong, Rose?" he repeated, prodded against his better instincts.

Something that seemed to resemble remorse flickered in her eyes before she averted her face as though she feared he could read the answer there. "It's nothing really."

"If it's nothing, then why are you bothered by it?"

She paled just a bit, glanced around as though she were expecting great hulking beasts to suddenly descend on her. "This isn't the place to discuss it."

"Then let's be away. My coach is here."

Relief washed over her face. He was certain she was going to acquiesce. Instead she said, "It's nothing with which to concern yourself. You should go play cards."

He was aware of the speculative looks being cast their way. At any moment they were going to be interrupted by the curious and prying. "I'm afraid I must insist."

Pressing his palm against the small of her back, he managed to communicate his willingness to make a scene if she insisted. She didn't. She moved with him, small, slow steps. "Avendale, I really don't want to bother you."

"It's no bother," he assured her.

He escorted her out of the building and ordered the young man standing outside the door to fetch his coach. While he and she waited, they spoke not a word. As he had yet to remove his hand from her back, he felt the shiver go through her. It was a cool night, but not overly so. He slipped his arm around her shoulders to offer her more protection from the slight breeze.

"This is inappropriate," she said.

"We've just exited a gaming hell. Seems a bit late to worry overmuch about what is appropriate."

"I suppose you have a point," she said, and moved in closer to his side.

He was not renowned for his ability to give comfort, but at that precise moment he wished he'd devoted more of his energies to mastering the skill. Whatever was bothering her needed to be set to rights.

His coach arrived, and he helped her inside. While he was tempted to sit beside her, he knew that choice could lead to a distraction that neither could afford at the moment. Not until he got the truth from her. So he wisely took the bench opposite her, stretched out his legs on either side of hers.

The coach jarred forward, the horses moving at a slow, steady pace.

"Where are we going?" she asked.

"Around the city, hither and yon, until such time as we decide on a destination." Until she was ready to come to his residence, his bed. He couldn't recall ever leashing his need so tightly. He wanted her, but he wanted her without furrows in her brow and something resembling defeat in her eyes. "I can wait all night."

She lifted her gaze to his. "Why are you interested in my troubles?"

"It's hardly a tempting seduction if your mind is elsewhere."

"You surprise me, Your Grace. I assumed you only cared about the physical aspects of a woman."

Normally he did. She was different. He didn't know why. It irritated him, confounded him, but the truth was he wanted every aspect of her involved. Every hair on her head, every thought in her mind. "Pleasure can be much more intense when it is the sole focus of one's efforts, when there are no distractions to plague us. So while it may seem I am being kind, it is pure selfishness on my part. I believe that bedding you will be a truly remarkable experience, but not if all of you isn't in my bed."

Her lips twitched, eased into a smile. "I believe what I like best about you is your forthrightness."

"I like that aspect about you as well. So be forthright."

She clasped her gloved hands together, knitted her fingers tightly together. "Will you extinguish the flame in the lamp? It is better said in the dark."

Most confessions were, or so he'd heard. He was not one for giving them or listening to them. She was turning his world topsy-turvy. Perhaps he would have two nights with her. He blew out the flame, settled back, and waited.

"This is so difficult, so foolish," she said quietly, her voice lyrical in the near-dark.

He could hear every subtle nuance, and wondered why he'd never noticed that she spoke in what seemed to be a mosaic of accents. Perhaps she was more traveled than he thought, her journeys not limited to India as she'd implied. Perhaps he would inquire again when this was done, but then what difference did it make?

"I can't see you being foolish," he said, truth in his words. She might be a lot of things, but he didn't think foolish was one of them.

"Naive is perhaps a better word." He heard her swallow, but he could see little more than the shadows dancing around her silhouette as light from the streetlamps flowed in and retreated. "I misjudged how long it would take for my husband's estate to be settled, for all that he left me to come into my hands. I've spent quite liberally on credit, expecting to cover my debt with my inheritance. But it has yet to arrive and the creditors are losing patience."

"Have they threatened?"

He thought he saw a nod.

"Yes, I fear so," she said.

"What does Beckwith say?"

"That it shouldn't be much longer, and he has helped where he can, has even lent me a tidy sum, but it's not enough. I don't want to run, I don't want to be cowardly. I know I must face the consequences, but the thought of prison—"

"One can no longer be imprisoned for debt."

"A few of them have banded together and are ac-

cusing me of thievery. I have only a day to pay what I
owe or they have threatened to go to Scotland Yard."

He couldn't recall hearing of such a thing, but he
supposed those who extended credit needed some
recourse. At that moment, light filtered in and her
gloves stood out in stark relief as she knotted her fingers. "How much do you owe?" he asked.

"I'm too embarrassed to say. I spoke with a bank
this afternoon, but they would not loan me the
funds I require. I can hardly blame them when my
husband's estate is still unsettled. Bless him. He was
not the most organized of men. He has left me in
quite the pickle. I am trying desperately not to resent
him, but it is becoming increasingly difficult when he
made such a muck of things."

The man sounded like a blistering fool. Leaning forward, Avendale worked her hands free of the
choking hold she had on them and wrapped his fingers around them. "Let me help you, Rose."

"I would only be exchanging one type of debt for
another." Through the dim interior he could feel her
sharp gaze homed in on him. "I know the sort of payment you would require."

Her words stung. A first for him. He'd never cared
what people thought of him or said about him. He'd
made himself impervious to slander. He lived a debauched life, held no moral high ground because it
was so damned difficult to defend. He'd never cared
how his actions were perceived, but her belief that he
would assist her in exchange for her coming to his
bed . . .

It rankled.

Releasing her hands, he leaned back. "I am not so
desperate that I have to pay for a woman to come to
my bed. If you join me there, Rose, it will be because

you want to be there and only because you want to be there. I have the means to lend you the money you need. It comes with no obligations, no expectations. If it will reassure you, we can wait until you have repaid me before we take things further."

"You don't think it will taint our relationship? I've heard the worst thing a person can do is loan money to a friend."

"I'm not certain I'd label you as a friend, but I am quite certain that I can lend you money and not hold it over you. It's not as though I need it. Pay it back at your leisure."

He heard her take a deep breath. "I don't know, Avendale. Am I not jumping from the pan into the fire? I like you, a great deal. I don't want to take advantage of what you feel for me."

"We can write out terms if you like, sign a contract."

She laughed lightly. "I don't think that's necessary. Unless you do, of course."

"No, I trust you, Rose." He gave her a devilish grin. "And I know where to find you."

She shook her head. "Still, I don't know. It's a ghastly amount."

"How much?"

"Five thousand quid."

"Pittance."

She laughed more fully this time and her gloved hand covered her mouth. "You are a godsend. So generous. I can hardly believe it. If you are certain it won't change things between us, I will gladly accept your offer."

With a rap on the roof, he signaled to his driver to go to his residence. "You'll have the money within the hour."

Chapter 8

Clutching her reticule, Rose swept into her residence. "Merrick!"

Avendale had taken her into the grand study of his magnificent residence. After opening a safe located behind a seascape, he'd handed her five thousand quid with the same ease with which she handed over a penny for candy. Without demanding anything else of her, not even a kiss, he had returned her to the Twin Dragons.

She'd promptly made her excuses—she needed to contact those to whom she owed money so she could settle her accounts—promised to play cards with him in a private room tomorrow evening, had a young man fetch her carriage, and quickly returned home. The fashionable carriage and four for which she'd promised to pay a ghastly sum were waiting in the front.

"Merrick!"

Carrying a mug, he finally wandered out from the hallway that led to the dining room and the kitchen beyond. "You're home early."

"Pack up. We're leaving."

His brown eyes widened. "Tonight?"

"Yes, tonight. Straightaway, as soon as we can."

"What do we take?"

"Only what we own. Leave the rest."

He scurried over to her. "How much did you get?"

"Enough. Now see to matters posthaste."

She hurried down the hallway from which he'd emerged. Outside the door to the library, she stopped for a moment, took a deep breath to compose herself. Then another. She could hardly fathom that Avendale had handed over five thousand pounds without so much as a blink. For a heartbeat she almost felt guilty about it, but she knew that was an emotion she did not have the luxury to feel. She denied herself most emotions, any that would deter her from her purpose. Another breath. She was about to deal with the most critical part of the plan.

Opening the door, she strolled in, glad to see that Harry was still awake. Sitting at the desk, scratching pen over paper, he looked up. She smiled with confidence. "Hello, dearest."

Moving around behind him, she hugged his shoulders, kissed his head. Then she came to stand in front of him because it was imperative that he understood the significance of what she was about to say. "I apologize for disturbing your writing, but you need to pack up your things. We'll be leaving tonight."

"Is it because of that duke?" he asked. "Did he hurt you?"

She was taken off-guard for a moment that he would draw that conclusion. Avendale would never hurt her. Pity she couldn't offer him the same courtesy. "Oh no. I simply decided I'd like to see Scotland." They could become lost there. "The streets of London are so crowded during the day that we want to leave now, while we can travel swiftly." Reaching across, she squeezed his hand. "Take your writing materials and your favorite books. We have only the one carriage so we can't take everything, only the items you truly treasure. Can you pack quickly?"

"Yes, all right."

She heard the hesitation, the sadness in his voice. They'd never lived anyplace quite this fine. She also knew his quickness would still be slow. As soon as she was finished getting her things together, she would assist him. "Thank you, dearest. I think you'll like Scotland."

Not that she'd ever been there to judge it, but she'd heard things. Leaving him then, she rushed to her bedchamber. She considered changing into something more practical for travel but she didn't want to take the time.

Pulling her small trunk from its place against the wall, she threw back the lid and got down to the business of stuffing her clothes into it. Unlike her instructions to the others, she would pack things that had not yet been paid for. She wished she could take everything but it wasn't possible, so she selected only the finest gowns because they might come in handy in the future.

It was half an hour later when her coachman came up to get the trunk. Joseph was nearly seven feet tall and as slender as a reed. She feared his bones might snap when he lifted the trunk up but he carried it with no problem at all. She wished she had jewelry. It wouldn't take up much room and selling it would have provided them with more money than anything else they might sell, but jewelers were not as quick to part with their treasures when one could only offer a letter of credit. She gave a last glance around the room.

She was leaving far too much behind but she
wanted to ensure Harry had all the room he required.

She traipsed quickly down the stairs and went outside to check on the status of things. Joseph was heft-
ing her trunk onto the roof. Several bags and boxes
were already there. It seemed they were making
great progress. Now if she could simply rush Harry
along—

"Sneaking off somewhere, Mrs. Sharpe?" a deep
voice, one she knew far too intimately, asked from
behind her.

Spinning around, she found herself squarely facing
Avendale. God help her. She was surprised the fury
burning in his dark eyes didn't ignite her on the spot.

Avendale was livid.

It had nagged at him—that he'd never been able
to read her accurately until tonight. Suddenly it had
been as though she'd opened the book of her soul to
him for a private viewing.

He'd been vain enough to think that he possessed
amazing powers of observation, that he had come to
know her, understand her. He'd even dared to consider that there might be something more between
them than the physical, that she stirred something to
life that had been dead for far too long.

He'd been playing a private game with several
lords, Lovingdon, and his wife, Grace. Grace, who
was so damned skilled at cheating, who could make
you believe she was bluffing until you had wagered
everything of value knowing—*knowing*—it would
all be yours, only to watch with a muttered curse as
she turned over her cards, smiled victoriously, and
swept everything into her little pile of ill-gotten gains.

Suspicion had reared its ugly head and he'd begun

to suspect that he might have been playing another game entirely from the moment he'd spied the lady in red walking into the club. If a lady wanted to swindle someone, she would be wise to select a fellow who wouldn't ask too many questions because all his interest rested in lifting her skirts, a known womanizer, a scapegrace with a reputation for having a singular purpose in life: pleasure.

That treacherous wench now angled her chin. "I returned home to a missive from my husband's mother. She's taken ill—"

"Don't," he commanded, his voice low, feral. "Don't further insult me with more lies."

"I didn't lie. I am in debt. It's only that five thousand isn't nearly enough."

The giant—the man had to be at least seven feet tall—who had been hoisting trunks, bags, and boxes onto the top of the carriage, blinked in wonder. Obviously he'd not been privy to the amount.

"What would be?" Avendale asked.

He could see the shrewdness in her eyes as she calculated. The bitch. He'd bet all he owned that she wasn't calculating her debt but how much he would willingly part with and the odds that she could convince him that she was a frightened woman instead of a conniving one.

She licked her lips, opened her mouth—

A small man stepped out from behind her skirts. A dwarf and a giant. Avendale was the fool she'd added to her odd mix of curiosities.

"Give him back the money, Rose," the little man said.

"Merrick—" she began.

"The money is yours for a week," Avendale interrupted, determined to regain and retain the upper hand in this situation.

Giving her attention back to him, she laughed. "What good is it to me if I have it for only a week?"

"I was referring to your spending a week with me."

"In your bed, I presume."

"Goes without saying."

"You want me to be your whore for a week?"

"Better than a thief. I'll call in Scotland Yard for a thief." It seemed he was intent on proving the full extent of his idiocy. If she gave back the money she was still going to leave and he would lose his leverage. He had a feeling this Merrick fellow could convince her to give back every ha'penny. Something in the small fellow's voice when he spoke to Rose alerted Avendale they had been friends for a good many years. He didn't want to consider that they might be more than that.

Didn't matter. Didn't matter how many men she'd had. He'd enjoyed his fair share of women. He wasn't hypocrite enough to hold it against her if she welcomed other men into her bed. Besides, when it came to pleasuring her, he'd already won that contest, and he had shared only the beginning. Her reaction in the coach had contained too much surprise for it to have been part of her ruse. No other fellow had made her feel what he did. He hated that he nearly busted the buttons on his waistcoat with the thought.

Her chin came up again and she leveled her gaze on him. "Three conditions."

"As long as they don't interfere with our trade, name them."

"Don't do it, Rose," the little man urged again. "Just give him the money. We'll find another way."

She rubbed his shoulder as though to ease the hurt that was going to come because she wasn't going to accept his counsel. Avendale knew she wasn't. He saw the determination in her eyes, a warrior's gaze, one that came from knowing the battle was lost but not yet giving up on the final outcome of the war. He could have told her the truth: she was going to lose it as well. But he was too angry, so he kept that little tidbit to himself. Let her learn the hard way.

She'd taken him for a fool, and he intended to ensure she regretted that folly—every second that she was in his company.

Clasping her hands in front of her, she said, "First, as we've been living here on only the promise of payment, you'll pay what I owe on the lease of this residence through the end of the month so my companions have a place in which to live without fear of being cast out. Then we do, in fact, have a few other creditors who need to be appeased. Pay them all that is owed to them. And last, each afternoon, for one hour, I may return here unaccompanied."

"You could pay off your creditors with the five thousand pounds."

"No. I walk away with the five thousand quid intact. Any expenses that occur during the next week, you will cover without questioning or quibbling over the cost."

"You're not in a position to negotiate."

"If I have accurately judged how badly you want what you want, I believe I am. I won't give it cheaply."

Had he truly told her only this evening that he wasn't desperate enough for any woman that he had to pay to have her? She was going to take his last farthing, the little witch. If he possessed an ounce of intelligence, he'd tell her to go to the devil and to return his money. If he possessed *any* intelligence at all—

Apparently he didn't possess so much as a drop.

"Is one of those trunks yours?" he asked.

She nodded. "The red one."

"My coach is at the end of the street. We'll take your trunk with us."

"You expect me to leave with you at this precise moment?"

"If you want to keep the money."

"You agree to the conditions?"

It grated. "I do."

"I require ten minutes inside."

"No. I've made all the concessions I intend to make." He signaled for his coachman to bring the coach forward. "We leave now or you immediately hand over the money. And even then I'll likely report you to Scotland Yard. You should know that an old family friend is an inspector there, and I'll have him hunt you down like a dog. As many a criminal can attest, he has the skills to do it."

Bending down, she whispered something to the small gent. Avendale almost grabbed her arm and jerked her away. She'd held enough secrets from him.

As his coach came to a stop, she straightened and walked forward until she stood by the door. She arched a brow. "Your Grace?"

The dwarf stepped toward him. "If you hurt her, I'll—"

"I won't hurt her," Avendale cut in. Sliding his gaze to her, he gave her his most devilish grin. "Causing her pain is the farthest thing from my mind."

*S*itting in the well-sprung coach, Rose wasn't quite sure she trusted Avendale's words or his smile. "I know you're angry."

"Angry does not even begin to describe my fury at being duped. Although I can hardly complain. I initially lent you the money to keep you near. Now you shall be all the nearer."

He crossed over to her bench, crowding her, but she refused to be cowed. She met his gaze head-on.

"I ought to put you over my knee, hike up your skirts, and give your bare backside a sound thrashing," he ground out.

"I believe you'll find our time together more pleasant if I'm willing, which I won't be if you're going to cast out threats of bodily harm. I know you won't see them through and it will merely serve to irritate me that you would think I would be intimidated by such poppycock."

"I'm far more dangerous than you think."

Reaching up, she cradled his bristled jaw with the palm of her hand. "I know precisely how dangerous you are." It had been part of the reasoning behind her decision to leave quickly, not so much for fear he'd uncover what she was about, but fear that she was very close to giving in to the allure of him. "I suspect by the end of the week that I shall be more scarred, scored, and branded than you can possibly imagine. Even as I dread how much I will ache at the end of it, I believe I shall relish every moment spent with you. You hold the power to destroy the very essence of me, and yet here I am. Do your worst."

"Damn you," he growled. "Damn you."

His arms tightened around her like strong bands as his mouth descended to claim hers. By now, she thought that she shouldn't be surprised by the power of him, the force of her attraction to him, and yet it always took her a bit off-guard. Pleasure swept through her, hunger for him roared to the surface. Suddenly his bare hands were in her hair and she felt the weight of it as it began to tumble, down, down, down.

He knotted a fist around the strands. "Glorious, glorious," he murmured as he rained kisses over her face before returning his mouth to hers. Within her, he ignited flames that began at the tips of her toes and rose ever upward.

Running her hands over his shoulders, his chest, she relished the feel of his muscles bunching with his movements. She wondered if she made him feel as hot, as tormented, as desperate for more. She was a fool not to return the money, to have bargained with this devil, but he'd given her a flavor of what he could deliver. She thought she might be more of a fool not to welcome the opportunity to share his bed. She was already ruined. She had nothing else to lose.

Slipping her hands beneath his lapels, she ran them up and over, striving to remove his jacket. He reared back, quickly worked himself free of the offending garment, tossing it across to the other bench. With nimble fingers, she unknotted his cravat, unwound the neck cloth, and cast it aside. Without thought or permission, she buried her face against his neck, inhaled the rich aroma that was he. She kissed, nibbled, suckled the soft skin.

He moaned, low and deep. His fingers tightened on her.

"I have long wanted to do this," she whispered, her voice raspy with her heightened awareness of him. "I've been rather envious of your neck cloth."

His dark chuckle echoed between them. "Do not dare deny yourself any aspect of me."

Once again he claimed her mouth, and the sensations swirled through her. She should be afraid by the storm of passion brewing between them, but she seemed capable only of standing in the midst of it and letting it have its way. It had been building between them from the moment she felt his gaze on her that first night, from the first word, the first assessing glance, the first touch. The accumulation of every encounter since had led to this journey within his conveyance, a journey over road, a journey into pleasure.

The coach jolted to a stop. Avendale was out the door in a flash. She made to follow him, and suddenly found herself in his arms, his long legs carrying him toward his grand manor. She'd thought it magnificent before, but the purpose of her visit had her paying little attention to details. Now his mouth on hers served as the distraction.

She was vaguely aware of them passing through the entryway door, the echo of his booted feet on marble before they were ascending stairs. He carried her with ease as though she weighed no more than a willow leaf. Clutching his shoulder with one hand, scraping the fingers of the other over his scalp, through his thick hair, she knew she had never felt so protected, so safe.

Odd when she knew where they were headed, where this encounter would end. She thought she should be trembling with trepidation; instead she was quivering with anticipation.

Marching into a bedchamber—no doubt his bedchamber—he kicked the door closed behind them. Dragging his mouth from hers, he tossed her onto the massive four-poster bed. She landed across it with a soft bounce. Grabbing her bodice, he ripped it asunder, buttons popping off, some clattering to the floor. She tried to do the same with his waistcoat, but she hadn't the strength and had to resort to attempting to unbutton it even as her hands wandered wildly over his chest, his taut stomach.

With a dark bark of laughter, he tore off his waist-coat, flung it aside. His shirt went next and her hands were skimming over the marvelous warm expanse of his chest.

He spread the parted material of her bodice wide, buried his face between her breasts. "You are so beautiful," he rasped as he stroked and kneaded with fingers, with tongue. He left a trail of tiny bites up along her throat until he was once again in posses-sion of her mouth.

There was a wildness to their actions, a despera-tion. She could not get enough of touching him, thought she would never get enough of it.

"We'll go slower next time," he growled, as his heated mouth trailed along her throat.

Suddenly her skirt and petticoats were pooled at her waist, his fingers were slipping through the open-ing in her drawers.

His breath was hot against her ear. "God, you're wet, so damned wet. So remarkably hot."

Straightening a fraction, he hastily unfastened his breeches. She barely caught sight of what he'd set free, had less than a second to wonder if she should be afraid before he thrust inside her.

She fought back the cry of pain, but a portion of it escaped in a whimper.

"Goddamn you," he ground out through clenched teeth as his head reared back, his body bucked, and he emitted a low groan that reverberated from deep within his chest. Then he went still, so profoundly still, only his harsh breathing echoing between them.

She looked up into eyes filled with molten fury.

"You said you were a widow," he fairly snarled.

"I lied."

Chapter 9

Without another word, he left her. Sprawled on the bed in a heap of sticky, blood-spotted skirts, the room echoing with the crash of the door slamming in his wake. She was surprised it remained hinged.

The burn of tears hurt worse than the burning between her thighs. She'd never felt so alone, so abandoned, so hopeless.

Struggling, she sat up and tried to secure her bodice with the few buttons remaining. Was he done with her? Was she supposed to stay now? Did her virginity alter the deal?

Surely not. She wouldn't stand for his reneging on their agreement. The money was hers, even if he never wanted to see her again. Why had he been so mad about it, like she'd done something awful? She'd thought he'd be pleased to know that no other man had ever come before him. Wasn't that what men wanted? What they valued? Virtue?

Noises echoed on the other side of a wall that contained a door. Was that another bedchamber? Was he in there, washing off her blood? Where was she to wash up?

Sliding off the bed, she grimaced at the slight discomfort. With her shoes still on, she tiptoed to the washbasin, not certain why she didn't want him to know that she was moving about.

No water. God, she needed water. She felt so unclean. The tears threatened again, and she forced them back. She would not weep for the loss of what he had so callously taken, for what she had freely given.

A soft rap sounded on a door leading to the other room. It slowly opened, and a young girl with a mobcap covering her brown hair smiled tentatively at Rose. "We've prepared you a bath, miss."

"Oh." She needed to say more than that. "Thank you."

Cautiously she walked into the tiled bathing chamber. It had an immense copper tub in which she could practically go swimming.

"I'm Edith," the young maid said, obviously striving not to be disconcerted by the sight of Rose's torn bodice or missing buttons. "Are you hurt?"

"No. He didn't force me if that's what you're thinking."

Relief washed over Edith's features. "I know it's not his way, but he seemed rather upset. He was barking orders— Apologies. I've spoken what I shouldn't." She cleared her throat, straightened her shoulders. "I shall begin anew. It will be my pleasure to assist you. A footman is bringing up your things now. I'll put them away while you soak in the tub for a bit."

So it appeared she was staying. "Thank you," she said again.

With Edith's help, she managed to get out of her clothing without incident and climbed into the tub, welcoming the warm water seeping in around her as she sank down. Edith put a small pillow beneath Rose's head.

"There now, you just rest for a bit," Edith said quietly, as though Rose were on her deathbed. "I'll be back to wash you once I've seen to your things."

Rose wondered what Avendale had told the maid to make her so solicitous. She took a deep breath, exhaled, sinking more deeply into the water. Taking a moment, she made note of the gold fixtures that were part of the tub and a nearby sink. He had plumbing up here. That must have cost him a pretty penny.

Closing her eyes, she allowed the lapping water to soothe her. It was so quiet, almost unnaturally calm within the residence. She heard movement in her bedchamber, no doubt her trunk being delivered, Edith putting her things away.

But where was Avendale?

She wanted him. She wanted him to take her in his arms, hold her near, comfort her—

With a moan, she buried her face in her hands. That was stupid. From the moment she'd run away from home, she'd relied on no one except herself. Her cunning, her plotting, her determination. She was strong. She didn't need Avendale.

But she *wanted* him. Somehow that seemed so much worse than needing him. It gave him control.

A soft rap.

They had an arrangement. It wasn't based on love, caring, or affection. It was pure lust, some animalistic attraction that had them clawing at each other whenever they got close. It was madness. She had to recognize it for what it was and keep her heart from becoming involved.

Another soft rap.

"Yes?" she called out this time.

The door opened. "Are you ready for me, miss?" Edith asked gently as though she expected Rose to shatter.

It irritated her that Avendale had thought she needed to be mollycoddled, just because he'd taken her maidenhead. Blast him. She wasn't weak.

"Yes," she answered with a bit more firmness in her voice. As she sat up, the pillow plopped into the water.

Edith retrieved it, before she began washing Rose's hair.

It wasn't long before Rose found herself in her nightdress, sitting on a sofa before a low fire, her hair braided. She supposed she shouldn't have been surprised by Edith's expertise at assisting her. She had no doubt that Avendale entertained lots of ladies here. She thought about inquiring but she was in no mood to have confirmed that she was one of many. Perhaps it was because of what she'd given up tonight that she wanted to feel special. Even though she knew she wasn't.

Yet one more soft rap on the door.

Merrick and Sally never knocked so softly. It was almost as though this residence was in mourning. Suddenly she wished she were back with those she cared for.

Edith set a tray with covered dishes on a low table in front of her. "Your dinner, miss."

"Where is the duke?"

Straightening, Edith interlaced her fingers tightly together. "In the library."

Rose got to her feet. "I should like to see him."

Edith paled. "I'm sorry, miss, but no one is allowed to disturb him when he's locked himself away."

Blinking, Rose stared at her. Surely she'd not heard properly. "He locked himself in?"

"Yes, miss. He does that on occasion when he's in an ill temper."

Rose had never heard the like. "Take me to the library."

"Oh no, miss. I was told to see to your comfort. To have you fed and put to bed."

"Put to bed?" Rose laughed. "I'm not a child to be put to bed. I go when I damned well please."

Edith's eyes nearly popped right out of her head. Rose assumed it was because she'd never heard a lady utter profanity. "If you won't take me to the library, I shall find it on my own."

She headed for the door. The patter of footsteps echoed through the room as Edith beat her to the door and opened it for her.

"I'll take you," Edith said, "but His Grace is not going to like it one bit."

Rose cared not one whit what he liked.

*B*rooding, Avendale sat in a chair in front of a low fire in the hearth and took another long swallow of scotch. For all his sins, he had never harmed a woman, never caused one pain.

Until tonight. Until Rose.

Why the bloody hell hadn't she stopped him, or at least slowed him down?

He didn't understand this obsession, this need to possess her that coursed through him. Never before in his life had he thought, *If I don't have this woman now, I shall die.*

In her presence he lost all reason. How else to explain his giving her five thousand pounds instead of having her arrested for swindling him? She had swindled him further. Not a widow, but a virtuous woman.

His dark laughter echoed around him. No, not virtuous. She might have never had a man between her legs but she was not virtuous. He didn't know what she was. Who was Rose Sharpe?

What did he know about her really? That she could bring his cock to attention so swiftly that he went dizzy. But other than that—

A loud knock sounded. "Avendale, open the door."

Bloody hell, what was she doing here?

"Go to bed, Rose."

"I've sent someone to fetch the housekeeper with the key. You might as well let me in."

He was master here, not her. And his servants understood not to intrude when he was in a dark mood. He'd seen his father in enough of them to know that they were not something he wanted others to witness. His staff was fully aware that if they unlocked that door, someone would lose his or her posi—

Click. Rattle. Creak.

Rose stepped through the open door and closed it behind her.

What the devil? Had the entire world gone mad or just his world?

He came to his feet and stormed to the sideboard. "You do not want to be in here."

"I quite disagree," she said calmly. "If I didn't want to be here, I wouldn't be."

Splashing scotch into his glass, he ground out, "You really need to leave before I do something that we shall both regret."

"May I have one of those?" she asked.

Jerking his head to the side, he wondered when she had approached. Could she not see his temper flaring?

Looking into her blue eyes, he felt his fury dimming—

"I could truly use it," she said.

—sputtering . . . dying out. Gone.

He handed her his glass, reached for another. "While you're here, I expect you to do as I command."

"I daresay that you're in for a time of it then as I have no intention of becoming your slave." When his glass was full, she tapped hers to it. "To an evening of surprises." Taking a sip, she nodded in approval. "Very nice."

Then she wandered to the sitting area by the fire and sat in *his* chair.

He walked over. "I was sitting there."

With a gamine smile, she peered up at him. "Yes, I know. I can still feel the warmth from your body. It's quite lovely."

She brought her legs up, tucked them beneath her. Any other woman would have scrambled to the other chair. But then she wasn't any other woman. He'd known it the moment he set eyes on her.

Dropping into the opposite chair, he stretched out his legs, took a sip of his scotch, and studied her. Her braided hair draping over one shoulder, she wore a plain muslin nightdress. Tomorrow he would purchase her something in satin and silk. What was the point? Two seconds after she donned it, he would have it off. It irritated him that he wanted her again with a fierceness that nearly unmanned him.

"So your being a widow," he began, "it was all part of the ruse?"

"Yes."

"There is no estate to settle?"

"No."

"But you had Beckwith jumping through hoops like a well-trained dog."

"Quite so. However he is becoming suspicious,

close to figuring out that I sent him on a wild-goose chase. That I had no husband, had no inheritance, had never been to India. Never so much as set foot out of England, to be honest. Therefore it was time to move on, a bit sooner than I would have liked, but necessary."

"Why didn't you tell me about your untouched state?" he asked quietly. "You had ample opportunity in the coach."

"Not really, not once your mouth landed on mine. All reasonable thought seems to scatter when you touch me. Besides, I didn't think it would matter."

"I tore into you like a battering ram trying to breach the walls of a castle."

"You weren't quite that uncivilized, and it wasn't that bad."

"You cried out."

"I'd have not expected you to be upset that you hurt me."

"This game we've been playing . . . I thought you were more experienced, that you understood—"

"I did understand. Lack of experience does not make one ignorant."

"But lack of knowledge made me so. Had I known—"

"What would you have done differently?" she demanded with a raised eyebrow.

"I intend to show you when I'm no longer angry with you."

She gave him a slow, sensual smile, and the last remnants of anger he'd been harboring melted away. Damnation, he was going to show her before dawn.

"Who are you, Rosalind Sharpe?"

"I am the woman who will warm your bed for a week. Then I shall move on."

His gut clenched with the thought of her leaving. "That easily?" he asked.

"Neither of us is looking for anything permanent."

She had the right of it there. He would grow tired of her soon enough, and she definitely wasn't the sort he'd take to wife. He needed a respectable woman who could cloak him in her virtuousness.

"I don't think I've ever met anyone as forthright—" He stopped, shook his head. "You speak in a forthright manner, but I fear you are full of deceptions."

"My desire for you is not false."

This time the tightening in his gut nearly doubled him over. "How have you remained untouched?"

"I never before met anyone with whom I wished to be so intimate. You could have gotten me for half the amount."

He laughed. "I like you, Rose. Damned if I don't."

"I like you as well, Your Grace."

"Not so well if you had no compunction about swindling me."

Lifting a shoulder, she peered at him over the rim of her glass. "As I said, I had creditors breathing down my neck. I was a bit desperate, and you did confess that money meant nothing at all to you."

"I was foolish enough to say that, wasn't I?"

She glanced around. "When you have so much it's easy to forget there are those who have so little."

He would not feel guilty for all that he possessed. In spite of his errant life, he had managed his estates well, ensuring they were profitable. "I make considerable contributions to charity."

She gave him an impish grin. "Is that the name of a harlot you frequent?"

He barked out his laughter. He'd never known a woman so open about matters of which ladies never spoke. "You are a contradiction. Until an hour ago, you were a virgin, and yet you have no compunction about spewing bawdy talk."

"I've led a singular life, which I will not discuss. I've been on my own since I was ten and seven, no chaperone to ensure I remain pure in thought and ignorant of all that transpires between men and women."

He knew many a girl who had married at seventeen. Why did he find it appalling to think of her being on her own at so tender an age? "How did you manage to survive?"

"With skill, cunning, and perseverance."

"And a fair amount of swindling?"

"I never take from those who can ill afford to be taken from."

"You believe that somehow makes you noble?"

"No, not at all. And I know I shall pay dearly for it. Just not yet."

"On the contrary, I believe it is time you paid for leading me to believe you are far more experienced than you are." Setting aside his glass, he stood. He didn't see fear in her eyes, but merely curiosity and desire. Always the desire. He'd never met a woman who made him feel as though she yearned to be with him. Oh, women certainly sought out his company, flirted with him, teased him, tempted him. But they never made him feel as though something deep within them called to something deep within him.

Crossing over, he took her glass and set it on the table. She didn't object, she barely moved, her gaze never leaving his. He no longer trusted himself to read her moods, to read what she might be communicating. She had fooled him once. She could be doing it again.

Yet she'd come here to his lair, to poke the tiger. She had to know that he'd have not bothered her if she'd stayed in her room and simply gone to sleep. He might have felt differently in the morning. His temper might have cooled by then.

Instead she'd joined him. She had to have known where her actions would lead. Bracketing his arms on either side of her, folding his hands around the arms of the chair, he leaned in and took her mouth. She responded as though she were kindling and he'd struck a match. In spite of his impatience and rough taking of her earlier, she opened her mouth to him, her tongue swirling over his. No shy miss. Not at all.

She gained nothing by pretending to want him. She had the money. He had met her terms, although he was already regretting that he'd agreed to let her have an hour alone in the afternoon. He wanted to be with her every moment, every second until the time of their bargain came to an end. Slipping an arm beneath her legs, another around her back, he lifted her and cradled her against his chest. He didn't want to consider how well she molded against him, how perfectly she fit. Nothing in life was perfect. Nothing fit exactly.

Yet he could almost swear that she did as she settled against him.

"I do know how to walk up stairs," she said.

"But my legs are longer, will get us there faster."

She dropped her head to the curve of his shoulder. "Why do you lock yourself in your library when you're in a foul mood?"

"I don't like others to see my temper." He started up the sweeping staircase. "I see it as a weakness."

"I don't think anything about you is weak."

She was wrong there. Where she was concerned,

he wasn't nearly as strong as he needed to be. Twice now this evening she'd diffused his anger with little more than a smile. If he weren't careful, she might change him irrevocably.

That he could not risk.

*S*he thought she could become accustomed to his strong arms holding her, to his carrying her where he wanted her to be. The thought angered her. She'd not needed anyone since she had run away from her father when she was seventeen. She hadn't exactly been on her own, but she was the one responsible for the others. They were with her because they believed in her, because she was the one willing to do anything to see them all safe.

Wasn't that the reason that she was now in the duke's bedchamber as he slowly lowered her feet to the carpeted floor?

It had to be the reason, the only reason. She wouldn't allow it to be more, to think that perhaps a week with her wouldn't be enough for him. That something grand could come from something steeped in retribution.

She would leave here with memories only. She knew that. He would not give her any part of himself that she could carry away. All he would give her was pleasure. Nothing deeper than that.

His large hands slowly worked free the buttons on her nightdress. A cheap thing that she could easily replace if he ripped it apart. But no, he had chosen to ruin something that had cost her a pretty penny. She smiled. No, it would cost *him* as it was included in the bills he would be paying. And then he would pay for it again when she had another ordered before the week was done.

She supposed she should have waited until all the creditors were paid before she came to be with him, but he was a blackguard with standards. A duke who would pay his debts, even if those debts were hers. Strange how she trusted him, trusted his word.

A little voice whispered for her to trust him with everything, but she couldn't. The time spent with him was as much for herself as anything. As her night-dress slid to the floor, she thought of nothing except him, except Avendale.

The satisfaction in his eyes, the admiration, the heat.

"God, but you are beautiful," he said, his voice rough with desire. "I could flog myself for going so quickly before and denying myself the sight of you completely unclothed."

"Perhaps I'll flog you for denying me the sight of you." She didn't know from where her boldness heralded. She only knew that it felt right, that with him there was no shame in the naked form, no mortification in what they would share.

He wasn't done up nearly as much as he'd been before. She merely had to release a few buttons at the front of his shirt, not even the cuffs. Then he was reaching back and dragging the cloth over his shoulders, over his head, slowly revealing a sculpted stomach and chest. Bronzed. And she wondered what he did to expose himself to the sun.

His eyes glinted with satisfaction. He knew he was beautiful. She wished she could bring him down a notch by telling him that she'd seen better, but it would be a lie and there was enough deception between them. Her fingers trembled slightly as she gingerly touched them to the heated flesh.

Avendale groaned low and she felt powerful to be able to affect him so. She flattened her hands just below his ribs and slowly caressed upward. Such firmness, such silk. How could he be both? She carried her hands on a journey over his chest, along his shoulders, and down his powerful arms. His muscles were like granite.

"I would tell you that you're magnificent," she said, meeting his eyes, "but I suspect enough ladies have told you that to swell your head."

"None of them mattered." His jaw tensed, a muscle there jumped, and she wondered if he'd fought to stop himself from saying she mattered.

What silly, fanciful thoughts. He cared nothing for her beyond what they would have here. He could have asked for a fortnight, for two, and she'd have granted it. But he merely wanted a week, and then he'd be done with her. As much as she might wish otherwise, she was one of *them*. The ones who, in the end, didn't matter.

But she wouldn't think of that. Not tonight.

She skimmed her hands up his arms, reversing the previous journey, until her hands rested where skin met cloth. She could see the bulge there, the strain against his trousers. She knew what it felt like buried within her, but she'd barely seen it.

Lowering her gaze, she flicked a button free of its mooring. Then another. Another. Setting him free. Pressing quivering fingers against the heat, she found it difficult to draw in air. "Had I gotten a good glimpse of this before, I might have been terrified."

"Had I known you were a virgin, I'd have assuaged your fears."

Easing down, she lowered his trousers, inhaling the musky, heady scent of him. When he stepped out of the cloth and nudged it aside, she glided her hands up his muscular thighs.

Slipping his hands beneath her arms, he brought her up. "You can explore later. For now I'm going to share with you what I was too selfish and consumed with need to share earlier."

Once more, he lifted her up and set her on the bed, only this time he placed her along its length, her head coming to rest on a pillow. Stretching out beside her, he took her mouth so gently that she almost wept. Always there had been so much hunger between them, clawing at them, and she knew that he was tamping it down, striving to make amends when there was nothing which required recompense. Yet neither could she deny that she liked the slowness of his tongue stroking hers. She wound her arms around his shoulders, relishing the closeness of him.

Taking hold of her wrists, he pulled her hands over her head and clamped one hand around the fragile bones. "No touching," he ordered. "This is all for you."

"But I enjoy touching you. I take pleasure from it."

His face hovering mere inches from hers, his gaze delved into her eyes. "You're remarkable."

"Surely other ladies have wanted to touch you."

"More out of obligation, I think. Because it was expected."

She gave him a sultry smile. "They may have wanted you to think that, but I suspect they were quite delighted at the opportunity to run their hands amok over you. You're quite splendid."

His eyes narrowed.

"It's not flattery when it's the truth," she added.

"For now simply relish what I am about to bestow."

Releasing his hold on her, he grazed his mouth along her chin, down her throat, eliciting tiny bubbles of pleasure that caused her toes to curl. He licked his way along the center of her chest, between her breasts, lapping at her skin as though it were coated in sugar.

She tried to keep her hands where he'd placed them, to grant him that bit of abeyance, but when he cupped her breast and closed his mouth around her nipple, she couldn't help but bury her fingers in the thick strands of his dark hair. Nor could she stop herself from moaning low, from arching her back. He suckled, lathed his tongue over the taut peak, suckled again, all the while kneading gently.

It was so marvelous, how he could touch her in one place and yet she seemed to feel it everywhere. She thought she might go mad with the sensations, and perhaps that was his intent: to drive her insane so she could no longer look out for herself, so she would have to surrender to his care for the remainder of her life.

What a silly thought. He didn't want her forever. He'd made that clear enough. He wanted her for only a week, seven nights. Then he would be done with her. Then she would stagger from his residence, a woman forever changed.

But she would neither resent nor regret it.

Not when he had the power to carry her to such heights as he had that night in the coach, as she suspected he intended to take her now. With him she could fly, she could be free as she'd never been before.

Once more, he placed her hands on the pillow. She almost cursed him. No doubt she would when she left. He would ruin her for anyone else, and a small voice echoed through her mind that that was his plan. To give to her as no other man ever would. To take from her as no other man had the power.

He shifted that incredible body of his, and she watched the play of muscles with his movements.

The bunching, the knotting, the smoothing out. She wanted to see him without clothing, engaged in every sort of activity imaginable. He was perfection, the possessor of a body that did not betray. If she believed in gods, she would believe him blessed, but she had looked in his eyes and she knew he was not a stranger to betrayal, that he carried the scars deeply within him. Yet for all the darkness that hovered below the surface, still he had the ability to gift her with the beauty of pleasure.

Wedged between her thighs, he folded his hands around the curve of her hips and trailed his lips over her stomach, licking, kissing as he progressed to her navel. He circled it with his tongue, dipped it inside.

"I'll have brandy here later," he rasped, and heat coursed through her with the image of him lapping at her flesh. Then he inched farther down until his breath was stirring the curls at the apex of her thighs.

It seemed decadent to see the top of his head between her parted legs. Reaching down, she threaded her fingers through his hair. She'd resisted touching him as long as she could.

Then his tongue laved a provocative path between the folds of her womanhood, and she pressed her thighs against him, tightened her hold on the strands of his hair. She'd thought he'd use his fingers again. Hadn't expected him to fairly worship her with his mouth. He nibbled, nipped, drew her in, tugged gently. Her head came off the pillow, her shoulders rolled forward.

"Avendale, what are you doing?"

He lifted his head. Within his smoldering dark eyes, she saw passion, desire, and possession. He owned her at that moment and he damned well knew it. "What I should have done earlier. What I want to do now. What I intend to do a hundred times before you leave."

"It can't be proper behavior."

"Do you want me to stop?" The challenge was there, but so was a flicker of doubt. He would cease his ministrations if she but asked.

She didn't trust him with her heart, but that wasn't fair because he didn't know it was part of the bargain. She trusted him without reservations when it came to her body. "No." It was a breathless sound, lower than a whisper, and yet it seemed to echo through the room like a shot fired from a rifle.

He gave her a devilish grin. "Then enjoy."

She slumped back down, stared at the velvet canopy above, as his tongue circled and swirled. She didn't want to take with her memories of velvet. She wanted memories of him. Lowering her eyes, she relished the sight of him between her spread thighs. Heat fanned out from her core to envelop her. Pleasure spiraled.

Sliding his hands between the mattress and her bottom, he lifted her slightly as though he were offering himself a tasty feast, and sensations zagged through her as though he'd delivered a lightning strike. She tightened her fingers in his hair. Her breathing became shallow, harsh. The pleasure ebbed and flowed as though he were the commander of the tides of hedonism.

She whispered his name, then screamed it as a tide of ecstasy enveloped her, carried her under, then lifted her up. She shuddered with a force that threatened to unhinge her bones. "Oh God, oh God."

Sliding up her body, he took her into his arms and cradled her close, burying her face in the curve of his shoulder, running a hand along the length of her spine. After all he'd given her, how could she find even more pleasure in something so simple, so comforting?

She was lethargic, and had been almost correct about her bones. They had dissolved. She'd never be able to leave this bed. Somehow she managed to drape her hand over his hip. "You should be . . . inside me," she forced out.

He pressed a kiss to her forehead. "Later."

"But I want you."

"I told you: this time was for you. I won't be so unselfish again, so make the most of it. Drift off to sleep in a sated state." He squeezed her bottom and said in a low voice, "It's the best kind."

In the coach, she thought she'd experienced the pinnacle of pleasure. She didn't know whether to be pleased or terrified to discover she'd been wrong. Before he was done with her, she thought she might very well die from all the sensations he was so skilled at delivering.

His body ached with the need to be buried inside her. He was not in the habit of denying himself what he desired, but then where she was concerned, it seemed all his habits were doomed.

He'd always enjoyed pleasure for pleasure's sake, but with her there was another element that he couldn't quite identify, that he didn't want to examine too closely. Examining her, however, was another matter entirely.

Holding her so near, he was well aware of her languid muscles relaxing even further as she succumbed to the lure of sleep. He did what he should have done earlier, and gingerly unbraided her hair, gently combing his fingers through the long strands without disturbing her. He could still barely fathom that she had marched into his sanctum—had convinced his housekeeper to unlock the door so she could—as though it were as much hers as his. With no other woman had he ever felt on such even footing.

He found that aspect to her as tempting as the alabaster skin which he'd revealed when he finally took the time to bare all of her to his appreciative gaze. They were going to have an incredible week together, although he already regretted that it wouldn't be longer.

Her soft breathing stirred the fine hairs on his chest. Her hand on his hip went limp, her fingers twitched. Never before had he noticed so much.

He could have had her for half the amount, could he?

He'd almost confessed that she could have named any price and he'd have paid it.

Moving slowly so as not to disturb her, he reached down, grabbed the covers, and brought them over her. Then as gingerly as possible he eased from the bed, retrieved his silk dressing gown, slipped into it, and walked to a table near the fireplace. After pouring himself a glass of scotch, he sat on the sofa and watched the embers dying on the hearth.

Who was this woman and why was he so obsessed with her? He had a million questions he wanted answered, and he knew she'd answer nary a one. He thought he could be with her for the remainder of his life and still he wouldn't know everything about her.

Why a dwarf? Why a giant? Why London? Why him? Who all had she swindled before? Why had she stepped onto that path?

He considered asking James Swindler of Scotland Yard to make inquiries, to discover what he could about her. The man was skilled at ferreting out information, but that way might lead to her incarceration. Besides, he didn't want another to provide the details of her life. He wanted her to do it.

Leaning forward, he planted his elbows on his thighs, held his glass between two hands, and stared more intently at the smoldering heat. What did it matter who she was?

It mattered.

As nothing else in his life ever had.

She mattered.

He didn't want her to. He didn't want her to provide anything other than surcease. He wanted her to be what every other woman in his life had been: a convenience.

But damnation, she was most assuredly not that.

Tossing back his scotch, he set aside the glass and stood. He was unaccustomed to deciphering relationships. This one would be short and sweet. They'd have no time for delving beneath the surface. Nothing would come of it if they did. She was a criminal, a swindler . . . a woman with secrets.

He had enough secrets of his own.

ℛose awoke to darkness and luxurious warmth, a large body curled around hers, a chest at her back, strong arms holding her near, a hand pressed to the flat of her stomach. He'd undone her hair. It would be a tangled mess in the morning. She didn't care. He made her not care about anything beyond the pleasure he was so skilled at delivering.

Up against her backside, the hard, thick length of him stirred.

She twisted her head back as far as she was able. "Are you awake?" she asked quietly, not wishing to disturb him if he wasn't.

"Mmm. I am now." The rasp of his voice sent pleasure through her. Everything about him sent pleasure through her. Moving her hair aside, he pressed the heat of his mouth to the nape of her neck. "Are you still sore?"

"No." It was a small lie, but worth the reward of him rising up and slowly turning her over. He was a silhouette encased in shadows, with only pale light sifting in through the windows, but she was able to follow the outline of him as he lowered his mouth to hers.

He smelled of sleep, of dreams, and she wondered at her fanciful thoughts. Normally she was too pragmatic for such whimsy, but he made her wish for innocence. The lady he eventually took to wife would be. She would be of the nobility, Lady Something-or-Other. Never kissed, never touched. She would be innocent to the cruelties of the world, and Avendale would ensure she remained so. He would protect her, and she would cherish him.

Rose was certain his wife would do so, because already she herself was feeling the spark of caring for him as he came to rest between her thighs. He nuzzled her neck. It seemed so wicked in the darkness. But then everything about him was designed for wickedness. This time, she wouldn't allow him to deny her everything, to deny her anything.

Working her hand between them, she felt the steel covered in velvet. She sighed as he groaned. Raising her hips, barely noticing the discomfort, she welcomed him sliding into the depths, stretching her, making her so aware of the fullness of him as he settled in. She pressed her soles to his calves as he slowly eased out, eased back in. Raised on his elbows, his hands cradling her head, he kept most of his weight off her as he continued to plunder her mouth.

Digging her fingers into his shoulders, she wondered if she would ever tire of his attentions. Each time was different, each time brought another aspect of him to her notice. The languidness of their motions made her wonder if perhaps they were both hovering on the twilight edge of sleep, where dreams beckoned.

She feared she might awaken to discover that he was a dream, that all of this was but fantasy.

Except the lovely sensations coursing through her assured her that everything was very much real. He tore his mouth from hers, his breath harsh in the quiet surrounding them. She dug her fingers into his shoulders, scraped her nails along his back. His guttural groan shimmered through her.

The pleasure built and built—

She cried out as the cataclysm rocked through her. With a feral growl, he threw his head back as he slammed into her, his back arching, his body going still. She could feel the tremors cascading through him. Without separating himself from her, he rolled to his side, bringing her in close, her leg draped over his hip.

Their breathing calmed, but she thought her heart might never cease its pounding.

"You shall be the death of me," he said.

"But what a lovely way to go."

"Much better than being a tiger's dinner, I suppose."

She nipped at his skin with her teeth. He merely released a tired laugh, drew her in more tightly against him, and held her as she drifted off to sleep.

Chapter 10

When next Rose awoke, she found Avendale still with her, his hand splayed over her hip as though to keep her there beneath the sheets with him until he was ready to let her go. They'd fallen asleep without closing the draperies so sunlight spilled in through the many windows of a room that was nearly as large as the entire floor that housed bedchambers in her residence. He was facing her, his long dark lashes resting gently on sharply defined cheeks.

Striving not to disturb him, as unobtrusively as possible, she pressed the flat of her hand to the center of his chest, smiled as the hairs there curled around her fingers similar to the way he'd been curled around her for most of the night. She'd not expected him to stay with her, but then there was a good deal about him that she had not expected. A good deal about herself as well.

The gladness that swelled within her because he was still here. The joy frightened her because she knew at the end of her time with him, he would bundle her into the coach without remorse, without any thought of missing her. Yet she already knew that she would miss him dreadfully, that she would have numerous regrets, that there would be an agonizing ache in her chest.

He opened his eyes. The brown depths seemed warmer than she'd ever seen them. A corner of his mouth tipped up slightly. "Hello."

His voice, rough with sleep, shimmered through her. She swallowed. "Hello."

He moved his hand over her bottom before gliding it up her back. "Are you hungry?"

If she were a light-skirt, he would probably expect her to say, *Hungry for you*. She almost said the words anyway, because she was, but they sounded so silly, so unlike her. "A bit, yes."

"Then we'll have breakfast in bed, shall we?"

She nodded. "That sounds lovely."

Pressing the flat of his palm to her spine, he brought them closer together until their bodies were nestled together, but they could still look into each other's eyes. "Are you still sore this morning?"

"A little," she reluctantly admitted.

"Mmm," he murmured as he leaned in and nuzzled her neck.

She sighed. "Not so very much."

The barest of laughs escaped, his breath fanned over her neck. "After breakfast then."

"Why not before?"

His laughter was deeper this time as he leaned back. "Because I want you to recover a bit more so you'll enjoy it to your fullest. I'm not a complete bastard."

"I enjoyed it very much last night."

"I was in a haze of sleep when we started, with no strength to resist you."

"Now you can resist me? Growing bored with me already?"

His mouth formed a wicked grin. "Not at all." His hold on her tightened. "We'll have it your way. Breakfast later."

They made love slowly, tenderly. While she experienced some discomfort, it wasn't enough to make her want to give this up. She loved the weight of his body over hers, the fullness of him filling her. She loved the sensations. She loved the sunlight for its gift of letting her see him clearly as he rode her, as he rode passion.

When they lay sated and content, she wrapped herself around him, held him near. Yes, she was going to have regrets when she left him, but they were the sort that in later years would make her smile with fondness. She should hate him for the bargain he insisted they strike. But then he should hate her for the advantage she'd taken of his generosity.

They were each getting what they wanted. Strange to realize that she needed something else entirely.

"Will you give me a tour of your residence?" Rose asked, wrapped in his silk dressing gown, her back against a mound of pillows at the headboard. Over her lap, a tray held an assortment of dishes and delicacies.

A small army of servants had delivered an abundance of food, setting it all on a long table against a wall. He and Rose could stay in this room for a week and not go hungry. She was torn between expressing amazement at the lavishness and anger for all the times she'd gone hungry while those with wealth let so much go to waste.

Stretched across the foot of the bed, wearing nothing except trousers and a loose shirt, he finished chewing the tiniest pie she'd ever seen. "If you like."

"Does it have a name?" The posh always named their residences.

"Buckland Palace, after my family name."

"So you're Benjamin Palace?"

"Buckland, you little witch, as you well know."

She loved teasing him, loved the twinkle in his eyes. He didn't smile enough for her tastes—not a true, genuine smile. He had his devilish smiles, his wicked ones, his caustic ones. But the ones that originated in the center of his soul were rare.

"I've never been in a palace before," she said, popping a grape into her mouth.

"I'm not sure this truly qualifies as such. People call their residences whatever they like."

To her it *was* without doubt a palace, she mused as they walked through it after they'd finished breakfast. She was still wearing his dressing gown. She suspected they'd have another romp in the bed before she left for the afternoon. He'd taken her through all the bedchambers in the section where his was. There was another section on the far side of the house where guests stayed. He'd shown her the formal dining room that she thought could accommodate the House of Lords, a smaller dining room, a breakfast one, a smaller one still where intimate dinners were held. She was familiar with his library. He'd walked her through the duchess's library, even though presently there was no duchess. All the books. So many. Even the rooms that weren't designated as libraries contained shelves housing books. Harry would love it here.

Now they were strolling through a portrait gallery. A house with a room designed specifically to display portraits. It seemed at once opulent and again, wasteful. Small sitting areas dotted here and there, but the paintings dominated. She could see shadows of him in each of the males.

Throughout the entire tour he often caressed her lightly—the small of her back, her shoulder, her hip—as though he could not stand the thought of going too long without some contact with her. She relished it, knowing that this time next week she would never know his touch again.

She came to a stop beside a gigantic portrait hanging over the fireplace. "Your father. I take it."

"Yes." His hand came to rest just above her backside.

"I can see you in his features, but he contains a hardness that you lack."

"If you believe that then you don't know me well at all."

Jerking her head around, she moved beyond his reach. "I think you're angry about something, something more than my deceptions. I noticed it that first night, seething beneath the surface. It gave me pause. But I found you too handsome to resist."

He barked out his laughter. "Did you? I think you thought, *Here is a man with heavy pockets I would like to lighten.*"

"That came later, after I made some inquiries."

He sobered. "Should probably send word to Beckwith to cease his efforts on your behalf."

She sighed. "Yes, I'll see to it on my way to my residence this afternoon."

"I'll take care of it. He's likely to be more forgiving if it comes from me." He arched a dark brow. "Besides, I have to pay him for his services rendered anyway."

With a smile, she strolled over to the next portrait. The woman had soulful brown eyes and mahogany hair. "Your mother?"

"Yes."

"She appears unhappy."

"I believe she was."

She looked over her shoulder. "And now?"

"Disappointed in me, but other than that I believe she is quite delirious regarding the other aspects of her life."

"Because you're a scoundrel?"

He gave a brisk nod. "She doesn't approve of my life."

"And that bothers you."

"Not really, no."

He was lying, but she wasn't certain he realized it. She refrained from pressing the point. Theirs was a surface relationship, one that involved flesh, sensations, and pleasure. It was best not to delve too deeply.

His steps matched hers. "What of your mother?" he asked.

"She passed when I was rather young."

"Your father?"

"I'm not really sure. I left him when I was seventeen. Never looked back."

"How did you manage at first? It had to be difficult."

She trailed a finger over the edge of a gilded frame. Not a speck of dust. "How many servants do you have?"

"Here in London? Thirty or so. You're avoiding the question."

She leaned against the back of a tall-backed plush chair. "My father had stashed away some money. I stole it before I left. It was enough to see me through for a couple of years."

"Then you began to survive by deceit."

"I prefer to call it cunning. The world is full of fools." Shoving herself away from the chair, she brushed up against his chest and wrapped her arms around his waist. "Some have very heavy pockets indeed. Although you turned out to be not quite the fool I thought you were."

He lifted her into his arms and began carrying her from the room. "Oh, I suspect I'm fool enough."

Nibbling on his ear, she relished his groan. He was not the only fool, it seemed. Because her heart sped up, her body thrummed with anticipation, and already she was wishing for more than a week.

"Why must you return to your residence?" Avendale asked, lounging in the bed, naked beneath the covers, sated and partially content. He would be completely content if she were still abed with him, but shortly after he'd taken her, she'd rung the bell for Edith. It irritated him that she could dispense with him so easily and quickly. Irritated even more that he could not seem to do the same with her. He should desire her less now that he'd had a taste of her, but he discovered he only wanted her all the more.

Watching as Edith dressed her, he'd cursed every bit of clothing that had begun to hide her flesh from his view. Now the servant was putting up Rose's hair and all he wanted to do was remove the pins and watch it tumble back down.

"I want to ensure that everyone is well after my abrupt departure last night," Rose finally said.

"I'll go with you."

"No," she snapped, at long last shifting her gaze from her reflection in the mirror to look at him. She softened her expression, her tone. "The condition was that I go alone."

"Why?"

"Because it's what I prefer." She turned her attention back to the mirror.

"What are those men to you?" He despised that he sounded jealous. He wasn't, but she was his at that precise moment. He wasn't about to share her.

"Friends."

"Why must you go alone?" he asked again.

With a deep sigh, she twisted around on the bench at the dressing table that he'd had temporarily moved in from another bedchamber, and glared at him. With a wave of her hand, she dismissed Edith. Once the girl was gone, Rose said, "I'm not going to have a tryst if that's what you're thinking."

He didn't know what to think. "I simply find it odd."

"That I should like a little bit of time to myself? Besides, I'm certain you'll welcome a respite from my presence."

He wouldn't. Not that he was going to confess that and give her absolute power over him. He also realized there was the matter of trust. She had given of herself so freely, so easily. He didn't trust it, didn't quite trust her. He'd known some truly diabolical women in his life. She didn't fit the mold and yet the others seemed more trustworthy.

"If you don't return here as promised, I shall hunt you down."

She pressed both hands in a cross over her heart. "Oh my word. Such romantic prose. Careful lest you cause me to swoon."

"I'm serious, Rose."

She got to her feet and walked to the foot of the bed. "We've made a bargain, you and I. I will keep to my end of it."

"Why should I believe those words when so many others were lies?"

She didn't appear the least bit offended or hurt.

"There was a purpose behind the lies. Nothing is to be gained with my not being truthful now."

Why couldn't he have faith in those words, and why did it matter that he couldn't?

With a duck of her head, she gave him a small smile. "I shall miss you while I'm away."

"I'm not quite certain I believe that."

"I shall seek to convince you when I return. I haven't time now." She crossed the room, picking up her reticule along the way.

"Why are you so secretive?" he asked.

Stopping at the door, she glanced back at him. "Why are you?"

His gut clenched. "I'm not."

"Of course you are. Our conversations involve only the surface of our lives. I find no fault with that since we are only interested in exploring each other's surface." She gave him a knowing smile. She had the right of it. He knew it. She knew he knew it.

"Bring me a list of all your creditors that I can send to my man of business. He'll see that they are all paid."

"I know you have doubts regarding my honesty, but consider this. I gave you what you wanted before the accounts were paid. Because I do trust you, implicitly."

"Have I ever done anything to make you think you couldn't?"

"There is that, I suppose. I know I've given you ample reasons not to trust me, yet here we are engaging in something that I believe requires absolute trust. At least for me. I'll see you in a bit."

She left then, closing the door quietly in her wake. Tossing back the covers, he leaped out of the bed and rang for his valet. While she was away, he had matters to which he needed to attend. Setting things right with Beckwith topped the list.

*B*eckwith buried his face in his hands. "A swindling female. How could I be such a fool?"

Sitting in a chair in front of the solicitor's desk, Avendale confessed, "If it's any consolation, I fell for her ploy as well."

Beckwith lifted his dark head, his blue eyes magnified by his spectacles. "My brothers are going to have a jolly good laugh at my naiveté."

"No reason for them to know. I'm here to make restitution for any expenses you've incurred and any fees you are owed."

Beckwith furrowed his young brow. "I should report her to Scotland Yard."

"I'd rather you didn't. You may add to your fees if needed in order to make you feel less a fool."

Beckwith's pride had an inflated sense of self, but Avendale paid the amount without quibbling. It seemed there was a bit of a swindler in everyone when given the opportunity.

Avendale then saw to the matter of Rose's residence. For reasons which he didn't examine too closely, he paid what was owed and an additional three months. He knew in all likelihood that she would leave London at the end of the week, but if she wished to stay a bit longer, he wanted to make the opportunity available. She was with him now because of the bargain, because she *had* to be if she wished to avoid dire consequences.

That knowledge grated. He wanted her with him because she *wanted* to be there. What passed between them was incredible, nearly earth-shattering if he were honest. But it clawed at his conscience that he had forced her into his bed. If he were any sort of gentleman, he would relieve her of her debt to him.

But he'd been a scoundrel too long to give up anything he wanted so badly.

And he wanted her.

He was damned anyway. Might as well ensure he took memories of the very best adventures into hell with him. So far she was proving to be the best of all.

"*D*id he hurt you?" Merrick demanded as Rose stepped out of the carriage with the footman's assistance. He'd rushed out of the door as though the hounds of hell were nipping at his heels. Her words to him the night before—*Tell Harry there has been a change in plans and we'll be staying in London a bit longer. I'll see him at two tomorrow.*—had ensured he'd be waiting for her.

"Don't be absurd," she answered as she walked past him into the house.

"I don't like him."

Reaching down, she rubbed his shoulder. "You don't have to, although I think if you removed me from the equation you'd like him very much."

"He took advantage."

She arched a brow. "I daresay he's not the only one. We'll be leaving with five thousand quid and anything else that we want as it's all paid for now."

"But at what cost?"

"One I was more than willing to pay. Now cease your harping. I want to spend some time with Harry. I can't be gone more than an hour or Avendale will seek me out. I've no doubt of that, as he doesn't trust me. Not that I blame him. I assume Harry's in the library."

"Yes. He's in a mood, though. I had to explain

a bit more than you wanted as he threatened to go after you."

That would have been disastrous.

"I trust your judgment, Merrick. Have Sally bring us some tea and biscuits." With a fast clip to her stride and her heels echoing through the hallway, she quickly made her way to the library. The door was open. Always a good sign. He wasn't in as troubled a mood as Merrick had indicated, although perhaps he was, but knowing her time would be short, he had decided not to waste it by having her trying to beat down the door.

She was reminded of the closed library door last night. It seemed all men had something in common when their pride was wounded: a need to lick their wounds. She was still amazed that Avendale had been upset to discover she was a virgin. She'd judged him a man whose pride would cause him to burn with anger, but not remorse or guilt. She'd thought he'd consider himself above those sorts of emotions. She'd never so erroneously misjudged a person.

Unfortunately she had also misjudged what this week in his presence was going to cost her. At the end of it, she was going to be irrevocably changed. But that was for dealing with next week. For now, there was Harry.

Striding into the library, she found him at his desk, pen in hand. "Hello, dearest. How is the story coming along?" she asked.

He leaned back, studied her with crystalline blue eyes that held a wealth of pain. "You simply left . . . without a word."

"I didn't have a choice, but I'm here now. Although I have less than an hour. Let's not spend it squabbling." Tugging off her gloves, she tucked them into her reticule. "Come sit with me by the window. It's a lovely day."

"It's going to rain."

She looked out at the cloudless sky. "Do you think so?"

"Yes. Tonight. Late."

He was remarkably skilled at predicting the weather. She thought about how lovely it would be to be snuggled in bed with Avendale while the rain pattered the roof and windows. She shook her head. She could not be thinking of Avendale right now.

Sitting on one end of a long sofa, she was grateful when Harry joined her at the other. Sally brought in tea and biscuits on a tray and set it on the table in front of them. She stared hard at Rose as though that were enough for her to decipher everything that had transpired since Rose had left. Rose blanked her expression, tried to make it as innocent as possible. With a narrowing of her eyes, Sally huffed before leaving.

Rose prepared the tea, set a cup in front of Harry, even knowing that he probably wouldn't touch it. Sometimes they both just needed a sense of being civilized.

"It was that duke, wasn't it?" Harry finally asked. "He forced you to go."

Rose took a sip of tea, set aside her cup. "No, sweeting, he didn't. I wanted to go. God help me, but I like him, Harry."

"Why?"

She scoffed. "*Why?* You would ask, wouldn't you?" Harry had an insatiable curiosity, wanted to know everything. She picked up her teacup, set it back down. How could she possibly explain to him what she didn't understand herself? "I like the way he looks as me—as though there were no women before me. Even though I know there were probably hundreds."

"What does he look like? I couldn't see him clearly the other night."

Pleasure tripped through her as she brought up an image of him. "He's tall, not as tall as you. He has broad shoulders. He likes to carry me around, which makes me feel protected. His hair is a deep, deep brown. Like sable, like Sally's winter coat. Sometimes when the light hits it just so, I can see the barest hint of red. His eyes are almost the exact shade of his hair. Although no red there. He's solemn. He spends a good deal of his time engaged in the pursuit of pleasure, but I'm not certain he truly enjoys it. He seems to be a little bit lost. Lonely I think. It's the oddest thing, when we are in a room crowded with people. They will acknowledge him with a nod or quick smile, but they don't talk to him or ask after his welfare. Not that he makes any inquiries either. It's as though he can't be bothered with anything other than his own needs, but I think that's just a façade. I think he's been hurt. He's awfully cautious." She was amazed she had spouted so much.

"You love him," Harry stated.

Rose nearly fell off the sofa with the proclamation. She laughed. "No, absolutely not."

Harry studied her as though he didn't quite believe her.

"That way lies disaster," she assured him.

"Knowing the dangers doesn't always stop things from happening."

"True enough." Leaning over, she squeezed his hand. "You should see his residence, Harry. So many books. In every room at least one book. Well, not the dining rooms. But you would be in heaven. I shall see if I can borrow some for you to read. You could read quite a bit in a week." She did wish she'd thought of that sooner.

"What does it look like, his residence?"

"It's called Buckland Palace. He says it's not truly a palace but it is. He's just accustomed to the opulence so he doesn't see it. But it's ever so grand. Paintings on the ceilings, gold edges along the wainscoting. Monstrously huge rooms. His bedchamber alone . . ." She hesitated, wishing she hadn't gone there, hoping she hadn't given him cause to conjure up images of her in the duke's bed. He was fairly innocent in the ways of men and women so her words probably gave him no naughty ideas. " . . . is almost as large as all our bedchambers put together. He took me on a tour. It was fascinating."

They talked then about how much longer they might stay in London. No reason to leave straightaway, with their debts paid. Although she suspected she would not want to linger overly long once she left the duke. She told Harry what she knew of Scotland, why she thought they would be happy there.

As she was leaving, she hugged him hard, promised to see him at two the following afternoon. She would not feel guilty about leaving him here. He had his story to write. He'd welcome the quiet.

Even as she welcomed a bit of it to settle her thoughts as the carriage rumbled through the streets. She didn't like how much she was anticipating returning to Buckland Palace, how much she longed to be with Avendale again. It was more than the fact that he knew so well how to make her body sing and fly to the heavens. She liked being in his company, liked the way he held her afterward. She liked the timbre of his voice, even if they didn't discuss anything of consequence. She even liked that he was a little jealous. Not that she wanted to spend a single moment of their time together with them at odds.

She was most disappointed when she returned to his residence to find that he wasn't about and that his butler, Thatcher, had no idea when His Grace would return. Not knowing if their evening would include more than romps in the bed, she wasn't certain how to prepare herself.

Shaking her head while standing in the foyer, she nearly laughed aloud. She was here for one reason and one reason only—because he wanted her in his bed. That was most certainly where they would spend the evening. She supposed she could bathe, make herself as alluring as possible. But first, while she was alone, she wanted to scour the shelves in the various rooms and see if she could determine which books Harry might best enjoy. Once Avendale returned, he would occupy all her time and thoughts—the rogue.

Not that she minded, not really.

She did hope that he didn't tarry too long, only long enough for her to locate some reading material for Harry, something obscure that Avendale wouldn't notice was missing. Sneaking it out was going to be the challenge, but she would find a way. She'd always been resourceful if nothing else.

She paused at a narrow table that held a silver bowl containing a myriad of vellum envelopes. They were not her concern, and yet knowing that they were probably invitations to balls, she couldn't stop herself from plucking one out and opening it. After pulling out the gilded invitation, she trailed her finger over the formal words. When she had first stepped into the Twin Dragons, her plan had been to make the acquaintance of those who would send her invitations such as these. She had the lovely one Drake Darling had sent her, but she had wanted to attend balls within residences, to be accepted, to take her time at selecting her quarry.

She had enjoyed dances held by country squires, merchants, bankers, and bakers. The towns she'd visited had offerings, but nothing as grand as what she had envisioned she would find in London. Over the years, she had honed her skills in out-of-the-way villages, among those who didn't rub elbows with the aristocracy. She'd had such exquisite goals for London: to linger, to enjoy, to move about in circles far above her humble roots. To attend every sort of ball imaginable: costume, masked, Cinderella.

But she would experience no aristocratic balls now because she'd allowed Avendale to get the better of her. Yet she couldn't seem to regret it.

She was in the smaller library—the duchess's library—searching through the books there when she became aware of the sensation of being watched. It was as it had been that first night at the Twin Dragons. Slowly she turned to find Avendale leaning against the doorjamb, arms folded across his chest. "I returned promptly as promised only to find you not here," she said.

"You sound disappointed."

She lifted a shoulder. "Had I known you wouldn't be waiting for me, I might have lingered."

"I had to settle things with Beckwith."

Her stomach lurched. "Did he give you any problems?"

"Nothing I couldn't handle."

His confidence, his arrogance. Neither should have appealed to her and yet they both did.

"I also saw to the lease on your residence," he continued.

Relief swamped her, a weight lifted that until that moment she hadn't realized had been so incredibly heavy. They had lodgings that no one could take away from them, at least for a time. "Seems you were quite busy."

"I even found time for something more pleasant."

With long even strides he crossed over to her. Indulging, she inhaled his magnificent masculine scent, almost took things a step further and leaned into him. She wanted her head on that broad chest, his strong arms around her. Ridiculous to want so badly what she would only hold for a little while. Perhaps that was what made it so appealing. If she knew she would have him for the remainder of her days, surely she would grow as bored with him as he would with her. It was the circumstance, the finite hours that were ticking by far too quickly. Why were they still down here anyway? Why hadn't he carried her up to bed already? Why were they still clothed when she longed for silken flesh over slick skin?

Leisurely, as though he had the power to stop the clocks, and minutes weren't passing that could never be regained, he slipped his hand inside his jacket and like a magician she'd once seen, he pulled forth a black velvet box that appeared too large to have been hidden so effectively inside a coat pocket. He held it toward her. "For you."

Now she was the one moving as though time had stopped, as though nothing was to be gained in hurrying. Slowly she opened the box and stared in wonder at the most beautiful set of rubies interspersed with tiny diamonds that she'd ever seen. She imagined the necklace around her throat, draped across her collarbone. Shaking her head, she closed the velvet lid and extended the box toward him. "I can't."

"What do you mean you can't?" he asked, his brow furrowing so deeply that it had to be painful.

"It's as though you're rewarding me for being in your bed. To accept it would make me feel like a whore."

"You do recall that I'm giving you five thousand pounds. Not to mention paying off your damned debt."

She'd angered him, not at all the mood she wanted for tonight. She didn't want drama. She simply wanted . . . peace. She wanted what had passed between them in the dark of the night. "I haven't forgotten, but this feels different. I can't explain."

He dropped into a nearby chair and stared up at her. "You are the most confounding person I've ever met. I've given jewelry to countless women. It doesn't mean anything."

His words stung, tiny barbs pricking at her heart. She'd thought she was special, had attributed some meaning to the gorgeous item, placed more value on it because it was coming from him. "I suppose that's it. You rain jewelry down on women who visit your bed. It makes me like all the others."

"Trust me, Rose, you are nothing at all like any of the others."

Slowly she sank into a chair. "Why?"

His jaw tightened. "Why what?"

"How am I different?"

Narrowing his eyes, he drummed his fingers on the arms of the chair, one at a time, rolling them along, over and over. "For one thing, you're not falling over yourself striving to please me at every turn. You prick my temper. You're argumentative. You challenge me. You—"

"You want it easy?" she asked. "Life, Your Grace, is not easy for everyone."

"You think my life is easy?"

"What else am I to think when you don't share anything of significance with me?"

"What you should think is that you should be damned grateful I don't burden you with the troubles in my life." Abruptly he stood and tossed the velvet case back into her lap. "You don't have to accept it but you will wear it while you're here."

She shot up, not reaching out to save the velvet when it plopped to the floor. "The terms of our agreement do not take away my choices. I agreed to be with you for a week, but I will not be controlled. What I wear during our time together is my decision."

"Fine, do as you please. We're going to the club this evening. I was going to ask you to wear the red you wore the night we met. But wear whatever pleases you as I no longer give a damn."

As he stormed from the room, tears stung her eyes. What the devil had just happened?

Chapter 11

*W*ithin his library, Avendale splashed scotch carelessly into a glass and downed it in one long swallow. He welcomed the burn, the heat, anything to counter the anger coursing through him. Anger at himself because sharp disappointment had gouged him when she rejected his gift. It felt like a rejection of him. Especially as he'd spent nearly an hour striving to find the perfect necklace for her. The red had to be the right shade, the diamonds not too many. The piece itself could not be overwhelming and yet it needed to be noticeable. Barely.

He poured more scotch, tossed it back. Generally when he selected jewelry for a lady, he purchased the first piece he saw. He didn't care if it was gaudy or too small. He didn't care how it would fall just below her neck. He didn't give any thought as to whether she would like it or it was suited to her.

He'd agonized over his decision today. Fretted over it, wanting so much to please her. Now it irritated the devil out of him that he'd given so much weight to his decision.

She was with him because of five thousand quid

and she drew the line at sparkling stones? He'd never understand her, and damn it all to hell but he'd never wanted anything as desperately as he wanted that. To know her thoughts, to not doubt that when she was with him she was his true Rose and not the swindler.

He wanted something real between them and that made him an utter fool.

He would use her body, as often, as hard, as quickly as he could while she was here. He would get his money's worth. If he hadn't already arranged for a private game at the club tonight, he wouldn't take her out. He'd simply drag her straight to bed. But friends would be waiting and he'd appear more the fool if he canceled.

After tonight, except for her afternoon visits, during the little bit of time left to them, they wouldn't leave the mattress. He would take her as many times as physically possible. She thought the gift of the necklace made her feel like a whore? He would bloody well ensure—

"I'm sorry."

He nearly crouched and swung around to defend himself at the soft voice. So lost in his temper, he hadn't heard the door open, hadn't heard her join him. He didn't look at her. Just poured more scotch and tossed it back.

"I've never been given such an exquisite gift before," she continued. "I may have placed more meaning on it than I should have."

He took a glass, filled it with scotch, and turning slightly, offered it to her. "I don't view you as a whore."

She took the glass. "Between us there is naught but the physical."

"I enjoy your company, Rose. Except when we're

at odds." He released a rough, self-deprecating laugh. "Hell, even then. You have the ability to anger me. No other woman has ever done that. It's odd. The things I notice when I'm with you. The things I consider. You are more than bared breasts and sweet thighs."

The lips he had intended to kiss the moment after he gave her necklace curled up. "There you are again, making me blush with such lovely prose."

He gave her a wry grin. "I've never had to spout drivel to get a woman into my bed. A title, wealth, power, prestige, influence—when they are the cloak of your character you need nothing else. All you have to do is crook a finger. Although you are here for the money, I don't think you're impressed by the others."

"I am very much impressed, Your Grace, but as you say, they are your cloak. I'm far more interested in what lies beneath it."

The grin he bestowed this time was the devilish one that he had practiced to perfection in his youth. "I believe you were introduced to that last night."

A red hue swept up her cheeks. "There's more to you than that."

"Not much more, I'm afraid." Setting aside his glass, he wandered over to a window, gazed out on the perfectly manicured gardens. "How was your visit to your residence?"

She joined him at the window. "Far too short."

He slid his gaze over to her. "Don't even consider that we'll renegotiate that part of our bargain. Our time together won't be nearly long enough as is."

"I assumed you would become quickly bored with me."

"To be honest, so did I. How fortunate for you that we were both wrong."

She laughed, a sound that shimmered through him clear down to his heels. She sobered. "I'll wear the necklace, but I don't think I can take it with me. After all I've done, I don't deserve a gift."

"It was a costly piece. You could sell it for a princely sum."

"I think I would treasure it far too much to ever sell it."

Her words would have appeased his disappointment if he thought she'd attach sentiment to the piece, but she was too pragmatic. She would treasure it because of its monetary value, perhaps for its beauty. Still, he said, "Then take it as a reminder of our time together."

"I'll need no reminders." Rising up on her toes, she brushed her lips over his, before placing her hand behind his head and bending him forward so her mouth settled more possessively over his, her tongue urging his lips to part.

It was the first time that she'd initiated a kiss between them and it caused a tight pain in his chest that he thought might be the death of him. No woman had ever been as aggressive with him, had ever taken as though it were her right to do so. He always led, guided, determined the dance. He liked that she didn't hold back, that she let him know what she wanted, when she wanted it.

Winding his arms around her, he pressed her flat against him, running his hands up and down her slender back. She could stoke the flames of his desire so easily. She drove him to madness with only the slightest of willingness. She was ruining him. He'd never be content with anyone else.

Although if he were honest, he wasn't certain he ever had been. Not as he was with her.

With her everything was different: the sensations, the passion, the hunger. Ten minutes after
he devoured her, he wanted to devour her all over
again. Without taking his mouth from hers, not that
he thought he could with the way she was clutching
him, the insistence with which her lips stayed moored
to his, he lifted her up and walked toward the desk.
When he got to it, with an awkward sweep of an
arm, striving not to drop her in the process, he sent
everything on top clattering to the floor.

With a laugh, she broke their connection. "Here?"

"Here."

Her eyes glittered as she began unknotting his
neck cloth. He hiked up her skirts. She quickly unbuttoned his waistcoat and shirt. Then her hands
were skimming over his skin, caressing, outlining.
He unfastened his trousers, before gliding one hand
up her thigh until his fingers were lost in the honeyed
heat that was ready for him.

Placing her hands behind his head, she drew him
back in, returning that wonderful, luscious mouth of
hers to his. He shifted her body, brought her nearer,
before plunging deep, growling low as she closed
tightly around him.

She rained kisses over his neck and chest while
he rocked against her. Harder, faster. Their harsh
breaths echoed around them.

Clutching him, she cried out his name, either a
benediction or a curse, he couldn't tell which. Her
name on his lips was definitely a curse as pleasure
ratcheted through him, unforgiving and furious. He
held her tightly while the spasms had their way, and
she tightened around him, her haven still undulating
from her own release.

Why was it always so intense with her? Why did

he feel weakened afterward, yet incredibly powerful? With a long, shuddering sigh, he pressed his forehead to hers. "We shall be late for our engagement."

"Must we go?"

He'd never known a woman who seemed to welcome the coming together with the fierceness that she did. "We're expected."

She leaned back until she could hold his gaze. "By whom?"

"A few friends. We've set up a private card game. The stakes are high, which makes it more thrilling."

"So I'll just observe."

"You'll play."

"I'm not putting any of the five thousand at risk."

He tucked stray strands of her hair behind her ear. He liked her flushed skin and unkempt state. "All expenses are on me this week, remember?"

"If I win?"

"Anything over what I give you is yours to keep."

"I don't see how I can say no."

She couldn't without reneging on their bargain. She was his tonight, however he wanted. He intended to make the most of it.

"*Y*ou swindled me," Avendale said, sitting opposite her in the coach. "You can swindle them. Never let them know when you've drawn good cards—or poor ones, for that matter. Keep your expression neutral, uncaring. You'll make out like a highwayman."

She'd chosen the red because it was what he wanted her to wear. The necklace weighed heavy against her throat because it, too, was what he wanted. While she wished it otherwise, the truth was that she wished to please him. "I'd not expected dishonesty from you, Your Grace."

"The game we play tonight involves more than cards. It should be to your liking."

"It's important that people not know the truth about me. I can't afford inquiries being made, so how will you explain my presence?"

"No explanation will be required. Besides I have no desire for them to know I fell for your ruse."

"Not completely. Otherwise, I wouldn't be here."

He looked out the window. "It stings my pride to know you could have left so easily with so much unresolved between us."

"Not so easily, and certainly there would have been regret."

His gaze came to bear on her as though he could see through the shadows, through her clothing and straight into her soul. "Were the others easy to leave?"

"Yes."

"I suppose I shall take some consolation in that. How many others were there?"

"I told you last night that I will not discuss my past."

"Yet I am fascinated by what it might entail."

With a sigh, she looked out the window, refusing to be baited. He knew far too much, enough to see her imprisoned if he chose. She had to trust that when their time was done, he would not seek retribution through the courts, he would hold to his vow and let her go.

The coach came to a stop. He stepped out before handing her down, and she discovered they were in the mews behind the Twin Dragons.

"Ashamed to be seen with me?" she asked, bothered by the knowledge that her past would prevent her from ever having anything more than a tryst with a man of his position.

"On the contrary, but it is the way we do it on nights such as this—when we want the game to be very exclusive."

Inside, they climbed stairs and traversed darkened hallways until Avendale stopped outside a door and rapped several times in a manner that reminded her of a children's lullaby.

A tiny portal appeared in the door. "What's the word?" a rough voice asked.

"Feagan," Avendale replied.

The door opened and he led her inside. The room was shadowed, but she made out various sitting areas and tables that housed decanters.

"Who's Feagan?" she asked.

"Some old blighter who taught the parents of those you are about to meet how to survive the streets."

"Sounds like a story," she said.

"Several of them, in fact."

With his hand on the small of her back, he guided her toward draperies, then pulled one aside and she walked into a brightly lit room where others had gathered.

"Ah, there you are," a dark-haired man said. At his side was a woman with the most astonishing red hair. "We thought perhaps you'd changed your mind."

"Not when I have the chance to take your money," Avendale said. "Allow me to introduce Mrs. Rosalind Sharpe. Rose, the Duke and Duchess of Lovingdon."

Rose curtsied. "It's a pleasure."

"We'll see how you feel by the end of the night, once I've taken all your money," the duchess said with a teasing smile.

"Go easy on her, Grace." Bringing her in more closely against his side as though he thought her in need of protection, he said. "You know Drake, of course."

She should have known Drake Darling would be here. "I've been enjoying your establishment."

He gave her a shrewd once-over, leaving her with the impression that he could see far more than she wanted. "I'm glad to hear it," he said.

Avendale turned Rose's attention to a tall gentleman. "The Marquess of Rexton."

Before she could curtsy, the marquess was carrying her hand to his lips, but the devil was dancing in his blue eyes, and she suspected he was having his fun at Avendale's expense, because she felt the duke's fingers jerk against her back. "It's always a pleasure to have a beautiful woman join us."

"You are most kind to say so, my lord, but I own a mirror and know I am no beauty."

"I think your mirror is broken. Perhaps I'll purchase you a new one."

She realized that with his flirtation, he no doubt understood her role in Avendale's life. They probably all did.

"She's not in need of a mirror," Avendale told him.

"All ladies are in need of mirrors." Rexton released his hold. He seemed pleasant enough but he didn't draw her as Avendale did.

"Finally, Viscount Langdon," Avendale said.

With eyes of pewter, Langdon smiled at her. "I never thought to meet a woman who could bring Avendale to heel."

"I've hardly brought him to heel."

"I suppose that remains to be seen."

"I wanted a game of cards," Avendale barked, nearly making her jump. "We can go elsewhere if you gents are going to keep tittering on like gossipy spinsters."

"By all means, let's play," Rexton said.

With Avendale at her side, Rose found herself sitting opposite the duchess, with the other gentlemen on either side of her. She was astounded by the obscene amount of money being brought out and exchanged for chips.

"No cheating, Grace," Avendale said.

"Certainly not when we have a guest," the duchess said, as though terribly offended he'd think otherwise.

"Do you cheat?" Rose couldn't help but ask her.

The duchess smiled. "Of course."

"I only recently discovered my sister is quite skilled at it," Rexton said, and only then did Rose see the similarities in their features.

Her observation skills were slipping. Normally she would have noticed right off. She could blame it on Avendale for distracting her. Only a part of her was paying attention to her surroundings. The majority of her was paying attention to him. How could she explain all of this to Harry if she didn't give it her unbridled attention?

"I can't believe you didn't figure it out," Darling said as he shuffled. Apparently his role was simply to dole out the cards, as he'd taken no chips.

"I never expected such duplicity from one so sweet," Rexton muttered.

"My duplicity is what landed me Lovingdon," she said, placing her hand over her husband's. Smiling at her, he turned his palm up and threaded his fingers through hers.

Avendale leaned closer to Rose and whispered, "They're disgustingly in love. I'm in need of scotch. What would you like?"

"I'll have the same." After he signaled a footman, she murmured, "I find them charming."

He scowled, but there was no heat behind it. She was quite flattered that he wanted to spend an evening with his friends with her in tow. Flattered and unnerved, surrounded by nobility, and yet they seemed not so different from her.

"Do you play poker, Mrs. Sharpe?" Darling asked.

"Please call me Rose. All of you. And I don't. Actually I'm not one for gambling. My coins are too hard-earned."

Avendale made a strangling noise that very much sounded as though he were choking. He cleared his throat. "Which is why she'll play with my chips this evening."

"Aren't you going to play?" she asked, as footmen began setting glasses of amber liquid before everyone.

"Not until I ensure you understand the game, the best hand for winning."

The duchess lifted her glass. "A toast, to our newest member. May fortune smile on you tonight, Rose."

"Cheers!" the gents echoed in chorus, lifting their glasses and downing the contents in one swallow.

She did the same, savoring the fire.

Chips were tossed into the center of the table. Darling began dealing cards. Rose waited until he stopped. Taking her cards, she fanned them out. Avendale leaned in, his arm resting on the back of her chair, his fingers skipping up and down her arm. She wasn't certain he was aware of his actions, while she was very much cognizant of them. How did he expect her to concentrate when he was so near, his sandalwood and bergamot fragrance teasing her nostrils?

She watched his long fingers plucking cards out, putting them in a different order, and she thought of his fingers, plucking her, squeezing her breast, pinching her nipple. He had such capable hands.

So masculine. The allure they held over her was ridiculous.

With his lips near her ear, his low voice a lover's caress, he explained the various combinations, how they ranked, which held more value—things he had explained in the coach on the ride over. She remembered every word he'd spoken, thought she would be able to recall every word from his lips on her death-bed. She wished he didn't have this effect on her, even as she relished the fact that he did.

He allowed her to select the cards to discard, didn't appear at all disappointed when they lost the round to the duchess.

"We'll win the next one," he told her.

We. Her heart hammered within her chest with such force, such a loud clamoring that she was certain everyone in the room was aware of it. She took some pride in the fact that her hand didn't tremble when she picked up the glass and downed a good portion of its contents.

She had never before been part of a *we*. While she was not alone in life—she had Harry, Merrick, Sally, Joseph—she took all the risks, determined all the plans, worked alone, faced her marks alone. She never involved the others. Harry hadn't a clue how she managed to secure lodgings or food or clothing. He didn't know she was a swindler. In that aspect of her life, there was only she.

If caught, she was the one who would be imprisoned, she was the one who would pay. She wouldn't risk the others. She carried the burden of her sins.

The next hand was dealt. She lifted the cards and stared at three tens. She did little more than furrow her brow in confusion, while Avendale moved them around in her hand as though he could find no way to situate them that made them pleasing. Slowly she let her gaze roam over the other players.

They were incredibly stone-faced. Not a smile among them, not any indication at all regarding whether they were pleased or disappointed in their hand. This, she thought, was why he enjoyed playing with them. It wasn't about the money or winning a hand. It was about outfoxing them. Had he brought her because she'd outfoxed him?

Only she hadn't, not at the end, not when it had counted. She'd never been discovered before. Afterward people came to understand what she'd been about, but never during the ruse. Why had she slipped with him? She didn't want to contemplate that perhaps she'd done so on purpose, that she had wanted him to catch her. That made no sense. At the time, she hadn't known enough about him to know that he wouldn't turn her over to the authorities.

Her three tens took that hand. She scooped up the coins. She might make a tidy profit tonight. She wondered why she wasn't filled with the same sense of accomplishment she usually experienced when she took from those who could afford to be taken from. None of the people at this table was going to suffer because she took a few of their coins.

Yet she found herself feeling not particularly triumphant with the thought of taking their money. It was an honest game of chance. They were all on equal footing here, their fortune determined by the whim of a card, but she didn't want to beat them.

She had always viewed the aristocracy as distant, sitting atop pedestals that reached into the clouds. In between hands, she watched as they lowered their gaming faces and took a moment to laugh, joke, tease. In spite of being Avendale's friends, they seldom included him in the banter. She realized it wasn't that they didn't want to, but he somehow held himself apart, as though he weren't quite comfortable within their circle.

Still, she found herself fascinated by them. They were kind, funny—and generous, she discovered when she had won three hands in a row.

"Appears the orphanages aren't going to benefit tonight, Grace," Rexton announced.

"Grace always donates her winnings to the orphanages our parents established," Darling explained.

Rose fought not to appear surprised. He was part of their family?

"Not any longer," the duchess said.

Around the table, several brows arched in surprise. Although Lovingdon did little more than place his hand over his wife's where it rested on the table. She smiled softly at him, before addressing the others. "I'm going to build a sanctuary upon the land that was my dowry."

"For what purpose?" Langdon asked.

"To provide a haven for women who have had devastating surgeries. A place for them to recover and to not feel quite so alone."

"Bravo," Langdon said, lifting his glass. "From tonight forward, my winnings will go to your endeavors."

She graced him with a beatific smile, and Rose wondered if all their winnings were donated elsewhere. Would she be expected to donate hers? Was that why Avendale had been so keen to let her have them? She couldn't take them with her? She would not feel guilty because she had never given any of her ill-gotten gains to anyone other than those within her close circle. She didn't possess as much as these people did. They could give without suffering. Yet it didn't diminish her respect for them as they seemed to give as a matter of course. They weren't selfish as she'd originally thought or consumed with naught but pleasure.

The knowledge made her more curious about Avendale. How did he fit in? How much was he like them? In many ways, he seemed to be very different.

He ceased arranging her cards, although he stayed near. When she lost a hand, he would explain how the odds would have favored her had she played differently, kept what she tossed, tossed what she kept. Sometimes, even when she won, he pointed out how she might have increased her odds.

"Very easy to decipher once you've seen everything that has been played," she said tartly.

With a grin, he trailed his finger along the nape of her neck, across her shoulders. "You'll thank me one day for the lessons I'm teaching you tonight."

She wondered if he was referring to more than the cards. "I doubt it. I shall never play with my own coin."

His grin grew. "We'll see how you feel when the night is done, especially if you win a particularly large pot. Once you've experienced that thrill of victory, you'll always be searching for it."

"Then I shall hope that I don't experience it, as I daresay, I'd have a most difficult time affording it."

"I've often said," Darling began, "that the worst thing that can happen is for a person to win the first time they gamble."

"I notice you don't wager," Rose said.

He merely shrugged.

"We don't allow him to play," Avendale said. "He's the most skilled cheater of the lot."

Rose laughed. "You've mentioned the cheating before. Are you serious? You all cheat when you play?"

"Sometimes," the duchess said, giving her husband a sideways glance and smile. "But if you're caught doing it, you must forfeit all your winnings."

"I never cheat," Rexton announced.

"You also seldom win," Darling said. "I'm more than happy to teach you."

"Mother would be appalled—are you free for a lesson tomorrow evening?"

Rose laughed. She didn't want to like these nobs, but she did. She didn't want to recall how she had entered this establishment searching for an easy mark. She'd certainly misjudged there.

They played a few more hands, then Darling cracked his knuckles. "Let's take a small break, shall we? I need to check on a few things."

"Your staff will let you know if anything is amiss," Lovingdon said.

"I'd like to see for myself. I shan't be but ten minutes."

Chairs scraped back as everyone stood. Rose knew a few seconds of light-headedness. She looked at her glass. It was nearly full. While she'd been sipping the scotch as they played, she hadn't had that much.

"Are you all right?" Avendale asked, taking her elbow.

She smiled at him. "Yes, I'm feeling rather lovely, actually. I like your friends."

"They like you as well."

"How do you know?"

"Because they're *not* cheating."

"Perhaps they are, but they're letting me win. I suspect people cheat for all sorts of reasons."

"If you're looking for a noble one, you won't find it here." She suspected he might be wrong. She was good at reading people. These seemed . . . genuine. They cared for each other, looked out for each other.

She was glad Avendale had them, although she wasn't certain he appreciated exactly what he held.

"Avendale, may I have a moment?" Lovingdon asked.

"Yes, of course." He looked at her. "Do you mind?"

"No, not at all."

They walked away several feet. Rose wished she had the ability to read lips, wondered what was so urgent that Lovingdon—

"He did it for me," the duchess said.

Turning, Rose found herself staring into kind, but inquisitive, blue eyes.

"I wanted a moment alone with you," the duchess explained. "It became obvious rather quickly that Avendale was going to hover. I've never seen him smitten."

"If you're implying he's smitten tonight, I fear you have misjudged things."

"How did you meet?" she asked.

"At the ball here, opening night."

"Are you a member then?"

"Yes." She wanted to deflect any further questions away from herself. "I was surprised that you and Mr. Darling seem to have the same parents."

The duchess smiled warmly. "My parents took him in when he was a lad. I grew up knowing him as my brother."

"Your parents are . . . ?" Inwardly she groaned at the habit that had her searching for details that would help her identify how best to take advantage.

"The Duke and Duchess of Greystone."

"With so many dukes fluttering about, I'm not certain I've ever been in such esteemed company before."

"We're really rather common, in an uncommon way I suppose. My mother and Langdon's father began life on the streets and managed to survive them. We're quite aware that not everyone is as fortunate as we are."

"Is that the reason you're building the sanctuary?"

"It's a bit more personal." Her eyes widened slightly and she smiled. "Here are the gents returning to us."

Lovingdon place his arm around his wife's waist and drew her in against his side. Avendale placed his hand on the small of Rose's back. She would not wish for more. It was foolish to want more.

"I've grown bored with the cards," Avendale said. "Let's be off to Cremorne."

"Pleasure gardens?" Rose asked. She'd heard of them. They were decadent by all accounts. Some were advocating they be closed. "I've never been."

"It's where wickedness—and I—thrive." He looked at Lovingdon. "Care to join us?"

Lovingdon shook his head. "No."

Avendale turned to the duchess. "You have made him dreadfully dull."

"She has made me dreadfully happy," Lovingdon said.

"We're off before I cast up my accounts."

Something was amiss. Rose wasn't quite certain exactly what it was. "It was a pleasure to meet you," she said.

"We must get together for tea sometime," the duchess said.

"That sounds lovely."

Then Avendale was nudging her away from them.

"You're forgetting your money," she told him as he walked her away from the table.

"Darling will cash in my chips, have the money delivered to me."

"You trust him?"

"He gains nothing by cheating me. I know precisely how much money is there. You're up five hundred quid. I'll give it to you later."

"Give it to the duchess."

He stared at her. "Which duchess? You mean Grace?"

She nodded, her stomach tightening. She could purchase Harry books with that money. What was she thinking to give it away? Perhaps she wanted to make amends, perhaps she was seeking to save her soul. As though her misdeeds were not worth a good deal more. "For her sanctuary."

"We'll talk about it tomorrow," he said, "when you're able to think more clearly."

"I'm thinking clearly now."

He grinned. "You only believe you are. I'm surprised you're still able to walk."

"I didn't drink much. My glass is nearly full."

"The footmen are paid to be discreet—and they are paid to keep the glasses nearly full. Trust me, you've had far more than you realize. And we shall have a good deal more before the night is done."

As the coach traveled through the midnight-enshrouded streets, Avendale had to admit that he had enjoyed watching Rose play cards much more than he had ever enjoyed playing them. He took pleasure from the way her face lit up whenever she won a hand, was impressed by the way she hid her disappointment when she lost. He thought she could make a living upon the stage.

"Are you certain we should go?" she asked. She sat opposite him. If he were beside her, he would have her before they reached their destination. He should take her straightaway to his residence. He didn't know why he wanted to spend time with her at

Cremorne, when it would be more rewarding to have her in his bed. "I have it on good authority that it's going to rain before the night is done."

Scoffing, he looked quickly out the window. The fog had yet to roll in. "It's not going to rain."

"I'll wager the five hundred quid I won tonight. If it doesn't rain before the sun peers over the horizon, it's yours. If it does rain, I keep the five hundred and you give the same amount out of your pocket to the duchess and tell her it's from me."

"She would appreciate the cunning behind that wager," he told her. "But I've no need of the money. If it doesn't rain, I get an additional night of you in my bed."

"Done."

He was surprised she capitulated so easily. Was it because she welcomed another night in his bed or was she arrogant enough to believe she couldn't lose now that she'd had a taste of winning? It didn't matter. He owned the wager. The scent of rain wasn't even on the air.

"I like your friends, but I have the impression your friendship doesn't run deeply."

She was far too astute. He should have known she'd pay attention to more than the cards. "I am closest to Lovingdon. He was the one with whom I sought out trouble before Grace got her clutches into him."

"You don't approve of the duchess?"

"I don't approve of any woman leading a man on a merry chase to the altar."

"Eventually you'll marry."

"I doubt it."

"But you're a duke. You require an heir. Your bastards can't inherit."

"I don't have any—" He stopped, grinned. "Clever girl. If you wanted to know if I had any children, why didn't you just ask?"

"You're not very forthcoming with answers when I pose questions."

"I've always taken precautions to ensure no off-spring come from my loins." Only he hadn't with her, he realized now. And she wouldn't have the knowledge to prevent conception. Damnation. He'd been so obsessed with her, wanted her so badly that he hadn't given any thought to protecting her. "If you find yourself with child, you're to let me know."

"Do I really strike you as the sort to come begging?"

The light from a streetlamp they passed caught the necklace at her throat, a gift she would leave behind. No, she wouldn't come begging. After their time together, he'd never see her again. A fissure of anger sliced through him at the thought and he tamped it down. He didn't need her, didn't need anyone. It grated to acknowledge that he might actually miss her when she was gone. "Still, I should like to know."

"As you wish. So do you visit Cremorne often?" she asked, and he was grateful she was taking the discussion away from the possibility of children. He didn't want to analyze why it was that the thought of having children with her wasn't abhorrent.

"Nearly every night," he said. He didn't understand this insane need he had for her to see how he lived.

"What shall we do there?"

"Drink, dance. Kiss in the shadows."

"We could have done all that at the Twin Dragons."

He chuckled low. "We could have, yes, but it all seems so proper there. Nothing at all is proper about Cremorne Gardens."

He had the right of it there, Grace thought, as she walked along beside him, her hand nestled in the crook of his elbow. She wasn't certain why it made her melancholy to imagine him here night after night, searching for something that she suspected would not be found within these gardens.

Music played. People danced—on the pavilion and off of it. Wine and drink flowed. Women—no doubt the charities to which he made donations—strutted about, flitting from man to man, some boldly taking their pleasures out in the open. She didn't want to contemplate that he might have found surcease with some of these women, that he had taken them against walls or trees.

No one acknowledged him, although surely there were people here who knew him. She supposed it was an unwritten rule: whatever happened within these confines was not discussed beyond them and identities were held secret.

Now and then Avendale would stop, cup her face, and lean in to kiss her. Here to kiss in public was acceptable. Although, so it seemed, was fornicating. She would not go that far. What she shared with him was for them only. It was personal, private.

But a man could bring his mistress here without experiencing censure. It fluttered through her mind to wonder how many nights a woman needed to be with a man to qualify as being his mistress. Avendale could share with her all the tawdry places because she wasn't decent or respectable. He could have the sort of fun with her that he couldn't have with a wife. That thought saddened her, made her want to leave.

Yet she wanted to stay, touched that he was sharing part of his life with her, even if it didn't shed a particularly good light on him. She wondered why he strove so hard to convince her that he was naught but wickedness and vice. Unfortunately her mind was not clear enough to discern his reasoning. On the morrow perhaps.

They'd been drinking since they arrived, and the spirits were having their way with her. She staggered against him. His arm came around her, held her near. She laughed. "This isn't you."

He looked down on her, and she wondered when he had become blurred. Squinting, she was able to make out his puckered brow. "I believe I am me," he said. "I haven't morphed into someone else."

She shook her head. The world spun. She flung out her hand. "No, this place. It's not you."

"You're wrong there. It's where I flourish."

"No, it's where you come when you want to be lost." She rose up on her toes and pressed a kiss to his luscious lips. "Why do you want to be lost? What are you striving to escape?"

"You don't know what you're talking about."

But she did know.

"Here, finish this off," he said.

Feeling a cool breeze, she welcomed the warmth that his scotch would bring. She downed it in one swallow. The glass slipped from her fingers, shattered. Avendale merely laughed and dragged her away.

Suddenly there was another glass in her hand. She didn't remember how it came to be there.

"Drink up," he ordered.

"I'm nearly foxed, I think."

"I want you completely foxed."

"Why?"

"Because this place calls for it."

She drank deeply, thinking nothing had ever tasted so marvelous. Tossing the glass aside, she moved in front of Avendale and wound her arms around his neck. "I'm going to win the bet."

"I don't think—"

A crack of thunder prevented her from hearing

the rest of his words. The skies opened, releasing a deluge. Stepping away from him, raising her arms in the air, she spun in a circle. "I win! I win! I told you it would rain!"

Snaking an arm around her waist, he drew her back to him. "I've never kissed a woman in the rain."

"Then kiss me, so you'll have the memory, so you'll never forget me." Quite suddenly, it seemed imperative that he never forget her, that something about her be different from the countless other women who warmed his bed.

"I shall never forget you."

He took her mouth with a savagery that surprised her. Was it this place? The decadence of it, the madness of people seeking whatever pleasure they could find?

It didn't matter. She was vaguely aware of shrieks, the patter of feet as people ran past them, seeking shelter, yet she and Avendale stayed as they were, not caring one fig that they were getting drenched. She thought how lovely it would be when they returned to his residence and he warmed her.

But for now, she wanted nothing more than this: his lips ravaging hers as though he could never have enough of her, as though nothing in the world were more important than holding her at this moment.

$\mathcal{R}$ose snuggled beneath the blankets until she was flush against Avendale, absorbing his warmth. He began slowly stroking her back, which she should have found soothing, but her head felt as though it had exploded sometime during the night and was only now starting to come back together, each piece locking into place with a snap that caused a pain behind her eyes. She couldn't recall ever indulging to such an extent. Why would Avendale do this to himself night after night? While she had to admit that the majority of the evening had seemed like jolly good fun, she wasn't certain it was worth this agony. She could have had as much fun with fewer spirits. She might have even remembered the night. At that precise moment it was little more than snippets, flashes. Arriving here. Avendale disrobing her. A deliciously warm bath. Snuggling against him. The world spinning when she closed her eyes, pulling her down into a vortex where her past circled around her, a thousand ravens pricking her conscience until she was bleeding. Avendale cooing to her, promising all would be well.

She'd wanted to tell him everything, but an instinct for survival stronger than the allure of a clean conscience overrode the taunting of the spirits. Now she was suffering from the indulgence.

She couldn't even enjoy the rain as she usually did because it was as though each droplet was pinging off her brain instead of the windowpane. A constant barrage of irritating noises. But at least she'd won her bet with Avendale. It had rained, was raining still.

Avendale cupped her backside, pressed her against him. He was hot and hard. Suddenly all the discomforts lessened.

"I thought you'd never awaken," he said in a voice roughened from sleep.

"You don't sound as though you've been up all that long," she answered, nipping his collarbone.

He laughed, a rich, deep sound that chased away the lingering cobwebs in her mind. "Oh, I've been up long enough and aching for you."

Rolling them over, he tucked her beneath him and began trailing his mouth along her throat, her bare shoulders. They hadn't bothered with clothes when they came to bed.

She heard the distant bonging of a clock. Four times. The one in the foyer, she thought dreamily. She briefly wondered why the servants hadn't stopped the chimes for the night.

"I thought it was later," she murmured as Avendale slid down and began to give attention to her breasts.

"Mmm?"

"It seemed we'd slept longer."

"I'm not sure how much longer we could have slept. It's afternoon."

She furrowed her brow. The curtains were drawn, the room dark, but surely it was morning beyond the windows. Not afternoon. Not four in the afternoon. "It can't be."

He eased down farther and circled his tongue around her navel. "I'm fairly certain it is, sweetheart. We've slept the day away."

Bolting upright, ignoring the jarring pain to her head, she shoved on his shoulders and scrambled out from beneath him. "Why didn't you let me know?"

Lying on his side, he grabbed her arm, preventing her from leaving the bed. "What the devil, Rose? We're having a pleasant lie in."

"I was supposed to be at the residence at two."

"What difference does a couple of hours make?"

"It matters. I promised." Jerking free of his hold, she clambered off the bed and hurried to the wardrobe. She selected a simple dress that would require no assistance to don. No corset, a single petticoat. "Can you please shout down for them to have a carriage readied?"

Leisurely he left the bed as though she had all the

time in the world. "Why this obsession with seeing your servants every afternoon?"

"I've told you before: They're not my servants. They're my friends." After securing the last of the buttons, she reached for a brush and began working the tangles out of her hair. She caught his disgruntled gaze in the mirror. "Please, Avendale."

He snatched his dressing gown from the floor at the foot of the bed. "I don't like this part of our arrangement."

Grabbing a ribbon, she pulled back her hair, secured it, and faced him. "Regardless, it is part of the arrangement. If you want me to return willingly this evening, you will hold to it."

She saw the familiar fury, wondered that it failed to frighten her.

"God help me," he snarled, "I should have had enough of you by now but I haven't."

With that he left to see about a carriage. After she fetched a pelisse to protect her from the rain, and her reticule, she followed him out.

She arrived at her residence to discover her worst fears realized: Harry was gone.

Chapter 12

Avendale sat sprawled in his library, slowly savoring his scotch, watching the clock on the mantel, listening to the chimes of the one in the hallway as the minutes dragged by. One hundred and twenty of them. Double what he had allotted her for the afternoon. The only reason that he was still here was because he was allowing for the rain and the likelihood that the carriage would be forced to travel more slowly.

It irritated the devil out of him that she was not with him for every hour of every day while she was supposed to be in his company. He had told her that she had to be with him for a week. He would deduct these hours when she was away from the total hours found in a week and insist she not leave until he'd had that many hours in her company. Perhaps he would deduct the time she was sleeping as well.

With a growl, he shot out of the chair, crossed over to the fireplace, pressed his forearm to the mantel, and stared into the fire. What was wrong with him? Why was he so bothered by her leaving for a spell? She would return and they would carry on. They'd dine, then tumble onto the sheets—after he'd stroked every inch of her body. He had some oils from the Orient. Perhaps he'd use them. Drive her mad first.

It was only fair, as she was doing the same to him. Why hadn't she returned? His driver had specific orders not to take any detours. What if she had slipped out through the back garden? She'd been unduly put out with him because he hadn't woken her in time to keep her appointment. How was he to know that the specific hour was so crucial? Why was it? Why would the little man or the giant care?

Everything within him stilled. He assumed the little man and the giant were the only ones in the residence now. Stupid assumption on his part, just because they were the only ones he'd seen. What if there was someone else? Someone she loved?

Just because she'd been untouched the first night didn't mean that she had no other man in her life. He lifted his gaze to the clock. Ten more minutes had passed. Suspicion reared its ugly head.

He wanted to trust her, but he didn't. She was a swindler. She'd lied, deceived him before. Why was she so secretive about her blasted hour that had now evolved into more than two?

He heard a soft knock and spun on his heel to find his coachman standing in the doorway, looking as though he were about to put his head on the chopping block. "Your Grace, I waited far longer than I should have and I apologize for that. Eventually when the lady didn't come out, I knocked on the door only to be told by that small gent that the lady wasn't about. I decided it best to let you know. The rain slowed my journey."

"We'll be going back out in it."

"I suspected as much, sir."

She had broken the terms of their agreement. He should not have been surprised, but he was not going to let her get away with such treachery. He was well within his rights to seek her out, demand an explanation and the return of his money.

Even though in truth he didn't give a damn about the money. He wanted retribution for yet one more deception. She would have to give him a month this time, a month without an afternoon trip to her residence.

As he journeyed through the streets, rain pelting his coach, he held on to his anger, refusing to acknowledge the disappointment because she was untrustworthy, because she would leave him so easily. He despised himself for enjoying her company so much, for worrying about a possible mishap. How many times would he fall for her lies?

His carriage had barely stopped in front of her residence, when he leaped out. He barged up the steps, threw open the door, and strode in. The little man—Merrick, as he recalled—stepped out of the parlor.

"You can't just come in here," he stated.

"I pay the lease on the damned place. I can do anything I want, including kick you out into the street. Where is she?"

He jutted up his chin. "Went for a stroll."

"In this weather?"

"She favors the rain."

It occurred to him that perhaps whoever it was she needed to see this afternoon didn't actually live in this residence. That she was delivered here and then snuck out to go wherever it was she wanted to go. He started off down a hallway.

"See here now, you've got no right to be going through our home!" Merrick shouted.

He did and he would. He realized it was the first

time he'd been inside her residence. It was not lavishly furnished. No portraits, no paintings. Nothing in the hallway. He paused outside a dining room. No sideboards, no hutches, nothing save a small square table covered in a white cloth. It sat four.

He carried on down the hallway until he spotted another door. He closed his fingers around the handle.

"You can't go in there."

He glared at Merrick. "It would give me unbridled pleasure if you try to stop me." He didn't know why it was imperative that he saw every inch of the dwelling. Jerking open the door, he marched into what was obviously the library. A dozen or so books adorned shelves. A large desk and chair occupied a space near a window. A sofa rested before the glass, and he imagined sunlight streaming in over Rose as she sat there. A comfortable sitting area was arranged in one corner near a fireplace. On the opposite side of the room was an immense bed, neatly made. Did the giant sleep here? No, it wasn't long enough for him. It was more suited to a man Avendale's size. He'd ask Merrick but the indignant fellow hadn't followed him in. He doubted her man would tell him anyway.

Slowly he walked through the room, trying to get a sense of it. He noticed a tall stack of papers on the desk. As he neared he could see ink bleeding through but the paper was turned so he couldn't make out the words. A rock, like one might find in a garden, was on top, as though that were enough to keep anyone from prying.

Avendale was too angry with Rose to respect the privacy of anyone living here. Setting the rock aside, he turned over the first page.

The Memoirs of Harry Longmore

Who the devil was Harry Longmore? Why did he live here? What was he to Rose?

Moving that page aside, he began reading the second.

> *My story is as much Rose's as it is mine. We were inseparable . . .*

Clenching his jaw with the thought of another man having such importance in Rose's life, Avendale wanted to crumple the paper, set it afire. Instead he very carefully returned it to its place before striding out of the room. He took no satisfaction in the knowledge that he had separated her from this Harry Longmore. She obviously cared for him or she wouldn't come here every day. Once her time with Avendale was done, she'd continue to carry on with this beastly fellow, leave the city with five thousand quid, and laughter echoing between them. What a fool he was to give in to this damnable craving he had for her.

"Happy now?" Merrick asked as Avendale started back down the hallway.

"Hardly."

A commotion in the entryway, door closing, voices, had him quickening his pace, lengthening his stride until Merrick couldn't keep up.

"It's all right, my dearest," he heard Rose's voice say sweetly, encouragingly. He could not make out the words that followed but they were deeper, obviously male, and his anger boiled anew at the thought of her with another man. She might have been a virgin, but she obviously had a love. He was more than ready for a heated confrontation that might even involve fisticuffs. He stormed into the entryway—

Staggered to an unsteady halt as though he'd slammed into a stone wall.

If he'd not spent his life conditioning himself to never reveal what he thought, what he felt, he might have gasped, recoiled, scrambled back. Instead he gave no reaction at all. Merely studied the tableau as though it were something he saw every day.

Rose and the giant stood there, between them supporting—he wasn't certain what it was. A man perhaps. Almost certainly. But grotesquely misshapen. His head far too large for his body, a body that had obviously betrayed him as it dipped, bent, jutted out in ways that should have been impossible.

Had he been in an accident? Blood poured from a gash in what might have been his skull and dotted his clothing. Scrapes and discolorations marred the skin of a hideously distorted face.

For some reason, his right hand and arm—which Rose clung to—appeared normal. The other was shaped more like a seal's flipper, the fingers barely recognizable as such.

Rose didn't appear horrified that Avendale was there but then she was obviously concerned with the fellow she was trying to help across the foyer. Avendale suspected her anger would arrive shortly enough. Without thought, he crossed over to her. "I'll relieve you of the burden of assisting him."

"He's not a burden," she snapped, and he realized he'd misjudged. She was furious.

And reluctant to trust him. It stung. It also hurt to see the bruise forming on her cheek, the sleeve in her dress torn at the seam. Her hair was loose, the ribbon gone. Someone had hurt her, and he hadn't been about to protect her. "It'll be easier for him if someone closer to his height is providing the support."

She hesitated but a heartbeat before saying, "Yes, all right. Just take care that you don't hurt him."

As though it were even possible not to cause him pain. Avendale slid his shoulder under this . . . person's arm. The man grunted. "Sorry, old chap," Avendale said, as Rose eased off to the side.

"This way," she said, and began leading them down the familiar hallway.

"What happened to him?" Merrick asked as he came forward.

"He was set upon by ruffians," Rose said.

Avendale understood her unkempt state now. She would have charged into the fray. He had a need to pound his fist into something, someone.

"I told him not to go out but then he snuck out when I wasn't looking," the dwarf muttered.

"It's all right, Merrick," she said. "Fetch some towels and warm water. We need to get him into dry clothes."

She guided them into the library. With as much gentleness as possible, Avendale and the giant eased the man onto the bed. Against the head of the bed, the giant leaned a walking stick he'd been holding in one skeletal-like hand.

"He needs to sit up against the pillows," Rose told them. "He can't breathe well if he's lying down."

When the man was situated, Rose sat on the edge of the bed and gently cupped what at one time might have been a cheek. "Everything's going to be all right, sweetest."

The man didn't say anything, but his blue gaze, one similar to Rose's, was homed in on Avendale. It was unsettling, the intensity of his scrutiny. "I'll have my coachman fetch my physician," Avendale announced. "He's one of the finest in London."

She looked up at him. "I can't afford the finest."

"Our time together is not yet over, Rose. They are my expenses to cover."

"This isn't what you bargained for."

"I bargained for whatever would keep you with me for a week. Don't start splitting hairs now." He felt an irrational need to claim her, to ensure she understood things between them were not yet over. That the man in the bed understood that she was his.

"All right, then, yes, thank you. I suppose introductions are in order." She wrapped both her hands around the man's good one. "Your Grace, allow me the honor of introducing you to Mr. Harry Longmore."

The man to whom she was supposedly inseparable.

"My brother."

Chapter 13

Rose sat on a sofa in the parlor, one of Avendale's large hands covering both of hers as they rested in her lap. How she longed for a bench in the hallway outside Harry's room. The physician was with him now. A Sir William Graves. Apparently, he was not only the best but he served the queen. He also had a very quiet, yet confident demeanor. Harry was not usually comfortable with strangers, yet he had seemed so with Sir William.

"Is your name Longmore as well?" Avendale asked quietly.

She'd known he'd have questions. That his first was about her name took her by surprise. "Yes. Rosalind Longmore. I change the surname, never the first. It's easier."

"I want Sir William to have a look at you when he's finished with your brother."

"I'm fine."

"You have a bruise forming on your cheek. I daresay you'll have a black eye by tomorrow. You have scrapes, your clothes are torn."

"I'm fine," she insisted.

"Could you find them again?"

She stared blankly at him. "Find whom?"

"The ruffians who accosted you and your brother."

"What are you intending?"

"To have them arrested after I give them a sound pounding."

No, not at all the conversation she'd expected. "They were cruel idiots. I didn't pay much attention to their features. Harry knows the dangers of going out. Even when he wears a hooded cloak people won't leave him be. He was out searching for me, because I was late. He was worried that I was in some sort of trouble. I don't know how he thought he would find me."

"Why didn't you tell me about him, tell me why you had to come here?"

She shook her head. How to explain? "I didn't know how you would react." He was a powerful man. He might have tried to take Harry away, to use him for his own gain. Others had. She trusted only Merrick, Sally, and Joseph with Harry. "I was trying to protect him."

"Has he always been like that?" Avendale asked.

She'd been surprised by the gentleness with which he'd helped Harry into the bed, more surprised by his lack of reaction when first catching sight of her brother. Most were appalled, afraid. A good many struck out at him.

"No," she said softly. "He was perfection when he was born. I was four, but I still remember the wonder of him. My father worked the fields, my mother had her chores, so I was left to care for him. He was around two when my mother noticed the first . . . lump on his head. My parents thought I'd been careless and dropped him. My father took a switch to my bare backside and legs until he drew blood, until I

couldn't sit down." Avendale's hand flinched around
hers, and she imagined the anger sparking in him
because she'd been mistreated. "My father was so
proud of having a son, a male. He thought it made
him more of a man, I think."

"You don't know where he is now?" Avendale
asked flatly.

She peered up at him. "My father?"

He gave one brusque nod.

"No. He can be rotting somewhere for all I care."

"I'd like to take my fist to him."

"No sweeter words have I ever heard."

Tenderly he skimmed his finger over her swollen
and bruised cheek. "Do you know what caused your
brother's condition?"

"No. Other lumps began to appear. Portions of
him began to grow oddly. His jaw twisted, his body
became misshapen. My parents took him to a physician. He had no answers. My father decided my
mother had consorted with the devil, because surely
nothing like the creature my brother was would
come from his loins. He had her placed in an insane
asylum. She died there."

"Do you believe she consorted with the devil?"

She shook her head. "Absolutely not. I think
nature is simply cruel. It picks people at random
and bestows upon them horrors they don't deserve.
I don't believe in a god who punishes people. Harry
was a babe. What could he have done to anger a god?
Why was he made to suffer and not me? It makes no
sense."

"There are many cruelties in the world that make
no sense. I assume your father's anger didn't diminish
once your mother was locked away."

"On the contrary, it seemed to flourish. He hid

Harry away for a time, but still people heard about him. They would journey to the farm, offer to pay a penny for a look. Eventually my father decided he could make a fortune on Harry's oddities. He began to exhibit him. People would pay tuppence to view the Boulder Boy. He would be dressed in a loincloth, so they could see the full extent of his deformity. Harry would stand there as proudly as he could while people gawked. Broke my heart. People see a curiosity, something hideous. I see a gentle soul who deserves so much more.

"Eventually we joined a tour of oddities, which is where I met Merrick and his wife, Sally—the Tiniest Bride and Groom in the World, they were called. And Joseph, the Stickman. When I was seventeen, I told Harry I was going to take him on a grand adventure and we ran off. The others came with us."

"You've been taking care of them ever since."

In his voice, she thought she heard admiration tinged with sadness. "It's easier for me. I'm the least odd."

His brow furrowed. "The least odd? You're not odd at all."

Her smile was self-deprecating. "My face is plain. It does not hold a man's interest, but my rather large bosom does. I learned early on how to use it to my advantage. It's the first thing men notice about me. It's where their gazes linger. They don't pay attention to my eyes so they miss the shrewd calculations going on in my mind as I measure their worth and gullibility. I miscalculated yours. It stung my pride."

He squeezed her hand just before he began stroking his thumb over her knuckles. She wanted to weep at the kind gesture.

"I didn't notice your bosom first," he said quietly.

"What caught my attention was the way you walked into the room as though you owned it."

Her gaze captured his, and within his eyes, she saw the absolute truth. All along she'd assumed he was like all the others, fascinated by an aspect of her body over which she had no control. But as she thought about it, truly thought about it, she realized he never lingered overly long there. He spread his attentions over her entire person. Even her toes did not go unnoticed.

"I didn't think you were nobility," he continued, "yet you had such a regal bearing. I was quite entranced and I hadn't been in a good long while. It felt good to be curious, to be intrigued. Like me, you seemed to be hiding something. That intrigued me all the more."

"What are you hiding?" she asked.

He merely shook his head. "Does your brother never leave here, then?"

She realized he wasn't going to share, at least not now. It was probably for the best. Her focus should be on Harry, had always been on Harry. "No. He doesn't even go out into the garden during the day because our neighbors might catch a glimpse of him from their upstairs windows. We don't want to attract the curious. He travels in books. Reads voraciously when he's not writing. He likes to write as well, but won't share his endeavors with me. Ever so private."

Hearing footsteps, she rose as Sir William walked into the room. Avendale moved in to stand beside her, placing his hand on her lower back as though she needed to be steadied for what was to come. She wondered briefly if he was even aware how often he touched her.

"Let's sit, shall we?" Sir William said.

That start didn't portend well. Still, Rose returned to her place on the sofa, with Avendale at her side. Sir William took a plush chair opposite them. For the briefest of moments, it seemed he was studying Avendale intently, as though the duke were suddenly unfamiliar to him, which seemed odd considering he was his physician. Clearing his throat, he shifted his attention to Rose. "The injuries your brother sustained during the brawl are quite minor. A few cuts, scrapes, bruises. Nothing that won't heal on its own with time."

Relief swelled within Rose. "Good. I was quite worried. He seemed to be finding it more difficult to breathe than usual."

Sir William nodded slowly. "He mentioned that he was finding a few things more difficult."

Rose smiled. "You understood him? Most people can't because of the way the shape of his mouth causes him to mumble and slur."

"There are also growths within his mouth, within his body. He may have as many inside as he does out."

"But you could remove them," Avendale said.

Within Sir William's blue eyes, Rose saw a well of sadness. "There are so many. The risks involved . . . I would hardly know where to begin. To be quite honest, I doubt he would survive any surgery—even at the hands of the most skilled physician."

"What caused his condition?" Avendale asked.

Sir William shook his head. "I've no clue. I've never seen the like. I would like to examine him more thoroughly at the hospital, consult with a few of my colleagues."

"Because he's a curiosity?" Rose asked. "Because you can't cure him, can you?"

"I can't cure him, no." He leaned forward. "There might be something we could learn."

Tears burned her eyes. "No. He's been stared at, poked and prodded enough. I won't put him through that again. Even for medicine."

"I can hardly blame you, I suppose." He released a long, slow sigh. "You should probably begin preparing yourself, however, as I don't think he's long for this world."

The words were like a solid blow to the center of Rose's chest. She was astounded her lungs could still draw in breath and that her heart still pounded. The tears she'd been holding at bay broke free and rolled along her cheeks. "I could tell he was worsening. They keep growing, don't they? Those things."

"I believe so, yes, based upon what he told me. I could feel some inside him, but to know the full extent I would have to cut into him. I don't think we'd gain anything by that, based upon what I can see on the surface."

"Do you know how long before . . ." She couldn't bring herself to say the words. He might be a monster to everyone else, but to her, he was her brother.

"I'm sorry," Sir William said, "but that is not in my hands. I can leave some laudanum to help ease his discomforts. I can come to check on him every few days. The more I observe, the more light I might be able to shed on the matter. I want to discuss his condition with other physicians I know."

She started to protest.

"I won't be obtrusive," he assured her quickly. "I will be circumspect and not mention that I am seeing him. I'll make discreet inquiries, and perhaps I'll learn something to ease his suffering."

"Yes, all right."

Sir William got to his feet. She and Avendale did the same.

"Thank you for coming," Avendale said.

"I appreciate your sending for me. It meant a lot to your mother."

"Be sure to send me a billing for your services."

"Now you've insulted me." Sir William turned his attention to Rose. "I'm sorry we couldn't have met under better circumstances."

"I can't thank you enough for everything you've done."

He jerked his head toward Avendale. "Keeping him out of trouble is a good start."

With Avendale at her side, Rose accompanied Sir William to the door, watched as he strolled down the path, and climbed into a small, simple one-horse carriage that he could drive himself.

"What would it matter to your mother that you sent for him?" Rose asked, closing the door and turning back to Avendale.

"Because he is her husband."

Angling her head, she studied him. She'd sensed some tension between the two. "Has that anything to do with your secret?"

"Has everything to do with it, and that's all I'll say on the matter. I assume you want to stay the night."

"I do, yes." She wanted to be angry with him for coming here uninvited, for forcing himself into her life, into Harry's but she had nothing within her with which to fuel her anger. Stepping into him, she wound her arms around his waist, drew immense comfort from his enfolding her in his embrace.

He pressed a kiss to the top of her head. "I'm not the caring sort so I'm at a loss here, Rose. Tell me what I can do to make it better."

She merely squeezed him all the harder, because his presence at the moment was enough.

*I*f Avendale had any doubts that Harry was indeed a man, they were put to rest when Rose and he entered the library to find Harry sitting in a chair near the fire. He shoved himself to his feet. He had to have known Rose would come in to see him before she left, that Avendale might be with her. Pride had hoisted him out of the bed. His clothes were similar to the almost sacklike apparel he'd been wearing before only they weren't wet, torn, and bloody. They hung rather loosely, but then how would one go about fitting clothes to that misshapen form? Leaning on a cane, he mumbled something. Avendale couldn't quite distinguish the words.

"Harry wondered if you'd join him in drinking some whiskey," Rose offered as though she understood his inability to decipher the words.

"I'm a scoundrel," Avendale said. "I never turn down drink." He thought the man's lips twitched, and Avendale realized Rose's brother was hindered from forming a proper smile because of the shape of his mouth, but his eyes twinkled with amusement.

"I'll pour," Rose said. "Avendale, will you fetch the chair from behind the desk so I have a place to sit?"

He did as she asked, but he had no plans to let her sit in it while the other chair appeared more plush and comfortable. She brought over the glasses on a small tray. Avendale took one, then watched as Harry did the same with a hand that was beautiful and elegant, and he wondered if it might have been kinder if there was nothing about him that was shaped to perfection.

Rose lifted her glass. "To London's finest physician."

They clinked their glasses, each took a sip. Avendale indicated where Rose should sit, and once she did, he and Harry settled into their chairs.

"I'm sorry I wasn't here this afternoon as promised," Rose said. "The duke and I went to Cremorne Gardens last night, and I drank a bit more than I should have. I slept in I'm afraid." She eased to the edge of the chair. "It doesn't look at all like our garden. It's a place for enjoying all sorts of pleasures. Shall I describe it for you?"

He gave an exaggerated nod, and Avendale realized his head was far too large for subtle movements. He listened as Rose described Cremorne in such minute detail that he could see it in his mind almost as clearly as he had last night. No, more clearly. He saw all the things he'd overlooked, taken for granted. The colors, the sounds, the smells, the tastes—even the things she'd touched. Banisters, benches, the pavilion.

He thought about how absorbed she'd been at the theater. He understood the reason behind it now. She was striving to bring the world to her brother, a world he couldn't visit without consequences.

Harry would ask questions that were almost inarticulate, yet she would provide answers that seemed to satisfy. Avendale concentrated on the sounds, focusing until he was able to decipher the words, to know by her response to Harry that Avendale had indeed managed to master the guttural murmuring. But mostly he watched her: the light that shone in her eyes as she shared the places she'd visited, the excitement in her voice. The joy on her face as though she truly adored her time with her brother, adored him.

Avendale felt small and petty because he'd resented her time away from him in the afternoon, had wanted to deny her this. If only she'd told him . . .

But of course she hadn't and why would she? From the moment they'd met, by word and deed, he'd led her to believe that he wanted nothing more from her than a romp in his bed. Because bastard that he was, that had been all he wanted.

He'd wanted to be lost in her heat, her fire, her passion. He'd acquired it, only to discover it wasn't enough. Never in his life, had he been so unsure as to exactly what it was he did want. He'd been focused on absolute pleasure at any cost. Now he wondered if the price had been too high. For who would care if he were suddenly unattractive, without means, without power?

They'd been visiting for less than an hour when Harry seemed to wither and shrink. Setting aside her glass, Rose got up, crossed over to him, and pressed a kiss to his forehead. "We'll leave you to sleep now."

After she stepped away, Avendale moved in and extended his hand. "It was a pleasure to meet you, Mr. Longmore."

"Harry," he replied, the word still slurred, but Avendale's ears must have become attuned to the tortured sounds because he clearly understood what was being said.

"Harry, then."

The man's hand, warm and strong, closed around Avendale's, and Avendale thought it more unfair that the remainder of Harry's body had betrayed him as it had. Nature could be both wondrous and cruel, creating immense beauty and then offsetting it with ugliness. Perhaps it did it so people would never take beauty for granted.

Avendale followed Rose from the room, closing the door in their wake. In the hallway, she turned into him and he folded his arms around her.

"Will you come over tomorrow?" she asked.

"I'm not leaving, Rose."

She craned her head back to meet his gaze as though she didn't quite trust his words, as though she didn't quite understand their meaning. He skimmed his thumb along the edge of the darkening bruise. "I'm rather insulted that you'd think I would."

Slowly she shook her head, staring at him as though she could not find the words. He envied the ease with which she'd spent an hour talking to her brother, and yet with him, she measured words as though she thought he would judge each one. "I haven't what you need here."

"You're here."

Instead of relief or even warmth at his words, which sounded far more sentimental and foolish than he'd intended, she appeared all the more worried. "I have no servants, no one to wait on you."

"I suspect I can manage. You won't convince me to go so you might as well save your breath."

"You don't have to worry that I'm going to leave London. Harry is far too weak to travel. I see that now. I think trying to take him to Scotland would have killed him."

So that's where she'd been planning to traipse off to the night he caught her loading her carriage. Was there someone there to care for her? No, if there had been she'd have gone there long ago. His money would have tided her over for a while, but eventually she would have had to resort to another swindle in order to survive. Or perhaps she would have found legitimate means.

She clutched his arms, gave him a little shake as though she recognized that he was sorting things out, and she needed his complete attention. "He's dying.

Sir William said as much. He's not long for this world. Help me, Avendale, help me make whatever time he has left as pleasant as possible. Afterward, you can ask anything of me and I'll comply. I'll stay with you as long as you want. I'll sign papers attesting to that. I'll sign them in blood. Life has been so unfair to him. I just don't want him to have to worry anymore."

"Anything at all?" he repeated.

"Anything."

"For as long as I want?"

"For as long as you want."

He could not imagine what it would be like to love someone that deeply, to be willing to give up one's own hopes, plans, dreams for someone else's happiness. It was beyond the pale, beyond his grasp. What was not beyond his grasp, however, was how badly he still wanted her. Already he had begun to regret that their bargain kept her with him for only a week. Now she was presenting him the opportunity to hold her near until he tired of her. A better man than he would have felt guilty for taking advantage of the situation. He supposed there was something to be said for his character that at least he recognized that he should feel some remorse. But she was offering what he wanted, and he didn't have to give up anything he cared about in order to acquire it. Only a fool would have turned down her offer. He was no fool.

"It seems we've struck another bargain," he said.

Her smile of gratitude was as bright as a thousand stars beaming in the heavens. "You won't regret it, I promise," she said, and he found it telling that she thought another promise was needed to seal the first. "However, I still want to stay here tonight, so I can look in on Harry periodically."

"As I said, I'll be staying with you. I sent my driver back to Buckland after he fetched Sir William. He'll return for me in the morning."

"You knew I'd want to stay." She said it with surprise.

Not that he blamed her, as he was taken off-guard as well. He *had* known. He hadn't really given it much thought, and it was unsettling now to realize that he'd had no doubt regarding what she'd want to do. He hadn't needed to ask. He'd simply known. "It was logical."

She gave him a skeptical look before saying, "Would you like a tour?"

"Upstairs, perhaps. I've already seen everything down here."

Straightening her shoulders, she became the confident, bold woman with whom he was familiar. "I should be angry that you broke the terms of our agreement. You were not to bother me when I was here."

"On the contrary, you were gone more than the allotted time. I was well within my rights to seek you out. I may be a scoundrel, but I do honor bargains made, expect others to do the same."

She began walking toward the foyer, and he fell into step beside her.

"Did you get me drunk on purpose last night?" she asked. "To ensure I slept the day away?"

It shamed him to admit the truth. "It might have crossed my mind that with enough drink you wouldn't be up to going out today."

With a wry smile, she slid her gaze over to him. "Even though they were the terms of our original understanding?"

"I'm a selfish bastard, Rose. I want what I want when I want it."

They reached the stairs. She went up two steps, before turning to face him, stopping him in his tracks. At eye level, she wasn't shy about assessing him. She'd done the same thing the first night, and just as he had then, he wanted now to puff out his chest. "You do realize with our new bargain that I shall spend more than an hour a day with Harry. I shall spend a good deal of my evenings with him."

"I understand the terms and that I shall get the scraps." But eventually he would get the entire feast. He wondered why it filled him with a sense of sadness, not for himself, but for her. He didn't want grief to visit her, but it would, and he wanted to be on hand to console her—which also confounded him because he avoided emotional entanglements like the plague. "But I intend to stay near. I'm making an investment here, and I'm in the habit of keeping a close eye on my investments."

Her lips curling up into a smile brought him a sense of relief. He'd feared it would be days, weeks before she smiled. That she was doing so at his expense was irrelevant. She slid a hand around his neck and leaned in. "Your command of sweet words continues to astound me. I'm surprised women aren't swooning at your feet at every turn."

She pressed her lips to his, and he wished that he had sweeter words, that he had mastered the art of kindness. He lifted her into his arms.

"Not here," she said quietly.

"No, not here." He'd known that and yet been unable to resist holding her near. He carried on, taking her up the stairs. When he reached the top, he asked, "Which room?"

"The first one on the right."

He should have known she'd prefer looking out

on the gardens to viewing the street. He should have known a lot of things. Should have noticed the sadness in her eyes, the small lines that marred her brow. Should have recognized that her walls were thicker and stronger than his, that they encompassed others.

He strode into a room that astounded him with its simplicity, especially when compared with the library. Ever so slowly he lowered her feet to the bare wooden floor, eased away from her, and walked through the room. Cheap furniture. A bedstead, a wardrobe, a dressing table, a bench, a stepping stool, a sofa. A small table that held a bottle of brandy and one snifter. Nothing more, nothing excessive, nothing that pampered. When he turned around, she had one hand wrapped around the bedpost at the foot of the bed.

"I told you that it wasn't quite up to your standards," she said.

"I'll survive one night." He strolled over to the window, gazed out. Darkness had fallen. He couldn't get a good look at the garden, but he could make out the brick wall. While in an expensive area, the property was small. Neighbors could indeed spy on them. He took so much for granted. Privacy most of all.

"When I walked through downstairs, I didn't find a ballroom," he said.

"I lied about that as well. I wanted to you to think that I possessed more than I did."

Closing his eyes, he wondered if there would ever come a time when she didn't lie to him about something. To gain what she wanted, she spun lies as easily as one stirred sugar into tea. He couldn't forget that, and yet he wanted to trust her, to take a chance that something real could exist between them. Her footsteps echoed over the wood. Glancing back, he saw her kneeling before the hearth.

"I'll see to that," he said, and crossed over to the fireplace.

"I can manage."

He took the matches from her. "I'll take care of it."

"Are you hungry? I can ask Sally to prepare dinner."

"I thought you had no servants," he said as he struck a match and set the flame to the kindling.

"She's not really a servant, but she assists as needed. She's a far better cook than I."

The fire caught, the warmth welcome. "Perhaps later."

She rose. "Brandy then?"

"That I could certainly use." Standing, he watched as she poured the liquor into the glass. There was a familiarity to her actions, a loneliness. How many nights had she poured herself a drink? How many nights had she sipped it alone in this room? Was she as lonely as he was? He filled his nights with women, wine, and wagering—but it was only so he could avoid the yawning abyss of loneliness.

She handed him the glass, before sitting on one end of the sofa. He joined her there, settling onto the other end, keeping some distance between them, when all he truly wanted was to be as close to her as possible. Now wasn't the time. It wasn't what she needed or wanted. If he got too close, he was going to take her to that bed where he would be cramped and uncomfortable; he was going to ease her distress by bringing her pleasure. She might have indicated that she didn't want it here, but he knew that sex could be an excellent distractor from dark thoughts, fears, and doubts. He'd relied on it often enough through the years.

He took a sip of the excellent brandy before handing the snifter back to her. He hated the worry, the sadness in her eyes. They would travel with her to his residence. He didn't want to consider the number of smiles she wouldn't bestow upon him, the amount of laughter that he wouldn't hear in the coming days. He couldn't limit her to an hour here each day. He would have to give her as much time as she needed. It would mean time away from him. He should resent the moments. Instead he would give up everything he possessed to spare her the sorrow that was coming her way.

She offered him the brandy. He took it, drank more deeply.

"You're not going to be comfortable in the bed," she said.

"I'll make do."

She turned slightly until she faced him more squarely. "There really is no reason for you to stay, to be put out."

The sofa was not so large that when he laid his arm along its back, he wasn't able to skim his fingers along her cheek. "I'm not leaving, Rose."

She placed her hand over his, pressed a kiss to the center of his palm—and he could have sworn he felt it in the middle of his chest. "I did not judge you to be a man who would stay with me. I thought you selfish."

"I am. Incredibly so. I am here because it is where I wish to be. If I didn't wish to be, nothing would hold me."

"So your staying has nothing to do with me?"

"Absolutely not." He tucked strands of her hair behind her ear. "As you're well aware, I care only for my own pleasures and wants."

She gave him a half smile. "I have noticed that

about you. Strange, though, how your pleasures and wants often seem to mirror my needs."

Taking another long sip of the brandy, he thought he should mention that he cared for her. He wasn't sure exactly when it had happened. Somehow she had become a part of his life that he was loath to give up. He offered her the snifter, watched as her delicate throat worked while she took a small sip. She licked her lips, no doubt savoring the taste that lingered there. He was tempted to lean over and take her mouth. But he feared he would do little more than increase her melancholy.

"I was wondering," she asked quietly, tapping her finger against the glass, "if you would allow me to bring some of your books here for Harry to read. He so loves reading, and he's read everything we have."

"Would it not be better to take him to the books?"

She looked at him as though he had proposed setting her brother on a flying carpet.

Still, he plowed on. "When we return to my residence tomorrow, perhaps he should come with us. He could stay in the guest wing. He would have a bedchamber, a small library, servants to assist—"

"No, I'll not have your servants gawking at him."

He skimmed the knuckle of his forefinger along her cheek. "I am a duke, Rose. My staff does not gawk."

Rising, she moved nearer to the fire, staring at it, holding the bowl of the snifter with both hands. "He's comfortable here."

"I daresay he would be more comfortable there. He would have space in which to move about, a thousand books at his disposal. Servants would see to his needs." She began shaking her head. Standing, he joined her by the fire. "You asked me to help you make his last days happy. My cook could prepare feasts for him unlike any he's ever experienced. My gardens are lavish. He could walk about them, enjoy them without fear of neighbors peering through windows. You would be within easy reach, anytime day or night. Your worry would lessen. You could check on him anytime you wanted."

"Why are you doing this?"

Because it lashes at my heart to see you so wounded, so sad.

"It seems the best way not to disrupt our current arrangements." He wanted to touch her desperately, but he feared she might toss the remaining brandy on him. He would not make himself vulnerable, not even for her.

"I think you care for me," she said softly, as though the notion had just flittered through her mind.

"Emotions, feelings, sensibilities—they are not my purview. Pleasure is. All pleasures. Pleasure of the palate when a well-prepared meal touches the tongue, the pleasure of fragrance when inhaling the aroma of wine aged to perfection, the pleasure of sight when gazing upon a masterfully painted piece of art, the pleasure of sound when a harpist plucks her fingers over the chords, the pleasure of touch." He outlined the shell of her ear. "I am given to believe that your brother has seen little of the outside world. I understand your fear of his discovery, your need to protect him from those who would judge him and wish him harm. My residence is more museum than home. He could spend hours browsing through it. I possess trinkets from all corners of the world that he could touch, examine to his heart's content."

"I don't say this to be cruel, but he is somewhat clumsy. If he were to break—"

"They are trinkets. Their value is in the joy they bring, not what they cost me to possess them. If they break, they break."

"I've seen them, Avendale. Some are priceless treasures."

"They mean nothing to me, Rose." *You do.* Why were those words impossible to say? "I shan't be upset if they break. Perhaps we would even sneak Harry into the Twin Dragons for a game of poker."

Her gaze roamed over his face, and within her eyes he saw the wonder of possibilities, all that they might share with her brother. "I desperately do not want Harry hurt."

"I give you my word that he won't be."

"You can't control others."

"I think you might be surprised by what a duke can accomplish and what people will do to please him. Even one as much a reprobate as I am."

Setting the snifter on the mantel, she faced him squarely. "How would we get Harry to your residence?"

"You have a carriage. We'll leave before first light. No one will see him depart from here. I doubt anyone will see him arrive at my residence."

She clutched her slender hands, furrowed her delicate brow. "If my dearest wish comes true and your physician is wrong, and death is not hovering in the corner to take Harry . . . should we limit it to a week in your residence?"

"No limits." He traced his finger along her cheek. "In for a penny, in for a pound."

"And if you grow weary of us?"

"I won't." That he knew without doubt.

"What of Merrick, Sally, and Joseph?"

"They'll stay here."

She nodded. "That will create less discord. Merrick doesn't like you."

"The feeling is mutual."

"But perhaps they can visit him."

"Occasionally, perhaps." With one hand, he cradled her cheek. "You've carried the weight of caring for your brother for a good many years. Let me help you."

Tears welled in her eyes, her smile quivered. "I'm afraid. I'm not accustomed to not being responsible."

With his thumb, he wiped away one of the tears that rolled along her cheek. "The night we struck our first bargain, you trusted me. Trust me now."

She nodded, inhaled deeply, blinked back the tears. He felt a sharp, painful poke in his chest. If he didn't know better, he'd think a wall was crumbling. Lowering his head, he pressed his lips to hers, tasted the salt of lingering tears.

"I'm going to borrow your carriage to return to my residence to see that things are readied for your brother's arrival. I will be back tonight, but you needn't wait up."

"I'll be awake when you return."

"Then I shall return in haste."

He kissed her again, wondering why it was so blasted difficult to leave her. He'd left countless women without so much as a backward glance. But she was different. He'd known that from the beginning.

Drawing back, he slid the crook of his finger below her chin. "Where will I find the giant?"

"In the kitchen, no doubt."

"Don't worry. Everything will be all right."

"If it's not—" She swallowed, licked her lips. "I promise to keep to my end of the bargain. Whatever you want for as long as you want."

He suddenly had a clear understanding of why she hadn't wanted to accept the necklace. He didn't want her gratitude. He wasn't quite certain what the bloody hell he wanted.

"I would expect no less," he stated succinctly, before striding from the room, wishing he'd been in possession of gentler words.

"*I* don't like it," Merrick said.

Once Avendale left, Rose returned to Harry's room, grateful to find him still awake. She suspected he slept little these nights, mostly in fits and spurts. There was a labored quality to his breathing, occasionally a whistling like the sound of air rushing through the narrow confines of a cavern. She'd asked Merrick and Sally to join her there. She'd just explained how she was taking Harry on an adventure to the duke's residence.

Harry's face had taken on the wonder of a child being handed a penny candy for the first time. No surprise, Merrick's face had taken on the appearance of a storm cloud.

Now he paced in front of the fireplace. "What do you know of this duke? He took advantage the night we were leaving. He could be doing the same now. Mayhap he intends to parade Harry before all his aristocratic friends. The nobility like to have something special to show off."

"He has no intentions of parading Harry about," Rose insisted. "But he is in a better position than we are to see to Harry's needs. He has servants, staff. I daresay he'd hire a nurse if need be." While he hadn't said as much, she'd wager her five thousand quid that he would do it. He fought so hard to give the appearance of not caring, and yet he had done little except show her kindness. And now he was extending it to Harry.

"We don't take such bad care of him," Merrick insisted, coming to a halt and jabbing his hands onto his hips.

She realized his pride was hurt. She hadn't considered that. She'd thought they'd all want what was best. "You take marvelous care of him, but this is an opportunity for him to experience a bit more of life. The duke has a billiards room. Harry has never played."

"It's a silly reason to take him away."

"You can come visit, every day if you like." She fought not to grimace. Avendale probably wasn't going to like that.

"It should be up to Harry," Merrick said.

"Yes, of course, it's completely up to Harry. We're not going to take him kicking and screaming from here." She looked at her brother. "Do you want to come with us?"

"Do you love him?"

What did that have to do with anything? "I like him very much."

"I like him, too." He turned his body slightly so he could see Merrick more clearly. "I'm sorry, Merrick. But I want to go."

"No need for you to apologize," Merrick groused. "If I was you, I'd probably want to go, too."

"I think it's wonderful," Sally said. Merrick glowered at her, and Rose knew he was thinking, *Traitor.* "Think of everything he'll experience. Lovely breakfasts that are more than my boiled eggs."

"I like your boiled eggs," Harry said.

Sally smiled. "You're such a sweet lad. But, caw, to spend time in the presence of a duke . . . it's a dream for some, you know."

"For you?" Merrick snapped.

She scowled at him. "No, of course not." But when Merrick looked away, Sally winked and nodded at Rose.

Rose almost laughed, then her thoughts sobered. She'd once judged Avendale by his rank, giving little thought to the man behind it. Now she hardly saw his rank anymore. She saw only the man.

Chapter 14

$\mathcal{H}$arry felt like the puppy he'd had as a boy. It had been an excitable creature, always jumping around, chasing its tail. His father had given it to him before Harry had become a monster, had become the Boulder Boy. In anger, when his father realized Harry was not his son but the devil's, he'd drowned the dog.

Rose had held Harry while he cried. She'd promised him that she would never let anyone hurt him again. She was seventeen before she'd been able to carry through on that promise. Harry often wished that he could make the same promise to her, that he could watch out for her.

Although he suspected that the duke was going to do it for him. Not that he thought the duke was aware of it as the carriage traveled through the London streets. But Harry knew. He was able to sense things like that. Just as he knew it was going to rain again.

The trunk Merrick had helped him pack was on top of the carriage. Rose sat beside him. He suspected the duke would have preferred that she sit at his side, but she was worried that Harry was afraid, that someone would hurt him. He wasn't afraid, at least not for himself, but he did worry about her. He knew that she'd often done things that she shouldn't, that she could go to prison if she were ever caught. She didn't know he knew these things. Because his speech was impeded and he had to communicate with simple words—his misshapen mouth had difficulty forming the more complicated ones—people often thought his brain was encumbered as well. But he was sharper, more aware than people realized.

And so it was that he was also very much aware that very soon he would die.

He was growing more tired with each day. Sometimes he could barely lift his head because of all the boulders that had grown from it. They were growing inside him as well; he'd known it for a while. The doctor had confirmed it when he'd pressed on Harry's stomach. He was certain the physician had felt them. He hadn't said as much but his eyes had filled with sorrow.

Harry had wanted to stay with Merrick, but it was more important that Rose be with her duke. Harry knew all about dukes and the power they wielded. He could protect Rose as Harry never could.

Harry wore his hooded cloak. He'd kept the hood up even after he settled into the carriage. Easier to observe the duke that way without the man realizing he was being studied. The duke's gaze seldom left Rose.

"You should know," the duke began, "that I instructed my butler to have a footman available to you at all times. Should you require anything at all, you need only ask him."

"That's very kind," Rose said.

The duke scowled. "I pay them, Rose. They might as well earn their salary."

The duke didn't like her feeling beholden to him. Harry found that interesting.

"You are welcome to spend time in any of the rooms, as often and as long as you like," the duke said. "Except for my bedchamber."

"Harry has difficulty traversing stairs," Rose said.

"I assumed as much, based upon the current arrangements in your residence. I've had one of the rooms on the lower floor converted into a bedchamber. You should find everything you need, but don't be shy about asking for anything you might require. I don't mean to come off as vulgar, but money is no object."

Beside him, Rose stiffened. She didn't like it when people took coins for granted. "Take advantage, Harry. It may be the only time in our lives when money is no object."

But it came with a price, of that he knew. He also knew Rose would never tell him the cost.

The coach pulled off the street and onto a cobbled path. Before them lay Buckland Palace. Harry knew his eyes were widening, his mouth was agape, because Rose was correct.

It was a palace. For a while, he would live here.

Rose clung to Harry's arm as he used his walking stick to transport himself from the carriage to the residence. Avendale was near her, carefully watching as though he feared her brother might topple her over. But when they went through the door, stepped into the foyer, she felt the excitement and wonder thrum through Harry as he took in the high ceiling, the sweeping staircase, the paintings, the glamour of it all.

Two footmen were already scurrying down a hallway, Harry's trunk in tow. If they had caught sight of him beneath the hood of his cloak, they gave no indication. But the morning was only just beginning, the fog hampering the arrival of sunlight. Perhaps they hadn't gotten a good look.

Thatcher stepped forward; a young footman—whom she had never seen—stood at attention slightly behind him. She suspected Avendale had a good many servants she'd never set eyes on before.

"Your Grace, all is prepared as you requested," Thatcher said, before turning to Rose. "Welcome back, miss." He shifted his gaze slightly. "Welcome to Buckland Palace, Mr. Longmore."

Harry pushed back his hood. "I'm pleased to be here."

Neither Thatcher nor the young footman indicated anything amiss. No gasps, no widening of eyes, no stepping back. They both reacted not at all.

Twisting slightly, Thatcher said, "This is Gerald. He'll be attending to your needs while you're in residence."

"Thank you."

Rose was amazed that there was no awkwardness. She wondered precisely what Avendale had told his staff. She doubted he'd tell her if she asked.

"Harry, would you like a tour of the place before we sit down to breakfast?" Avendale asked.

Harry nodded slightly, and Rose fought not to be nervous. Everything was going splendidly well, but she had come to expect that trouble rested just below the surface.

"Shall I take your cloak, Mr. Longmore?" Gerald asked, stepping forward, hand extended.

Shifting his cane to his bad hand, Harry managed to loosen the button on his cloak with his good hand. Rose wanted to help him, but she understood his pride, so she waited patiently while he awkwardly removed it and held it out to the footman.

Gerald took it, draped it over his arm. "While you're touring, I shall see to putting your things away if you've no objection."

"Thank you."

Gerald exchanged a nod with Avendale before heading for the hallway that led into the wing where Harry would reside.

"I shall ensure that all is readied for breakfast," Thatcher announced, then he, too, was gone.

"Let's start to get you familiar with the place, shall we?" Avendale asked. "Although I suggest you keep Gerald near should you decide to go wandering. It's quite easy to get lost in the maze of hallways."

He led the way with a leisurely gait that didn't leave Harry behind. He explained things as he went, much as he had with her. As Harry walked beside her, Rose was very much aware of his awe and wonder. She wished she could take him on a tour around the world.

Then they entered Avendale's library. Harry gasped. Rose realized that within the pages of all the books here, Harry would travel farther than she could ever take him. Cautiously he approached the shelves, placed his good hand on the leather spine of several books.

"Look at them, Rose."

"They're yours to read while you're here," she assured him.

"You're to let Gerald fetch the ones that are too high for you to reach," Avendale told him.

"I shall never get through them all."

"You'll find a smaller library in your wing," Avendale said, "but I fear most of the books there are love stories and might not be to your liking."

Turning slightly, Harry bestowed upon him his rendition of a smile. "I enjoy romantic stories. They never leave me feeling sad at the end."

"My mother preferred the same sort of tale. You should find an abundance of them there."

Rose had not expected the camaraderie she saw developing between Avendale and Harry. All her doubts about bringing him here were easing away as she realized Avendale was truly welcoming Harry into his home.

When they arrived at the breakfast dining room, Harry's eyes grew wide at the assortment of food spread out along the sideboard.

"It's quite lavish, isn't it, Harry?" Rose asked.

He shook his head, looked at Avendale, looked at her. "I could never eat all that."

"You don't have to," Avendale said. "Whatever remains is distributed to those in need."

Rose stared at him. He lifted a brow. "Did you think we simply tossed out whatever remained?"

"Why would I think anything else? You live with such excess."

"A good many people make a rather nice living off my excesses," he said.

She'd never considered that. So much about him, she'd never considered. She'd told him that their relationship was naught but the surface because he refused to provide her with the details of his life. Perhaps it was merely that she was not as observant as she'd always thought.

Holding a plate, Gerald stepped forward, and Rose wondered when he'd arrived. "What would you fancy, sir?" he asked Harry.

"Everything."

"As you wish." He made his way along the sideboard, placing an assortment of food on the plate while Harry followed.

Avendale moved in closer to her. "He seems to have taken to the place. I hope you're feeling more at ease about his being here."

Nodding, she touched his arm. "I'll never be able to repay you for all this." No matter how long she stayed with him, no matter what he asked of her.

"Don't worry about that now."

Unsaid was that she should enjoy whatever time she had left with Harry. The sentiment was in Avendale's dark, somber gaze. When they were all settled at the table, she watched as Harry took his first bite of deviled egg. With a sigh, he closed his eyes. She thought he was going to be even more delighted with dinner.

Gerald discreetly sliced the ham on Harry's plate, prepared his tea, was quick to replenish his glass of water. She did hope Avendale was paying the man well. She gazed across the table at Avendale. His attention was focused on pushing food onto his fork with his knife. Harry's features often dimmed others' appetite. Even Merrick, Sally, and Joseph seldom joined him for meals. Avendale seemed not the least bit bothered.

Her chest tightened. He would pay his servants well. He was a man of wealth, but he wasn't stingy with it. He'd opened his home, his books to Harry. He was expanding her brother's world. Perhaps they would play a game of chess. Perhaps they would talk.

He was not a man who judged. Even knowing she survived by swindling others, he'd never brought her to task for it, had never made her feel like the criminal she knew herself to be. She could even forgive him for the deliberate night of debauchery that had resulted in her missing her appointment with Harry. Left to her own devices, she never would have told Avendale about her brother, not because she was ashamed of Harry—because she wasn't—but she had judged the duke to be a man without compassion. She wondered what else she might have misjudged.

When Harry pronounced that he was on the cusp of bursting his buttons, they took him to the guest wing, and once more he was as a child surrounded by wonders. They walked into a study and there, resting on the desk, were the pages of his manuscript.

He approached it slowly, as though it were somehow different within these walls, not quite recognizable. Head bowed, he pressed his good hand to the neatly arranged stack of papers.

"You'll be able to work on your story here," Rose told him. "Perhaps get it finished."

Nodding, he lifted his head, zeroed his gaze in on Avendale. "Would you like to read it?"

Rose stepped forward. "You finished it? How marvelous."

He shook his head. "No, but I thought the duke might find it . . . interesting. But you can't let her read it. Not until it's finished."

With a huff, Rose planted her hands on her hips. "You barely know him and you're going to let him read it? And not me? The sister who loves you more than life?"

Harry's gaze never left Avendale. "I think he should read it."

"I will be most delighted to do so."

Harry shoved it toward the edge of the desk. Avendale gathered it up. "Thank you for trusting me with it."

"Don't let her see it."

"Honestly," Rose said indignantly, "if you ask me not to read it, I won't."

"She lies," Harry said.

Avendale chuckled low. "So I've discovered."

"I'm insulted. Harry, I've never lied to you."

He swung his head toward her, his blue gaze intense, and she realized she'd not done as good a job at protecting him as she'd intended. He knew she was conniving, that she'd not always been honest with him.

"Make yourself at home," Avendale said. "I'm going to see that your sister lies down for a bit. She didn't sleep well last night."

How did he know that? Was he aware that she was exhausted, thought she might drop at any moment? The worries had taken a toll.

She hugged Harry, told him to send Gerald for her if she was needed, then she quit the room with Avendale at her side. With orders to take the manuscript to his library, he handed the pages to a footman they passed in the hallway. Then with his hand at the small of her back, he led her to the bedchamber.

She'd expected him to tear off their clothes, to take her before they'd even reached the bed. Instead he merely said, "I'll send Edith in to assist you with your clothing. Get some rest."

She sat on the edge of the bed. "How do you know I didn't sleep?"

"Because I was holding you and was very much aware of how tense you were. You never relaxed a muscle."

"I thought coming here might be a disaster."

He crossed over to her, cradled her cheek. "Even though I told you it wouldn't be?"

"I've been in charge for so long. I find it difficult to hand over the reins where Harry is concerned."

"You haven't handed them over. You just have someone else to help you hold them."

Reaching up, she trailed her fingers along his bristled jaw. "Every time I think I know you, I discover that I don't. Why are you not staying with me now?"

"Because I have some matters to which I must attend. While it may appear that I live a life of leisure, I am only allowed to do so because I attend to my business when I should."

"Are you going out then?"

"No, I'll be in the library, studying reports, making decisions. It's boring and tedious, but it must be done. When I'm finished I'll join you here."

"I know I said it earlier, but I can't believe how kind you're being to Harry."

"You say that as though you are on the verge of recommending me for sainthood. I'm far from being a saint. I'm merely keeping to my end of our bargain."

He brushed his lips over hers, before leaving the room. Her heart would remain safer if she believed him.

The problem was—she didn't.

But even if he professed undying love, what would come of it? He was a duke. She was a criminal, with a past that shadowed her and would one day blot out all the light. Until then, she could serve as his mistress for as long as he wanted her—or until he took a wife. Her transgressions were many, but taking a married man to her bed was not going to be one of them.

Chapter 15

It always hurt to know that she was hurting, to see the sorrow and tears welling in her eyes. Sometimes I imagined that I could actually hear her heart cracking, tiny fault lines spreading out.

For her, I fought hard to stand with pride as people gathered around, pointed, whispered, gaped. Once a woman became ill, brought up her breakfast. After that my father decided it best to have hay spread around me, as though I were an animal with no control over my bodily functions. When it was the gawkers for whom the straw was necessary.

I never spoke, never let on that I was mortified by my nearly naked form being displayed as an oddity. Because I ceased to speak, my father thought I'd become mute. But Rose knew the truth of it. In the darkest hours of the night, she would creep over and kneel beside my bed.

"One day, we'll run away," she promised with such earnestness that even the boulders after which I was named would have wept. "As *soon as I have determined how we can survive."*

Then she would tell me a story of a beautiful place with beautiful people where I was loved, and I would drift off to sleep feeling not quite so ugly.

"Your Grace?"

Avendale jerked his head up from the words he'd been reading, surprised to discover that nearly an hour had passed. He'd meant merely to read a page. He'd read dozens. It was disconcerting to have been caught so absorbed by the tale that he'd not heard his butler enter his library. "Yes, Thatcher?"

"Mr. Watkins is here, sir."

"Excellent. Send him in." Avendale stood, walked to a side table and poured a splash of scotch into two glasses. He turned to the doorway just as a man of medium height and width, his clothing impeccable, strode in.

"Watkins." Avendale extended a glass toward him.

The man staggered to a halt. "It's not yet noon, Your Grace."

"Trust me, Watkins, you're going to need it."

His tailor took the offered glass and sipped cautiously, while Avendale leaned his hips against the edge of his desk. He downed his own scotch, sighed. "A gentleman is staying with me. A Mr. Harry Longmore. He requires clothing. Something simple for moving about during the day as well as evening attire."

"My specialty, Your Grace."

"Which is why I sent for you. I require a man of your skills, but I fear the task will present a challenge. To put it bluntly the man is deformed, hideously so."

Watkins finished off his drink, licked his lips. "I see."

"I doubt you'll be able fit him to perfection, but a close proximity would be well rewarded. And haste doubly so. We need the items within the week."

"I shall do my best. I can begin straightaway if you like."

"Excellent. Come along then. I'll introduce you."

Harry was busily scribbling at his desk when the duke walked in with a man who had a thick thatch of black and white hair swirling over his head, bushy side whiskers, and a heavy mustache that hid much of his mouth. For a moment Harry knew a spark of despair. Had the duke brought him here to display as a curiosity to his friends as Merrick had thought? If he had, it was without Rose's knowledge; he was certain of that. She would be furious when she discovered the treachery. She would take Harry away, and he would have to leave all the marvelous books behind, unread.

But the man's eyes didn't even so much as widen when his gaze fell on Harry.

"Harry," the duke began, "allow me to introduce Mr. Watkins, my tailor. He's one of the most accomplished London has to offer. I would like you to allow him to take your measurements for some new clothing."

Harry's face grew hot with shame because he'd jumped to the wrong conclusion regarding the duke's intentions. He was no different than those who looked upon him and judged what he was. He should have known the duke was only trying to make him feel more comfortable in these elegant surroundings. He knew he walked about in clothes that hung loosely, more like a potato sack, over his odd frame. Sally was a fine seamstress but not one of London's most accomplished. He nodded with eagerness at the prospect of proper clothes.

"Splendid," the duke said. He raised a finger. "But we're to keep this a secret, just between us gents. I have a surprise planned for your sister, and I don't want her to know about it just yet."

Harry liked giving Rose surprises. When he was a boy he would pick flowers for her, find pretty rocks. But he hadn't been able to give her anything since he'd begun spending so much time indoors. His writing was for her, would be a gift to her when the time came. He was filling the pages with all the love he held for her so it would remain with her when he was gone.

But to be able to share a surprise with her now— he was fairly certain it would be a surprise she would like because the duke's eyes were warm with mischief laced with anticipation. He was looking forward to surprising Rose. Harry put his finger to his lips. "Shh."

"Precisely. I'll leave you two to it."

As the duke strolled from the room, Harry wondered if the duke was even aware that he loved Rose.

After a marvelous sleep, Rose wanted to stroll leisurely through the gardens with Harry, but they got only as far as the fountain where a nude couple carved in stone embraced in such a way that very little was left to the imagination.

"It's really quite scandalous," she felt obligated to point out. "The detail"—the taut buttocks of the man; the firm, uplifted breasts of the woman—"is designed to shock those with proper sensibilities."

"I think they're beautiful."

"I quite agree," a voice boomed behind her, and she nearly leaped into the fountain.

Avendale came to stand on the other side of her, and she had to fight not to reach out to him, not to step nearer and curl against his side. Her resistance where he was concerned was nonexistent. She just didn't know if she could be content to be a mistress for the remainder of her life. Considering her past, marriage was not feasible. "There is beauty, truth, honesty in the naked form," Avendale said. "I find it a crime that society is so bothered by it that it must be covered with an abundance of clothing." With a grin, he shook her skirt as though to demonstrate what clothing entailed, in case she wasn't aware.

"Would the sight of it not lose its appeal if it were always visible?" she asked, even knowing that she would never tire of seeing him without clothing. "Perhaps we would begin to take it for granted."

"I continue to find this couple arousing and they've been here for years."

"But then you're debauched. I'm sure your wife will have them taken away."

"No doubt, so I must enjoy them while I may. What do you think, Harry? Should I have chosen a fountain that displayed fish cavorting about?"

"Don't bring him into this," she chastised.

"Why? He has an opinion, doesn't he? I'd like to hear it."

Harry grinned, his face turned red, and he wouldn't quite meet Rose's gaze. "I like this one very much."

"All men do. I think women do as well, but they have been trained to deny it. You like it, don't you, Rose?"

She could not believe she was standing here discussing the naked form in front of her young brother. "I'll admit it's provocative, but decadent."

"Do you know, Harry, I've had gatherings where women have danced naked in that fountain?"

Harry's jaw dropped only slightly more than Rose's did.

"I suspected you were a libertine," she said.

"I've never denied it." He touched her cheek. "Do you want the fountain gone? I'll have it taken away if it makes you uncomfortable."

It only made her uncomfortable when she was standing here discussing it with her brother. Otherwise she thought it the most beautiful piece of artwork she'd ever seen. It was a ridiculous offer he made when she wasn't going to be in his life all that long. "I rather like it, but I enjoy the roses more. Shall we explore the flowers, Harry?"

"Yes, before it rains."

"Is it going to rain again, then?"

"Yes."

"Wait a moment," Avendale said, his dark brown eyes narrowed. "Is he the reason you knew it was going to rain the other night?"

She couldn't help but feel a bit smug. "He has an uncanny ability to predict the weather. That does not negate our bet as I admitted to having the information on good authority."

He chuckled low. "So you did. I'll leave you to enjoy the gardens then, while you may."

He walked off, and she'd rather hoped that he would join them. She appreciated that he wasn't constantly hovering, that he was giving her a little bit of time alone with Harry. It was silly that she should miss him. She needed to shore up her heart or she was going to leave here a broken woman.

She slipped her hand within the crook of Harry's arm. "Shall we go exploring?"

Using his cane for support, he shuffled along slowly, admiring every flower. She thought every sort imaginable had to be in these gardens. Harry stopped to feel the petals, to inhale the fragrances, to admire the colors. The other residences in the area were far enough away that no one would be able to see him clearly. And if they did, she suspected Avendale would handle the matter admirably.

Harry was examining a pink rose when he asked quietly, "Will you dance in the fountain for him?"

"What? No! Most assuredly not."

He gave her a shrewd look, her brother who had never been shrewd in his life to her knowledge. "Do you dance for him out of it?"

She'd always considered her brother an innocent, had assumed he didn't know what happened between a man and a woman, but of course he knew. After all he was a man. It saddened her to think he would never experience the closeness of a woman or the sort of love that could exist between two people who weren't related through blood. What was she doing mooning about? She wasn't going to experience that sort of love either.

"Avendale and I have an understanding," she said, quite certain her cheeks were the same shade as the rose.

"What do you understand?"

"That we're only together for a little while."

"Because of me."

Yes. "No. We enjoy each other's company but neither of us wants anything permanent."

"He's doing a lot for us, Rose."

"Yes, well, he can certainly afford it."

"I don't think that's why."

She didn't want to consider that her brother was right, that perhaps she meant something to Avendale. "We shouldn't examine our time here too closely. We should simply enjoy it."

*B*efore winter would settle in, we'd return to the farm. Rose was happiest then. I think part of it was because I would not be displayed as much, but more she was able to see Phillip. His family had a farm next to ours and he would often come to visit Rose.

One evening as I was looking for her, I heard voices behind a shed.

"I'm going to Manchester to work in a factory. I want you to marry me. To come with me. It'll be a good life, Rose," Phillip said.

I heard her squeal, imagined her hugging him about the neck as I'd seen her do before. Perhaps she was even kissing him.

"Yes! Yes! I love you, Phillip. I think Harry will love Manchester."

"Why would it matter to him?"

"Because he's coming with us."

"No."

"Phillip, I can't leave him."

"He's not your child, not your responsibility."

"He's my brother. My father treats him horribly. It's getting worse. I promised to take him with me when I left."

"He's not coming with us. He turns my stomach. I can't eat for a day after looking at him."

"I thought you loved me."

"I do, but I don't love him."

Rose didn't leave with him. I often think of the life she might have had if she'd gone. It would have been much easier. Sometimes I feel guilty for being a burden, but I am selfish

*enough to be glad that she didn't leave me. If
our roles were reversed, I don't know if I would
have had the strength to stay behind.*

A little over six months later we ran off.

"Your Grace?"

When his butler's voice intruded, it took Avendale a moment to pull himself from the words, from the images. No wonder Rose hadn't told him of her brother. He would like to find this Phillip fellow and pound his fist into the man's face for the pain he'd caused her, the pain he'd no doubt caused Harry by his unkind words.

"What is it, Thatcher?" Was he going to have to lock his door just so he could read in peace?

"A small fellow who insists he be allowed to see Mr. Longmore is in the foyer. Quite formidable for a gent his size. As you instructed the staff to protect Mr. Longmore from any who might wish him ill, I wasn't quite certain what to do with the chap as he doesn't seem to fall into that category, and yet he doesn't appear to be the pleasant sort either."

With a sigh, Avendale shoved back his chair and stood. Dismissing his coachman the night before had meant relying on Rose's driver for transportation and thus giving his address to the giant. So now Merrick had known where to find him. "I'll see to the matter."

Thatcher had neglected to mention that a woman was also in the foyer. No doubt, the other half of the World's Tiniest Bride and Groom. She was only a little shorter than the man fuming at her side, her hair black, her eyes brown. Her hopeful expression was quite the opposite of her husband's belligerent one.

"I demand to see Harry." Merrick was fairly frothing at the mouth. His wife merely rolled her eyes. Avendale immediately liked her immensely.

"Within my residence you're not in a position to demand anything. I assume the giant brought you and is still here."

Merrick looked as though he was on the verge of having an apoplectic fit.

"Yes," the woman said. "Joseph brought us." She took a tiny step forward. "You must understand that we've looked out for Harry for so long that we just want to see that he's happy with his new surroundings."

Even without her explanation, he had planned for his next sentence to be, "Would you care to join us for dinner?"

Books were set on chairs so the tiniest couple were elevated enough to reach the table comfortably. They sat on one side together, Harry and the giant on the other. Avendale had taken his place at the head of the table, while Rose sat opposite him. She seemed rather amused by their dinner guests, or perhaps he was the one who amused her. Because he'd been soft, because he hadn't kicked the little man out.

On the other hand, he found the entourage quite entertaining. If Rose wouldn't reveal her past, he was quite certain he could garner information from them. That had been his original plan, and yet he couldn't quite bring himself to invade the privacy she clung to so tenaciously. Perhaps he shouldn't even be reading her brother's writings.

"Caw, wish I could cook like this," Sally said as she enjoyed glazed partridge.

Avendale sipped on his wine. He was indulging more in drink than food. "I'm certain my cook will be happy to share her recipes."

"That would be lovely."

He tapped his glass. "I assume you don't miss your life from before."

"Wasn't so bad," Sally said, apparently more of a talker than the rest. "Merrick and I would just stand there while people had their fill. Much harder on poor Harry, because he was so different."

So different. That was a genteel way to describe him.

He studied Rose, the bright hue of her cheeks. She'd been surprised that he'd invited the others to dinner, but had also thanked him. He didn't want her gratitude. He wanted to know everything about her life. He suspected he would discover far more than he wanted to know within the pages that Harry had written, but he wanted Rose to tell him more of herself. Which wasn't fair since he wasn't going to reveal anything about himself.

"Were you ever displayed?" The words were out before he could stop them. He thought he might destroy something if her answer was yes.

Delicately, she blotted her lips with her napkin before settling it in her lap. "Not exactly. My father bottled an elixir that he claimed would prevent any sort of deformities if a woman would drink it before she got with child. He said he had developed it after Harry was born and that his wife had taken it before she was expecting me. Then I would skip across the stage and twirl about. It didn't matter that Harry was born four years after me. Because of his condition it was difficult to judge his age. So a tuppence to see Harry, and a shilling for the magical elixir."

"And of what precisely was the magical elixir composed?"

"River water with a dash of gin."

"From a particular river?"

She shook her head. "Whichever river we were passing."

"Quite the charlatan, your father."

"He thought God owed him, and he was within his rights to do what he could to make his life better. It didn't matter who he hurt along the way."

Like her father, she had chosen the path of swindling others, yet he was hard-pressed to think of her as a swindler. Selfishness certainly hadn't guided her. He couldn't say the same for himself. From the moment he'd met her all he'd considered was his need to possess her.

"He invited these others to join you?"

"No, that would require too much work—to be in charge of the entire menagerie. It was a little traveling circus of oddities. An elephant, a camel, uh . . ."

"A giraffe," the giant barked out, and Avendale stared at him. It sounded as though his voice came up from the depths of his soles. It was the first time Avendale had heard him speak. He'd begun to think he was mute.

"Joseph liked the giraffe," Rose said, shaking her head. "The world is full of oddities. I daresay we are all peculiar in one way or another."

She might be right, although he found nothing about her peculiar. Instead he found her to be quite remarkable.

After dinner, he dispensed with the usual custom of the gentlemen retiring for a bit of port, and invited the ladies to join them in his library. They were sitting near the fire, enjoying a bit of drink, when he became aware of the rain pattering against the window. He met Rose's gaze. She gave him a soft smile, a moment shared that the others—talking and laughing—missed.

He'd never been one to care about domestic tranquillity or quiet nights or remembering peaceful moments. He'd always favored the ribald, the loud, the coarse. He never wanted to examine the aspects of his life that he'd abandoned.

Strange how, looking at her now, he experienced a flash of contentment, surrounded by this unusual assortment of people.

"*I* may have seen Tinsdale lurking about the streets."

Standing on the bedchamber's balcony, with the fragrance of the earlier rain wafting on the slight breeze, her fingers gripping the iron railing, Rose replayed Merrick's parting words whispered to her as he and the others were taking their leave, letting the unwelcome refrain tumble through her mind, surprised that after more than a dozen repetitions, it still had the power to cause cold fear to knot her gut.

The former bobby who now sold his investigative skills to those willing to pay for them had been on her trail for several years now, ever since she'd duped a solicitor in Manchester in much the same way that she had fooled Beckwith. It didn't help that in the north two warrants had been issued for her arrest. Not to mention the promise of a small bounty offered by a widowed landowner who had taken exception to her leaving after he'd provided her with a residence for three months. When she'd first begun her trade, she'd been too young and naive to realize that her efforts were best served by selecting men who had too much pride to let on that they'd been deceived.

Over the years, eluding Tinsdale had become as challenging as swindling.

He wouldn't search for her within the nobility. He wouldn't think her bold enough for that tactic. He would scour for her among the untitled wealthy, merchants, railway investors. Briefly she wondered if she should make arrangements for the others to be moved elsewhere. No, they were guilty of nothing. Tinsdale wouldn't intentionally risk alerting them to his presence by approaching them. Joseph wouldn't have traveled here without ensuring they weren't followed.

Still, if not for Harry, she'd begin making plans for her departure. If not for her bargain with Avendale—

She squeezed her eyes shut. If not for Avendale himself. The bargain had little to do with her desire to stay. It was the man who awoke something deep and profound within her, the man who without even being aware of it was revealing to her the incredible cost of the life she'd led. Always looking behind her, waiting for the ax to fall, to be found out, she could never be more than his whore, relegated to the shadows.

"I wasn't expecting to find you here," Avendale said quietly.

Glancing over her shoulder, she gave him a soft smile. He'd invited her to join him for a cognac after saying good night to Harry, but needing a few moments to shake off Merrick's troubling news, she'd feigned a headache and the need to retire. Suspicion had glittered in Avendale's dark eyes. Why was she so inept at lying to him?

"I thought you'd avoid my bedchamber with your brother in residence," he continued. "I was prepared to seek you out."

Escaping him when the time came would involve an inordinate amount of planning and deception. She'd broken a thousand promises in her lifetime, but not keeping the one she'd made with him would cause her the deepest regret. But if Tinsdale were about, she'd have no choice.

"Your residence is large enough that with Harry in the other wing, we won't be heard," she said now.

Stepping forward, he closed his arms around her waist and settled his warm mouth against her nape, creating a circle of dew that branded her as thoroughly as scorched metal might. "Are you issuing a challenge, that I should have you screaming rather than crying out?"

The heat of embarrassment warmed her face. "Absolutely not. If you brought me any more pleasure, I might expire on the spot."

"What of your headache?"

"It's gone. Preparing for bed seemed to have eased it." While he was helping her care for Harry, she would give to Avendale all that she could—even if it wasn't everything.

"This nightdress is ghastly unflattering," he said.

"But it's familiar and comforting, like an old friend."

He moved so he was beside her, his gaze landing on her profile with such intensity that she well imagined she heard a thud. "Speaking of old friends, what did Merrick say when he drew you aside just before he left?"

He would notice that quick exchange, wouldn't he? He noticed everything. It was one of the things she loved about him: that he didn't go through life ignoring the little details. "What he always says. He doesn't like you."

"Why don't I believe you?"

"What else could he have said?" she asked as innocently as possible.

"I don't know, but he looked too worried and you had a moment of looking too frightened."

She twisted around to face him squarely. *Always*

*meet your opponent's gaze head-on when you're
lying.* Or so Elise, a fortune-teller, had claimed. "I'm
not one to be scared."

Again the doubt in his expression, then he shut-
tered away the emotions. "After all I'm doing for
you, for you and Harry, don't I deserve the truth?"

She almost told him that honesty between them
wasn't part of the bargain. "I told you that I would
never speak of my past, yet tonight you caught
glimpses of it. Be content with that."

"And if I can't be?"

Everything within her went still, quiet, and she felt
as though the balcony had disintegrated beneath her
feet and she was falling. She almost reached for him,
grabbed him, but she had learned long ago that she
was responsible for saving herself. "I never should have
agreed to bring Harry here. We'll leave tomorrow."

"What about all the things you want for Harry?"

"I have the five thousand quid."

"Not unless you finish out your week. Otherwise
all you'll have is a trip to Scotland Yard."

"You're bluffing."

"So are you. You're not going to leave. You're not
going to give this up, not as long as your brother is
the beneficiary of my good graces. After that, I'm not
even certain your promise to me will keep you here."

It wouldn't, dammit, but she wasn't going to confirm it, wasn't going to confirm that she might have
no choice. Even with a choice, she couldn't swear
she'd stay. Hoping to turn them off this path, she
placed her palm on his chest. "I don't like when we're
at odds."

"Then be honest with me."

"I can be honest with you regarding my feelings
for you, my desires where you are concerned. But not

my past. I'm a criminal, Avendale. You need know no more than that."

"How much of a criminal?"

She laughed lightly. "That's like asking, 'How much with child are you?'"

"There are degrees of criminality. Murder is worse than picking a silk handkerchief from a gent's pocket. How many have you swindled?"

"Enough to survive."

"You were much more forthcoming last night."

"Last night, I was upset, lowered my defenses for a bit." Stupidly lowered them, revealed far too much. As kind and generous as he was, he could never truly understand all her transgressions. "I've regained control, and the drawbridge has been effectively raised."

"I don't like that you continue to hold secrets from me."

"Ours is a temporary arrangement. My secrets have no impact on it." Another lie.

"And if it wasn't?" he asked.

She was again hit with the sensation of falling. "I don't see how it can be anything else. You're a duke. I'm a swindler. You might be comfortable introducing me to a few of your intimates in the back room of a gaming hell, but publicly? To every peer of the realm? To the queen? I know precisely what I am, Your Grace, and what my place in your life would entail. I'm relegated to being your mistress. I should hope that when you marry, you would care enough about your wife to send me on my merry way. Care enough to spare me the torment of sharing you." Dear God, she thought it would be worse than prison.

He slid his hand around her neck; his thumb stroked the underside of her jaw. "It seems you've given this a great deal of thought."

"I have spent a good portion of my life calculating and weighing the ramifications of my actions. I may not be honest with others, but I've always been honest with myself."

"While I'm the opposite. Brutally honest with others, seldom honest with myself."

"Why aren't you honest with yourself?"

"It would involve flaying my conscience and I have an aversion to pain. Which I suppose is the reason that I focus on pleasure. If you don't want that hideous nightdress tattered, you're going to need to remove it out here. Because once you step into my bedchamber I'm ripping it off."

It took her three heartbeats to realize that he was abandoning the discussion. That they were moving on to more pleasant things, more daring things. While only the pale lamplight washed over him, she could still see the challenge in his eyes. What was it about him that made her want to pick up every gauntlet that he tossed down? She wanted him to remember her when she was gone from his life, when he climbed into bed with a woman of sterling reputation and gave her children.

She flicked a button free of its mooring, heard his sharp intake of breath, saw his eyes darken. "I suppose the next thing you'll want is me dancing in your fountain," she said.

"Would you?" he asked, desire causing his voice to come out raspy with need.

Heat pooled between her legs, and she thought he could bring her to the pinnacle without ever touching her with his hands. It took only his voice, his gaze. Just knowing that still he yearned for her as though he'd yet to possess her. Another button freed. "You should have asked before we had a guest."

"His room doesn't look out on the fountain."

"But he likes to walk about at all hours of the night." Another button.

"I should make arrangements to keep him occupied one night but . . ."

Her fingers stilled on a button. "But?"

He shook his head. "I'm not sure I want you dancing in the fountain. I grew bored with the ladies who did."

"You'll grow bored with me eventually." She released the final button, eased the nightdress off her shoulders so it could slither down her body. He watched the journey of cloth until it all gathered at her feet. Then he lifted his gaze back to hers.

"Eventually. But not tonight."

Taking her hand, he led her into the bedchamber.

Chapter 16

"Rose, we need to get up now."

Pressing her nose into the hollow of Avendale's chest, she tried to ignore the lure of his throaty voice, still heavy with sleep. After bringing her to bed, he'd made love to her so slowly that she'd almost wept. Made love. That was the word that seemed to fit when they were together.

Squinting, she peered through one eye. "It's not light yet."

"I know. We need to be away before it is. It's more spectacular that way. Now, come on get up." He smacked her bottom before rolling away from her.

Still she shrieked her indignation as she scrambled back until she was sitting against the headboard. "What are you on about?"

He took a plain dress from the wardrobe and tossed it onto the bed. "Wear this."

Clutching the covers to her, she said, "I'm not wearing anything until you explain what's going on. Are you in trouble? Are we running away? Have you decided to get rid of us?"

He fairly pounced, his hands coming to rest on

either side of her, his arms effectively caging her in. "I have a surprise planned."

Unfurling her fingers from the blankets, she touched them to his cheek. "It might be too soon to leave Harry all alone."

"He's coming with us."

"Where are we going?"

He kissed the tip of her nose. "Someplace I doubt you've ever been before. Now be quick about it."

Abruptly leaving her side, he dropped into a chair and began to pull on his boots. When had he drawn on his trousers?

She scrambled out of the bed. "Why must you be so mysterious?"

"Because it's more fun."

She wanted to trust him, but he'd only just found out about Harry. He didn't understand the limitations, her need to protect him. She knelt before him, and he stilled, his eyes delving into hers. "Will there be others around?"

He sighed, obviously disgruntled with her. "If you must know, we're going beyond London for a picnic in the country."

That didn't sound as though it had the potential for Harry to be hurt. Rising up, she pressed a kiss to the top of his head. "Thank you."

She began dressing. As he finished before her, he assisted her, but his mouth remained in a straight line. She hated that she'd ruined his surprise. "I've never been on a picnic," she said quietly, hoping to assuage some of his disappointment in her.

"I'm hoping this will be one that you'll never forget."

She didn't think she'd ever forget any moment she spent in his company. Because it was to be a picnic, she decided to wear a straw bonnet to give her some protection from the sun.

She followed Avendale from the room, took his arm as they began to descend the stairs. She'd expected him to lead her out through the front door, but once they reached the foyer, he directed her back down the hallway toward his library.

"Shouldn't we fetch Harry?" she asked.

"Gerald should have him waiting for us. We're a bit behind schedule." He gave her a pointed look. Apparently he hadn't allowed time for her questions when he made his plans for the morning. They walked past his library to a door that led into the gardens.

She staggered to a stop at the sight that greeted her. The morning had lightened just enough that she could see Harry walking around a basket that was attached to a gigantic balloon. She'd seen one before at one of the fairs where her father had displayed Harry. "What's that doing here?" she asked, fearful that she knew the answer.

"It's going to serve as our conveyance."

He wrapped his hand around her arm and began propelling her forward.

"Is something wrong with your coach?" she asked.

"Not at all."

Glancing over, she saw that he was grinning. The picnic was not the surprise, blast him. The balloon was. The place he was taking her that she'd never been? The clouds.

"Rose, look!" Harry exclaimed as she neared. In the darkness she thought Gerald appeared as pale as she was certain she was.

"Yes, dearest, it's quite amazing, isn't it?"

"Would you like to take a ride in it?" Avendale asked.

Harry nodded with as much enthusiasm as his limitations allowed.

Avendale turned to her. "Rose?"

"You don't seriously expect us to climb into a wicker basket and go into the air."

"Think of the view."

"Think of the splatter when we fall from the sky."

"Mr. Granger"—he nodded toward a man standing near the balloon—"is an exceptional pilot. I've ridden with him before. I assure you that it is an extraordinary experience." He turned her until she faced him squarely. "Isn't that what you wanted for Harry? He'll see the sunrise coming over London as few have seen it. We'll go without you if we must, but I'd rather have you there."

"Come with us, Rose, please," Harry pleaded.

"Yes, all right." She'd never been able to resist granting him his wishes, and she detected the slightest disappointment in Avendale's eyes because it was Harry's words rather than his own that would sway her.

"Good," Avendale said. "Now we must be away or we're going to miss the best part." He swept her up into his arms, lifted her over the side of the basket, and settled her inside. She grabbed a rope that held the balloon tethered to the wicker. After helping Harry climb in, he followed, with Mr. Granger finally joining them. She thought he should have been the first one in. What if the blasted thing had taken off without him?

Avendale slid his arm around her and tucked her in against him. "Here I thought you were fearless."

"I'm pragmatic. If we were meant to fly we'd have wings."

"If we were meant to fly, we'd figure out how to do it."

Gerald removed the moorings. Granger did something and she heard a whoosh of air, the basket lifted slightly, swayed. She clutched Avendale's arm, wishing she could reach out and hold Harry, but that would have required she release her stranglehold on the rope, and she was certain as long as she held it, somehow she could keep the balloon afloat.

And it did feel as though they were floating . . . up, up, up. Until she was staring at the roof of Avendale's residence.

"We've gone up far enough, don't you think?" she asked.

"Relax, Rose. I'm not going to let you fall."

She leaned back against his chest, and his other arm came around her, bringing her near. "Shouldn't you be holding on to something?"

"I'm holding on to you."

"Yes, but if we start to fall—"

"If we start to fall, nothing we're holding on to is going to keep us up here."

"Thank you for the reassurance."

"Nothing is going to happen." Leaning down, he pressed a kiss to the nape of her neck. "I won't allow it."

For some reason, even knowing that he didn't command the air or the heavens or the movement of this contraption, she believed him.

"Just close your eyes," he said. "Absorb the peace of it."

She did as he instructed. It was so quiet, the din from below faint and obscure. Although she knew they were moving, they did so at a snail's pace and she could almost imagine they weren't moving at all.

"Rose, look!" Harry crowed.

Opening her eyes, she saw the Thames below them. The boats and barges. The sun easing over the horizon, painting the landscape in glorious shades of sunlight.

"We can see everything. Are we going around the world, Duke?" Harry asked.

"Not today," he answered.

Glancing over her shoulder, she saw Harry's smile larger than she'd ever seen it. Tossing his head back, he laughed as she'd never heard him laugh. Her chest tightened painfully. She'd have never given him this. Even if she could afford it, she'd have never *thought* to give him this.

Tilting her head back, she found Avendale watching her instead of everything unfolding below them. "Do you do this often?"

"A couple of times a year. There are no worries up here, no disappointments, no regrets."

"What do you regret?"

He shook his head slightly. "They don't exist up here."

But she knew it for a lie. They always existed; they stayed a part of you forever.

*R*ose sat on a blanket, Avendale stretched out alongside her. Harry was walking along the stream with Mr. Granger. The pilot had brought the balloon down in this beautiful field, awash with purple, yellow, and blue petals. Fully aware of Avendale's gaze on her, she plucked a flower, twirled it.

They'd enjoyed a lovely breakfast, packed in a wicker basket. "I'm going to miss your cook when our time together is over."

"Don't even contemplate stealing her away from me," he groused.

She peered over at him. "As though I could."

"I suspect you can do anything you set your mind to."

"Even fly in a balloon. I can't believe I did that."

"You enjoyed it, though, didn't you?"

"Immensely. Although not as much as Harry. I shall never forget the amazement on his face when that flock of birds flew by."

Reaching out, he traced his finger across her forehead, down her cheek, along her chin, and she wondered how it was that his touch could still send her heart to pounding. She almost wished it were only the two of them, so she could lean over and kiss him.

"I shall never forget the astonishment on yours," he said.

"I can well imagine what I must have looked like, probably all eyes."

"Almost."

She glanced around. "I do hope the fellow who owns this land doesn't come barging over the rise to chase us off before we're ready to leave."

"I have it on good authority that he is too stuffed with meat pie to go barging anywhere."

She eased down, raised on an elbow, so she could see him more clearly. "It's your land."

"It is."

"Part of your estates?" The lesser one perhaps. She was fairly certain they'd not traveled to Cornwall. She would dearly love to take a tour of his manor house.

"No, just some pretty property I fancied and so I purchased it."

"Why? A dowry for your daughter perhaps?" She could see him with a little girl, holding her hand, protecting her from anyone who would take advantage. For all his gruffness and his claims to not being a caring sort, she could easily see an imp of a lass wrapping him around her littlest finger with no trouble at all.

"No, simply for occasions like this when I want to get away from London. My estates are too distant for a short retreat."

"Will you build something here?" she asked.

He trailed his finger over her hand. "I was thinking of it."

"I should like to see it when you're done."

He lifted his gaze to hers, and with the intensity of it she felt as though a spear had lanced her heart. "Perhaps it will be for you."

A place for his longtime mistress, she thought, for that was what she would become, for as long as he wanted. She didn't want to think about that now, didn't want to acknowledge that she fully recognized what her place in his life would be. She would not regret her role, would not resent the price. He'd already proven that his part of the bargain would far exceed anything that she could give her brother, would far exceed anything she could give Avendale. She wouldn't give him bastards, though, God help her, she would love being a mother to his child. Although it wouldn't be fair to the child. Even if Avendale acknowledged him, he could never inherit, would never have a proper position in Society.

She forced back all those thoughts, fought back his implication that they would be together long enough to warrant his building her a house, and simply laughed. "I am a woman who will not accept a gift of jewelry. Do you really think I would accept a residence?"

"I suppose not, not without a great deal of arguing."

"There you are then. You shall have to find another purpose for the land. Share it with your family perhaps."

Slowly he shook his head and glanced toward the

stream where Harry was tossing pebbles into the water. "He's fortunate to have you as a sister."

"I'm the fortunate one. While my father did not set a sterling example, Harry embodies all that a family should be."

Mr. Granger handed Harry another pebble. She wondered if he had recognized that if Harry bent over to retrieve one, he would in all likelihood topple into the water.

"What will you do when he's gone?" Avendale asked quietly, yet Rose felt as though he'd bludgeoned her.

She gave him her most menacing glare. Here she'd thought he was understanding and kind—

"You have to have given it some thought. And no one would blame you for doing so. You're a realist, Rose, and you claimed last night not to lie to yourself, so you've thought about it."

Damn him. He was coming to know her too well, learning to read her far too easily. Her strength rested in remaining an enigma. And if she had to leave him before the bargain was done, how would she do it if he could read through her lies? "Doesn't mean that I don't feel guilty when I do."

"So what will you do?"

Arching a brow, angling her chin, she said succinctly, "Honor the bargain I made with you."

"And if there were no bargain to be honored?"

"What good comes from speculating on theoretical scenarios?"

"I'm simply curious. Before you met me, what were your plans for when the time came that you didn't have to watch over him?"

"Why do you care?"

He trailed his blunt-tipped finger along the back

of her hand, and she was astounded as always that his faint touch in such a small area could lure her in, could make her want to kiss him. "If you're not comfortable with thoughts of Harry being gone, what will you do when you're free of me?"

Weep uncontrollably for days, nights, weeks. No, she was too pragmatic for such nonsense. She would cry for a few hours, then straighten her spine and carry on. Rolling onto her back, she stared at the blue sky, still finding it difficult to believe that she'd journeyed through it. She would never forget this day. He was creating as many memories for her as for Harry. How could she ever in a thousand years repay that debt? "I shall awaken each morning and go wherever I want. Perhaps even to India. I'll have no responsibilities, no duties, no obligations. I'll wander, with nothing to tie me down. I'll have no plans, no strategies, no compelling need to do anything except breathe."

"How will you survive?"

She shrugged. "The occasional swindle."

As he moved nearer, she could no longer see the brilliant blue. Only his face as he gazed down on her. "I thought you did that out of necessity."

"I still must eat." Had she claimed she was always honest with herself? "I don't know if I can give it up. I thrive on the challenge of it." Reaching up, she brushed the hair back from his brow. "Sorry to disappoint."

"Life has other challenges you could embrace."

"But none would give me the freedom to live on my own terms, worrying only about my own whims and fancies." She swallowed hard, forcing the words past her tightening throat. "I've spent a little over a quarter of a century caring for Harry." She licked her lips, swallowed again, pushed back the tears. "I don't resent it."

Abruptly she sat up, barely aware of knocking her shoulder against his chin. "I don't," she insisted again. "But sometimes I yearn to be beholden to no one, to only have to think about me. My wants, my needs, my dreams. I'll part ways with Merrick and the others. I'm selfish, terribly, terribly selfish. I want no children, no husband, no one claiming me. I want to answer only to myself."

Avendale pushed himself up and, with his thumb, he wiped from her cheek a tear she didn't realize had escaped. "Yet you agreed to answer to me."

She traced her fingers over his face, noting the deep lines that a man of his age should not yet possess. "So I did."

"And you'll keep to it, because of Harry."

More so because of Avendale, but she could not give him that power over her. Self-preservation forced her to let him believe his words were true. "I'll keep to it."

"Even though you're not in the habit of paying your debts?"

"This one I'll keep."

"Why don't I believe you?"

"You must believe me or we wouldn't be here now."

"I'm sure you'll stay with me as long as Harry breathes. After that, I think you'll take off the moment my back is turned."

"Then why are you doing all this?"

"Because I enjoy watching you smile."

The words devastated her. Why did he have to be so good when she was so rotten? "I will not break my promise to you." She meant the words, intended to keep them—if she could. Always there was that caveat. Always the words could prove false.

"How did you learn to lie so well?" he asked.

"I'm not lying."

His scrutiny was almost a physical caress. It took everything within her not to look away.

"I should hope not," he finally said, and she was able to slowly release the breath she'd been holding. "But I find it difficult to believe you learned everything from your father."

She smiled. "You're right on that score. I learned some skills from a fortune-teller. Elise. She was part of the traveling ménage of oddities. Claimed to be a Gypsy. I don't know if that's true. But she had black hair and black eyes. When she looked at you, it felt like she saw into your soul."

"Did she ever tell you your fortune?"

"At least once a week. I was fascinated by the ritual of it. From her I learned the importance of setting the scene. With her scarves and flickering candles and whispers, I could not help but believe she could see my future."

"What did she predict for you?"

"It was always a variation of the same: before I see thirty years, I will lose what I treasure."

"Harry."

"I don't see that it could be anything else."

"When do you turn thirty?"

"In two months." She took a deep breath. "So yes, I have considered what my life would be after I'm thirty. And you, Your Grace, what do you see in your future?"

"An upstanding wife who can bring respectability to me and the family name. A lady whom Society will view with reverence for bringing me to heel."

A woman with a sterling reputation, one far different from hers. "Someone of whom your mother will approve."

Nodding, he looked out toward the stream. "I should at least give her that, as I've not been a good son," he said quietly.

Although he was still gazing out, she wasn't certain he saw Harry any longer. Instead he saw regret, perhaps the reason behind it. They were no longer among the clouds, so regrets were once more prevalent and weighing heavily on shoulders.

She was not surprised by his proclamation. He'd alluded to his mother being disappointed in him. "I suspect you are a better son than you realize."

He slid his gaze to her. She could easily fall into those dark depths and lose her way. Perhaps she had already. "Where do you find your optimism?" he asked.

"How do you not find yours?"

He laughed darkly. "Because I know my transgressions."

"They can be forgiven."

"But not forgotten."

"I believe we chose how we remember them, how we perceive them. Take my father, for example. I could choose to remember his treatment of Harry beneath the light of ignorance. I could be more tolerant of his actions. Instead I view him through the lens of cruelty. I shall never forgive him. With my dying breath, I shall curse him. I know that makes a part of my soul black and ugly but there are other parts of it that are bit brighter thanks to Harry. Your mother will have no choice except to look at you through the lens of love. She will forgive you because she can do little else."

"She is hosting a dinner tonight. She wished me to attend."

Rose would love to go, to see the splendor, to dine with the duke's family, but she was well aware that he could not share her with those above reproach. "You should go. Harry and I can entertain ourselves."

He shook his head. "I can't go."

"She's your mother."

"She killed my father."

He'd never said the words aloud. Echoing around him, they sounded harsh, cruel, and untrue.

They'd propelled him to his feet, sent him striding over the field, crushing petals beneath his boots. He didn't know why he'd told her. Why he'd blurted it out.

Her family was far from perfect, yet when he saw her with her brother, witnessed the love and devotion they shared—

He had three brothers and two sisters—half siblings—and he doubted he'd be able to pick them all out in a crowd of six. He couldn't recall the last time he'd seen them. He stayed away because he didn't want to be a bad influence, not that his reasons were entirely noble.

"Avendale, slow down," Rose called behind him.

He couldn't. He needed to outrace his thoughts. They were traveling back in time and he didn't want to go there, never wanted to go there.

"Avendale." She grabbed his arm. "Hold up."

He wanted to shake her off, even as he wanted to wrap himself around her. He was aware of a tug as she tripped, began to fall—

Spinning around, he caught her, steadied her, looked into eyes that had seen cruelty worse than he could have imagined, and yet she'd been forged into

a remarkable woman who didn't belabor the unfair-
ness in life but simply sought to balance it.

"You told me your father died in a fire," she said
softly.

"That's what they led me to believe." Releasing his
hold on her, he dragged his fingers through his hair.
"I did not bring you here for this."

Taking his hand as though they were children, she
led him to a tree, slid down its trunk, and sat on
the ground, seeming not to care that her skirt would
become stained. She looked up at him, the invitation
there. He should announce that it was time for them
to depart. Instead he sank down, raised a knee, and
draped his wrist over it.

"Tell me," she urged.

He plucked a flower, pulled off a petal. "Tell her."
Plucked another. "Tell her not." Another. "Tell her."

She snatched the flower from between his fingers
and tossed it aside. "You know my secrets," she said.

"Do I?" He doubted that he knew them all.

"The ones that matter."

In part, due to Harry's writings, he knew far more
than she probably realized. It did seem only fair that
he reveal some of his, but he had harbored them for
so long that it was difficult to share them now, even
with her. Yet if he were going to share them with
anyone, it should be she. He was coming to care for
her, more than was wise, more than he'd thought
possible. He'd always kept himself divorced from
his feelings, because he'd learned early on that they
couldn't be trusted. As much as he wanted to trust
her, he couldn't. Not completely, but perhaps enough
that he could unburden himself somewhat.

She waited patiently, quietly, as though she knew
exactly how difficult it was to bare his secrets. He

reached for another flower and found instead her fingers threading through his, holding firmly, providing strength, her blue eyes searching. He cleared his throat and began.

"Memories of my youth are tattered, blurred at the edges. I don't remember how it came to be, but we were staying with Sir William—he wasn't Sir William at the time; he was simply Dr. Graves—when word came that my father died in a fire. Mother didn't cry when she told me but there was this sense of relief. I remember that most. Graves was with her, holding her. I believe he and my mother were lovers. I was too young at the time to make that assumption. It was only as I got older, came to understand what passed between men and women, that I could look back on that time and speculate why he was always about."

"You think they arranged for his death so they might be together?"

"I know it sounds preposterous. It's the reason I've never spoken of it. At the time I didn't quite understand death. I knew only that I would not see my father again, because he'd gone to heaven. But I did see him. Three years later."

Her eyes widened. "You mean you saw his ghost?"

He shook his head, tucking away the little tidbit that she believed in things such as that. "No, he was flesh and blood and very much alive. He kept to the shadows: at the park, the zoological gardens. One night I awoke to find him at the foot of my bed."

"You must have been terrified."

"Strangely I wasn't. I'd begun to think of him as the shadow man, because I couldn't see his features clearly. That night he told me that my mother and her lover had tried to be rid of him, but he wasn't so

easily gotten rid of. He would make them pay. None
of it made sense to me at the time as I didn't know
what a lover was or where he'd been. He also told me
he was there to protect me, that my mother didn't
love me, but wished me ill. I was to tell no one. But
I'd drawn pictures of him. My mother saw them. One
afternoon she took me to Lovingdon's and ordered
me to stay the night. But when it grew dark, I ran
home. I saw her strike him down with a fireplace
poker. He didn't get up."

"Did she see you?"

"No. I was hidden away in the shadows of the ter-
race. For hours I made no sound. My tears fell in
silence. I might have even fallen asleep. I can only
recall snippets of the night. Graves was there. So was
Inspector Swindler of Scotland Yard. I thought she
would be arrested, but she wasn't. Eventually I ran
back to Lovingdon's. My mother came for me and
acted as though there was no blood on her hands.
I thought there would be another funeral. But there
wasn't. Nothing was ever said."

Leaning toward him, she cradled his face. "And
she married Graves?"

Taking her hand from his cheek, he traced the lines
along her palm. It was easier to speak with a distraction. "Shortly afterward. Sometimes she would look
at me, and I saw the guilt. And I wondered when she
would kill me, too."

Shock tightened her features. "You can't truly
have believed your mother would harm you."

"I was a child. His words, her actions haunted me. I
lived in fear until I went off to school. Even then I wasn't
completely certain I was safe. I kept to myself, trusted
few. Over time, it became a habit. Which is why, I suppose, I didn't quite trust you in the beginning."

"But you trust me now."

"Not entirely."

Her mouth formed a little moue of displeasure and he wanted to kiss it away. Why was it, no matter what she did, he wanted to kiss her? He slid toward her until his hip touched hers, until his arm crossed over her lap, pressing his palm to the firm ground, and he was able to balance himself so he had one hand free to cradle her face. "Should I trust you?"

She gave him a self-deprecating smile. "Probably not, but you should talk to your mother about that night. Perhaps there's an explanation for all it."

"Do you think she would feel better knowing what I saw?"

"I think she would feel better if you were more a part of her life. And I think you would benefit from knowing the truth."

But what if it was worse than he'd ever imagined? "I've let it go on for too long. No good would come of it."

"I'd not have thought you a coward."

Her words served as a punch to the gut; the challenge in her eyes nearly felled him. "Careful. You don't want to make an enemy of me."

"I know that well enough." With her fingers, she gently feathered the hair back from his brow. "Go to dinner."

He wasn't half tempted, only he wanted her at his side, but one didn't bring his paramour, especially one who skirted the law, to his mother's dining table. Although it wasn't as though his mother's friends hadn't done a bit of skirting themselves. Still, the dinner party wasn't where he should begin reconciliation. "There will be time to make amends later."

Weary of revisiting the past, wanting to be ensconced in the present where passion loomed, he covered her mouth with his. An image of the future flitted through his mind, and he saw her there, strolling over his land, his children tugging at her skirts. All the responsibilities and duties that she didn't want.

She had agreed to stay with him for as long as he wanted, but already he regretted the bargain, because he was discovering that he didn't want her with him unless it was where she wished to be. And she had already told him that it wasn't. The carefree life she craved would not be found at his side. Unfortunately, he wouldn't be unselfish enough to let her go.

*S*tanding in the gallery, Rose studied the former Duke of Avendale's portrait.

After they'd returned from their outing, Avendale had taken his leave to attend to some business in town. It amazed her to discover that he was not quite the man of leisure she'd thought. It seemed there was always some detail that required his attention.

Hearing the familiar shuffling, she turned to her brother and smiled. "You should have sent for me, sweeting. No need for you to traverse stairs."

"I wanted to." He gave her an almost bashful grin. "Besides, I wasn't looking for you. I just like to explore."

"It is an amazing place. I try to imagine all the care that went into arranging each room, and it's quite beyond me."

"It speaks of permanence."

"Yes, I suppose that's it. I'm not of a mind to view anything as permanent. It's all fleeting."

Sadness touched his eyes. "You should have permanent, forever."

She smiled, to soften her words, to ensure they brought no guilt his way. "I wouldn't know what to do with it." Usually by now she was itching to move on with her nomadic life.

Harry looked past her shoulder, to the portrait that took up a great portion of the wall, more than any other painting, as though the man's ego demanded it. "Avendale's father?"

"Yes."

"I don't like him," he whispered.

"There is something sinister in his eyes, isn't there?"

"The artist didn't like him either. He didn't hide that Avendale's father wasn't nice."

Briefly she wondered what sort of rendering an artist might do of Harry, if given the chance. It might be interesting. Her father had been gifted with handsome features but his hatred and self-centeredness had twisted them until his demeanor made him unattractive. Harry might have been graced with the same pleasing lines beneath the misshapen masses, but even without them she found him quite beautiful.

"You should have a portrait done," Harry said.

What a disaster that would be, to have a likeness created that would provide police with more clues to her identity. "Perhaps someday."

Harry limped over to study the portrait of Avendale's mother.

"Harry, if you were to awaken one morning, and I weren't here—"

He turned. "Why wouldn't you be here?"

"Something might happen and I would need to leave."

"What?"

"Anything is possible. It's just a hypothetical, but I want you to know that even if I'm not with you, I still love you more than anything."

"The duke won't like it. You leaving."

"No, he won't."

"Are you going to tell him you might leave?"

"No, but if it should happen—"

"It won't." He turned his attention back to the portrait.

"But if it should and Avendale wants you to leave, you're to return to Merrick. You're not to try to find me."

"It won't happen," he repeated. "But if it does"—he gave her a shrewd look—"I won't have to look for you because the duke will find you."

A shiver went through her with the acknowledgment that Avendale would be ruthless in his search. "You give him far too much credit."

"You don't give him enough." He returned his attention to the portrait. It wasn't often that she wanted to smack her brother but at that precise moment she thought he could do with a good wallop.

"You can be most irritating when you want to be," she said, not bothering to hide her irritation.

"But you love me anyway."

She rubbed his shoulder, forgiving him far more easily than she should. "I do, yes."

"And you love the duke."

Her fingers jerked, and she quickly removed her hand before he could sense her tension. "That would be a silly thing to do."

"Why?" He'd turned completely around, his gaze on her intense.

"He could never marry me."

"Why?"

She sighed with exasperation. "Honestly, Harry, we need to work to expand your vocabulary."

"Is it because of the things you've done, the way we live?"

Reluctantly she nodded, not surprised he'd figured things out. He was so astute, observant. "I'm not a very good person, not really. A duke requires a wife who is above reproach."

"He needs a wife who loves him."

"I should think he won't have any trouble finding that once he sets his mind to it."

He wouldn't have any trouble at all. She did hope she'd be gone by then. A small voice in the back of her mind cautioned her to be careful of what she wished for.

Chapter 17

*R*ose secured for us a small cottage by the sea. At night, the crashing waves would lull me to sleep. On nights when there was a full moon I would walk along the water's edge. I wanted to wade out into the surf, but I was afraid that I might topple over and not be able to get up, that I would drown. My left side had developed more protrusions, and I'd begun to have difficulty maintaining my balance.

Although she never said anything, I think Rose knew about my midnight walks. One day, she gifted me with a walking stick of beautiful ebony with a dog's head carved at the end. The carving reminded me of the dog I'd once owned.

Rose began to go out in the evenings. I thought perhaps she had a swain. One night as I was walking, she appeared out of the darkness and I wondered how many nights she may have been there watching me.

"Would you like to step into the sea?" she asked.

"*I might fall.*"

"*I'll catch you.*" *I was all of fifteen, still a lad but on the cusp of manhood, although not as large as I would become. She knelt down and removed my shoes. Then she took my hand, and we counted the steps as we waded into the sea.*

Six. The water swirled around my ankles, and I imagined that the waves had touched distant shores, that the water was free to journey wherever it pleased. For a moment I was envious.

"*We're leaving this place,*" *Rose said quietly, but still I heard her over the rush of sound that belongs to the sea.*

We were gone by morning.

As the faint knock of ebony on parquet and shuffling feet disturbed Avendale's concentration, he looked up to see Harry slightly inside the library doorway. It seemed Avendale wasn't the only one unable to sleep tonight. His conversation with Rose earlier in the day weighed heavily on his mind. Had he been unfair to his mother all these years? Was he being unfair to Rose now?

Following dinner, he'd lost himself in her for a while, but after she'd drifted off to sleep he'd come here to become lost in *her* past because it was easier than dealing with his own. Or it should have been. He was discovering that hers troubled him far more than he was willing to admit. She had been strong for so long. But without meaning to, he'd taken choices away from her. He shoved himself to his feet. "Harry."

"I'm sorry to disturb you. I didn't think anyone would be here this time of night."

It was well past midnight, the shadows hovering in corners. "Where's Gerald?"

"Sleeping."

"You shouldn't wander about without him."

Although only a solitary lamp on the desk provided light, Avendale was still able to make out Harry's smile. "I won't get lost. I wanted to be in this room because it has the most books. Their fragrance is heavier here. I like the way they smell. But I'll come back later."

"Stay. Take a seat by the fire. Join me in a drink." His guest nodded, and Avendale strode over to the marble table and poured scotch into two glasses before joining Harry. After taking his seat, Avendale lifted his glass. "To a day of adventures and getting your sister into the balloon."

Harry grinned, drank. Avendale did the same.

They sat in comfortable silence, as Harry gazed around the room and Avendale watched him. Finally he asked, "How did you learn to read? I can't imagine that you went to a schoolroom."

"Rose."

"Of course."

"She attended school for a short time before Father decided to share me with the world."

Share me with the world. Phrasing that made what his father did sound less sinister, less unconscionable.

"I know numbers, too," Harry said. "I don't like them as much. There's beauty and magic in letters and words and the way they come together."

"There's beauty and magic in numbers as well, my friend. They have come together in ways that allow me to do quite a bit that I wouldn't be able to otherwise."

"Am I?" Harry asked.

Avendale angled his head. "Pardon?"

"Am I your friend?"

It seemed there was also truth in words. Avendale had used the term without thought, without considering the weight of it. Without realizing how Harry, who wrote with such honesty, might interpret it. "Yes, I believe you are."

Harry grinned, nodded. "You are my friend as well."

Avendale lifted his glass. "I'm honored. To friendship."

They both sipped, savored. With a blunt-tipped finger, Avendale tapped his glass. "I'm enjoying reading your story very much."

"It's all true."

"I thought as much. Your sister is an extraordinary woman. You should know that I shall see to it she's well cared for."

In spite of his limited facial expressions, Harry gave Avendale a grin that could only be described as cunning. "I know."

Avendale realized very little got past Rose's brother. He could have accomplished anything he wanted were the world more accepting of those who were different.

Harry craned his head back slightly. "How do you get to the books up there?" He pointed at the balcony—its walls composed of more shelves laden with literary treasures—that circled the room. "The ladder isn't high enough."

"No, it's only useful in getting to the books on the top shelves at this level. To get to the balcony—come. I'll show you." Setting his glass aside, he took Harry's and placed it beside his. Then he stood there, fighting not to reach over and help Harry to his feet. He had a too keen understanding of pride, and he could see it reflected in Harry's struggle. There would come a time when he would not be able to get up on his own, but the time was not yet.

Avendale never would have described himself as a patient man. Odd that he was being so now.

When Harry was finally as upright as possible, leaning on his cane, Avendale jerked his head in the direction behind him. "This way."

He led Harry to a section of shelves not far from the fireplace. "Now watch."

He gave the shelves a quick shove at the seam that separated one section from the other. A click sounded as an inner latch was released, and the shelves sprang forward a tad. He slipped his hand behind the fissure and opened the door fully to reveal a spiral staircase nestled inside a small alcove.

With a gasp, Harry widened his eyes in astonishment as he whispered in awe, "A secret passage."

"Indeed. It was my favorite place to sneak about when I was a lad. Go on in."

With a deep breath, Harry stepped inside as though he thought the small room would transport him somewhere. In a way, perhaps it did. He touched the black metal railing with wonder, released what might have been a muted laugh. He peered over at Avendale. "May I go up?"

Damnation, he hadn't considered that Harry would make that request. He should have merely said the balcony was ornamental. "I was given to understand that you have difficulty traversing stairs."

Disappointment dimmed the sparkle in Harry's eyes. "I'm awkward and slow."

"Is that all?" Avendale asked. "I've no pressing appointments. Have you?"

$\mathcal{R}$ose stood in the library doorway, quiet as a dormouse, and watched as her brother explored the balcony while Avendale patiently answered his questions. From time to time their laughter rolled out through the room, causing tears to prick her eyes.

She'd awoken in a lethargic haze to discover Avendale absent from the bed, and so she'd gone in search of him, assuming he would be in his library. She'd not expected the sight that greeted her.

They were an odd pairing—the handsome duke and her misshapen brother—but to see them together, a friendship forming, caused a tightness in her chest that might prevent her from ever being able to inhale a deep breath again. It was so obvious that Harry adored Avendale, that Avendale was the older brother he'd never possessed.

Avendale's kindness . . . she'd not anticipated it. She'd expected him to be tolerant. She hadn't thought he would embrace Harry as he had. Although in spite of Harry's imperfections, he possessed the ability to charm when given the opportunity. The problem was that so few gave him the chance. Far too many judged him by his appearance and went no further.

Although the same could be said of her: men saw her bosom and assumed it comprised the whole of her. Except Avendale hadn't.

As he pulled down a large book, set it on a small table, and opened it, he was a danger to her heart. Pointing to something, he turned aside, spoke, and Harry moved in to look at whatever was displayed on the page. Even from this distance she could see the surprise cross his features before he laughed.

With a broad masculine smile that conveyed a secret shared between men, Avendale clapped him on the shoulder. Harry looked up—

"Rose!" His delight at spying her was evident in his expression. She rather wished he hadn't spotted her. Standing there for days watching them would have pleased her more.

Harry limped to the railing and her breath caught with the possibility of him toppling over it. "Careful, sweeting!"

"There's a hidden staircase," he called down, and pointed. "Come up it."

She saw it then, the shelves that were a door slightly ajar. Harry would have loved discovering the hidden alcove, exploring it. She was grateful to Avendale for sharing it with her brother.

Traversing up the winding spiral stairs, experiencing a sense of vertigo and dizziness, she was amazed that Harry had handled them. At the top, Avendale was waiting for her.

"I fear your brother has decided this is his favorite part of the residence," he said, wrapping his warm fingers around hers and leading her onto the balcony. Their footsteps echoed hollowly around them as the cavernous ceiling reflected the sounds.

"I daresay I can hardly blame him."

"Look at it all, Rose," Harry said as she joined him. "Some of these are extremely old books. Ancient. They smell different than the ones below."

He would notice. He was aware of so many subtleties. "They do, don't they?"

She saw the table was now empty. "What of the book Avendale was sharing with you?"

Harry blushed; Avendale cleared his throat before

leveling his hooded gaze on her. "Just a bit of naughtiness. I'll show you later if you like."

"Are you corrupting my brother?"

"Absolutely."

Unable to help herself, she laughed. There was no contrition whatsoever in his manner. She'd tried so hard to shelter Harry. Had she done him a disservice? He was a young man, with a young man's curiosities. In that regard, Avendale would no doubt serve as the perfect tutor.

"Perhaps I should leave you to it," she said.

Harry's eyes widened with surprise, while Avendale merely gave her a devilish grin. "I believe we're finished for tonight. Harry tells me you often read to him. Perhaps you would do so now."

They settled into a very cozy corner of the balcony, near the windows. The chairs were large and plush, perfect for curling in, although Rose was the only one to take advantage of that aspect. Harry leaned forward, ever alert, while Avendale lounged back.

After peering over at Avendale, Harry struck the same pose as much as he was able, and Rose's heart twisted. She was remarkably glad that Avendale had suggested they bring Harry here.

He handed her *Arabian Nights* and she began to read "Aladdin's Wonderful Lamp." She found herself wishing they might have a thousand and one nights such as this.

Chapter 18

As Rose dressed in a gown of red, she could not help but acknowledge that Harry had settled in rather nicely during the week since he had first come to Buckland Palace. He was devouring books, walking in the garden, and twice more Merrick, Sally, and Joseph had joined them for dinner.

Each afternoon, Avendale presented him with some surprise: a windup acrobatic clown; a mechanized racetrack that took up a good portion of the parlor and had Harry enthusiastically wagering on the outcome even though the same horse always won; a kaleidoscope, a telescope. Last night the skies had been clear and they'd taken to the gardens to observe the stars.

So when Avendale had asked her to accompany him to the theater this evening, she had not felt that she was in a position to decline the invitation. He was giving far more of his time to Harry than she'd expected, and it wasn't fair that Avendale's hours alone with her only occurred late at night when they retired.

They deserved an evening out together. Harry had been terribly understanding. When she had suggested sending for Merrick to keep him company, Harry had told her he preferred to be alone. The duke had granted him permission to disassemble the racetrack, and Harry was looking quite forward to deciphering how it worked.

Looking past her reflection in the mirror, she watched as Avendale shrugged into his evening jacket. By now she shouldn't take such joy in observing him as he dressed, although she preferred his clothing being removed. Shouldn't the novelty have worn off, shouldn't they be tired of each other?

Edith secured the last pearl comb in Rose's hair, then reached for the necklace.

"I'll handle that," Avendale said, coming up behind Rose.

With a quick curtsy, Edith took her leave. Rose barely moved as Avendale draped the gorgeous piece at her throat. She watched him, saw appreciation light his eyes, and decided to take the jewelry with her when she left, because it would so well serve as a reminder of their time together. She would be able to recall the sensations he stirred as he placed it on her.

"Thank you," she said when he was finished.

She began tugging on a glove, and he stepped back. In the mirror, she saw his brow furrow.

"Hmm," he murmured.

When the glove was in place above her elbow, she began on the next. "What is it?" she asked.

"Something doesn't seem quite right."

With the last bit of kidskin in place, she stood and moved to the cheval glass. She turned one way, then another. "I don't see anything amiss."

"Perhaps it's this." Taking her hand, he draped a ruby and diamond bracelet over her wrist before securing it.

"Avendale—"

"Don't say no," he said, cutting off her objection, lifting his gaze to hers. "Leave it behind if you like, although it is from Harry."

"Harry has no money with which to purchase something like this."

"I taught him to play poker this afternoon. He gave me a sound thrashing."

She knew beyond any doubt that he had cheated to receive that thrashing. She cradled his jaw. "I did not expect you to be so kind."

"I'm not certain I expected it of myself either, but I'm not entirely unselfish. If we don't leave soon, we're going to miss the curtains opening. It will ruin the entire evening if we don't see the play from the beginning."

Draping her wrap over her arm, she followed him out into the hallway and began descending the stairs.

"What play are we seeing?" she asked.

"Some Shakespearean drama no doubt. Does it matter?"

"No, I suppose—"

She staggered to a stop at the sight of Harry standing in the foyer grinning up at her. He wore black trousers, a black swallow-tailed jacket, white shirt, gray waistcoat, and a perfectly knotted cravat. He held in the hand leaning on the gleaming cane a tall beaver hat.

"Avendale," she whispered. He'd stopped one step below her, and she turned to him now. Her heart was breaking at his kindness, but it was also breaking for the cruelty he was unintentionally inflicting. "We can't take him with us."

"Trust me, Rose."

Her throat clogging with tears, she shook her head. He didn't understand what it was like when people first caught sight of Harry. He'd created a safe haven within his residence, but beyond it he couldn't control others and their reactions. He couldn't save her brother from the embarrassment of being reminded how very different he was.

Avendale cradled her face with one hand. "My box is in shadows. He'll sit in the back, and no one will see him."

"But he has to get there."

"I was once involved with an actress. I know a back way in. The only ones who will see him are those I paid well to show no reaction and to hold their tongues." His gaze delved into hers. "I remember your awe that night we went, the way you scrutinized every aspect. I know now that you were trying to carry all the details back to Harry. Give him the opportunity to experience it on his own."

It was her nature to be protective of her brother, to try to spare him all the suffering possible, but even fledgling birds wouldn't fly if they were never forced out of the nest. She took a deep breath, cursed her corset for not allowing her to breathe as deeply as she needed. "Yes, all right."

Placing her hand in the crook of Avendale's elbow, taking comfort in his strength, absorbing it until her trembling fingers stilled, she carried on down the stairs. Reaching the foyer, she smiled brightly. "Oh, Harry, don't you look dapper!"

He nodded, his gaze traveling between her and Avendale. "The duke has an accomplished tailor who came to see me."

"I should say he does."

"We need to be away," Avendale said quietly, his hand coming to rest on the small of her back assuaging any remaining fears that this was a horrible idea.

Harry placed his hat on his head but it didn't sit quite properly. Rose straightened it as best she could, then declared, "Perfect."

Once they were in the coach, Rose found herself sitting on the bench alone with the two gents opposite her. Obviously, Avendale had instructed Harry on the proper etiquette regarding where gentlemen sat. The lamp was lit, but the curtains were drawn over the windows.

"Were you surprised, Rose?" Harry asked.

"Quite."

"Harry has been busting to tell you all day," Avendale said. "Why do you think I entertained him with cards all afternoon?"

"I beat him. Every hand," her brother crowed, and she refrained from informing him that it was bad form to boast of one's victories.

"You're very clever, Harry." But then so was Avendale. Clever and kind. While he proclaimed to know nothing at all about caring, it seemed he knew a great deal indeed.

And she realized with dread that she was falling in love with him. How would she survive when he was no longer in her life? It wasn't her person she was concerned with, but her heart, her soul. He nurtured them, fed them.

She'd held herself distant from everyone except those in her small circle. She loved them dearly, but not in the same manner that she did Avendale. It was as though he had somehow become part of her. She was beginning to know the things he would say before he said them. Each time she saw him, she overflowed with gladness. It didn't matter if only five minutes had passed since she'd last seen him. She wanted to reach across now and touch him, hold him, cradle her head on his shoulder.

"How long have you been planning this?" she asked him.

"Almost from the beginning."

"You might have mentioned it."

"And ruin my fun? Not likely."

"I had no idea my little brother was so skilled at keeping secrets."

"I'm the best," Harry said.

"Between the balloon and this secret, I'm beginning to think I shouldn't leave you two alone to plot things."

"The duke and I are friends. Friends plot adventures."

The words flowed over her, through her, and she wondered if Harry was aware how remarkable it was that a man of Avendale's station in life was his friend. But then was the duke aware that Harry was his friend for no other reason than that Harry liked him? Harry wasn't influenced by wealth, rank, or position. He judged people by what he saw inside them. Which also made it remarkable that he could love her.

The coach clattered to a stop, rocked, and Rose felt her nervousness kick back in.

"Wait here," Avendale ordered, before stepping out of the coach.

Rose peered behind the curtain to see him marching up some steps to a door. Using the head of his walking stick, he knocked, waited, glanced casually around.

"What's he doing?" Harry whispered.

"Waiting for someone to answer his summons.

We seem to be in an alleyway." She saw the door open, heard voices, although she couldn't decipher the words exchanged. Then Avendale was heading back toward them.

A footman opened the coach door as he neared. Reaching in, Avendale took Rose's hand. "All is arranged."

He handed her down before assisting Harry. He led them up the stairs and through the doorway into a small, shadowed room that opened onto stairs.

A finely dressed gentleman holding a lamp greeted them. "If you'll be so kind as to come with me."

With Avendale providing support for her brother, Rose followed the gentleman up the narrow stairs. At the top, they waited with bated breath while he parted heavy draperies and peered between them. Holding the fabric aside, he stepped out into the hallway and indicated they should precede him.

They made their way to Avendale's box with no incidents. Releasing a breath she didn't realize she'd been holding, Rose settled on her chair between Harry and Avendale, very much aware of the excitement thrumming through Harry as he took in his surroundings.

"It's just as you described," he whispered, "only better."

"I knew my descriptions wouldn't do it justice."

"How can you capture its soul? It can only be experienced." Harry leaned forward slightly. "All the people. They can't see me?"

"Not as long as we stay back here," Avendale said. "But even if they do see us, they shan't disturb us."

Harry looked over at him. "Because you're a duke?"

Avendale gave a confident grin. "Precisely."

But Rose realized it was more than that. It was because he wouldn't tolerate it. He would stand his ground just as his ancestors had on battlefields. She did wish he'd never learned about Harry, because everything was changing, because she'd been so worried about shielding Harry that she had failed to take precautions to protect her heart. Avendale had slipped beneath the wall, made his home there. Yet she could not seem to regret it, even knowing the pain their parting would cause. But that time was not yet.

Reaching over, she folded her hand over his where it rested on his thigh. Shifting his dark gaze to her, he lifted her hand and very slowly peeled off her glove, inch by agonizing inch. Everything within her went still. When he was finished, he removed both his gloves before interlacing their fingers. This man feared nothing, not Society's censure or doing things one ought not. For the briefest span of a heartbeat, she dared to dream that he might claim her. That he would move to the edge of the balcony, pull her against his side, and shout that he loved her, that she would become his duchess.

In the next heartbeat she imagined Tinsdale in the crowd, jumping to his feet, pointing at her, and revealing her for the fraud she was. A thief, a swindler, a charlatan. No better than her father with his magical elixir. The shame her trial would bring to Avendale. The pain it would bring to her if he didn't stand beside her, the agony if he did.

A duke's wife could not disappear into shadows.

"What's wrong?" he whispered.

Shaking her head, she lifted their joined hands and pressed a kiss to his knuckles. "I'm just grateful for tonight."

His eyes narrowed, and she knew he didn't believe

her. It made it all the more difficult that he could read her lies so easily.

Hearing a gasp, she looked over to see Harry leaning forward and the curtains below drawing back to reveal the stage. She almost cautioned him to take care, but she couldn't seem to bring herself to risk squelching his excitement. Tonight was an incredible opportunity, another that she could have never given to him. But Avendale had the power, the wealth, the influence to make almost anything happen. So Harry was attending the theater.

As the performance began, she leaned toward Avendale. "Is your actress on the stage tonight?" She didn't know why she'd asked, why she felt this spark of jealousy that he might spend his evening reliving moments with another woman.

"No," he said quietly.

"She must have been very beautiful."

"To be quite honest, I barely remember what she looked like."

Years from now, after their time was over, would he say the same of her? "That does not speak well of your feelings for her."

"A month ago, I could have described her in detail, but now she pales. They all pale, Rose."

He was striving to reassure her, to imply she was somehow special, but she knew that someday, for him, she would pale as well. While in her mind, her memories, he would always remain strikingly vibrant. She could not imagine, no matter how many years she lived, no matter how many men she encountered, that she would ever find anyone to fill the niche he had carved in her heart. Unfair perhaps to any future gentleman whose fancy she might catch, but then she'd long ago learned that not everything was fair.

Squeezing his hand, she didn't release her hold as she returned her attention to Harry, who was enthralled, absorbed by the pageantry, the action, the grandeur. Not once did his eyes stray from the tableau before him. Not once did he speak. He made nary a sound. She wished for a portrait of him lost in this world of make-believe.

When the curtains finally drew closed, he stood with the rest of the audience, clapped madly, smiled brightly. Leaned over and hugged her as though the gift of the night had been from her.

Drawing on her glove, she looked over at Avendale to find his expression one of immense satisfaction. "Thank you," she said quietly.

He slid his hand around her neck, pressed a light kiss to her temple, and whispered, "It was for you."

Her breath caught, her chest tightened with the knowledge that everything he was doing was for her, to give her memories, to ease her guilt because she couldn't give her brother a better life. Had she truly thought that, even if Tinsdale was breathing down her neck, she could walk away from her promise to stay?

They waited until the hallway was cleared to make their way to the stairs and out the back. Harry didn't speak until they were once again in the coach, traveling home. Only this time Avendale sat beside her, as though, having her near in the box, he wasn't quite ready to be separated from her. He interlocked their hands, and she regretted that she'd put her glove back on.

"Thank you, Duke," Harry said.

"My pleasure."

"What are they doing now, do you think? The people on the stage?"

"Turning in for the night, preparing for another performance tomorrow."

"Did they mind us watching them?"

"No, it's what they want."

"It isn't as it was with you, Harry," Rose tried to explain. "They want to entertain people."

"Is it wrong that I didn't?" he asked.

"No, sweeting. It's one thing to have a passion for bringing plays to life, to have a desire to perform. It's something else entirely to be forced into doing something you don't want to do."

He nodded, and she hoped he understood. She certainly didn't want him wishing he'd embraced their father's attempt to take advantage of Harry's unusual condition.

"Are you forced to do things?"

Beside her, Avendale stiffened, no doubt waiting for her to explain about the bargains they'd made. But she'd had a choice. The first time she could have walked away. No, she couldn't have. She'd wanted him as badly as he'd wanted her. The second bargain—she'd had a choice there as well. Or perhaps he was considering the whole of her life, and how it had involved caring for Harry since she was four years old. "You should know me well enough, Harry, to know I don't do anything I don't wish to do."

He blinked, considered, then said, "It was a splendid night."

"Yes, it was," she replied, grateful that he wasn't going to pursue the path of things she'd done. Just because she'd often felt she had no choice did not mean that she felt as though she'd been forced.

When they arrived home, Gerald was waiting to assist Harry. She kissed her brother on the cheek. "See you tomorrow, sweeting."

"Good night, Rose, Duke."

She watched him walk down the hallway, his step

a bit slower, his gait more imbalanced even with the cane. "Perhaps Sir William should see him tomorrow."

"I'll send word."

"Thank you." Turning, she faced him. She would never owe anyone as much as she owed him. If she voiced the words, she knew he would become irritated, his jaw would tighten, his lips would flatten into a hard line. She understood so much about him, until it was almost as though she was part of him. She could read his moods as she'd never been able to read another's. "I find it interesting that Harry didn't comment on my bracelet, considering it was a gift from him. I would have thought he'd be pleased that I was wearing it."

"I think he was simply occupied with his adventure of going to the theater."

Stepping up to him, she wound her arms around his neck. "I believe, Your Grace, I am not the only one who lies."

"I am found out."

He didn't seem at all upset about it as he lifted her into his arms and began carrying her up the stairs. With nimble fingers, she unknotted his neck cloth, fully aware that anticipation thrummed through her. "I suppose I shan't need Edith tonight."

"I'll be doing the honor of undressing you."

He did make her feel as though it was an honor while he undressed her slowly, provocatively, pressing kisses to revealed skin that never seemed to displease him. He had ruined her for any other man. When he was done with her, she would spend the remainder of her life in solitude and not regret a moment of it. She hoarded these moments, collecting the details until the madness of their coming together overwhelmed her. But years from now, she would be able to recall the smallest of specifics because she had trained herself over time not to overlook anything so she could describe every aspect of the things she'd seen to Harry.

Not that she would ever share any of this with him. No, these memories were for her alone, to keep her warm when her bones were frail and her skin like parchment. She would recall the way she lounged on the bed and watched as he removed his clothes, his eyes never leaving hers. The manner in which he prowled toward her like some big cat, all long limbs, sinewy muscles stretching out beside her. Beautiful perfection.

He could have served as the model for the male portion of the sculpture in the fountain. She was hit with the realization that he probably had. In his youth, arrogant and bold, and confident of his masculinity. She'd been so absorbed by the enticing shape of the figure that she'd barely noticed the face. Shame on her. She who had always hated how her body distracted men had been guilty of the same thing.

But then why would she look at any other man's face—whether cast in flesh or marble—when such an incredibly handsome and well-formed one was above her now. His dark eyes burned with desire and she marveled that he still yearned to be with her, that after these many nights, the passion continued to flare hot and unyielding.

Dipping his head, he took her mouth. Lifting her hips, she welcomed the marvelous length of him. They moved in tandem. The sensations spiraled, consuming until they alone existed, until they shattered.

And she knew a day would come when her heart would do the same.

Chapter 19

*H*arry buttoned up the shirt that the duke's accomplished tailor had made for him to wear when walking about the house. The soft material was heavenly against his skin, made him feel as though he were being continually caressed by the gentlest of hands.

"It won't be long now, will it?" he asked quietly.

Sir William snapped his black bag closed. "I don't think so, no."

"Don't tell Rose."

His eyes reflecting regret that there was no more to be done, the physician met his gaze, nodded. "If that's how you wish the matter handled, I'll oblige."

"Normally I like to give her surprises. This won't be one of them but it's better that way."

"You don't think it would be kinder to prepare her?"

"She knows I'm dying. You told her that already."

"Yes, I'm afraid I did."

"She doesn't need to know how soon it will be, how bad things are now."

"I wish I could do more for you."

"You've done a good deal."

"I'll leave some additional laudanum."

Harry didn't object, although he wasn't going to use it. It made him drowsy. He did not want to spend whatever time was left sleeping. It was imperative he finished writing his story. So many more books were waiting to be read, so many things left to be done. He didn't know if it was a blessing or a curse to know that his time was short, that so much would not be experienced.

We arrived in London in the dead of night, for that was how we always arrived anywhere, as though we were miscreants intent upon causing mischief, but I knew it was my disfigurement that prompted our secretive arrivals. Although I wore a hooded cloak whenever I went out, it did not have the power to save me from those who would inflict harm. People fear what they do not understand, and they seldom took the time to understand me.

Our residence was the finest in which we'd ever lived. One night Rose went out and the next morning, she described to me a gaming hell. I was at once shocked and intrigued that she would visit such a place. But she did not seem herself as she sought to create a vivid portrait of all that she had seen. I had the sense that there was a good deal about her adventure that she was not sharing, a part of it that even frightened her. I tried not to worry, as I knew there was nothing I could do, yet it seemed I worried all the same.

"Thatcher said you wished to see me."

Pulling himself from the story, Avendale stood as Rose crossed his library to stand in front of his desk. It had been a few days since their foray to the theater. He was growing bored. He imagined Harry was doing the same. Mechanical toys could hold his interest for only so long. "I'd like to take Harry to the Twin Dragons Tuesday next, and before you object—"

"I trust you."

The words slammed into him with such force that they nearly sent him reeling. He hadn't realized how desperately he wanted her trust, how desperately he wanted so much he wasn't certain he could acquire. She was here with him now because of her brother. She would stay with him for as long as he wished because of all the things he did to ensure her brother's last days were memorable. He would not resent her reasons, but he found himself wishing for more between them. Even if he considered overlooking her past to make her his duchess, the responsibilities there were far more than she could fathom. How could he ask her to accept the duties that came with being his wife when he knew that she craved freedom?

His entire adult life he'd been a selfish bastard, caring for his own wants and needs. It was an uncomfortable fit to consider changing for her, to think of letting her go when he so desperately still wanted her. He didn't know how she'd done it all these years, caring for her brother at the expense of her own desires.

"Excellent," he said cheerfully, not wanting to reveal the doubts creeping through his conscience. "Let's keep it a secret from Harry for now, shall we?"

"You like secrets."

"I like surprises." But secrets did little more than lead a man to ruin.

$\mathcal{A}$vendale stood in the modest parlor of his mother's residence and waited while the butler informed her of his arrival. Above the fireplace was a portrait of her with her husband and their children. She had asked him to be part of the gathering but he'd been too busy at the time, with scotch in need of drinking and a woman in need of pleasuring. He regretted it now because she asked so little of him. And he was about to ask of her an immense favor.

"Whit!"

Hearing the joy in her voice, he turned from the portrait. "Mother."

Crossing over to him, she gave him a quick hug, then held him at arm's length to study him as though she possessed the power to read his thoughts. He wondered why he had failed to notice during their last visit how her hair had faded to silver and the lines at her eyes and mouth had deepened into wrinkles. Before Rose, he noticed so few things.

"You're looking well," his mother said now. "Yet you're troubled. What's amiss?"

"Nothing really. I just— May we sit?"

"Oh yes, of course. Forgive my lack of manners. Shall I ring for tea?"

"No, I—" He almost told her that he wouldn't be there that long, but what he wanted couldn't be explained easily. "Scotch if you have it."

Her mouth formed a moue of displeasure. Still, she rang for the butler. When tea, biscuits, and scotch had been delivered, Avendale savored the fine amber liquid while his mother sipped her tea. Leaning forward, his elbows on his thighs, holding the glass between two hands, he said, "I have a favor to ask. While I believe I could get assistance from my acquaintances—" Rose was correct. His only friend was Lovingdon. The others were merely acquaintances. "I believe I would have more success if the request came from you."

"What do you require?"

Just like that. No hesitation, no doubt, as though he'd been a good son, as though he deserved her loyalty, as though he weren't taking advantage of her influence, the goodwill others had toward her. Her face was wreathed with hope that she could assist, that she could help him acquire what he sought.

During the past decade, how often had she—with the same hopefulness—waited for him to arrive for a special dinner, waited for him to visit? How many invitations had he ignored? Once he'd been old enough to move out, he'd rarely crossed her threshold. Setting aside his glass, he stood. "I'm sorry. I made a mistake in coming here today."

With swift movements, he headed for the door.

"Whit, my darling son, whatever you need, whatever trouble you might be facing, we are here for you."

Stopping in his tracks, he knew if he walked through the door, he would never, ever be back. He could no longer live without the truth. He just wasn't certain he wanted it. He thought of the truth with which Rose dealt. She was going to lose her brother. Yet she courageously faced each day. Compared with her he was a blistering coward.

Turning, he faced his mother, watched as the hope returned to her eyes. He was going to dash it, bluntly and cruelly. It was the best way. No mincing of words, no more dancing around something that should have been faced years ago—when it had happened. "I saw you kill my father."

She staggered back as though he'd thrown the mass of his body at her. Probably felt as though he had. Tears welling in her eyes, she cupped a shaking hand over her mouth, shook her head, and sank onto the settee.

Where was her anger, her offense, her repudiation? It infuriated him that the tiny seed of doubt he'd nurtured all these years was crushed beneath the weight of horror marching over her features. "You're not going to deny it?"

Her mouth moved, but no words sprung forth, as though she couldn't decipher where to begin. Finally, in a barely audible tone, she asked, "How is it . . . that you think you saw . . . something so horrible?"

"You'd taken me to Lovingdon's but after we were put to bed, I slipped out and raced home, because I missed you. I came in through the gardens, but sensed something wasn't right and became frightened. The door into the library was opened. As I approached, I saw you bash him with a poker."

She shook her head more briskly, held up a hand as though she had the power to stay his words. "I didn't mean to kill him, only to stop him."

"But why would—"

"She was protecting me," a deep voice cut in quietly but forcefully.

Avendale jerked around to find himself facing the wrath of Sir William. He'd always thought the man gentle, almost too kind, but at that moment, Avendale saw a man who would kill to protect what was his. And the duchess was his.

"She was protecting me," Sir William repeated.

"Because you and my mother were lovers?" he spat. "You were found out, so you sought to rid yourself of my father?"

"No!" his mother cried out. "Is that what you thought all these years?"

"What else was I think to when Sir William was always about?"

"That you and she were in need of protection. Your father was a beast. We tried to rid your mother of his presence once; it didn't work."

"*We?*" He looked back to his mother.

"She had nothing to do with it the first time."

He returned his attention to Sir William. "Who did?"

Sir William's face went blank. "It's not important."

"Was this when he supposedly died in a fire?"

"I would invite you to sit, but I suspect you'd prefer to hear all this standing," Sir William said. "There was a fire, which he started, but he was rescued from it. Would have been better for all if he'd been left where he'd fallen, but he wasn't. Arrangements were made for him to travel as a convict on a prison hulk to the far side of the world. Smart man, your father. He managed to escape and made his way back here."

"Once I realized he was alive and back in London, I knew he would come for me," his mother said softly, sadness in her eyes. "I sent you and the servants away. I'd changed while he was gone. I was happy. I wanted him to understand that I would not allow him to take that away from me; I would not allow him to take you. But he had trussed William up like a Christmas goose. He was going to kill him, send me to Bedlam. Who would protect you from him then?"

Avendale shook his head. "I don't remember Sir William being there, not trussed up. I recall him later, telling you the man was dead."

"Trauma can affect one's memory," Sir William said. "And it's been a little over twenty years."

He nodded. So much of his early years was a blur, so many things he hadn't wanted to remember sharpened into clarity with his mother's confession. He recalled his father beating her.

"Is that why you've kept your distance all these years?" his mother asked. "Because you knew what I'd done and can't forgive me."

He thought of all the things Rose had done to protect her brother. How she had once told him that she knew she would pay a price for them. His mother had done the same, paid a price to protect him. They both had. He knelt before her. "He came to me one night, told me you were trying to rid yourself of him, that you also wished me harm."

She gasped. "No."

"When I saw you kill him, I feared I was next."

"Oh my dear God, Whit." Tears brimmed in her eyes, overflowed onto her cheeks. She cradled his face between her hands. "I would never hurt you. You are my precious boy."

How was it that he had so badly misjudged? He wrapped his arms around her waist, rested his head in her lap. "I'm sorry, so sorry that I distanced myself. I was angry, didn't understand what had happened but was too cowardly to ask."

"It's not your fault. Damn your father for putting such notions in your head. I swear if he were alive I'd kill him again."

Straightening, he looked into eyes that were not those of a murderer, but a lioness who would protect her cub. He could hardly countenance what he'd believed at the age of seven, the fears he had allowed to guide his life. "As I got older, it made no sense, but the damage was done."

She cupped his cheek. "I am not completely without fault. I felt such guilt. I was always afraid that somehow you would discover the truth. Now you have. If only I'd taken you aside and told you everything years ago. But I feared what you would think of me."

"I suspect I would have thought what I think now: that you are a remarkable woman."

Once more tears filled her eyes. "Not so remarkable. Defending my life and those I loved was thrust upon me. My actions were not what I would have chosen, but sometimes we don't have a choice."

How did one know, he wondered, when one had a choice—when one should have a choice?

"If he had told you that you could leave, would you have gone?"

"Yes," she said softly. "He had beaten my love for him out of me. William came into my life and refilled my heart. I will always choose love above all else. It is the only thing that matters. My dearest wish is that none of my children will go through life without it."

"I'm sorry I've not been a good son."

"Oh, Whit, I could not have asked for a better son."

He knew it for the lie it was, but he let her have it.

Leaning back, she brushed his hair from his brow in the same manner that she had when he was a small boy. "Now, you came to ask a favor of us. What is it?"

The years of separation melted away as though they'd never been. His heart swelled with all the love he held for his mother. Then he told her what he needed done.

Chapter 20

This time when Rose descended the stairs to see Harry dressed in evening attire she didn't stop partway, but carried on and forced her trepidation into submission. She trusted Avendale, absolutely, unconditionally.

"Are you ready for a night engaging in wicked things?" she asked her brother as she neared him.

Nodding, he grinned. She suspected he had no fear of being delivered to hell for any sins committed tonight since he'd spent most of his life in it. Surely that had to count for something, and the pearly gates would be thrown open to welcome him when the time came.

"Let's be away then," Avendale said, and she thought he'd never looked more handsome, more at ease, more confident. Something had changed in the past few days but she couldn't quite put her finger on it.

He sat beside her in the coach. Relishing his nearness, she was determined to enjoy the night, to welcome the deceptive belief that their time together would never come to an end. He certainly gave no indication of tiring of her, but surely the novelty of her would wear off. She pushed back those troubling thoughts.

The coach came to a stop. The curtains were drawn, and yet it seemed she heard far more sounds than she'd heard in the alleyway the last time they were here: the whinny of horses, the whir of carriage wheels, rapid footfalls, leisurely ones, voices. The door opened. Avendale stepped out and extended his hand to her. As she emerged, her gaze fell on the front façade of the Twin Dragons, and she had to fight back the panic, the wrongness of it.

Trust him. Trust him.

"I assumed we would go in through the back where we would have more privacy," she said.

"Not tonight," he said, leveling a pointed stare on her. Did she trust him? Swallowing hard, she nodded. He signaled the footman, who reached in to the coach.

"Master Harry." He then proceeded to assist Harry. Once her brother was standing on the pavement, his eyes widened. "Beautiful architecture."

"I always found it rather gothic-looking," Avendale said.

"Fits the name," Harry said.

"I never considered that as I abhor the name. To me, it shall always be Dodger's Drawing Room. Are you ready to explore it?"

"Yes, indeed."

"Gentlemen," Avendale said, before offering Rose his arm, and she realized there were two additional footmen.

As one helped Harry up the steps, the others flanked them. They were large, bulky men providing a shield. No one was going to approach Harry. She doubted anyone was going to get a good look at him. As they topped the stairs and neared the door, a footman bowed slightly. "Your Grace."

He then pulled the door open. Only she, Avendale, and Harry walked in. Her brother's face was wreathed in wonder, while Rose was surprised by the absence of a crowd, even more surprised that no one seemed to take note of their arrival.

"They're not very busy," Rose said. She did hope the business wasn't failing.

"Invitation-only tonight," Avendale said.

She looked up at him. "At your request?"

Before he could answer, Harry proclaimed, "Merrick!"

Roe turned to see Merrick, Sally, and Joseph greeting Harry. The gentlemen were dressed in evening attire as finely tailored as Harry's. Sally wore a blue silk evening gown that had not come cheaply. She smiled at Avendale. "Thank you, Your Grace, for the invitation."

"A night with friends is much more enjoyable than one without."

She gave a quick bob of a curtsy. "Also, thank you for the lovely gown. I've never had anything so fine before."

"My pleasure. And let me say that the color suits you."

Her eyes twinkling, she looked at Rose. "He sent a seamstress to the residence. And a tailor for the gents. Merrick has never looked more handsome."

"I daresay I've learned that the duke is quite generous and enjoys surprising people," Rose admitted.

Merrick walked over, stuck out his hand. "Duke."

Avendale took it, gave it a shake. "Merrick."

"Quite the place here."

"I can take no credit for that."

Joseph approached, gave him a hard look. "This is a place of improper behavior."

"It is indeed."

The man smiled. "I like that."

Avendale laughed. "As do I. To ensure you all enjoy it to its fullest, you'll find a generous amount of tokens has been set aside for your use. Anything you earn over that is yours to keep."

"Well, then," Merrick said, rubbing his hands together in glee, "we need to tempt Lady Luck to smile on us. Are you coming with us, Harry?"

"In a moment."

As the others walked off, Rose squeezed Harry's hand. "You should go off and enjoy the night with them."

"I will, I just . . ." He looked around. "No one is staring at me. No one is taking much notice at all. It's like being in a play." Shrewdly he studied Avendale. "They are your friends."

"Which makes them yours as well."

Harry's gaze darted to Rose before it settled back on the duke. He didn't look quite convinced. "But they don't know me."

"They will before the night is done."

Stepping forward, Rose laid her palm against brother's misshapen cheek. "What a wonderful thing it is that they will have the opportunity to meet you, to see you as a person and not something on display. I've no doubt they'll adore you as much as I do."

"How long will we be here?"

"Until you grow weary of the entertainment," Avendale said. "The club never closes, so we'll leave whenever you're of a mind to go. Right this moment if you want."

"No, I want to stay."

Miss Minerva Dodger, resplendent in a lilac gown, approached. "Your Grace," she said with a slight tilting of her head.

"Minerva," Avendale said. "Allow me the honor of introducing Miss Longmore and her brother, Harry."

"*Miss Longmore*," Miss Dodger said. "I suspected you weren't being quite truthful the night we met. Fortunately for you, I'm not one to judge, although I do hope you'll share your tale with me at some point."

"I fear it's rather dull," she assured her.

"Oh, I very much doubt that." Miss Dodger then turned to Harry. "Mr. Longmore, I've looked forward to making your acquaintance. My father once owned this establishment so I'm very familiar with it. I hope you will grant me the pleasure of giving you a tour."

Harry blinked, seemed too stunned to speak, and Rose suddenly regretted that there had been no marriageable women to lavish attention on him during his short life.

"Harry, you always say yes when a young lady offers you anything," Avendale explained.

Blushing, Harry visibly swallowed. "I would be most delighted, Miss Dodger."

"Excellent, but you must call me Minerva as I suspect we're going to become fast friends before the evening is done." She wrapped her hand around the crook of his arm. "I'm going to introduce you to some rapscallions who will no doubt attempt to lure you into a private card game. Play at your own peril."

Rose watched as the young woman led Harry away, chattering as she went. Her brother already seemed a bit smitten. "You have remarkable friends, Your Grace."

"I only told Harry they were mine to put him at ease. The people here tonight are more my mother's doing."

Surprised by his words, she turned to him. "You've spoken with her?"

"Faced the past, more like. I'll tell you about it later. Presently, I believe I shall introduce you to her."

Rose looked over to see Sir William approaching with a diminutive woman at his side. Although her hair was more faded than in the portraits, Rose recognized her. She possessed an elegance and refinement that Rose could never capture no matter how many hours she spent practicing in front of a mirror. Dear God, she couldn't remember the last time she'd given any thought to being something she wasn't.

Avendale hugged his mother, before straightening and bringing Rose into the cozy circle. "Mother, I'd like to introduce Miss Longmore."

"It is a pleasure, Miss Longmore."

"Your Grace, please call me Rose," she said with a curtsy.

"It's been a good many years since I've been a duchess. Lady Winifred will suffice quite nicely. I appreciate that you have given purpose to my son's life."

"I'd hardly say that although he has been most kind regarding my brother's situation."

"Life can be so unfair and we are often given not what we deserve."

"I understand that you are responsible for the kind people here this evening."

"Oh bosh. Don't make more of my efforts than they were. I merely extended invitations."

"In person," Avendale said.

"Well, yes. I've discovered it's more difficult for people to refuse a request when looking in your eyes."

"Which is how she has managed to raise an abundance of money for so many charities," Sir William said, pride evident in his voice.

She patted her husband's arm before returning her attention to Rose. "We must finish making the rounds. We look forward to making your brother's acquaintance. Although rest assured that Minerva shall ensure he has a jolly good time. I do not understand why the girl is not yet spoken for. Young men these days, sometimes they can be quite blind."

"Forgive my wife," Sir William said. "She also likes to play matchmaker."

"Only because the right match is crucial to happiness."

"Be sure to point your Cupid's arrow elsewhere," Avendale said.

His mother rose up, pressed a kiss to his cheek, and murmured in a low voice, "Only if you open your eyes, darling." Then she winked at Rose. "A pleasure, my dear. You must join us for dinner sometime. I would so love for you to meet my other children. They were desperate to come tonight, but they are still far too young for a night such as this filled with such scandalous amusements."

"Thank you, my lady. I would like to meet them." Although in truth, she knew if the woman understood Rose's role in her son's life as well as her past, she would be appalled by the notion of entertaining Rose in her home and introducing her to impressionable children.

As Sir William and his lady wandered away, Rose could not help but think they were a perfect match. "I like your mother," she said.

"She is to be admired, except when she is trying to tend to my heart."

"She loves you, wants you to be happy. That's probably what most mothers want for their children. I didn't get to experience it firsthand. You shouldn't take it for granted."

"I won't, not again, but that doesn't mean I want her meddling."

"She'll find you a proper wife."

He swung his gaze to Rose. "I'm not certain I'm suited to a proper wife."

"But you are thinking you want a wife." In spite of his claims not to want a proper wife, she also knew she was too improper to fill that place in his life.

"I'm thinking I want a drink. Let's see what we can find, shall we?"

But she was bothered by the conversation, the possible implications, needed to remind herself as much as him of her place. "You used my real name."

He'd taken two steps, stopped and looked back at her. "Pardon?"

"When you introduced me tonight it was as Miss Rosalind Longmore."

"I'm weary of the lies, the deceptions, all the blasted secrets that do nothing except cause misunderstandings and put distance between people." He stepped back to her. "Does Miss Rosalind Longmore have a bounty on her head?"

She didn't hesitate. "No." But Mrs. Rosalind Pointer did. As did Mrs. Rosalind Black.

"Then why the concern?"

"Habit, I suppose. I simply never use my real name."

"Then it's high time you did. Come now, let's find a drink, and then I want to introduce you around."

Rose began to get dizzy, overwhelmed as the introductions continued: the Earl and Countess of

Claybourne, the Duke and Duchess of Greystone, Sir James and Lady Emma, Jack Dodger and Olivia. Throughout the night, she met some of their children although she wasn't altogether certain that, if she were pressed to do it, she could have sorted them all into their proper families.

She was grateful to have a quiet moment in the balcony to catch her breath, to look down on the gaming floor and see her brother tossing dice. Those surrounding him cheered, Jack Dodger slapped him on his back. Harry's joyous laughter rang out, reached her where she stood, curled through her, warmed her.

"I'm not certain he's ever been so accepted," she said.

"He was always accepted by you."

She peered up at Avendale as much as she was able with his arms circling her, her back to his chest. "That's different. He's my brother."

"It would make little difference to some."

She didn't think she was so very special. Those who took the time to get to know Harry fell in love with him. How could they not when his was such a generous heart?

"I am torn between being at his side tonight and giving him a chance to spend the evening in the company of others."

"Let him enjoy the others for a while. Come dance with me."

She might have considered his request selfish if she weren't acutely aware that for almost a fortnight he'd been settling for scraps of her attention and time. "I would like that very much, but first . . ."

Turning in his arms, she rose up on her toes and kissed him, welcomed his drawing her nearer. She almost told him that she loved him, but she doubted he would welcome the sentiment. There was also the chance that he wouldn't believe her, that he would believe she felt obligated to voice the words because of all that he'd done. In a way all that he had done was responsible for her feelings—but only because they served as evidence of his kindness and generosity. Both of which she was discovering knew no bounds.

She had sought to take advantage of him, only to find herself falling madly in love with him.

*H*arry was overwhelmed by the night, the people, the games of chance, the astounding luck he seemed to have with them. Everyone was so kind, but it was all too much. He had met two young ladies who looked exactly alike. He couldn't remember their first names now, only their last: Swindler. Their father was an inspector with Scotland Yard, and for a moment he'd worried about Rose, but then he'd seen her strolling with her duke, and he'd known nothing would happen to her.

Still, he'd told the two ladies that he would like a moment with her, so they'd been kind enough to escort him to the ballroom. Only a few couples were dancing in the magnificent room with the gorgeous crystal chandeliers and the orchestra playing in the balcony.

Rose and her duke were on the dance floor waltzing. Harry knew the dance because Rose had once circled a room with him, shown him the steps when he was still able to walk without the cane, before he was so easily thrown off balance. Now he simply enjoyed watching the grace of her movements, the joy reflected on her face as the duke held her close. She was happy, and Rose deserved that so much.

And that made him happy. Happier than he'd ever been.

"Mr. Longmore."

His name was a soft, slow purr. Turning slightly, he saw the most beautiful woman he'd ever set eyes on. Her hair was woven from moonbeams, her eyes were sparkling sapphires. She was tall, but composed of curves. He felt the heat warm his face because he noticed the dips and swells. The duke wouldn't grow warm like this. The duke would merely look until he was content. No, his friend would take her to the shadows and hold her, kiss her. Harry wanted to do the same. He was embarrassed, ashamed that he would have such a thought. She would no doubt scream if he got too close.

She smiled, joy wreathing her face as she met and held his gaze. "I've been searching some time for you."

"Have you?" he croaked, wondering what had happened to his voice to make it go so deep, so rough.

"Indeed I have. I'm Aphrodite."

He wasn't surprised she was named for a goddess. He envisioned her in a diaphanous gown, the wind swirling around only her as though the rest of the world didn't require gentle breezes. She was worthy of poetry, and words began flittering through his mind.

"Will you dance with me?" she asked.

The poetic words, all thought stopped. He wanted what she asked for more than he wanted to breathe, but no choice remained except to shake his head with regret. "I'm sorry, but I can't. I might lose my balance." And the wonderful night would be ruined as everyone witnessed his clumsiness at its worse. He would no longer be able to pretend he wasn't a great oaf.

"I'm extremely skilled at ensuring men don't lose their balance." She moved in, placed one delicate hand lightly on his shoulder, another on his arm, on his hideous arm, but she appeared not at all revolted. "We don't have to follow the music. We can just sway if you like."

He liked it very much, liked her nearness. She smelled of oranges.

"Are you a friend of the duke?" he asked.

"Sometimes. But tonight I'm your friend."

Harry was relatively certain it was because the duke had asked her to be. The duke had answered a good many of Harry's questions regarding women, but each discovery led to another question until he felt as though he were being swallowed in a vortex where a thousand queries swirled, waiting for him to pluck out the next. The duke had assured him that if he lived to be a hundred, he'd never uncover all the answers.

"Women are a mystery, my friend, which only serves to make us want them all the more," the duke had said.

At long last, while swaying extremely slowly with this woman incredibly near, her breasts brushing against his chest, her long, slender legs in danger of becoming entangled with his, Harry finally understood what the duke had been striving to teach him. That no one question, no one answer applied to every woman. Each woman was unique, each provided a very different experience. He knew so little about Aphrodite, but he discovered he wanted to know everything, but already he knew that a lifetime wouldn't provide all the answers.

But there were certainly adventures to be had in trying to uncover them.

*D*ancing with Avendale was different from when she'd danced with him the first night when they'd met. She was as aware of him, but she wasn't frightened that he would discover her secrets, that he had the power to ruin all her plans. Before he'd been an enigma, a curiosity, a possible means to an end. She had wanted to use him.

Now she wished there had never been any deception between them, no bargains struck. She wished that she had trusted him sooner, that they had come to where they were through mutual wants. On the other hand, she was pragmatic enough to realize that she would never be more than an ornament in his life.

While those closest to him might have been bold enough to cast societal rules aside and marry those not of their class, Avendale would want nothing to do with her if he understood the full extent of her deceptions and swindles. Oh, he might still want her plump breasts and sweet thighs, he might still yearn to skim his hands over every inch of her flesh, he might still desire her body cradled beneath his, but he wouldn't want her for a wife. He would tire of her eventually.

And she would tire of the life he provided. Not that she didn't appreciate all the comforts, but her daily routine would offer no challenges—just pleasing him, doing whatever he wanted, even if what he desired was exactly what she wished to bestow. She would grow bored without her plotting and conniving.

When the time came for them to part all she would have were the memories. The wonderful, glorious, marvelous memories. The way his eyes never strayed from hers as they waltzed. The slight smile that promised another sort of waltz later in the night, in his bed, where the music would be a crescendo of their moans, sighs, and cries.

Oh, she was going to miss him. While she knew it could be years before that came to pass, she could not help but believe that their parting was going to come much too soon.

He circled her around the floor, and out of the corner of her eye, she caught sight of Harry in a beauty's arms. Dancing—at least as much as he was able. Her heart tightened, swelled at the pleasure written on his face, and yet she worried that the woman might ask more of him than he could deliver.

"Who is that woman dancing with Harry?" she asked.

Avendale didn't even bother to look to the side, so she knew he must have been aware of their presence. For how long? she wondered.

"Her name is Aphrodite."

"Truly?"

He shrugged. "Probably not. Just as you are not Mrs. Sharpe. People change their names for all sorts of reasons, so I wouldn't judge her too harshly if I were you."

"I'm not judging her, but I do want to ensure she doesn't take advantage of Harry."

"Oh, I suspect he wouldn't mind if she did."

"Is she the sort who would?"

"With the proper incentive."

"Which you no doubt provided. Is she one of the charities you've given to over the years?" She despised the jealousy that rifled through her voice.

He gave her an understanding smile and that irritated her even more. "She is one of the women with whom I grew bored, even though she is remarkably talented and quite free with her affections."

In his voice, his tone, she heard no lingering desire for this Aphrodite. He might as well be explaining how a gentleman put on his trousers. Still, she had come to understand his relationship with her brother well enough to know the incentive behind the woman's appearance. "You brought her here to entertain Harry."

"He's a man, Rose. We talked about a good many things late at night in my library. He's curious about women. It seemed a sin for his curiosity not to be sated." He pinned her with a daring stare. "You said you trusted me."

"I do. I'm just not certain if I can trust her."

"She has a heart of gold."

As she glanced over, she saw that Harry had stopped dancing, that he and the woman were leaving the ballroom, arm in arm. "What if she hurts him?"

"What if the building crumbles in on top of us?"

She jerked her gaze back to Avendale. He gave her a gentle smile, one she'd never seen, one that captured her heart, squeezed it. "You can't always protect him, sweetheart. Let him be a man tonight, enjoy the pleasures found in the company of a willing woman."

"It hurts so to grow up."

"I know. I spent years of my life trying not to. But for all its pain, there are rewards aplenty."

Reaching up, she cupped his jaw, feathered her fingers through his hair. Sometimes she wished she hadn't grown up at such a young age, been forced to run off and survive by any means possible, but then if she hadn't, she might have never met him. There would have always been something missing in her life. She would have felt its absence without truly understanding what it was. This man had taught her what it was to share a goal with someone, to work together, to have a common bond. "Where my brother is concerned, you think of so many things that he might want or need that never occurred to me."

"He's your baby brother. You would protect him with your dying breath. For me, he's a reminder of youth, how fleeting it is, often filled with unfortunate choices and yet some of them provide us with the best memories. And he's someone with whom I can share all the wicked things I've done through the years. He's replaced Lovingdon as my partner in debauchery."

"You've proven my point," she said. "Do you know how much it would please him to know that you hold him in such esteem? It would make him feel ever so manly, ever so accepted."

"Perhaps you can tell him later. Meanwhile, let's finish the dance, then find a darkened corner. I'm in want of another kiss."

And she fell just a little bit further in love with him.

It was half past one when Rose found Harry sitting in the gentlemen's parlor with Merrick, Sally, and Joseph. And Aphrodite. She sat beside him on the sofa, holding his good hand, stroking it with her long, slender fingers, while her smile radiated warmth and gentleness. When Harry looked at her, Rose could see that he, too, had fallen a little bit in love.

"Is it time to go?" Harry asked.

It might have sounded like an inquiry to the others, but she heard the weariness in his voice, knew that he was ready to leave—no matter how desperately he might wish to stay. She also knew that he had no desire to hurt anyone's feelings, that he didn't want their leaving to be on him. So she took on the responsibility. "I'm afraid it is," she said kindly. "It's quite late, my feet hurt, and I'm dreadfully tired."

He turned his attention to Aphrodite. "I have to leave now."

She cupped his face, kissed his cheek. "Thank you for a lovely evening."

Rising with grace and elegance, she began to walk away. Avendale stopped her and exchanged hushed words that Rose couldn't decipher.

Sally got out of her chair and gave Harry a hug where he was sitting. "Thanks, duck, for the fun evening. We miss having you with us, but what adventures you've been on."

"They've been the best, Sally, but I've missed you, too."

"We'll come see you for dinner tomorrow," Merrick said as he clapped him on the shoulder.

Harry nodded, although his movements seemed more laborious and slow. "Yes, all right. That would be grand."

Joseph stood and helped Harry to his feet. He merely gave Harry a sharp bob of his head, which Harry returned before walking over to Rose. "I'm ready."

Avendale was waiting for them at the door that led into the main gambling salon. When they arrived, Rose saw the gauntlet of people—footmen, croupiers, musicians, commoners, and nobles—queued up across the gaming room until they reached the entrance.

"They'd like to say good night," Avendale said.

And so they did. The gentlemen shook his hand, the women kissed him on the cheek or gave him a hug. Kind words flowed.

"Lovely to meet you."

"Thank you for joining us."

"Pleasure."

"Take care."

Rose thought she would never, ever be able to thank Avendale enough for the gift of this evening. No matter what she promised him, no matter what he asked, it would never be enough.

They were quiet in the coach as they traveled home. Rose was absorbing the night. She suspected Harry was doing the same. Gerald was waiting in the foyer when they arrived.

"Master Harry, I take it you had an entertaining evening."

"I did." He looked at Rose. "I would like a drink, though."

"Didn't you have enough at the club?"

He nodded. "But I want one more with you, with you and the duke."

"My library or yours?" Avendale asked.

"Mine."

They walked down the hallway to Harry's smaller library. Gerald saw to it that a small fire was burning in the hearth.

"Ring for me when you're ready for bed, sir," Gerald said.

"I will," Harry promised. "Thank you, Gerald, for everything."

"It is my utmost pleasure, sir." Back straight and stiff, he strode from the room.

"Here, Harry," Rose said, tugging on his jacket. "Let's get you comfortable while Avendale pours the drinks." She helped him out of his jacket, unbuttoned his waistcoat, loosened his neck cloth. "Go ahead and take a chair."

"A gentleman—"

"I know what a gentleman does, but you're my brother, and I can see how weary you are. Sit."

He didn't argue further, but dropped into the large plush chair. Avendale brought over their drinks and guided Rose to the settee. She watched as her brother slowly drank his scotch, seemed to savor it.

"Did you enjoy yourself tonight, sweeting?" she asked.

"Very much indeed." He nodded toward Avendale. "I like them all, your friends. Especially Aphrodite. Even though I know you paid her to keep me company."

"I offered. She refused. Seems she's never met anyone she likes more than she likes you. Perhaps she can keep you company some afternoon."

"I would like that."

"I'll send word to her tomorrow."

Rose wasn't going to worry that Harry might be disappointed, that tonight's attentions had been merely a result of the occasion. He possessed an innocence, a charm that would appeal to the most hardened woman.

"When you do, address the missive to Annie," Harry said.

"Who the deuce is Annie?" Avendale asked.

"That's her true name."

Grinning, Avendale bowed his head slightly and lifted his glass, a warrior saluting an opponent who had bested him. "She never shared that with me. I'd say she liked you a great deal."

Harry blushed, but looked remarkably pleased

with himself. He was also extremely tired. Rose could see it in the slump of his shoulders, the listing of his head to one side.

"We should let you get some sleep." As she rose to her feet, so did he. "We shall all sleep late in the morning. It's what one does after a night such as this."

"It was a wonderful gift, Rose. A wonderful gift. For one night, I was normal."

She hugged him hard. "To me, you're always normal. I love you, Harry."

She felt the squeeze of his arms. "I love you, Rose."

Leaning back, she smiled up at him. "Sleep well, my dearest."

"I will." Then he shook Avendale's hand. "Good night, my friend."

"Good night, Harry. I'll have Gerald sent in."

"Not yet. I'm going to write for a bit. I'll ring for him when I need him."

"As you wish. We'll see you tomorrow."

Reaching out, Rose squeezed Harry's hand. She didn't know why she was so reluctant to leave him. She might not have if Avendale's arm hadn't come around her, propelling her forward.

"The evening tired him out," she said as they headed for the foyer and the stairs leading to his bed-chamber.

"I believe it tired us all out."

"Not completely," she said, as she nestled against him. "I have enough energy left for you to tell me about your visit with your mother. I rather liked her."

"The next time she invites me to dinner, we'll go."

She released a weary laugh. "I can't go into your mother's home, sit at her table. I'm a criminal."

"As were a good many of the people you met

tonight—at one time or another. One can change, Rose."

"Not our past, not what is already done."

"I wish you would tell me everything you've done."

"Not now." Never, if she had her way. "I don't want to ruin what has been a lovely night."

"But for us it is not quite over." He lifted her into his arms and carried her up the stairs.

After dipping the pen into the inkwell, Harry scrawled out the final words, the ones that belonged at the front of the story but that he had waited until last to write. He was finished, in more ways than one. Glad to be done. Glad to have the story written. Sad about it as well, for now he had no purpose.

As he did every night, he wrote a letter to Rose and set it on top of the pages—

Just in case.

Chapter 21

Avendale had slept only a couple of hours when he awoke with Rose snuggled against him. He didn't want to disturb her, but he couldn't resist the temptation to skim his hand lightly up and down the bared skin of her arm. She didn't stir. She'd been so worried about Harry being exhausted that she'd overlooked the fact that she was as well.

With a lamp on the bedside table still burning, he was able to look down on her profile. How was it that she considered her features unremarkable? How was it that he had the first time he'd spied her?

If he were honest, he had to acknowledge that an armada of ships would never sail to reclaim her for her beauty, but they might damned well sail to reclaim her for her courage, her grit, her determination, her unwillingness to be cowed. She always stood her ground with him. He wasn't certain he'd ever met a woman more his equal.

And dammit all to bloody hell, he'd fallen in love with her.

Probably that first night when she had turned to refuse the champagne he was offering. He'd recognized the refusal in her eyes before she'd assessed him, the acceptance afterward. Or perhaps it had been when she'd told him that she held all the cards. Such cocky confidence.

He loved that aspect to her. No mewling miss.

He had begun to fall in love with her long before he knew the truth about her, but when he had uncovered her secrets, his feelings for her had merely cemented. Would she honor the bargain to its full extent? If he wanted her with him forever, would she be willing to stay that long?

Or had she made the bargain expecting their time together to be short?

A soft rap on the door stopped him from driving himself mad with the questions and speculations. Easing out of bed, he snatched up his silk robe and drew it on as he padded to the door. Opening it, he found Gerald standing there. The man's face said it all.

"Your Grace—"

"It's all right. I'll be down shortly." Closing the door, he pressed his forehead to the wood. Why did it hurt so much? If only he could spare Rose—

"Is it Harry?" she asked softly.

Glancing over his shoulder, he saw her sitting up in bed, the covers clutched to her chest. "I'm so sorry, Rose."

Pressing her lips into a straight line, she nodded. "Right. There are things that will need to be done."

She tossed back the covers. He crossed over, sat on the edge of the bed, gently folded his hands over her shoulders to still her actions. "You've kept an upper lip for years, I suspect ever since you were accused of dropping your brother. You don't have to keep an upper lip for me."

She shook her head. "Avendale . . ."

He held her gaze. "You don't have to put on a show of being strong for me."

"If I don't," she rasped, "I shall fall apart."

"I'll catch you and help you put yourself back to-gether."

Tears began welling in her eyes. A loud, harsh sob that sounded as though it came from the pit of her soul broke free. Then another. Another. Holding her tightly as her shoulders shook with the force of her grief, he rocked her and cooed her name.

While his own heart broke at her anguish.

*H*arry looked at peace. That was what Rose thought as she sat on a footstool beside the chair where her brother had begun the journey for his final rest. She'd been holding his hand for nearly half an hour now. For at least twice that, she had wept within Aven-dale's embrace.

She would have to send word to Merrick and the others, but she was not yet prepared to pen the mis-sive. No, she wouldn't write them. She would tell them in person. They had loved Harry nearly as much as she had. He had loved them.

"Rose, the coroner is here," Avendale said quietly, yet firmly.

Nodding, she got to her feet, leaned over, and pressed a kiss to Harry's forehead. "No more boul-ders, my love. No more pain. But oh how you shall be missed."

She looked at Avendale. "I should go see Merrick now."

"I need to show you something first." With his arm around her shoulders, he led her from her brother's bedchamber to the small library where Harry had written, read, and indulged in spirits.

"I do hope he finished his story," she said.

"I believe he did."

He escorted her to the desk. On top of the neat stack of papers was a folded piece of parchment with her name on it. Very carefully she opened it.

My dearest Rose,

For some time now I have written a letter to you every night. In the morning, if it was not needed, I would burn it. I suppose that if you are reading this one that it was needed.

The life I shared with you has come to a close. I will not be so selfish as to ask you not to weep, but I do hope that you will also smile. For I have gone to that beautiful place with the beautiful people you used to tell me about.

I know you believe that life was not kind to me, but it was, you see, because it gave me you.

I finished my story, Rose. Last night in the wee hours. Although it is really our story, perhaps even more your story, which is why I wanted the duke to read it. I think you love him. I also think he loves you, although I am not sure he is a man who would voice the words. You wouldn't believe them if he did. I do not know why you always thought yourself unlovable, while I—as hideous as I was— never considered myself so. But then I always had your love and was able to view myself through your eyes. I wish I could have done the same for you.

Please thank the duke for the grand time I had in his company. He gave me so many gifts but best of all, he gave me his friendship. That above all else, I treasured and took with me. That and your love. Hopefully mine stayed with you.

Read the book now, Rose.

Always,
Harry

Without glancing at Avendale, Rose folded up the paper and stuffed it into her pocket. Harry was wrong about Avendale loving her. He hadn't known about the bargain she had struck with the duke. "He treasured your friendship."

"As I did his."

She really hadn't expected them to get along so famously. Looking down at the stack of papers, she touched her fingers to it. "He said he finished."

"I thought he was close to the end. He asked me to return to him what he'd given me. I assumed he wanted to put it all together. Are you going to read it?"

She looked at the title written in his perfect penmanship. He'd always been so proud of it. "He said I should read it now."

She moved the first page away, and tears filled her eyes as she read the words.

This story is dedicated to my sister, my perfect Rose.

She shook her head. "I was not perfect."

"To him you were."

Stepping into Avendale's embrace, she welcomed his arms closing around her and wondered if a time would ever come when her heart would not ache.

Chapter 22

*O*ver the next few days the ache did lessen as Avendale's staff took the time to offer her their condolences. Merrick, Sally, and Joseph wept almost as much as she did. They were with her in the parlor when those who had been part of their night at the Twin Dragons had stopped by. Those who had managed the games, played the music, served the food. Then all of Avendale's family, friends, and acquaintances who had been there that evening. They spoke fondly of their time with Harry, shared parts of the night that Rose hadn't realized had occurred—card games and laughter. He had been in their lives but a short while and yet it seemed he'd left an indelible mark never to be forgotten.

Rose thought it a lovely legacy.

Harry was laid to rest in a garden cemetery surrounded by beauty. She was not surprised, as Avendale had seen to the arrangements. It seemed where her brother was concerned he was determined not to spare any expense.

When she wept, he comforted her. When she couldn't sleep, he held her. When she walked the gardens, he provided an arm upon which she could lean. One day rolled over into the next until a fortnight had passed, and she knew it was time that she forced away the melancholy. She had made a pact with Avendale to be with him however he wanted for as long as he wanted. Surely he didn't want this mourning woman.

She was standing in front of the fountain when she heard the footfalls over the cobblestones. Glancing at Avendale, she smiled. In spite of her sadness, she was always glad to see him, although for some strange reason he was carrying the silver bowl littered with invitations that usually remained in the foyer.

"Enjoying the fountain?" he asked.

"It is odd, but my favorite memories of Harry occurred while he was in your residence. Every aspect of it reminds me of him. You truly went above and beyond to make his final days grand. I'm not certain I'd ever seen him smile so much. I don't know how to thank you."

"I don't want your gratitude," he said gruffly.

"Yet still you have it." She nodded toward the bowl. "What are you doing with that? I've never seen you give it a glance."

"While I've seen you give it a hundred. Every time we go into the foyer, your gaze darts over to it. And I've wondered: Is it the beauty of the bowl that fascinates you or what it holds?"

The beauty of what it contained: to have so many who wanted him in their lives. Did he even grasp how precious that was? "You receive countless invitations, and yet you ignore them all."

"Perhaps it's time I stopped."

She thought she could hear each drop of water pinging into the fountain. Not that she blamed him for having enough of her. She wasn't keeping to their bargain by giving him what he wanted, because surely he didn't want the sad creature she'd become.

"You'll send mothers' hearts a-fluttering with the hope that you're searching for a wife." While her own might cease to beat.

"I'm not searching for a wife but rather something that might bring you some happiness. Have you ever been to a ball, other than the one at the Twin Dragons?"

The lie hung on her tongue but she couldn't spit it out. "I've attended country dances, but I suspect they pale in comparison to a ball hosted by someone in the aristocracy."

He extended the bowl. "Pluck out an invitation and it's the one we'll accept."

Scoffing, she rolled her eyes at him. "You can't take me to a ball."

"Why not?"

"For one thing I'm in mourning."

"Which Harry would heartily disapprove of. You would know that if you read his book. Have you even started it?"

"I can't. It's too soon."

"Trust me, then. He would be sorely disappointed." He shook the bowl.

"Avendale, this is wrong on so many levels. I'm your mistress."

"I don't think of you as such."

"Lovers?" she asked pointedly.

"I can't deny that."

"Semantics, then, because they are one in the same."

"People take their lovers all the time."

"With a past as wretchedly filled with deceit as mine?"

"Why do you keep flaying yourself with the past?"

"I know what it is, I know what I've done." Taking a deep breath, she held his gaze. "I know who I am."

He skimmed his fingers over her cheek. "I know you as well, know how stubborn you are. I won't push you on this, but I've decided you should have a new gown anyway. Don't bother to protest that you're in mourning. You promised to do anything I wanted, so the black must go. I want to see you in red again. Something new and vibrant. We'll leave for the seamstress in half an hour."

With that, he turned on his heel and marched off, leaving her to stare after him. Stubborn man. Blast him for using the bargain against her. Still, a thread of excitement thrummed through her, a sense of being alive again. She looked back at the fountain, at the couple lost in a heated embrace.

Perhaps tonight she would dance in the cascading water.

While the coach traveled through the streets, Avendale sat across from Rose, which gave him a clear and enticing view of her. He was glad to see that some color had returned to her cheeks. She wasn't one to care about acquiring things for herself—otherwise she would have snapped up the jewelry he gave her—but he did think it was doing her some good to get out of the residence.

She would always miss her brother. There was no hope for otherwise. Damnation, but he missed Harry, so he knew it was far worse for her. He was always listening for the echo of a walking stick meeting the parquet flooring, the shuffling of large feet. He waited for the welcome interruption that would never come again.

Strange, the influence that one person could make in such a short time.

Although he didn't know why he was surprised. It hadn't taken Rose long to have absolute sway over him. He loved her. It was an emotion he'd never thought to experience, and sometimes he wished he didn't because it brought with it as much pain as it did joy. He hurt when she hurt. When sorrow visited her, it visited him. But when she smiled, it was as though that smile encompassed his entire body, his entire being. He would do whatever was required to return the smiles to her—even if it meant taking her to a boring ball.

It had pleased him to discover that he'd accurately read the longing in her gaze whenever she looked at the silver bowl. He could give her an incredible life, filled with balls, dinners, and elegance. Yet he suspected that for her one ball would be enough. Then she would again yearn for freedom.

"I needed this outing, I think," she finally said. "I feel as though I can breathe again, as though the oppressive weight of grief is lifting."

"You do seem a bit perkier."

"What woman doesn't perk up at the thought of a new gown?"

"You don't."

She blushed. "You read me too well, even better than Harry did."

"I've had considerable practice. I suspect you lied to me more than you did to him."

"Only when necessary. But you're right. I've always viewed clothing as a tool, going for something that would serve as a distraction. Now I want something that pleases you. It'll be a new experience."

"I've never watched a woman be fitted for a gown."

"And you won't today. I want to surprise you." She arched a brow. "It will be red, but other than that you'll have to wait until I'm ready to wear it. So you'll need to entertain yourself elsewhere this afternoon."

He would do so by purchasing something for her. Not that he was going to tell her that. She wasn't the only one wanting to provide a surprise.

"I suspect Merrick and the others will need to seek employment," he said casually.

She tilted up the corners of her lips, and in her smile he saw understanding and assurance. "Yes. I need to speak with them, explain that I won't be providing for them anymore. It's time for them to make their own way again, although I suspect they know it. It was Harry that kept us together. While they saw to his care, I was more than happy to see after their needs. But he doesn't need their care anymore."

"The lease on the residence is paid for two more months."

Her eyes widened in surprise. "When did you do that?"

He lifted a shoulder. "In the beginning. I didn't want you to feel as though you had to run off immediately after our original bargain was met."

Her smile grew. "They'll appreciate it. You might win Merrick over yet."

"Not my goal." Keeping her happy was.

𝒲hen the coach came to a halt, Rose was surprised by the anticipation humming through her. As Avendale handed her down, she took a moment to glance around—

Trepidation sliced through her as she saw a man

emerge from a hansom cab, but she kept her expression neutral, her smile soft. Not too big, not too small. Just right.

Give nothing away. Not to Avendale, not to the man, not to anyone passing by.

"There's a bookshop nearby," Avendale said. "I'll browse through there for a while, be back in an hour for you. Will that be enough time?"

"It should be plenty."

He turned for the coach.

"Avendale?"

He looked back at her.

"All you've done for me, for Harry, means everything to me." *You mean everything to me.* But she couldn't leave those words with him. He'd think they were a lie, and she didn't want him thinking their final words of parting were a lie.

"Rose—"

"I know you don't want my gratitude, but you have it all the same." Rising up on her toes, she brushed a kiss over his lips. He couldn't have looked more taken aback if she'd disrobed on the crowded street. She gave him a saucy smile. "I couldn't resist. I'll see you in a bit."

Wishing she could have given him a more heartfelt and proper good-bye, she strolled into the shop and stood at the window until the coach disappeared from view. Knowing she would never see him again caused a harsh ache in the center of her chest. She turned to the proprietor. "Is there a back way out?"

The dark-haired woman arched a brow. "Trouble with your lover?"

So the woman had seen the kiss. Not that it mattered. Rose was never going to see her again. "A bit. Can you help me?"

"I shouldn't. Avendale is a powerful man."

"You know him?"

"He asked me to make a ball gown for a very small woman. He seems to have quite diverse tastes in women."

Rose didn't have time for this, for denying or confirming such an accusation. Glancing back out the window, she saw the man leaning against a lamppost studying his nails. Straightening her spine, she delivered her most formidable look. "I'm powerful as well. I'll find my way."

As she went through to the back, she ignored the women stitching away, the one woman being measured. The door came into sight. Without hesitation Rose went through it and into the alley. She hurried down it until she reached a street, turned—

And slammed into a brick wall. Arms banded around her and she dropped her head back to stare at a mouth curled up into an insidious smile.

"Well, if it ain't Mrs. Pointer."

"Mr. Tinsdale. I don't suppose you'd unhand me?"

He unwound his beefy arms but his large hand immediately wrapped painfully around her wrist, not that she was about to give him satisfaction by crying out, but with the tiniest pressure he could snap her bone in two. "How did you know where to find me?"

"With your brother's death, the others weren't so careful with their comings and goings as they sought to comfort you and themselves. I even followed you all to the cemetery. Once I figured out where you were, I just had to bide my time until the big bloke weren't around. You were living quite swell. But now you're mine."

As Avendale browsed the books, he realized that he didn't know what sort of story Rose preferred.

He would have liked to purchase her a book, but suspected most of her selections were based on her brother's preferences. Better to go with jewelry. Something simple this time. A cameo. A brooch. A choker. A ring.

The possibilities tumbled through his mind as he left the shop and climbed into his coach. It hadn't been quite an hour since he left Rose, but arriving early might provide the opportunity to catch a glimpse of what she wanted in a gown. He imagined it would be less revealing, a little more demure. She had no reason to distract him now.

Not that she could if she tried. He was on to her, knew her moods, her movements, her expressions. In the days following Harry's death, an honesty had developed between them, a bond had strengthened. He'd never known anything like it. She could rely on him wholeheartedly. He wanted to be there for her— during the good times and the bad.

The coach drew to a halt and he leaped out as soon as the door was opened. He strode into the shop, surprised not to see Rose looking over fabric samples.

"Your Grace," the proprietor said, with a small curtsy.

"Mrs. Ranier, I've come for Miss Longmore."

"She is not here, Your Grace."

"Did you finish up quickly then?"

"We did not even begin. She came in through the front door, departed through the back one, with hardly two minutes in between."

Surely he'd not heard properly; the woman wasn't communicating well. "She left through the back?"

"Yes. She implied she was having trouble with her lover. I assumed she meant you as I saw the kiss just beyond my windows. Quite scandalous."

He took a step toward her, not certain what his expression conveyed, but she hopped back. "Are you telling me that she came in here and immediately left, using the alleyway?"

"I am, Your Grace."

He almost asked her why, but the woman wouldn't know. Although he did. *Help me make whatever time my brother has left as pleasant as possible. Afterward, you can ask anything of me and I'll comply. I'll stay with you as long as you want.* She'd even offered to sign her name in blood. She'd turned to him in her hour of need and he'd been fool enough to fall for her lies. It was inconceivable, unconscionable that she would swindle him again—

But she had, damn her.

"Where is she?"

Avendale had barged into Rose's residence and cornered Merrick in the parlor.

"Who?" Merrick asked.

"Rose. Who else would I be looking for?"

"Ack! What are you doing?" Sally asked as she entered the room, and he swung around at her, irritated that she scrambled back as though his anger were directed at her when it was all for Rose.

"Rose ran off this afternoon. I want to know where I'd find her."

"Ran off? That makes no sense."

"You haven't seen her?"

She wrung her hands. "Not since poor Harry was laid to rest. Why would she leave?"

He took a deep breath, expelled it, studied both Merrick and Sally. They seemed confounded. Maybe she hadn't left him. Maybe—but why go out through the back?

"You love her," Sally said.

He might have, but now . . . dammit all to hell, he still did.

"We had an agreement. She was supposed to—" He broke off the words because they sounded silly, childish. She was supposed to stay with him. When he'd never declared his feelings, his love, his admiration of her. When he had never truly trusted that she would stay.

"She's free now," Merrick said. "With Harry gone."

"Merrick!" Sally scolded. "Don't say such things."

"But it's true." He came to stand in front of Avendale. "She loved him. We all loved him. But she never had a chance to be a girl, not really. To be carefree. She always had the responsibility of him, from when she was a child from what I understand. You can't know what a burden that was."

Only he did know. He'd read Harry's writings. Maybe she'd run off to be with that stupid factory worker in Manchester. She'd known she was leaving, when she'd kissed him publicly on the street outside the seamstress shop. He could see it now, in retrospect, in her voice, her eyes. He thought he'd learned how to read her, that she could never swindle him again. She was an incredible actress and he was more the fool.

"If she comes here—" What, what was he going to do? Force her to stay with him? "Tell her to knock on the servants' door at my residence, and Edith will deliver her things. She won't have to see me." And he wouldn't have the opportunity to beg her to stay.

*A*vendale sat in a chair by the fireplace in the library and tried to drink himself into oblivion. One moment he was cursing Rose to perdition and the next he was in danger of going in search of her.

She hadn't come here to get her things. How was she going to survive with only the clothes on her back? Why hadn't she just told him that she wanted to leave? Because he had made asinine comments about going after her if she left. She must have felt like a prisoner, mourning not only Harry but the complete loss of her freedom, of choice.

"Your Grace," Thatcher said.

He lifted his head. He'd gotten out of the habit of locking the damned door when he wanted to be left in peace. "What is it, Thatcher? Can't you see I'm indisposed?" Or would be soon if he had his way.

"Inspector Swindler has come to call."

Swindler? What the devil did he want? A husband for one of his daughters? "Tell him I'm not at home."

"I'm not certain that's an option, sir. He says he's here on Scotland Yard business."

A fissure of unease ratcheted through him. After downing what remained in his glass, he set it aside and stood. "Yes, all right. Send him in." He counted the seconds—twelve—before Swindler strode into the room. "Swindler."

"Your Grace."

"How might I be of service?"

"I fear I'm the bearer of bad tidings. Miss Longmore has been arrested and charged with theft, deliberately misleading merchants into believing she would pay for items bought on credit, and for deceiving more than one person regarding her true nature."

Avendale stared at him dumfounded. "When . . . how?"

"This afternoon. A gentleman brought her in, collected the reward—"

"There was a reward offered for her capture?"

He shrugged, sighed. "She has left quite a trail of unhappy folk."

Was it possible that she hadn't been running away from Avendale but had been trying to outfox this man who might have been after her? Guilt gnawed at him because he hadn't trusted her, because he'd thought the worst. "Make this go away."

"I can't. She's not denying any of the accusations. As a matter of fact, she willingly confessed to them all."

Avendale charged across the room, heading for the door. "I must see her."

"I thought as much."

*R*ose sat at a table in a small room, alone with little except her thoughts. They traveled the road of regret. She'd been so young when she began walking this path, had thought it the only one she could successfully traverse. Perhaps Merrick had been correct, and she should have sought another way, but it had been easier to carry on as she'd begun.

At least Harry hadn't witnessed her downfall. Avendale would no doubt think she'd simply run off. No, he wouldn't think that. He would worry until he saw the account of her arrest in the newspaper. It was bound to be news. Then those she'd swindled would descend like avenging demons wanting a pound of her flesh, leaving her with no way to adequately repay Avendale for all he'd done for Harry.

The door opened and Inspector Swindler strode in. He'd questioned her earlier—

Avendale followed on the heels of the inspector. Her breath caught, the air backing up painfully in her lungs. She should have known the inspector would alert him. They were connected by some strange sort of history.

Swindler closed the door, then stood in front of it, arms folded over his chest. Avendale pulled out the chair opposite her and sat.

"Are you faring all right?" he asked.

A silly question considering her circumstances, but still she nodded when she desperately wanted to reach out and cradle his face, assure him that she'd had every intention of honoring their bargain.

"Inspector Swindler has explained your situation to me." He set a piece of paper in front of her. Several names were scrawled over it. "These are the people who claim that you . . ."

His voice trailed off as though he found the word unpleasant. She supposed it was one thing to know that in the beginning she'd been dishonest with him. Another entirely to see the evidence of all her transgressions spelled out in such neat script.

"Swindled," she said briskly, finding the word repugnant on her tongue, not blaming him for feeling the same. "The word for which you're searching is swindled. Or perhaps fleeced."

"Is this all of them?"

She heard the temper scoring his tone. She wanted him mad, angry, hating her. It would be easier for them both that way. "What difference does it make?"

"I need to ensure that everyone is paid what they are owed so this doesn't happen again."

He might as well have hit her with a battering ram. Just when she thought it was impossible to love him any more than she already did, he did something like this that made her love him all the more. She blinked back the tears stinging her eyes and threatening to make their presence known. But she could not resist

the temptation to lay her hand over his in order to
soften the blow of her words. "This is not your debt
to pay."

"Now is not the time to quibble."

But it was. She would hold firm on this. She would
not allow him to save her when she was not worthy
of being saved. Sitting back, she merely studied him.
She knew every line, every curve, every sharp edge of
his face. She would miss seeing them in the future.

"Rose—"

"No." She wouldn't succumb to his pleas.

The dark eyes that had so often warmed with passion when he gazed on her now turned brittle and
hard. The jaw she had so often kissed jutted out with
his anger. His nostrils flared. "We had a bargain,
you and I," he ground out. "You would do all that I
wanted for as long as I wanted. I want you to give me
every name until I have them all."

"You can't fix this."

"I can. Once they are paid, they will drop the
charges."

She laughed. "I'm a criminal, Avendale. Accept it.
Let it go. But I do have a favor to ask."

"No. You won't give me what I want. Why the
bloody hell should I do something else for you?"

Because he cared for her. He wouldn't be here if he
didn't. She didn't know if what he felt was as deep as
love, but it was something. In spite of his anger, his
harsh refusal, somehow she knew he would do this
for her. "Take my trunk to Merrick. There's a secret
compartment. He knows how to access it. He'll find
the five thousand there. He and the others are to use
it to begin their lives anew."

"And what of your life?"

"I always knew that eventually it would end here.

The guilt over what I'd done weighed so heavily—as heavily as the boulders that poor Harry had to carry. I'm relieved, really, that it's over. I do regret that I was not able to hold to my end of the bargain I made with you. I came to care for you."

"Then tell me what I need to know."

"And then what? We carry on as though nothing happened? Do you not think this will make the newspapers? Tinsdale will see to it, otherwise those who hired him to find me will not pay him. So your mother will know the sort of woman who has been cavorting with her son. And your friends? Do you think they will be pleased to know that a woman who had no compunction whatsoever about taking things and not paying for them sat among them, laughed with them, and took their money? They will be appalled, as well they should be."

"I don't give a bloody damn! I love you."

She felt as though the noose were already about her neck and the trap door sprung. He closed his mouth tightly, squeezed his eyes shut.

"You can't," she whispered.

He opened his eyes, resignation swimming within the dark depths. "I do. I have for some time now."

She scoffed, released a quick burst of laughter. He loved her. She wanted to curl against him, hold him near, but she had to protect him. She couldn't allow him to ruin his life for her. "What a fool you are. I swear, Avendale, you have been my most successful swindle yet. Dear God, you probably had plans to marry me, have applied for the license."

"Don't, Rose."

"Don't what? Be honest with you? From the beginning you were my mark. I lied to you that first night at the Twin Dragons and I have lied to you ever since about everything except Harry. Do you really think that I was going to stay with you, do whatever you wanted, for however long you wanted? I said those words because I knew you would respond to them, just as you respond to my touch. I never planned to stay for overly long."

"You're lying."

"Am I? Ask the seamstress. I walked in, I walked out. I wasn't going to order a gown to wear for you. I was ready to move on. Unfortunately, before I could hail a cab, I ran into Tinsdale."

"How were you going to pay for this cab? You didn't have the five thousand with you."

"As I pay for all things. With promises."

"I don't believe you."

"Be that as it may, they are the most honest words I've ever said to you."

Eyes narrowed, jaw taut, he studied her. "Have it your way then." He stood. "I'll have the trunk delivered to Merrick."

"Thank you."

"This isn't over between us."

But it was. He had to see that. He headed for the door.

"Avendale, one more favor."

He stopped, turned, and her heart nearly broke at the look of stoicism on his face.

"Please don't attend my trial," she said quietly.

He gave a brusque nod before walking out of the room. With his leaving, she felt herself wither, felt the tears she'd been holding at bay pushing to be set free. But if she began to weep now for all that she'd lost, she feared she'd never stop.

He'd never know how much he'd given her, never know that she loved him more than life itself. Never know what it had cost her to lie through her teeth and send him away.

*T*here wasn't going to be a bloody trial. If it took every last farthing he possessed, every favor owed, his soul sold to the devil.

Avendale walked out of that tiny room and into the hallway at Scotland Yard. She'd looked so brave, so stoic, so alone. As though she'd given up on him, given up on them. He should leave her to rot in prison. But he couldn't because she'd come to mean everything to him. He knew her, understood her. Knew she had spouted lies in an attempt to protect him. It was what she did.

She knew how scandalous it would be for him to have a swindling female at his side.

"What now?" Swindler asked.

Avendale turned to face him. "I intend to find them all. I could use your help."

Swindler gave a brusque nod. "I'll do what I can."

"I know where to begin."

Avendale suspected that Swindler did as well, but as he had other pressing matters to see to as a result of his position with Scotland Yard, Avendale carried on without him. The three who gathered within Rose's parlor were shocked, but not the least bit surprised when he announced that she'd been arrested. They were, however, understandably distressed.

"She was taking too many chances," Merrick stated as he paced before the empty hearth. "I tried to warn her, but she's a stubborn one, won't listen."

"There's nothing to be gained in placing blame," Sally said, swinging her gaze to Avendale. She'd offered tea, which he'd declined. She now sat in a chair, her feet not touching the floor. She should have

LORRAINE HEATH

looked like a child. Instead she appeared to be a lioness, determined to find a way to protect her cub. "At
least now we know she wasn't running from you but
from Tinsdale, the little weasel."

Silent as a grave, Joseph sat in a nearby chair, his
knees nearly touching his chest.

"I told her he was about," Merrick said. "She
should have been looking for him."

"She knew?" Avendale asked.

Merrick nodded. "That first night we ate dinner
at your fancy house. We weren't there to check on
Harry but to let her know that we'd spied Tinsdale."

"We did want to see Harry as well, though," Sally
said, but Avendale was still processing Merrick's rev-
elation.

"Are the whole lot of you swindlers?" he asked.

"Liars, more like," Merrick said. "When the need
arises, I suspect you lie, too."

"We're not discussing me," Avendale ground out.

"But we should," Sally said. "You're a duke. Get
Rose out of there."

"While it might seem otherwise, I'm not immune
to the law," he admitted.

"Then what good are you?" Merrick asked.

"Merrick!" Sally scolded. "Don't take that at-
titude. He's done plenty for us, but his hands are
tied—"

"I didn't say that," Avendale said.

Merrick took two steps forward. "Then what did
you say?"

Avendale removed the paper from within a jacket
pocket. "I have the names of four men who have
brought charges against her. I need to know the
names of any others she may have swindled."

Merrick crossed his arms over his chest. "Why? So

they can tell the authorities everything and she can spend the rest of her life in prison?"

Avendale briefly wondered what made Merrick so distrustful of every blasted word that came out of his mouth. "So I can offer them restitution, pay them what is owed to them, so they can bring no charges against her."

"Oh." Merrick offered a mulish expression that Avendale thought he might think passed for contrition.

"How many?" Avendale asked.

"Think you was number nine."

Not as bad as he'd thought. He arched a brow. "Names?"

"Don't know that I know them all or even where you'd find them. She didn't always share everything if she could find the information herself."

"I know them," the giant said in his deep voice. "And where to find them all."

Eyes wide, Merrick swung around. "Why would she share everything with you and not with me?"

"Because I was the one driving her about." He lifted a bony shoulder until it nearly touched his ear. "Had to know where I was going. I also know all the merchants she said we'd pay but never did."

"You can't remember all of it," Merrick said. "It's been years."

Joseph touched his finger to his temple. "Remember everything. Everything. It's a blasted curse."

"Well, then, between the two of you, perhaps we can get an accounting of everyone and where I might find them," Avendale said. Sitting, he withdrew a pencil from his pocket. "Shall we get started?"

*T*wenty-seven days. As she sat on the terribly uncomfortable cot in her cell, Rose wished the days

would roll one into another until she could claim to
have lost count of them, but despite the monotony,
each one stuck in her mind like a sore thumb that
throbbed and ached and would never be forgotten.

Daniel Beckwith had visited with her twice to
assure her that his oldest brother would handle the
trial "if it came to that." She wasn't quite certain why
it wouldn't and when she questioned him on it, his
response was "You never know."

Perhaps his cryptic words were his attempt to get
even with her for deceiving him when they originally
met. The first time he'd visited, he'd brought her Harry's story and she had spent her time reliving their life
through his eyes. Perhaps she hadn't done so badly
by her brother after all. The price she would now pay
was worth it.

She heard the clatter of a key turning in the lock.
Slowly she rose to her feet. The door opened to reveal
a matronly woman dressed in blue.

"Gather up your things. It's time to go," she
barked.

Into a cloth bag, Rose placed a towel, her brush,
and a blanket. Beckwith had offered to bring her more
to make her stay comfortable, but she had asked him
not to. She knew anything he brought would have
been at Avendale's expense and the man had spent
enough on her. She picked up Harry's book. "Is it
time for my trial?"

"You're going elsewhere."

"Where?"

"I don't know. I was just told to fetch you."

Rose followed her out into the hallway. "Is Mr.
Beckwith here?"

"I seen a gent, but I don't know who he is."

"What does he look—"

"No more questions."

Rose pressed her lips tightly together. She'd learned fairly quickly that she had absolutely no power here. She ate when they brought her food, washed when they brought her a bowl of water. But she would not complain because her transgressions had led her to this. She'd known they would.

The woman opened the door. Rose followed her through into a larger room.

And there was Avendale. She wanted to chastise him, yell at him, tell him to go away, even as she wanted to run to him, fling her arms around him, and beg him to take her away from this. But she just stood there as though she had turned to stone, was a statue that he could place in a fountain in his garden.

He looked as though he'd lost weight. Lines in his face were deeper. She hated that she might be responsible for his weariness.

Self-consciously, she patted her hair, wishing it was pinned up instead of braided. That absurd thought almost made her laugh hysterically. She hadn't had a proper bath since she arrived. Her dress was filthy. She was filthy.

In long, confident strides, he marched over to her, slid his arm around her, and began propelling her forward.

"What are you doing?" she asked.

"Getting you out of here."

"My trial—"

"There's not going to be one."

Planting her feet, she managed to stop them both just shy of the front door that would lead them out of here, that would take her away from this madness. "What have you done?"

He faced her. "What I told you I was going to do. I paid them all off."

"All?"

"All. Merrick, Joseph, and Sally helped me to find them. Took longer than I'd hoped but it's done now. We had struck a bargain, you and I. How the devil did you think you were going to keep your part of it from within prison walls?"

She studied his beloved face, the seriousness in his eyes, perhaps even a spark of anger. "I told you the bargain was a lie."

"I told you that I didn't believe you."

And he had declared that he loved her. "Avendale—"

"We'll discuss everything later, Rose. Right now, let's get the bloody hell out of here."

She sighed. "Yes, please."

Chapter 23

The first thing she did was strip out of her clothes to luxuriate in a steaming hot bath. The water could not be too hot for her. If Avendale hadn't cautioned her that anything hotter would peel the skin from her bones, she would have gone hotter still.

"Burn them," she told him now as he sat on a stool beside the tub. "The clothes. Have them burned."

He rang for Edith, who took them away. When he returned, in one hand he held a glass of dark red wine, and in the other a plate with an assortment of cheeses and fruits arranged on it.

Taking the goblet, she held it aloft. "To freedom and to you for giving it to me."

"Was it so awful in there?" he asked.

"Lonely. Cold, harsh. Unpleasant. But I deserved all of it." She took a sip of the wine, moaned low. "We should let Merrick know I'm here."

"He knows. You'll see all of them tomorrow." He tapped a red, ripe strawberry against her lips. She took a bite of the succulent fruit, moaned again.

"Everything tastes so marvelous, so much richer than it ever did before. I shall never take anything for granted again."

"I don't think you did before."

"Not often, but now I shall never take *anything* for granted." Especially not him.

Pineapple was next, then cheese, more wine.

"As grateful as I am for what you did," she began, "I never meant for you to pay for my misdeeds."

"I paid for them with money, Rose. What good is money if it is not spent?"

"But you had to spend so much. I know what I owed. It must have nearly cost you your last farthing."

"You underestimate how heavy my pockets are."

"I will make it up to you. Anything you want—"

He touched his thumb to her lips. "Tonight you can make it up to me by not mentioning what you owe me."

She nodded. She would never be in debt to anyone more than she would be to him. "I'll return the five thousand—"

"That was a different bargain. It's yours."

"I so misjudged you, Avendale."

"I doubt it. Let's get your hair washed, shall we?"

She'd expected him to call for Edith. Instead he set the plate aside, moved in behind her and washed it himself, slowly massaging her scalp as he did so. She wished she could eliminate the guilt she felt for all he had spent on her behalf. Perhaps it would help if she told him that she loved him, but would he believe her? Knowing how much she owed him, that her debt to him was now one that could never be repaid, would he think she was merely spouting words, striving to flatter him, to bestow upon him a false gift?

Did he truly love her, or had the words been spoken in haste? Did he regret saying them, especially when she'd said such cruel things to him?

"I didn't mean it," she said quietly.

His fingers stilled, and he moved around until she could look into his eyes, and waited.

"When I said it had all been a swindle," she continued. "That I'd been running from you. It was a lie. As I was stepping out of the coach, I saw Tinsdale. I was running from him."

"Why didn't you tell me about him?"

She shook her head. "Embarrassment. Shame. I never talked about my past because I didn't want you to know the awful things I'd done. But now you know. I don't know why you didn't leave me to rot."

He cupped her chin, skimmed his thumb along the soft edge. "You know why."

"You said you loved me and I threw it in your face. Yet still you saved me. You have no reason to trust me, no reason to believe me, not after all the lies. But I've fallen madly in love with you, and that's why—"

His mouth, his wonderful luscious mouth claimed hers with a fierceness that should have frightened her, but only served to fan the flames of her desire. She wanted him, every inch of him. She wanted to touch and taste, stroke and lick. So many nights she had tossed and turned, thinking of him. From the moment she'd fleeced her first gent, she'd known she'd eventually pay for her crimes, but having known Avendale, the harshness of her punishment had seemed to increase tenfold. Knowing him had turned into a blessing and then a curse . . . and ended as a blessing.

He had saved her from more than prison. He had delivered her from a lifetime of regret where Harry was concerned. All the lovely moments they'd shared, all the experiences she would never have given him. Avendale had rescued her from a lonely existence. Life with him would never be dull. They would make passionate love often, wildly and madly. They would visit gaming hells and play cards. They would gamble, wager with each other, laugh, and talk.

For as long as he wanted. Unfortunately, she also knew that as long as he wanted would never be long enough for her. She would never want to leave him, never want to let him go. She would relish each day, but she would also end each with the bittersweet knowledge that it might be her last. That any morning he could awaken and decide he no longer loved her. Another had claimed love for her and turned away. Avendale might as well, someday.

But for tonight she was here. His wet hands were caressing her slick skin. The sensations began to build and she latched her mouth back onto his. His tongue delved deeply, claimed and conquered. He could conquer her so easily, and yet each time he did felt like her own victory.

He tore his mouth from hers. "Your skin is covered in chill bumps."

When had the water gone cold? "Doesn't matter."

"It matters. I've been without you for twenty-seven days—"

"You counted," she stated, both surprised and pleased.

He grinned. "It seems you did as well." He skimmed his fingers over her face. "I don't intend for us to spend our time together tonight with you shivering and catching your death."

He helped her out of the water. Her heart nearly broke with his gentleness as he patted the towel over her body. Then he lifted her into his arms, carried her into the bedchamber, and set her on the bed in a manner that barely stirred the sheets. So unlike the first time he'd tossed her there.

"I won't break," she said as he removed his clothes. So many times she had tortured herself with images of his nude body. It was comforting now as she realized that she had been able to recall him exactly as he was: every perfection, every imperfection. The corded sinewy muscles of his arms and legs. A small blemish on his left shoulder. A mole resting just below his right rib. His broad chest, his firm back. His taut buttocks.

"I'm well aware," he murmured as he stretched out beside her. "I've never known a woman as strong as you. I wanted to shake you when you wouldn't give me the names."

She combed her fingers through his hair. "But you went after them anyway. I don't know if I've ever known a man as singular in purpose as you. Even that first night when we met, I knew you would not give up easily."

"I had no plans to give up at all. I wanted you then, and if it's at all possible I want you more now."

"Yet you're being so careful with me."

"I want to savor every moment." He lowered his lips to her throat, peppering kisses over the length and width of it, before moving his mouth to the valley between her breasts. She scraped her fingers along his scalp, relishing the feel of his thick hair curling around her fingers.

He shifted his attention to one of her nipples, his tongue outlining it before he closed his lips around it and drew it into his mouth. Sensations shot through her, curled her toes. She might have never had this again for the remainder of her life. But she had it now. She'd never take it for granted.

She was acutely aware of every kiss he bestowed,

every flick of his tongue, every suckle, every soothing stroke, every press of his fingers. Slowly he went while her body mapped out the touches.

Pressing on his shoulders, urging him to roll over, she took hold of his wrists, carried his hands over his head, and proceeded to torment him as he had her. With kisses, strokes of her tongue, caresses of her fingers. Now she was mapping out his body. The long length of his torso, the firmness in his arms, the hardness of his thighs. The heated hardness of other parts. She stroked the last, her fingers closing around the hard length of him. Magnificent, bold, strong.

Lowering her mouth, she took in as much as she was able.

"Ah, Christ," he groaned, his hands cradling her face.

She lifted her eyes to his face, a mixture of agony and rapture. Feeling powerful, she swirled her tongue, watched as he squeezed his eyes shut, pressed his head back. She suckled, kissed, tormented. While she was away, she'd had moments when she'd thought of this, had regretted that she'd never given him this when he had so often brought her pleasure with his mouth pressed to her most intimately. She'd wondered at his taste, at how it would feel to have her way with him as he had with her.

Taking her arms, he brought her up. "It's been too long," he said. "I can't go another moment without having you."

Lifting her hips, he lowered them, and her body took him deep, closed around him. A shudder of delicious pleasure went through her. It felt so good, so very good to have him there, to be one with him. Almost too good.

He raised her, slammed her down, and she began

to ride him fast and furiously, while he cupped her breasts, kneading them with expert fingers. She leaned over him, her hair forming a curtain around them. She took his mouth, thrusting her tongue inside as he was thrusting into her lower. Sensations spiraled, curled, unfurled.

She kissed the dew from his throat. "I love you."

Pleasure ratcheted through her, carried her higher, burst forth. He growled as he bucked beneath her. He closed his arms around her, held her tightly. She lowered her head to his chest, could hear the rhythmic pounding of his heart.

Lethargic, she was vaguely aware of his kissing her crown as she drifted off to sleep.

Chapter 24

*S*he awoke to sunlight streaming in through the windows and a bed absent of Avendale. She jerked upright, saw him sitting in a chair beside the bed, and breathed a sigh of relief.

"I don't know if I've ever slept so well," she confessed.

"You barely stirred when I got up."

She studied his fine clothes: his tan trousers, his brown brocade vest, his white shirt, his black jacket, his perfectly knotted neck cloth. Something was amiss. A shiver of trepidation went through her. "Why are you dressed?" She lifted the covers a bit to reveal her nude body. "Come back to bed."

"You have an appointment."

He extended something toward her. A narrow bundle. Taking it, she untied the string, folded back the paper to reveal tickets. She studied them. Passage on the railway to Scotland. She shifted her gaze to Avendale, not certain why a fissure of anger went through her. "As much as I owe you, I expected you to require more than one night."

Slowly, he shook his head. "No, our bargain is

done." He stood. "The others will be waiting at the railway station. I purchased passage for them as well. I'll send Edith in to help you prepare for the journey."

She wanted to cry, scream, beg him not to send her away. He loved her; he said so. She'd dared to say the words back to him and make herself vulnerable. Then a coldness settled through her. Last night, he hadn't told her he loved her. Not once. Why would he? In striving to grant her freedom, he had uncovered all her secrets, all her shameful actions. As haughtily as possible, fighting to hold in the pain, she angled her chin. "What time do we leave?"

"In an hour."

She nodded. "Well, then, I'd best get to it."

He walked from the room without a word. In that moment, she hated herself for falling in love with him, for giving him the power to break her heart.

Walking out of that room was the hardest thing that Avendale had ever done, but he knew he had no choice, had known he would have no choice when he paid off the man she had first swindled. And the one after him, and the next. As her debt to him had accumulated, risen ever higher.

He wanted her love for as long as he lived. But that was not something for which he could ask. He cursed the damned bargain. If she stayed, he would always doubt the words whispered in the night, whispered in the throes of passion. He could not live with the uncertainty, the doubts regarding her true feelings for him.

Nor could he ask her to give up the carefree life she craved. As his duchess, she would have more responsibilities heaped on her than she could imagine. He had to let her go, give up his own hopes, plans,

dreams in order to ensure her happiness. He understood it fully now, the sacrifice, the pain of setting
aside everything one wanted in order to ensure that
someone else realized his or her dreams. It was odd
that in the ache of loss there was also some joy in
knowing that she would be happy. That she would
not feel like a slave or a whore.

That by sending her away, he would ensure that
she not awaken each day feeling beholden to him.

As he headed to his library, he knew that if he
weren't a selfish man, he would have taken her to the
railway station the day before, but he was a selfish
man and so he'd given himself one more night with
her, one more night of memories that he would carry
with him for the remainder of his life. No woman
would ever replace her. He knew that as well.

In the library, he went to the window and looked
out on the garden. When he returned later in the day,
he would lock the door and drown himself in drink.
Perhaps tomorrow he would fill his residence once
again with loose women and young swells who only
wanted a good time. They could frolic naked in his
fountain—

No, he wanted them nowhere near the fountain. He
wanted nothing that would tarnish his memory of Rose
standing there striving to explain to her brother how
naughty the stone couple in the fountain were. He had
posed for the blasted sculptor. He'd thought it a grand
idea at the time. Funny, how now when he looked at the
woman carved there, he saw Rose. She had not been the
model, and yet she was the one he saw.

He feared he would see her in everything. A silly
thing to fear when it was what he wanted: to never
forget her.

"My trunk is being loaded," her soft voice said behind him.

Turning, he caught sight of the clock on the mantel. An hour had passed. How had that happened?

"I want to thank you for everything you've done for me," she said, her voice flat, unemotional. The swindler who could make him believe anything, even that she didn't care that she was leaving, stood before him. If she had torn up the tickets, objected to his offering, he might have asked her to stay.

"It was nothing." His voice was equally flat. But then he'd spent a lifetime mastering the art of not appearing to care.

"Well, then, I'll say good-bye."

"I'll accompany you to the station."

For a moment, she almost appeared panicked, but then once again all emotion was wiped from her face. "That won't be necessary."

"I insist." Although things between them were strained, he still wanted a few more minutes with her. Offering his arm, he was surprised when she slid her hand around the crook of his elbow.

Uttering not a word, they walked from the room, down the hallway. It was odd to feel this unnatural tenseness between them when they'd never had it before. From the moment they had met, whether he was angry or irritated with her, he'd never felt this widening chasm. He knew that in short order it would be too broad to breach. It was for the best. He told himself it was for the best. It was for her.

In the coach, he sat opposite her. If he sat beside her, he might find his resolve weakening. It was bad enough with her scent filling the interior, taunting his nostrils. He could see only her profile, because she was looking out the window as though the passing scenery were infinitely fascinating.

"What will you do with yourself?" he asked.

She looked at him. "I don't know, but I do recognize that you have given me a great gift. My life is a blank slate. I shall take advantage of that to do something worthwhile. Perhaps I'll teach. Or write. Although unlike Harry, I would want to write fiction. The truth is too sobering. What will you do with yourself?"

"Return to the pleasure gardens." It was a lie. Going with her had ruined them for him. He would see her there. Everywhere he looked.

"What of the responsibilities to your title? You should marry. Have an heir."

So easily she could give him to another when it nearly killed him to think of her with another man. "I have a cousin. He can see to them."

"You should do it."

That would involve marrying a woman he didn't love, because he couldn't envision that he would ever love another.

Finally they arrived at the railway station. The footman saw to her trunk. The others were waiting on the platform. Avendale stood to the side while she greeted them with exclamations of joy and long, hard hugs. That would be her life: joyful reunions and friends.

Merrick approached him, craned his head back to hold his gaze. "You're not such a bad sort." He stuck out his hand.

Avendale shook it. "High praise indeed."

"We can never thank you enough," Sally said.

"My pleasure."

"If you ever need anything," Joseph said.

He needed Rose, but he couldn't have her, not under the circumstances to which they'd agreed. Even with declarations of love, the debts were there.

She stepped forward, his beautiful, courageous Rose. "I wasn't expecting to say good-bye to you so soon. Seems so much needs to be said."

"Just make the most of the opportunity you're being giving here."

"Why did you do it?" she asked. "Pay off all my debts?"

"I promised Harry."

Slamming her eyes closed, she nodded. "Of course." Then she opened her eyes, and within the depths, he thought he saw understanding, but she couldn't possibly understand it all. "My brother knew far more than anyone ever gave him credit for. He would have asked you to look out for me."

He would have done it without his promise to Harry, but telling her that would only delay the inevitable. A whistle sounded. "You all had best be off."

Very quickly, she leaned in and kissed his cheek before striding away, her head held high, her back straight. The others quickly followed, leaving him standing there, fighting not to rush after her, struggling not to call out to her and beg her to stay.

He had to let her go, even if he died in the process.

Sitting on the bench seat, Rose looked out the window. She wanted one last glimpse of Avendale to carry with her. She could hardly believe he was sending her away, not after everything he'd done for her.

She saw him standing on the platform. How forlorn and lonely he looked. How alone.

Harry, who had known so much, hadn't known everything. She remembered the words in his final letter to her.

I also think he loves you, although I am not sure he is a man who would voice the words.

But he had voiced them—in anger and frustration, to be sure. Yet when it had mattered most, when he'd come for her, they had been so formal. When she had dared to say the words, he hadn't repeated them. Now he was sending her away to a land she had mentioned, to a life with no responsibilities other than to herself. She could do anything she wanted: sleep in, eat cake three times a day, travel in a hot air balloon—

Her thoughts rushed back to the picnic, to lying in the field, when he'd asked her what she would do when Harry was no longer in her life.

I'll have no responsibilities, no duties, no obligations. I'll wander, with nothing to tie me down. I'll have no plans, no strategies, no compelling need to do anything except breathe.

He was giving her that. All of it. He hadn't stopped loving her because of the journey he'd taken to pay off her debts. If he didn't love her, he'd have left her to rot.

"Oh dear God." The train began to move. She shoved herself to her feet. "Wait for me at the next station."

"What is it?" Merrick asked.

"Love."

Then she was running down the aisle. She reached the door, threw it open, and, as the train picked up speed, she leaped out.

Avendale could hardly believe his eyes. Knocking people out of his way, he rushed forward, reaching Rose as she finally rolled to a stop on the platform. Grabbing her arms, he pulled her to her feet. "Are you completely daft?"

"I promised to stay with you for as long as you wanted. Are you already so tired of me?"

He looked to the train growing smaller in the distance, looked back at her. Dammit. Where was he to find the strength to let her go again? "I will never tire of you, Rose."

"Never is a long time."

"Yes, but where you are concerned it is not long enough."

"Then why are you sending me away?"

"I'm not sending you away. I'm setting you free of our bargain. I want you in my life more than I've ever wanted anything. But from you I learned what it is to be unselfish. I shall never again know happiness but as long as you are happy, that is all I care about."

"You are an idiot, Avendale. How in God's name am I to be happy if I am not with you?"

"Rose—"

"I love you."

"You say that because you owe me."

"No. I say it because it's what I feel. I don't give a fig about your money. Something I thought I'd never say. You could be a pauper. That you paid my debt . . . Avendale, I can never repay that. Not if I live to be a thousand. But I loved you before you paid it. I loved you before I was arrested. I loved you before Harry died. I wished to God we'd never made the bargain so that you could believe me. I'm so skilled at convincing people of lies, but I don't know how to convince you of the truth. I love you with all of my heart and all of my soul. I will love you until I draw my last breath. Please believe me."

"How can I not? You jumped out of a blasted moving train to tell me."

"I would jump out of a balloon if I needed to."

"You would splatter."

Moving up against him, she wound her arms around his neck. "No, I wouldn't, because you would catch me."

Rising up on her toes, she kissed him. Yes, he would catch her, he would always catch her. He kissed her back because he had no choice. Cradling her face, he drew her back.

"I love you, Rose."

"I don't deserve your love, but I will take it because there is nothing in this world that I want more. I will be your mistress as long as you want me."

He angled his head. "You don't understand how much I love you." He dropped to one knee, took her hand, pressed a kiss to it before looking up at her. "I want you with me for the rest of my life. Will you marry me?"

She blinked, her mouth opened slightly. "You're a duke. You can't marry me. That would be scandalous."

He grinned. "I've told you before. I'm nothing if I'm not scandalous."

She dropped to her knees, cradled his face. "I love you so much. I will be the best wife that any duke has ever had."

Pulling her in close, he blanketed her mouth with his, kissing her deeply, thoroughly, not caring one whit that people were staring at them. He was going to kiss this woman as often as he could for the remainder of his life.

"Shall we head home now?" he asked when they broke away from the kiss.

"I would like that very much, but I told the others to wait for us at the next station."

"Let's go get them then."

"Are you sure you don't mind?"

"Rose, the woman I love has agreed to marry me. I can't wait to tell Merrick."

She laughed. "I don't think he's going to object. I think he's come around to you."

"How could he not? After all, I'm a duke."

"You're much more than that," she said, tightening her arms around his neck. "You're the man I love."

Epilogue

From the Journal of the Duke of Avendale

A dark secret shaped me into the man I am . . .

Another's set me free.

In my youth I witnessed something that I wasn't supposed to. Had I not disobeyed my mother and returned home that night, I'd have never seen her striking out and killing my father. I understand now it was an accident, but at the time, in my young mind, I saw villainy. When my mother married William Graves shortly afterward, I saw duplicity. Over the years, I held close these treacherous thoughts along with my father's words that my mother wished me harm. They haunted me, conspired to separate me from my family.

My Rose carried burdens as well, but with far more dignity. She had a brother the world treated unkindly. To make amends to him for others' sins, she turned to swindling. In some ways she was a female Robin Hood, taking from the wealthy to give to those Society had branded as curiosities, those that life had not treated fairly. While I fully comprehend that her actions were not commendable, I also understand how and why they came to pass. She wanted to create for her brother a better world than the one in which they lived, and she knew that time was not on her side, so she took a shortcut which eventually led her to me.

And she, along with Harry, changed my life.

Not a day goes by that I don't consider the fortuitous night when

I glanced out over a balcony and had my attention snagged by a lady in red. Two minutes later, two minutes earlier, and I might have never seen her. I might have simply wandered off for another game of cards, another journey into decadence.

Instead that night I stepped onto a path that would eventually reveal what I'd been searching for all along: a love so profound, so deep, so true that I would do anything to protect the woman who captured my heart. Because through her, I came to understand the unmeasured lengths to which one would go for someone he or she loved. Through knowing her I regained my family. Through loving her, I regained myself. Through marriage to her, I gained a life far richer than all the coins in my coffers.

Our first son, my heir, we named Harry. He was perfection when he was born. Rose worried that her brother's affliction might visit our children, but it didn't. To this day, they remain perfect in appearance. More importantly, they are perfect in heart.

Merrick, Sally, and Joseph found employment at the Twin Dragons. They stayed in London and often joined us for meals and holidays. Our children viewed them as family.

In my library, on a gilded stand, rest the pages that Harry so painstakingly filled with his story, with Rose's, one that eventually became part of mine. I often read the final words of the story that Harry wrote:

> My tale must come to an end now, but Rose's will carry on. While I cannot see into the future, I do believe that Rose and her duke will live happily ever after.

Indeed we did.

Author's Note

I have always been fascinated by the life of Joseph Merrick, the Elephant Man. The cruelty he suffered at the hands of some, the kindness bestowed upon him by others. It was 1884 before he came to the attention of the physician Sir Frederick Treves, ten years after this story takes place. It would be another two years before Treves took him in and began to study him more thoroughly. But it would be long after Merrick's death that his condition would be diagnosed as neurofibromatosis, although there are some today who question the diagnosis.

Harry suffered from the same condition, but he had a sister who fought to protect him, would do anything to spare him facing the cruelty of the world. Even today there is no cure for the condition, so neither I nor physician extraordinaire Sir William Graves could save Harry. But he was loved, and in the end, by far more people than he ever expected. I hope you loved him as well.